**S0-AZU-536**

"*Alone, I have renovated more than ninety thousand major worlds, satisfying the widest array of clients. Perhaps a trillion sentient souls live in nests assembled by these hands. But my finest work lurks in those secret places that I build for myself, from nothing. On occasion, I'll invent some unique biology and hide it away inside dust clouds or faraway globular clusters. . . .*

"*It's the hiding that is intoxicating. The enticement of having something unique and entirely our own . . . and we must keep it secret . . . and really, isn't that the best way to protect whatever you cherish . . . ?*"

—Alice's testimony

"See some names—Pohl, Ellison, Gibson, for example—and you don't have to wonder if it's a good science-fiction novel: It is. Add Robert Reed to the list."

—Amarillo News-Globe

"Teen sf fans will be enthralled by the setting and will identify with young Ord."

—Booklist

BOOKS BY ROBERT REED

The Remarkables
Down the Bright Way
Black Milk
The Hormone Jungle
The Leeshore
* *Beyond the Veil of Stars*
* *An Exaltation of Larks*
* *Beneath the Gated Sky*
The Dragons of Springplace (story collection)
* *Marrow*
* *Sister Alice*
† *The Well of Stars*

* denotes a Tor book
†forthcoming

SISTER ALICE

ROBERT REED

TOR®

A TOM DOHERTY ASSOCIATES BOOK
NEW YORK

This is a work of fiction. All the characters and events portrayed in this book are either products of the author's imagination or are used fictitiously.

SISTER ALICE

Copyright © 2003 by Robert Reed

edited by James Frenkel

A Tor Book
Published by Tom Doherty Associates, LLC
175 Fifth Avenue
New York, NY 10010

www.tor.com

Tor® is a registered trademark of Tom Doherty Associates, LLC.

ISBN 0-765-34147-6
EAN 978-0765-34147-1

First edition: October 2003
First mass market edition: December 2004

Printed in the United States of America

0 9 8 7 6 5 4 3 2 1

TO JESSIE RENEE REED
BORN SEPTEMBER 5, 2001

Acknowledgments

A special thanks to Gardner Dozois for publishing the original novellas, and to my editor, Jim Frenkel.

BOOK ONE

SISTER ALICE

One

*"I found myself daydreaming, remembering my
childhood as a wonderful time clothed in simple fun
and sweet easy victories ... I was reveling in how
perfectly carefree my first taste of life had been ...
and that was the moment when my instincts first
warned me, whispering in my countless ears that our
work had gone seriously, tragically wrong ..."*
                                              —Alice's testimony

XO TOLD THEIR squad this was a lousy place to build and
their fort was sick with flaws, and the Blues were sure to
crush them, and, of course, every disaster would be Ravleen's fault. He said it with his best whiny voice, making
it impossible to ignore his grousing. She had no choice but
to come over, interrupting their drills to tell Xo to quit. But
he wouldn't quit. He laughed in her face, and said, "You're
no general." Ord heard him plainly. Everyone heard him.
Ravleen had no choice but to knock him off his feet and
give him a good sharp kick. Xo was a Gold, and she was
their Sanchex, the Gold's eternal general. She had every
right to punish him, aiming for his belly and ribs. But Xo
refused to cooperate. He started cursing, bright poisonous
words hanging in the air. "You're not Sanchex," he
grunted. "You're just a Sanchex face stuffed full of shit,
and I'm not scared of you." Ravleen moved to his face,
breaking his nose and cheekbones, the skin splitting and
blood spattering on the new snow. Everyone watched. Ord
stood nearby, watching their snow melt into the blood, each
diluting the other. He saw Xo's face become a gooey mess,
and he heard the boy's voice finally fall away into a sloppy
wet laugh.

Tule stepped up, saying, "If you hurt him too much, he
won't be able to hurt anyone else."

Ravleen paused, panting from her hard work. Tule was
right. Their general dropped her foot and pushed her long

black hair out of her eyes, grinning now, making sure everyone could see her confidence. Then she knelt, making a ball out of the bloody snow, asking, "Who wants to help this shit home?"

Tule was closest, but she despised Xo. She didn't approve of disobedience; it was her endless duty to keep their clan working smoothly, bowing to every one of Ravleen's demands.

On the other hand, Ord was passingly sympathetic. Xo wasn't his best friend, but he was a reliable companion. Besides, for the time being they belonged to the same squad. A soldier had a duty to his squad, and that's why Ord stepped up, saying, "I'll take him."

"Then come straight back," Ravleen added.

He gave a nod, and asked Xo, "Can you stand?"

The bloody face said, "Maybe." A gloved hand reached for him, and Ord thought of the battered ribs as he lifted. But the tortured groans were too much; Xo had a fondness for theater. "Thanks," he muttered, then he reached into his mouth, pulling out a slick white incisor and tossing it at the half-built fort. With a soft *ping*, the tooth struck one of the robots and vanished.

They walked slowly, crossing the long pasture before climbing into the dark winter woods. Xo stopped at the first tree, leaning against it and carefully spitting out a glob of dark blood. Ord worked to be patient. The tree's rough bark formed words, and he spent the moment reading about the Chamberlain role in some long-ago treaty. Then he stared back down at the pasture, watching the robots strip it of snow, building their fort according to Ravleen's exacting designs. A simple titanium pole, topped with a limp golden flag, stood in the future courtyard. Tiny figures wearing clean white snowsuits were drilling again—six squads honing themselves for snowfare. It looked like an easy pasture to defend. On three sides, it fell away, cliffs and nearly vertical woods protecting the fort. The only easy approach was from here, from above. Ravleen was assuming that the Blues would do what was easy, which was why the nearest wall had the thickest foundation. "Keep your strong to their strong," was an old Sanchex motto. But what if Xo was right? What if their general was leaving the other walls too weak?

"I can't walk very fast," Xo warned. His swollen face was inhuman, ruined flesh and bits of bone floating in a masticated stew. But the bleeding had stopped, scabs forming, and the smallest cuts beginning to heal. Speaking with a faint lisp, Xo admitted, "I sound funny now."

"You should have left your tooth in," Ord countered. Gums preferred to repair teeth, not replace them. "Or you might have kept your mouth shut in the first place."

Xo gave a little laugh.

Something moved in the distance. Ord squinted, seeing an airship carrying sightseers. The distant sun glittered against the ship's body, and he imagined curious eyes watching only him.

"Let's go," he urged. "I'm tired of standing."

They walked on a narrow trail, their pace more leisurely than slow. Snow began to fall, and the woods were already knee deep in old snow. They weren't far from the lowlands, and sometimes, particularly on clear days, city sounds would rise up from that hot flat country, forcing their way through the acoustic fence. But not today. The snow helped enforce the silence. To step and not hear his own footfall made Ord a little anxious. He was alert, as if ready for an ambush. The war wouldn't start until the day after tomorrow, but he was anticipating it. He was ready. Unless the fight had made him anxious, which meant that he was distracted and sloppy.

"Know why I did it?" asked Xo.

Ord said nothing.

"Know why I pissed her off?"

"Why?"

The battered face grinned, Xo proud of the gap in his teeth. "I don't have to play this war now."

"Ravleen's not that angry," Ord countered. "She isn't even half-enough pissed to ban you."

"But I'm hurt. Look!"

"So?" Ord refused to act impressed. Glancing over a shoulder, he observed, "You're walking and talking. Not talking fast and your words are dumb, but still, you're not that hurt."

But Xo's Family—the great Nuyens—were ridiculously cautious. A sister might see his suffering and order him to remain home for a few days. It wouldn't be the first time, particularly if Xo moaned like he did now, telling Ord, "I don't want to play snowfare."

"Why not?"

Wincing, Xo pretended to ache. But by now a cocktail of anesthesias was working, and both of them knew it.

"If you can stand, you can fight," Ord reminded him. "When you became Gold, you took a pledge to serve—"

"Wait." The boy waded into the deepest snow, heading for an outcropping of cultured granite. He found a block of bright pink stone and carried it back, dropping it at Ord's feet. "Do me a favor?"

"No."

"But not too hard. Just nick me here." He touched his stubby black hair. "I'll pay you back sometime. That's a promise."

Ord lifted the stone without conviction.

"Make it ugly," the boy prompted.

Ord shook his head, saying, "First you've got to tell me why you don't want to fight. Is it Ravleen?"

"I don't care about Ravleen."

"Tell me the truth, or I won't help you."

With his white gloves, the boy touched his scabbed and unnaturally rounded face. "Because it's stupid."

"What's stupid?"

"This game. This whole snowfare silliness."

Calling it a "game" was taboo. Snowfare was a serious exercise that taught you to give orders and obey orders and think well for yourself when there was nobody there but you.

"We're too old to play," his friend persisted. "I know I am."

This wasn't about Ravleen, which left Ord with no easy, clear rebuke. He asked, "What will you do instead?" He assumed there was some other diversion waiting for Xo. Perhaps a trip somewhere. Not off the estates, of course. That wasn't permitted, not at their age. But maybe one of Xo's siblings wanted to take him on a hunt, or somehow else share time with him.

But the boy said, "Nothing. I'm just going to sit at home and study." He paused for a moment. "Put the pointed end here, okay? Drop it next to this ear. And I promise, I'll tell my sisters that Ravleen did it."

Ord watched the boy lie on the hard white trail, his face cocked a little bit to his right. He was waiting calmly for his skull to be shattered. The stone couldn't hurt him too badly. Eons ago, humans gave up their soft brains for better ones built of tough, nearly immortal substances. The worst Ord could manage would be to scramble some of the neural connections, making Xo forgetful and clumsy for the next few days. The body might even die, but nothing more. Nothing less than a nuclear fire could kill them. Which was the same for almost every human being today.

"Are you going to help me?" the boy whined.

Ord watched the hopeful face, judging distance and mass, deciding what would make the ugliest, most spectacular wound. But he kept thinking back to Xo's comment about being too old, knowing he was right. Some trusted spark for the game had slipped away unnoticed, and that bothered the boy.

"Ord?"

"Yeah?"

"Will you hurry up?"

He let the stone slip free of his grip, and the earth pulled it down with a smooth perfection, missing Xo's head by nothing.

"No, I shouldn't," Ord said. "I won't, forget it."

"Be that way!" The boy lifted the stone himself, groaning as he took aim, trying to summon the courage to finish the job. He was invulnerable, but so were his ancient instincts.

This was not easy. His arms shook, then collapsed. The attempt looked like a half accident—a slick wet *thud*—and his head was left dented on one side. But not badly enough, they discovered. Xo could stand by himself, a little dizzy, but still on his feet. He touched his wounds one after another, telling himself, "At least I'll get tomorrow to myself." He wasn't looking at Ord, and he was talking to himself. "This is good enough," he claimed with a soft wet voice that instantly got lost in the muting whisper of falling snow.

Two

"In the universe, there is just the one ultimate law: Life always devises some ultimate means to put an end to life."

—Alice's testimony

THERE WERE EXACTLY one thousand Families.

Nothing about their existence had come easily. Not their laws, not their restrictions, and not even their numbers. Ten million years ago, with the Great Wars still raging, an alliance of desperate leaders met on a frigid, barely named world. Everyone who traveled there, enemies and friends alike, agreed about one vital issue: Without substantial, immediate change, the human species would soon be extinct. Populations were collapsing in every district; entire worlds were being reduced to dust and crumbled bones. Moreover, if the wars continued to spread, every other flavor of life in the galaxy would be battered, and many species would cease to be.

It was that atmosphere of terror and unalloyed despair that brought out the unsuspected genius in mere people. Suddenly the unthinkable was obvious, the impossible appeared easy, and the coldest, most bloodless bureaucrat found himself speaking in verse and dreaming in brilliant color. A war-weary prime minister sketched out the roughest imaginable plan for the future. With a quavering voice, she described the Families, giving them that inadequate name because she didn't have time or inclination to think of any better title. The Families would begin with a few carefully selected individuals, she explained. Each of those few would be given every imaginable power. A kind of godhood would be set on their shoulders, and because they had to be good ethical people, they would have no choice but to fill the role of worthy gods, helping normal citizens and old prime ministers steer a worthy course through the coming eons.

But how many people deserved such an honor? And how would they be chosen? And how many of these Families would be required to serve this pitiful humanity?

The prime ministers and presidents and even the scruffiest little despot had brought powerful quantum computers with them. Each asked his or her machine for its opinion, and after careful deliberation based on nearly infinite factors, plus a hard stare into the imaginable future, the machines blessed the outrageous plan. But they couldn't agree on any single perfect number of Families. There were too many variables, they confessed. The future was vast and unknowable and imperfect and probably malicious. It was left to the human minds to arrive at a target goal, and after a heartbeat's pause, some little voice in back cried out, "How about a flat thousand? It's a simple, memorable number, and it gives us a lot of them, but not so many that they'll be getting underfoot . . . you know, so they won't seem cheap . . . ?"

ORD WAS A Chamberlain.

Probably no Family was known by more or wielded more power. Near the center of the sprawling estate, perched on a broad scenic peak, stood a great round building, tall and massive, built from the cultured granite with a shell of tailored white corals living on its exterior. It was the Chamberlains' ancestral home. The interior, both above ground and below, was a maze of rooms and curling hall-ways, simple laboratories and assorted social arenas. There were enough apartments for fifteen hundred brothers and sisters, should so many ever wish to come home at once. And there were other fabulous buildings scattered about the property—elegant cottages and ancient hunting lodges and baby mansions built from the rarest or most modern of materials. The entire Chamberlain family could reunite on this one patch of holy ground, if there would ever be the need.

But it was the simple cylindrical house that embodied the Chamberlain legacy and legend. Humans throughout the galaxy would see the image of it, and they would think about Ord's family—how they helped the Sanchexes win the Great Wars, and afterward, the Chamberlains and Nuyens were instrumental in building the institutions and customs and laws and muscular organizations that had brought about the Ten-Million-Year Peace. Success brought wealth, and wealth gave new opportunities. The Chamberlains turned their vast energies on the stars. They explored the farthest reaches of the Milky Way, and farther, finding the bones of lost species and making first contact with hundreds of important alien species. And afterward, for these last long eons, it had been the Chamberlains who had mastered the rapid terraforming of empty worlds. Age and disease had been conquered, and death rates were vanishingly small, leaving an endless demand for new homes, and novel homes, and lovely places for which aliens and humans both would pay substantial fees, particularly for inspired work done on schedule.

Ord knew enough of his Family history to fill volumes, and he knew nothing. What he had mastered was a speck compared to the true history. He knew the Great Wars were fought with savagery, billions murdered, and the Earth itself left battered. But the Peace had endured for a hundred thousand centuries, and throughout, the Families had given it backbone and the occasional guiding touch. Ord himself was a whisper of a child, not even fifty years old. His powers as a Chamberlain lay in the remote future. Imaging himself in a million years, he saw a semigod who was busily building green worlds at the Core, or perhaps flying off to some far galaxy, exploring its wilderness while making new allies. But the actual changes between today and tomorrow were mysterious to him. His mind and energies would swell, but how would that feel to him? His senses would multiply, and time itself would slow to where seconds became months. But what would such an existence be like? He had asked the brothers and sisters who lived with him. He had worn them down with his inquiries. Yet not one could ever offer a clear, compelling, or even halfway believable answer.

"You're too young to understand," they would profess, their voices distant and bored. Even a little shrill. "Just wait and see," they would recommend. "Patience. Try patience. You'll learn when you're ready, and that isn't now."

But Ord sensed the truth. Like him, his siblings had no idea what the future held. Like all reasonable questions, his were completely unoriginal. And the Chamberlains that he saw day by day—siblings younger than a single millennium—felt as if they were trapped inside the same proverbial spacecraft, adrift and lost and a little bit scared.

Three

"When I lived here, when I was every kind of child, the mountains were new. The estates were new. Our mansions were modest but comfortable homes meant for modest and deserving gods, and the Families were utterly victorious . . . while the galaxy at our feet seemed vast and nearly empty, full of endless and intoxicating potentials . . ."

—Alice's testimony

THE FORT WAS finished by midafternoon that next day, exactly on schedule, and after it passed the standard inspection for volume and materials, the clan celebrated, walking up to the tube station together, arms linked and everyone singing ancient Gold songs in a well-practiced chorus.

It was a brief ride home for Ord. He was deposited at the base of the long yard, looking up at an expanse of smart snows and shaggy blue-green trees. A dozen giant bears came charging between the trees, their broad faces smiling and their bellowing voices calling out, "Him, it is . . . him, him . . . it is . . . !" Each bear had to be scratched behind the ears. There was no room for debate. Then all of them repaid Ord's affection, putting his head into their mouths, holding him carefully while a rumbling purr moved through his bones.

Done with that duty, Ord jogged up to the house, entering through one of its smaller doorways. Over the door hung a thick granite slab. "PRIDE AND SACRIFICE," said the ageless letters engraved into that exceedingly pink stone. He touched the words with his right hand, always. The gesture was a habit, almost a reflex. Then he ran to the first stairwell and rode up to his floor and sprinted to his apartment, finding a pair of mothering robots waiting for him. They were at least as smothering as the bears. They asked about his day and his accomplishments. Was there enough snow? "Plenty," he allowed; it had fallen all night. Good for forts, was it? "Perfect," he told them, removing his warm snowsuit. "Good wet stupid snow." The pasture was close to the lowlands, and that gave it a milder climate. "We built a strong fort," he boasted. "We broke three presses, squeezing the snow down to glacial ice, nearly. So it could be the best ever . . ."

The robots paused, saying nothing where they might have said, "We're so glad to hear it."

Ord hesitated, alert to the silence.

"Lyman just asked to see you," said synchronized voices.

Lyman was the oldest brother living in the house. *He wants to see me?* Ord assumed that something was wrong.

And he would have been in trouble, if he had bashed Xo with that rock . . . but he was innocent, and nothing else remarkable had happened during the last few days. "What does Lyman want?"

"We're curious, too," they replied, ruby eyes winking. "You're supposed to go to his apartment as soon as you are clean and dressed."

Ord looked outside. His longest wall faced east, and it was set to show what he would see if there was an old-fashioned window in place of the granite. Somewhere below, hidden in the gathering darkness, was his new fort. On clear nights he watched the glow of the cities, wondering about the people living beneath the mountains. Everyone on Earth was rich to some degree; space was too crowded and far too expensive for those without means. But only the Families could afford having winters, putting their trees and lakes to sleep. These weren't mountains so much as enormous sculptures, and like any artwork, they were not meant to produce meaningful food; nor had they ever housed more than a very few people.

"Lyman sounds impatient," the robots warned.

Ord nodded and ran through his bath, then dressed and left. His brother lived several stories above him. He had visited enough to know the way, and enough to hesitate at the door. Lyman liked to entertain girlfriends; caution was required. Ord announced his presence, and the door opened instantly, a distant voice telling him, "Wait out there. I'm almost done."

It was Ord's voice, only deeper. Older. Lyman had a larger apartment complete with several universal walls and a vast bed, plus a swimming pool as big as a pond. There were flourishes meant to say *Lyman* but always felt more *Chamberlain* than anything. Chamberlains liked mementos. Where Ord would have displayed his collection of alien fossils, his brother had set up small light-statues of the girlfriends—women of every variation, uniformly disrobed. The girlish faces smiled at Ord, showing him how pleased they were to stand before him. One of the universal walls was activated. A live feed showed some banded gas giant, each moon encased in a warm atmosphere, the nearest moon blued by an ocean. Had a Chamberlain built that ocean? It was likely. Lyman was training to become an apprentice terraformer. Once he was declared an adult, probably in less than a century, he would embark on his first assignment. Something easy, no doubt. Probably work on some little comet between the stars, most likely for a semiwealthy client who wanted a vacation home—

"How's your war?" asked Lyman, striding out of the bath, his loose-fitting trousers shrinking to a more fashionable size. "Done with your fort?"

Ord muttered, "Yes."

"Any more fights?"

Was he referring to Xo and Ravleen? Or maybe Lyman was trying to tease him, making fun of this silly kid's game. Either way, Ord guessed that his brother knew every answer, that he had already received updates from the robots and the estate's sentries. "No fights," Ord reported. "Not until tomorrow morning, at least."

But Lyman was only pretending to listen. He started to speak, aiming to make another little joke, but then paused, his pale pink mouth hanging open for a long moment.

Ord waited, feet fidgeting.

"Do you know where I was this morning?"

"Where?"

"Antarctica." Lyman liked to tease his little brother, reminding him that one of them could travel at will across the Earth. No farther, but still, it seemed like an enormous freedom.

"What were you doing there?" asked Ord.

"Having fun, naturally." Lyman tried to smile, scratching his bare belly. Taller than Ord, he had old-fashioned adult proportions, his body hairy and strong with an appropriate unfancy penis dangling inside his trousers. Red hair grew to his shoulders. Like Ord, he had the telltale Chamberlain face, sharp features and pale, freckled skin and brilliant blue eyes. Their sisters were feminized, with breasts and estrogens and such; physical forms were standardized, and they were eternal, every Family built around its immortal norm, every norm patterned after its founder and ultimate parent.

Lyman stood in front of his brother, sighed, and asked, "Do you know why I came home? Have you heard?"

Ord shook his head, his breath quickening. What happened that would demand that Lyman abandon his fun?

"Listen."

But then his brother said nothing, his mouth left open and the blue eyes gazing at the blue moon on the wall.

Finally, Ord asked, "What is it?"

"In the next few days . . . soon, although I don't know when . . . we'll have a guest here. Are you listening? You need to wear your best behavior."

"Who's visiting?"

Lyman seemed troubled, or at least deeply puzzled, pursing his lips and shaking his head. "One of our sisters is dropping by."

Sisters came and went all of the time.

"An old sister," Lyman added.

Every sister was older than Ord, and so was every brother.

Then Lyman grinned, as if realizing just how mysterious this must sound. "A very old, much-honored adult. She is."

Ord glanced at the universal wall, and the image changed. A small dull sun was setting over a glassy sea. An ammonia sea, perhaps. He found himself dealing with this news by distancing himself, working on the peaceful dynamics of that other world as if it was one of his tutor's lessons.

"You're not listening," Lyman warned him.

"You're barely talking," Ord replied. Then he blinked, asking, "How old is she?"

"Her name is Alice."

Alice—

"She's our Twelve." The words were incredible to both of them. Lyman repeated himself, saying, "Yes. Twelve."

Ord was stunned, closing his hands into fists and using them to drum on his thighs. "Why would she come here?"

"We received her message this morning . . . deeply coded . . . and everyone's excited, of course . . ."

Ord nodded. "But why—?"

"A Twelve is coming." Lyman was astonished, but his smile seemed nearly joyless. "I looked up when the last Fifty or higher came for a visit. Our Forty-Two touched down for less than sixteen seconds, and that was nearly twenty-eight thousand years ago. A handshake visit, she called it." He paused, rubbing at the stiff red hairs on his chest. "But Alice wants to linger. She's requested the penthouse and given no departure time. Even though she'll be bored in a nanosecond, she claims that she wants to live here. Here." He pointed at the white-coral ceiling. "Here."

This was landmark news. Ord imagined telling the other Golds. Tonight? No, tomorrow. On the eve of combat. It would give him a sudden importance, a renewed worthiness. Even Ravleen would be impressed, and jealous, and he felt himself beginning to smile, imagining that sweet moment.

"There's more," Lyman said, anticipating him. "This news is secret. Alice made it explicitly clear—"

Secret?

"And I'm giving you fair warning. You won't tell anyone. Not friends, and not even enemies. This is Chamberlain business, and what does that mean?"

"It's private."

"It belongs to us. Nobody else, Ord."

The boy offered a weak, confused nod.

"No other Family can know that she is here."

"Why not?"

"Because that's what she wants."

"But why visit us? And why stay—?"

"Why not?" Lyman interrupted. Then his face grew puzzled again. "I honestly don't know why. Nobody seems to know where she's been. But I'm sure she'll explain, if it's important."

A Twelve. Among Chamberlains, only five siblings were older than Alice. The rest had died long ago. And of those surviving five, two were currently bound for Andromeda as part of a cultural exchange. By contrast, Ord possessed a five-digit designation, as did Lyman and everyone else living here. Ord could never live long enough or become famous enough for his arrival to stun anyone. "Twenty-Four Four-Eleven is on his way. Behave, children!" Ord nearly laughed at the preposterous image. If he lived a billion years—a possibility, in theory—and if he did many wondrous things, then yes, he might just generate the kind of excitement that he felt now. Maybe.

"We don't even know where she's been," Lyman repeated. "We've asked and asked, but the walls won't tell us."

The famous Alice: She had been born after the Wars, in those first years of the Peace. She was an explorer and a pioneer at the high art of terraforming, and her techniques in building living worlds were still the standard, and her name didn't even need "Chamberlain" attached to it. Alice was famous enough in her own right.

"Not a hint to anyone. All right, little brother?"

Ord said, "Yes," with a soft, disappointed whisper.

Lyman made fists and drummed at his thighs, saying, "I bet it's nothing. Here and gone in two seconds, she'll be."

The universal wall changed again, showing a ringed gas giant. World-sized continents built of hyperfoams floated in its atmosphere, linked together like chains, the winds carrying them with a dancer's precision. Where was this place? Terraforming on that scale required time and great wealth, and there probably weren't ten thousand worlds like that in the galaxy. Ten thousand was nothing. Shutting his eyes, he knew that Alice had built it. Lyman had asked the wall to show him her work; and like his brother, Ord could only marvel at her skills.

Why would she come here?

Why bother?

And why would any enormous, wondrous soul want her presence to be kept secret . . . ?

Four

"Consider this. Our Families have never been wealthier, our reach never so great, yet in the same moment, we have never been so weak. Our portion of humanity's worth has shriveled throughout the Peace, which is exactly as it was planned. We are pledged to reproduce slowly. We patiently clone archaic bodies, then in measured stages fit them with the latest talents. But while we've kept a monopoly on many talents, other peoples and the aliens and even the machine intelligences grow in abundance each day, in numbers and wealth and in their capacity for accomplishment . . . their insectlike tenacity gradually winning the Peace, which, of course, is precisely why they agreed to it in the first place . . ."
—Alice's testimony

THEIR FORT WAS genuinely beautiful, tall and with a blue-iced skeleton draped with a heavy white flesh left behind by last night's snow. Yesterday, after the last drills and before the official inspection, everyone had added some touch of his or her own. Except for Xo, that is. Decorating the parapets were snow fists and starship prows and big-eyed skulls. Ord had fashioned a snarling wail-hail on his portion of the wall—a fierce beast with spiked wings extended forward, its curved white teeth glowing in the early light. He was standing behind his wail-hail, on the broad rampart, his squad flanking him and everyone at attention. Ravleen was speaking, her voice coming through headphones embedded in their golden face masks. "From now on," she promised, "our enemies, these awful Blues, are going to suffer every flavor of misery. We'll beat them once and again, and we'll beat them so badly that a million years from now, they'll still ache from what we've done to their miserable bodies today."

It was a famous quote, the "every flavor of misery" line.

An old Sanchex general had uttered it on the eve of victory, and Ravleen made a point of repeating it every year or two. She and Tule were sitting inside the thick-walled keep set at the back of the courtyard, watching the countryside with hidden watchdogs. Ord knew how much she wanted to win. The war's losers would make medals for the winners—the standard rule—and nobody would treasure her disk of iridium and diamond more than Ravleen. Some said that the Ten-Million-Year Peace had only tempered her Family. Without question, when the Golds grew too old to play war, nobody would miss the games more than Ravleen. Shutting his eyes, Ord almost felt sorry for her . . . then he let his mind drift back to the topic that had kept him sleepless all night . . .

"What are you thinking?" asked Xo. Save for a few golden bruises, his face had healed. He was proud that he healed so easily, and he showed his wounds to Ord before putting his mask back on. "You look like you're thinking hard," Xo observed. "So what's in your head?"

That his sister was coming. *Alice. My Twelve.* The words surfaced in his consciousness, begging to be spoken. But the news was still secret. Last night and twice this morning, he had promised Lyman to say nothing. And maybe this was a wise restriction, he sensed. Alice had no genuine reason to come here. None at all. And he would look horribly foolish if he ever told his enormous story, and then it turned out to be untrue.

"I wish we'd start," Xo groused, forgetting his question. "Waiting is boring."

Last night, following a long tense dinner with a dozen brothers and sisters, Ord returned to his apartment and requested a slender biography of their great sister. Then he read pages and watched holos until well past midnight, trying to absorb some fraction of her enormous life. But it was an impossible undertaking. The history of the Earth seemed simple by comparison, and in so many ways, trivial. Alice had been everywhere, and everything that her great hands touched had been saved, or improved, or, at the very least, appreciated in some new way.

"I'm bored," Xo repeated.

As if she heard him, Ravleen interrupted their long wait. "Enemies in the woods," she called out. "On the west. On the move."

Three squads were stationed on the strong west wall, including Ord's unit. Saying nothing, they stared up into the leafless black woods, waiting for any motion, a delicious hint of drama riding in the wind.

"Mortars," Ravleen cried out. "Firing!"

Whump-whump. The Blues had a pair of mortars, cell-powered and air-driven, their size and range dictated by ancient rules. Everyone dropped to their knees, hugging the parapet, and a pair of heavy snowballs fell into the courtyard, bucket-sized and hitting no one. But they were only meant to judge range and the wind. The next rounds did the damage, someone crying out, "Heat," as a crimson sphere struck behind Xo. A chemical goo broke free of its envelope, activated by the air and melting the ice beneath it. A thick red cancer was spreading. Ord and Xo jumped up, using shovels to fling the worst of the goo below, then they used last night's snow, making a fast, sloppy patch.

It was fast and fun, and everyone, including Xo, seemed to enjoy themselves.

"Return fire," Ravleen ordered.

Their own mortars were loaded, aligned by hand and guesswork. *Whump, whump. Whump, whump.* They fired only snow, harassing their invisible enemy. And then half a dozen Golds shouted, "Look!" just before the Blues broke from the woods above.

"Guns on the shoulders," said their general.

Ord had an old snowgun—a favorite. Untold numbers of sisters and brothers had carried it before him. The old carbon stock was worn smooth, but the over-and-under barrels were perfectly aligned with the simple laser sight. A potent compressor built up a cylinder of angry gas, and a slug of dense milky ice was made inside each barrel, each round as big as a healthy thumb and spinning for accuracy, able to hit someone in the teeth at forty meters.

"Ready," Ravleen whispered into Ord's ears.

He looked over the wail-hail's right wing, snow-colored figures with deep blue face masks charging across the fresh snow. A practiced scream grew louder as they closed the gap. There were two dozen soldiers, including the eight who were quickly rolling cannons into position . . . and where were the others . . . ?

"On my command," Ravleen roared. "Cannons . . . fire . . . !"

Thunk-thunk-thunk. Three cannons were set on the west wall, a fourth held in reserve. Big fat rounds followed golden laser beams, snow striking snow. The Blues were zigzagging, a thin line of them charging. Fifty meters, then forty. Then thirty, and Ravleen said, "At will. Fire."

Just like in the drills, Ord's squad rose together, aiming and squeezing off double shots. Flecks of laser light danced over their targets. It sounded like the popping of fat beetles, the air filled with white streaks flying both ways. Ord selected his target and hit it in the belly, then the face, then missed when it ducked and danced sideways. But he anticipated the next move, leading and firing and the double shots smacking the face between the eyes, snapping the head back, leaving the Blue sprawled out on the snow.

"Reload," said his gun. He dropped and opened the stock, shoving in handfuls of fresh wet ammunition. Then the lone squad on the east wall was shouting and firing. Not only were there two attacks, but Ravleen hadn't seen the other troops marshaling. "Squad Aspire," she shouted. "Change walls. Support the east. Now."

The Blues must have disabled the watchdogs on the east. With a fair trick? Every war had its strict rules—so much snow per fort, so much heat allowed the attackers, and a finite number of crude machines to keep the mayhem shackled. Squad Bash—Ord's squad—had to spread out and cover for Aspire. He would fire and drop, then come up somewhere else along the rampart. Someone's lucky shot caught him in the face, a warm thread of blood making the eye blink and water. He ducked again and wiped the wound with a sleeve, then moved and rose again. But now the Blues were in retreat, their attack always meant to harass and nothing more. Their cannons fired at the sky, sacks of red heat streaking high and plunging into the east wall, bursting with a sickly thud and gnawing away at the thin barrier of cold blue ice.

Ravleen pulled Squad Carnage next. She had no choice. They had to make repairs while Bash was left alone on the west wall, six soldiers fighting more than a dozen. And, of course, the Blues attacked again, in tight formation, pushing right up under the massive wall. Squad Bash closed ranks and fired down at them. A heat grenade lodged in the wailhail's mouth, and the fierce head collapsed into mush. Then the Blues started teasing them, shouting, "You're next, you're lost, you're dead!"

Ord dropped and reloaded, moved and rose again, and the Blues happened to guess right. When he rose, every gun was fastened on him, blue sparkles half-blinding him and the double shots already on their way. He had no time to react. The entire salvo caught his face and throat; and what startled everyone, Golds and Blues alike, was how he managed to stay on his feet, bloodied and stunned but undeniably upright.

The Blues fired again, in unison.

That second salvo lifted Ord off the rampart, snapping his head back, and he fell into the courtyard, landing on his back in a pool of greasy red heat, bruised and sore and suddenly tired enough to sleep, and blind with all the blood burning in his eyes.

Five

"Why did we attempt such a thing? The simple, single--word explanation is 'greed.' The two-word clarifica-tion adds 'charity,' because wasn't this for your good as well as ours? The third word is 'arro-

SISTER ALICE :: 23

gance,' I would propose. And the fourth, without question, is 'stupidity' . . . "

—*Alice's testimony*

ORD REMEMBERED WHEN his blood tasted salty. Now it was sweet, in taste and in odor reminding him of overly ripe oranges. His biochemistry was changing, new genes awakening, his body progressively tougher and faster, and faster to heal. He had been able to fight again by afternoon, and by dusk he felt almost normal, picking at the hard scabs as he slipped into the house. As always, he touched the PRIDE AND SACRIFICE emblem on his way to the stairs. But after a few more steps, something caused him to pause— something subtle to the brink of imperceptible—Ord standing on the balls of his feet while listening, hearing what wasn't exactly a sound emerging from an adjacent hallway.

He changed direction, suddenly aware of his heartbeat.

The old house had been built in stages, like in any coral reef, one layer set on top of the last. The oldest rooms were in the deepest interior. The original mansion was long abandoned—a five-story structure not particularly grand even in its day—and Ord knew that he had reached it when the floor changed to natural stone, cold and dirty white. Lights woke for him. House robots had carefully maintained every surface, yet the place felt old, tired and a little frail. Ord touched the simple brick walls, new mortars blending with the old but nothing else changed, and with senses half-born, he felt thousands of centuries focused squarely on him, barely allowing him to breathe.

A central staircase led up to dozens of sealed doorways. Ord had brought his friends here, just once, showing off the Chamberlains' humble beginnings. Next to the staircase was a heavy door, always sealed and a little mysterious. Not even Lyman had permission or the means to open it. But today, for no apparent reason, the door was ajar. No, Ord realized, it was missing. He stepped closer, blinked, and hesitated. Ancient hinges dangled in the very dark air. It was as if the great door had been stolen, or erased, and he couldn't guess why.

Ord did nothing. The room beyond was dim and vague, dust floating with a graceful ease. He heard a sound, a faint dry click, but couldn't guess its direction. "Hello?" His voice was weak, practically useless. The room seemed to swallow his noise, then him, his snowboots falling silent on the old rotted carpet and his face caressed by a sudden deep chill. He was inside the room before he made any conscious decision to take the chance. He told himself, *I shouldn't be here.* He thought, *I'll leave. Now.* But the promise seemed as good as the deed, and Ord walked on, following a straight, certain line.

It wasn't a large room, even in its day. A round wall stood on his left, the tighter curve of the staircase on his right, and both walls were buried behind cabinets and framed paintings and various decorations that made no sense to him, their styles and logic long extinct. The place felt like a storage closet, not a room where people would gather. Despite careful treatment, the relics were degrading, wood eaten by patient fungi, paintings faded and flaking. A faint yellow lamp came to life, illuminating an enormous portrait. Ord paused, glancing at the face, then at the plaque beneath, the subject's name etched into a piece of greenish metal.

"Yes, he's our father."

The voice didn't startle him. It came wrapped in a calmness that soothed and nourished him. Removing one thin glove, Ord touched the name, *Ian Chamberlain* written in the dead man's neat, circumspect script. It was nearly identical to Ord's handwriting . . . the same smooth curves, the same even spacings . . . and he felt a sudden deep reverence for the man. Ian was shown posing before the original mansion, the building and the man both blurred by the tired paints. Ord had seen Ian countless times, in holos and interactive fictions; but here, quite suddenly, he felt close to the man, and nervous, his mouth turning small and dry. This was their father, their One. Ord shivered, and he smiled, and the voice said, "Look at me," with a mild, flat tone that couldn't startle anyone.

It was his sister's voice—every sister's voice—yet it was wrong, reaching deeper than simple sound could manage.

"I'm standing behind you," he heard, and he turned, discovering a woman in the middle of the room, smiling at him. Her face was the same as any sister's face, only rounder. She wore a body that was a little fat, wrinkles crowded around the eyes and a softness to the flesh, pudgy hands trying to straighten the shoulders of her simple dark blouse. She took a step toward him, and Ord felt a tingling sensation, smelling ozone. Achieve a certain age, he knew, and you ceased to be merely tough meat and an enduring mind. Succeed at being an adult for tens of thousands of years, and your Family would teach you how to use new energies, plasmas and shadowy flavors of matter. Eventually you were built of things more unseen than seen, the prosaic nonsense of sweet blood and slow neurons left for only the most special occasions.

"Look at you," she whispered, a dry hand touching Ord on the cheek. "Do you know how perfectly perfect you look?"

"You're the Twelve," he sputtered.

She gave an odd little laugh.

Ord managed a clumsy sideways step. Could she be anyone else? It seemed preposterous to think that a Twelve would speak to him. Was she a younger sister, perhaps some assistant to their Twelve? Or an empty facsimile carved from light and dust, set in this room where it could be safely out of the way?

"My name is Alice," she warned. "Not Twelve. And you? You must be the baby. You have to be Ord."

He offered a very slight nod.

Curiosity and a mild empathy showed on the smiling face. Alice touched him again, on the other cheek, saying, "There. All gone."

His scabs had dissolved, bruises absorbed.

She laughed without making noise, tilting her head as if to look at him from a new vantage point. Invisible hands passed through his flesh, studying him from within; then she was saying, "I used to enjoy a good snowball fight. Isn't that remarkable to think?"

It seemed unlikely, yes.

"Quite the fort you have." She closed her eyes, a wisp of red hair dangling over her chalky forehead. "Not elaborate, no. But sturdy. A good solid structure, for being made of nothing but water."

"Can you see the fort?"

"Easily." She opened her eyes, smiling as she added, "You fought on the west wall, near the middle—"

"Did you watch me?"

"I can tell from the bootprints and the blood. There's a thousand obvious clues, and I can reenact the entire struggle for my own eyes, yes." Then she announced, "This is yours," and held up his snowgun.

Surprise slipped into nervous guilt. They weren't supposed to remove equipment from the battlefield. Ord watched while Alice went through the motions of a careful examination, placing her right eye to the end of the upper barrel and tugging on the trigger. He grimaced. But nothing happened, and she seemed amused by his response, smiling at him, her soft voice saying, "My, my. I didn't have such fancy toys when I was a girl."

The gun wasn't fancy, but he didn't correct her.

"I am jealous," she assured him.

That was a remarkable thing to hear. A Twelve envying him? Because of a toy gun? "How are my Radiant Golds?"

Radiant?

"What kind of war game is it?"

"A forty-hour scenario," he reported. "Heavy snows and the Golds defend a place of their choice—"

"Against the Electric Blues," she interjected.

Ord swallowed, then said, "They have to capture our flag."

She kept smiling, and something about Alice made him feel happy, as if she couldn't contain her own joy, and it was flowing into him, sweetening his mood. She shut her eyes again, savoring the instant. "Here." She handed him the weapon. "I don't mean to leave you defenseless."

"I can't have it . . . not here . . ."

"Pardon me?"

Ord swallowed, then used a careful, certain voice. "I leave my gun wherever I was standing. Where I was when we quit for the day."

"Marking your position. How reasonable."

The gun vanished from his grip, fingertips tingling for an instant.

"I am sorry. I didn't know." Yet she sounded more amused than sorry. Turning, she did a slow stately walk around the room, absorbing all of it with her eyes and perhaps other senses. Fine china plates were collapsing into dust. An ornamental sword was speckled with corrosion. Countless twists of dust had gathered on a pair of historic fusion batteries, hiding them under soft gray mounds. A quantum computer's infinity-drive had fallen to the floor when its mag-coupling failed, leaving it separated from the thinking world, and by now, probably insane. But what captured Alice's attention was inside the adjacent cabinet. A crystal sphere had broken in two—that seemed to amuse her—and she opened the door and picked up the larger piece, explaining, "In my day, we threw our snowballs. We made them with our hands and threw them, and I wasn't particularly good at it. The sexes differed too much in ability, and I had a girl's arm." The crystal depicted the Earth as it was ten million years ago. Carefully, she set Asia and the Pacific back where they belonged, then turned and stared at the ceiling for a long while. "That pasture you're defending? I fought for it once. I can recall . . . well, everything. It was a one-day war, and my shoulder was sore afterward. Because I didn't have much of an arm, I suppose." She paused, then looked at him. "Do the Swords still exist?"

"They're the Silvers," Ord replied. There were twenty clans, twenty colors, and fifty children in each clan. He had to ask, "Were you a Gold?"

"One of the first, and worst."

Ord imagined this woman running in the snow, attacking a cowering line of Silvers. In the early Peace, childhoods were quick and simple. A person became a full adult in just a century, and then was she given a new body and mind, endowed with the powers necessary to handle the Family's responsibilities. Slow growth, like Ord's, allowed for quality. Patience allowed a more perfect maturity. He had been told that many times, and he believed it, yet part of him envied Alice, thinking how she had to be a child for just a few winters.

"And who's your general?"

"Ravleen."

"A Sanchex. Am I right?"

Ord nodded.

"Mere crystal grows tired and shatters," she said. "But some things are too resilient. If you see my point." Alice gave a satisfied nod, then added, "I would love to hear everything. Soon. It's been too long since I last visited . . . and took in the pleasures of this lovely old house . . ."

Her voice fell away, as if she was hunting for the best words.

Then she said, "Pleasures," again.

"Why are you here?" Ord heard himself blurt the question, then too late, he added a respectful, "Alice."

She didn't seem to hear him. Stepping past him, she lifted her hands to touch the old portrait. With means powerful and obscure, she rearranged the molecules in the tired paints, re-creating the image of their father's face and body, then altering the artist's original work. A rope of glass fibers dangled from the dead man's chest. Through those fibers he would have controlled a multitude of primitive machines, his body linked to whatever warship or world he was residing on at that moment. Few humans used these systems anymore. No Family member bothered with them. But Ord recalled that exposing the glass rope, whether in public or in a portrait, would have been rude, even vile. After the Wars, and for a very long time, it was one of the Chamberlains' most important duties—keeping their powers tactfully and gracefully out of sight.

"What do you think, little brother?"

He stepped close and studied the portrait. The cylindrical white house and green lawn were unchanged, as if out of focus. That vagueness made Ian all the more real, set against an exhausted background. Ord stared at the face—ageless and wise; the seminal patriarch—and he noticed a quality in its expression. It was as if the artist had told the great man to smile, and he had done his best, but inside him was some massive, deeply felt sadness that no mere face could hide away.

Ord was uneasy. Restoration was noble work, but what Alice had done was vandalism. The past always should be respected; yet she had plainly twisted that work of art, making it into something else entirely. Self-righteousness left him bold, and he asked again, "Why are you here?"

Alice appeared composed, giving him a watery grin, while asking in turn, "Why can't I come here?" Then she looked at their father, a thin colorless voice saying, "When she wants, a person should be able to visit her home."

He had no simple, quick response.

"Desire," she said, "is reason enough, little brother."

And when he next glanced at the portrait, she vanished. He found himself standing alone, standing in a dark little room where he didn't belong, the air suddenly frigid and his blood-caked snowsuit warming itself and him in response, his breath visible, rising up into the weak yellow light like thin puffs of tepid steam.

Six

"Alone, I have renovated more than ninety thousand major worlds, satisfying the widest array of clients. Perhaps a trillion sentient souls live in nests assembled by these hands. But my finest work lurks in those secret places that I build for myself, from nothing. On occasion, I'll invent some unique biol-

ogy and hide it away inside dust clouds or faraway globular clusters. And yes, these are very questionable acts, legally and ethically. I know that perfectly well. But a terraformer always dabbles in such work, and I don't mean just the bored Chamberlains. The multitudes do their work in drawers and under their mattresses. And not just the thrill of the forbidden lures us. It's the hiding that is intoxicating. It is the enticement of having something unique and entirely our own . . . and we must keep it secret . . . and really, isn't that the best way to protect whatever you cherish . . . ?"

—Alice's testimony

ORD RODE THE stairs up to his apartment, telling no one what had happened. Tonight the house felt exceptionally empty. He assumed that his siblings were with Alice, treating her to some ceremonial party, and there were probably many good reasons not to include their youngest brother. Snow was falling again, he noticed. Eating alone, Ord studied the day's lessons without actually concentrating. Poetry and mathematics seemed all too ordinary, and he eventually set them aside, ordering his universal wall to show him more of Alice's worlds. Light-velocity feeds were piped to him; a new vista offered itself every few minutes. He let his pajamas dress him, and he sat on his bed, in the near darkness, nothing to watch but a numbing series of fabulous images streaming from the ends of the galaxy.

Alice's worlds were always rich with life. More than most terraformed bodies, they were productive and robust, and interesting, and in ways that he could only dimly perceive, inspired. Sometimes Ord asked to see who lived there, and he was shown city scenes and up-to-the-second census figures. Like him, the people were built of ordinary matter. Like him, they had limited talents laid on top of an open-ended life span. Barring the spectacular accident, they might live forever. Yet unlike Ord—unlike any member of the Families—they could manipulate their human forms.

Instead of enlarging themselves with trickery, they bent themselves with genetic tailoring, adapting to odd niches or simply embellishing those physical traits that most pleased them. It was a basic feature of the Peace; different sects were given different strengths. Wandering past Ord was the multitude of humanity: tall bodies and tiny ones, people with golden fur or elephant noses or dragonfly wings or outrageous sexual organs. On older, more crowded planets, it was best to make everyone physically small and split them into a carefully structured array of species. The Earth itself was home to several hundred thousand distinct forms of humanity, every foodstuff and every waste product metabolized by someone. Brother Lyman had a passion for the strangest local ladies. He brought them to the mansion now and again. Once, mostly by accident, Ord had walked in on him and a girlfriend, at the very worst moment. An embarrassing, instructive lesson, it still made the boy blush twenty years later: Eyes closed, Ord could see that finned beauty in the swimming pool, floating on her back with fins billowing and deep-sea eyes blinded by the soft lights, and his brother naked beside her, struggling for a handhold, absolutely unaware of the gawk-jawed intruder staring from the doorway.

The Peace was built on rules. The Families began with old-fashioned bodies, and no profession was theirs alone. Yet they remained the best terraformers, commanding respect and the highest salaries. Ordinary humans and teams of AIs couldn't build with the relentless beauty that Alice achieved, even on her smallest project. What's more, she worked for aliens. Methane seas; nitrogen seas; or water seas scorched by hard radiations—she was equally comfortable in every biology. She worked on vast scales, too. A brown dwarf appeared on Ord's wall, partly encased in some kind of scaffolding. Densely packed stars implied that this was a globular cluster. Or was it the Milky Way's core? Whatever the project, the work was only partially completed, and Ord knew just enough about the mechanics and scale of the undertaking to appreciate just how absolutely little he knew. When he saw Alice next, he would compliment her on this work. *If I see her,* he cautioned himself, lying back in bed, letting the sheets crawl up over him.

But he didn't sleep. Tired eyes had barely closed when a brother called to him, asking, "Did you tell? Anyone?"

Lyman was standing in the open door, his long hair and broad shoulders set against the light of the hallway.

"Tell them what?" Ord teased.

"About our sister," Lyman muttered, painfully nervous.

Ord shook his head. "I didn't, no. No one."

"I was just making sure." He drifted into the room, trying to smile while staring at the universal wall.

"Does she like the penthouse?"

Lyman blinked and remarked, "She isn't here yet. But she won't like it. I'm sure she won't."

The boy felt something. A caress, perhaps. Or his own adrenaline, or whatever stimulant was saturating his growing body. His fatigue had evaporated in a moment, his mouth hanging open but his voice stolen away.

Lyman noticed his odd expression, blinked, and stepped back.

"I saw her," Ord whispered.

"Where?"

Ord closed his mouth, summoning courage.

"Where did you see her?" Lyman came to the foot of the bed, suggesting, "It might have been another sister."

"She said she was Alice." Then he told the story, describing the missing door and the room full of relics, and Alice, and how she had easily managed some odd tricks. Would he get into trouble for entering the room? Or was the worst crime not telling Lyman about it afterward? "I thought you already knew she was here," Ord claimed. Then he asked, "Why hasn't she told you that she's here?"

His brother leaned against the bed, mouth open and his eyes empty. And around both of them lay a ghostly sense of amusement, thick enough to taste, and sweet.

"Where is she, Lyman?"

The older brother merely shook his head, never saying what was obvious. *She's here now . . . with us now . . .*

Seven

*"It isn't the most original idea, but it always capti-
vates ... that notion that our dear Earth was someone's secret garden, built long ago and soon lost,
and all of us are merely its lucky sons and happy little daughters ..."*

— *Alice's testimony*

THE SKIES WERE clear by morning. Dumb snows and smart
made the land look soft and new. The Sanchex mansion—a
great gray pyramid—covered the tallest peak to the north.
Ord was half-dressed, watching the sunrise while eating his
breakfast. Lyman returned to his room, announcing,
"Someone is living inside the penthouse. We're mostly sure
now."

Ord didn't know what to say.

"For some good reason, she doesn't want to respond to
us. Yet." Lyman shook his head with an easy gravity. "Just
the same, keep her presence secret. Understood?"

Of course he did. But Ord went through the ritual of
promising silence.

"Do what's normal," his brother insisted. "Act as if
everything couldn't be more ordinary."

Ord imagined his siblings crowding around the penthouse door, asking if Alice was inside. And Lyman, fighting his nervousness, merely nodded to himself, saying,
"Isn't it ... a lovely day ... ?"

THE ENEMY WAS entrenched east and west of the fort,
their main force clinging to the cliff face, using ropes and
narrow wooden platforms. The Golds knew that much because Ravleen cheated, asking the Families' security net
for help. Scans proved that the Blues hadn't broken any
major rules. They had used accepted methods to blind and
move, nothing but determined work responsible for their
early success. It was frustrating for Ravleen, her foes near

enough to touch and completely out of reach. Hugging the cliff, they couldn't be bombarded. They were free to gather, then rise en masse, flinging heat grenades and enduring a few good shots but always escaping before they were truly hurt.

Ravleen and Tule abandoned the keep. Separately, they strode along the ramparts, giving orders with sharp, worried voices. "You two," said Ravleen, pointing at Xo and Ord. "Take that cannon and harass theirs." The Blues continued to fire from the high ground, sending heat into the east wall. "And don't look at me with those eyes," she growled.

"What eyes?" Xo countered.

She glared at him, breathing loudly.

"Go away," Xo whined. "We'll smack them, don't worry."

Except Xo didn't work with conviction. Ord found himself loading the breech and aiming the long plastic barrel. Xo was content to fire the cannon, and when they missed—normal enough at this range, aiming uphill—Xo would shake his head and say, "Higher." Or he would state something else obvious. Ord tried to ignore him, knowing how Xo could be full of himself. Anger just made it worse. Then Xo declared, "I'm tired of winter. I hate this snow."

But winter had just begun, thought Ord. And with a hard jerk, he pulled on the wire cord, a strong dull *whump* sending a white streak up to a point just short of its target, a pair of happy Blues waving at them from behind their gun.

"Too bad." Xo's mask showed only his eyes and mouth, each of them grinning. "Aim higher, why don't you?"

Better to cut the snow instead. Ord knelt and counted handfuls, trying to decide what was perfect. Their next shot was closer still, and Xo, who hadn't been paying attention, remarked, "See? It's better this time."

It was a brilliant day, and lovely. In the quiet moments, they could hear the city on the lowlands—horns and bells and a suggestive gray murmur that could be a billion voices whispering—and Ord remembered when he crept down to the estate's boundary, hiding in the deepest grass, watching ordinary people moving through their lives. His universal wall would give closer, more intimate views; but sitting on the edge of that other world, knowing he could, if he wished, walk straight into it . . . well, that was a different type of watching, and intoxicating . . .

Chimes rang in the distance, very softly, and Ord wished he didn't have to be here.

The sunshine felt hot, and he broke a big rule in a small way. Rolling up his mask, Ord massaged the wet face with wet snow. Xo saw him, and asked, "What happened to your scabs?"

Ord pulled the mask back into place.

"It looks like you weren't even hit yesterday."

"I slept a lot." Ord couldn't invent a better excuse.

"Sleep did that?"

No, Alice did . . . and suddenly he couldn't stop thinking about her. He had pushed her aside all day; but now he found himself wondering what she was doing, and did she like the penthouse, and would he see her again? "I wasn't hit that badly," he offered, hoping to deflect suspicions.

But Xo didn't care. His mind had already shifted again, his voice too loud when he announced, "Oh, she's a good general in the open. Good enough. But not with this stand-and-fight shit, she isn't."

Teasing Ravleen was a better game. More dangerous, too.

"If I were her," Xo claimed, "I'd send out a couple squads. I'd assault the cannons right now—"

"And lose the squads when they counterattacked," said Ord.

"If we don't do something," the boy maintained, "we're going to be dead here. Dead."

Ord ignored him, aiming again, forcing himself to concentrate. The icy slug had an imprecise size and density, plus an imperfectly smooth surface. His tutor loved to explain how the universe was a tangle of simple suppositions and principles woven together in chaotic ways. Nonlinear mathematics helped navigate through the chaos, but only to a degree. Ord barely understood them . . . yet he had a sudden premonition, numbers and intricate symbols converging into a smooth, highly polished answer that made his hands lift, the right hand grasping the wire cord and hesitating . . . wait, wait . . . now . . .

He tugged at the cord with a careful, perfect strength.

The slug was in flight, traveling on a neat arc, when one of the Blues pulled on his wire, firing at the worst possible moment.

Ord's slug hit the barrel's mouth, plugging it; hot compressed air caused the breech to shatter, some old flaw exposed, steel-colored plastic shards driven backward into a boy's arm and face. He collapsed, limp and bloodied. A cheer rose from the rest of Squad Bash. Even Xo was impressed enough to say, "I can't believe it." Everyone took a break from the fighting to run over and watch while the unconscious body and the ruined cannon were dragged away. It was a sterling moment, and ugly, one less Blue to fight now. Ord tried to be thrilled, but instead he felt sorry. A few days would heal the boy, and no lasting harm had been done, but all those fine reasons didn't seem to have much weight behind them.

"You got a lucky shot," said his morose companion.

But it wasn't luck. Ord was certain.

And one shot wasn't the entire war.

The east wall continued to be hammered through the day. When it was time to quit, the hard ice had turned red and rotten. The Golds had fifteen minutes to make repairs, in peace. But they wasted most of that time. Someone approached Ravleen, telling her what Xo had been saying about her. She marched over to him, asking, "How would you like to be banished? Is that what you want?"

"If you were any kind of Sanchex," Xo countered, "I'd fight and keep quiet."

Ravleen wasn't wearing her mask. She had a sharp face that could be pretty, if she wished. Right now her features looked ugly and hard. Ord decided to step between them, trying to defuse things. But the best he could offer was, "We should work together—"

"Quiet," Ravleen warned him.

Then Xo said, "A real Sanchex would have won the war by now—"

Ravleen swung with her right arm and shoulder.

Ord pushed her back. But then she swung again, aiming at him, and the bony fist caught him on the temple. Yet he stayed on his feet. He shook his head, the world blurring for an instant. Then Ravleen was past him, pinning Xo against the soggy red wall, punching him with a blind rage . . . and Ord grabbed her forearm, giving it a quick little twist.

The tough bone failed, making a sharp *crack* as it split.

Ravleen collapsed to the ground, her arm useless and its shoulder dislocated. With a tight, furious voice, she said, "Wait." She looked only at Ord, saying, "Banishment's too easy."

She said, "You wait. You'll see . . . !"

Eight

"My closest childhood friend was a little Vondalush boy. He belonged to my clan, which meant that we often played together, and he genuinely adored me. If I were cynical, I would suggest that his older siblings encouraged his love and devotion for me. His Family was a robustly mediocre bunch—Vonda-lushes have always been that way—while Chamber-lains plainly had nothing but greatness waiting in their immortal futures. Everyone knew it, and the poor boy was part of some painfully obvious scheme, his Family hoping that our little War and Peace games would seal some deep and eternal bond.

"I was barely ten centuries old when I saw him for the final time. Afterward, I missed the boy when I bothered to think of him. We spoke often—the Milky Way practically glows with all the messages

relentlessly racing between the likes of him and me—
but every attempt at a rendezvous was a failure. I
had pressing business; that was my usual excuse.
And then, after another half million years, my child-
hood friend was dead.

"It was an accident. He belonged to a team work-
ing with a millisecond pulsar, trying to create an
enormous power plant . . . and by every fragmentary
account, his death was heroic and swift and tragic
and painless.

"After hearing the news, I sought out the first
available Vondalush boy, and for several thousand
years, he was my protégé. I gave his Family lucra-
tive work and weighty responsibilities. And then my
mood for charity found new directions, and I left the
boy, letting all the Vondalushes fall back into their
noble, godly obscurity . . ."

—*Alice's testimony*

"You FOUND MY message, did you?"

"Oh, yes." It was set on his desk, handwritten on the most ordinary parchment . . . or at least it had looked handwritten. "I came as fast as I could."

"Alice."

"Pardon?"

"Call me by my name, Ord. Please."

He whispered, "Alice," to himself.

"Have you ever been here?" She stepped back from the satin-crystal door, beckoning to him. "I mean the penthouse, of course. I redecorated today. What do you think?"

The penthouse was an enormous room with no apparent walls or ceiling. Ord had been here for special dinners, but the comfortable furniture and freestanding universal walls had been replaced, a jungle standing before him. The foliage was gray-green and thin, probably meant for a low-gravity environment. Ord took a step, discovering that he was lighter now. How did she manage it? Only expensive machines could dilute the Earth's pull, and he was very much impressed with his sister's skill.

"A quiet lad, isn't he?"

Ord said, "Sorry."

"Why? You had a busy day. You're entitled to your silence."

He looked at the ceiling, nothing to see but a deep, damp, blue-white sky. "What world is this?"

"A secret world."

He didn't understand. But before he could ask questions, Alice asked, "Are the others jealous? That only you received an invitation?"

Ord nodded. He had shown the note to Lyman—that was only right—and Lyman had sputtered, "What did you say to her?"

In plainer words: *What makes you so special?*

"You know, our brothers and sisters keep wandering up here." Alice smiled at the leaf litter on the floor. Tonight she looked thinner, wearing a flowing gown, deeply blue and soothing. She showed Ord her smile, saying, "They've stopped asking me to open the door. But they come and stare at it all the same. In their lives, I doubt if they've ever felt so curious."

Lyman had only looked tired and frazzled.

"And they're rather pissed off, I think."

The words were unexpected, as incredible as this little alien forest and the diluted gravity. That a Twelve would say "pissed off" seemed contrary to some law or principle. Straightening his back, Ord said, "I think they're scared. I think."

"Well," said Alice, "isn't that their right?"

It was a strange reply, but he managed to shrug and nod.

She touched his face, telling him, "You look well. You must have ducked at the right times."

He dipped his face. "How much did you watch?"

"Every moment," she reported happily.

"You . . . you did things . . ."

"Twice, and you're welcome." Alice played with her own hair. It was longer than last night, fuller and bright as fire. "I helped your aim, once, and I helped with the Sanchex girl."

"Now she hates me."

"Yet she will heal, won't she?"

What could he say?

"Twenty centuries from now, she won't think about what you did. Tragedy is perishable, little brother. Believe me. Ravleen will reach a point where these memories will elicit a smirk and little else."

What mattered was tomorrow, not the remote future. Ord almost wished that Alice had never come here, or at least she had ignored him. At this moment, Ravleen was sitting in her mansion, dreaming up a thousand suitable revenges. She was an impossible, brutal tyrant— "And yet," his sister interjected, "she might grow into a courageous warrior, a glorious success, vital to the Families and to humanity."

"Can you read my thoughts?" he asked.

"In limited ways. But then again, anyone can read another soul's thoughts, within limits." She offered a long laugh. "I feel sorry for Ravleen. Your house is very different from hers. Enormous pressures are bearing down on that little girl, which help explain why she is as she is."

"She's a monster," Ord offered.

"Yet she will become a special Sanchex. She possesses that essential spark."

"Does she?"

"Or I'm wrong, which can happen." Alice shrugged her shoulders. "Perhaps she'll even disappoint me."

Sanchexes loved dangerous work. Lacking wars, they kept busy by wrestling with stars, delaying novas close to populated worlds, and sometimes demolishing isolated suns, using titanic energies to create rare and expensive materials.

"Isn't it odd?" Alice continued. "We begin as perfect copies of our parent, and then countless factors, tiny but irresistible, have their way with us. For good and for not." She paused before adding, "Xo isn't much of a Nuyen. Which may or may not be an insult, depending."

Nuyens were talented governors and administrators. The Earth had them in high posts, serving as links between Families and the multitudes.

"I don't like Xo," Alice insisted. "I've met him a thousand times, and I have never trusted him."

Ord hesitated, then asked, "What about me?"

"What about you?"

"What kind of Chamberlain will I make?"

"I learned ages ago, never predict what Chamberlains might do." The smile seemed fragile. "Now come over here and sit. Rest, little brother." She put a fond arm around him, reminding him, "I invited you to dinner, so let's eat and enjoy ourselves. What do you think?"

THE MEAL WAS exotic—an alien stew made edible by inverting its amino acids—and the sky darkened slowly, easing into a starless night. They sat on the twin stumps of dead trees that didn't even exist yesterday. For now, the stage was Ord's. Alice demanded stories of his snow wars and other adventures. He told her about canoeing mountain rivers and breeding bears, preferring them to other pets; and he described the arrow wars fought in the summer, face paints in lieu of masks but the same essential rules. And, of course, he had private games, bloodless fictional contests that he played against AIs. Were any of the Blues his friends? Alice asked. Not yet. He had met them, and of course he knew which face belonged to which Family. And some of the older Blues came to visit Lyman and the others—

"Why?" asked Alice.

Why what?

"Why do we build these careful antagonisms, passionate but essentially harmless? Ancient clans, elaborate rules . . . what's the overriding purpose of this contrivance, Ord?"

His tutor claimed it was to teach cooperation.

"Cooperation," she echoed. "That's a key reason why the Families have thrived. But wouldn't bridging one of your little rivers serve the same noble function?"

Lyman had a different explanation. He claimed that war games were like tails on embryos—vestiges of something not needed anymore.

"Sounds a little truer," Alice replied.

Her face had grown empty. Did the topic bother her? Then why did she bring it up?

"Tell me, little brother. Why did we fight the Great Wars?"

There were thousands of would-be gods. They had embraced the new talents and tried to enslave humanity, and the Wars defeated them. Sanchexes and Chamberlains helped save the innocent multitudes, and in gratitude, they were allowed to keep their vast powers. They were given these lands, and, together, the Wars' survivors fashioned the Peace.

"Noble images," Alice conceded.

Ord had stopped eating, but he discovered that he couldn't muster the will to push the half-empty bowl aside.

"Here's the crux of it, little brother. Somewhere in its history, every technological species stands on the brink of godhood. Immortal citizens will be capable of building worlds, or obliterating them. How a species responds to that challenge . . . well, that's what determines its fate, more often than not."

The galaxy was littered with ancient civilizations torn apart by warfare. Sometimes Ord dreamed of sifting the rubble on some unmapped world, pulling out chunks of burnt bone and catching a glimpse of those lost souls.

"Our powers aren't cheap," said Alice, "and they're never plentiful. When the Wars began, there were only a few hundred billion people. How many of them could be fitted with those new technologies? Only a few. And many of them were corrupt. Perhaps, as you say, evil. But then our species saved itself with a single wise deed. Ordinary people sought out the best thousand from their own ranks. Not the wisest or strongest, but those odd souls who'd be least corrupted by their new talents."

The ideas were perfectly familiar, and Ord kept nodding.

"Ian Chamberlain was a thoroughly unimportant man until he was selected. A decidedly unsuccessful man, by most accounts."

The boy looked at his bowl. A tiny bug with long lacy wings was helping itself to his gravy.

"How is your dinner?"

He said, "Fine."

Alice nodded, saying, "The Families are pledged never to injure others, by act or by omission."

It was a fundamental law, a set of memes rooting in Ord's own mind.

"To you," she said, "the Peace looks immortal. Everlasting. Isn't that so, brother?"

He began to shrug.

"Yet ten million years is no span at all. You'd be amazed how brief it feels to me."

Ord was tired of being amazed.

Alice rose to her feet. Before them lay a shallow pond, bony fishes, alien and primitive, swimming lazily over soft white alien mud. She watched their motions for a long while, or pretended to watch them. Then she told Ord, "Your brother is terrified of me. Of my presence here."

Lyman?

"Did you know that he's left the Earth?"

"He's too young," said Ord, a boy's surety making his voice rise. "He isn't allowed to go anywhere."

"Yet he has. Many times." She laughed gently and easily. Her blue gown was becoming muddy, a sticky white fringe building as she strolled around the pond. "He was on the Moon when I announced that I was coming home. Seducing women, no doubt. Being a Chamberlain has its relentless advantages."

"Where else has he gone?"

"Around the solar system. Nothing too astonishing, don't worry." She paused. "Haven't you slipped out of these old mountains? The sentries aren't perfect. Nobody needs to know."

"I haven't."

"But please tell me that you've been tempted." She seemed disappointed, even hurt. "Haven't you been tempted?"

Endless times, yes.

"Yet you obey the rules. How nice." She knelt, cupping a hand and dipping it into the pond, then drinking it dry. "Lyman doesn't obey, and that's why he's scared. I'm going to punish him or embarrass him. Somehow, this visit of mine will make his little indiscretions into something important."

Again, Ord remembered the finned girl floating in Lyman's clumsy grasp.

Standing again, Alice dried her hand with the gown.

After a long moment, Ord asked, "Where's this world?"

"Inside a dust cloud. Hidden."

"Is this where you were? Before you came home, I mean."

She closed her hands into fists, sighed, and said, "Everyone wants to know where I was. What I was doing."

Ord's belly was aching, and not because of dinner.

"Tell them, brother. I was at the Core." She paused, a smile beginning and failing. Her face seemed to wrestle with her mouth, a strange lost expression winning out. Then she said, "I came straight from the Core. Which was a very long journey, even for me."

The oldest people in the Families didn't require starships. They could convert themselves to nearly massless particles, then move at the brink of light-speed. Ord tried to imagine such an existence. To say something, to be involved in this conversation, he mentioned, "Lyman wants to work at the Core someday. As a terraformer."

Tilting her head, Alice tried the same failed smile again. "A good Chamberlain goal, isn't it?"

The Core was famous for black holes and dust clouds, plus billions of star systems left sterilized by explosions and intense radiation. Over the last millions of years, the Families had made the Core remarkably safe. Humans and aliens had room to expand, no legal claims held by any species.

"The Core," Alice whispered, smiling at Ord, no light in her face and her words leaden. "It's a lovely place. Too many stars for me to count, little brother."

He doubted it.

She strolled over to him. Her bare feet left narrow prints in that strange white mud. With her damp hand, she held him beneath the jaw, blue eyes locked on his eyes, a cold voice telling him, "You could grow a tail. I could activate the old genes, and you'd grow one now. You still have that talent."

"I don't understand," Ord whispered. "What do you mean?"

"What do I mean?" She let go of him and turned away, her gown seeping a watery blue light as night fell. "Whatever I'm talking about, little brother, it isn't tails. You can be certain of that."

Nine

"While we're on the subject, I might wish to plead guilty to the tiny crimes that come to mind. I stole toys in my youth, and many times since. And I have built unregistered, illegal worlds, as stated. Plus on numerous occasions, to help friends and accomplices, I have used improper means to alter elections and overthrow some ugly governments that nobody misses . . ."

—*Alice's testimony*

"AND THEN WHAT?"

Ord took a deep breath. "We talked about tomorrow."

"What about tomorrow?"

"About snowfare—"

"Nothing else about the Core?" Lyman was pacing, crossing and recrossing his apartment while Ord sat on the enormous bed, watching his agony. "Well, at least we know where she came from. If she's telling the truth, that is."

Why wouldn't she?

" 'I'm not talking about tail.' Is that what she said?"

Ord nodded. "Basically."

"War." His brother's voice was soft. Ominous. "She was at the Core, and some kind of war has erupted."

"I don't think so."

Lyman stopped and stared at him. "Why not?"

"It's just a feeling." He could offer nothing more, but hearing the words, his reasons sounded treacherously thin. "It's not war. I'm pretty sure."

Lyman's girlfriends smiled at him from their perches.

"Alice gave me a plan," Ord continued. "For tomorrow. It involves Ravleen—"

"But what else did she say about the Core?"

"Nothing."

"Nothing?"

Ord shook his head, trying to appear certain.

Lyman picked up one of his tiny statues. The girl giggled and squirmed in his hand, then laughed quietly when he set her back down again. "You don't know," he began, softer than a whisper. Then he gasped and looked at the baby Chamberlain, admitting, "None of us understands what Alice can do. Her fantastic powers, her incredible reach. We live like fossils in this place. Old seashells set on a dusty shelf. All the children . . . we think we understand the universe, but we don't. Shit, we don't even hear rumors about her talents, that's how secretive and fucking strange she is . . ."

Alice had spoken to Ord about snowfare.

"What you need to do is earn your redemption," she had claimed. "Redemption with the Golds, and Ravleen, too. And here's how do it, easily."

Though to Ord, it seemed like a very complicated scheme.

Lyman moaned abruptly, throwing his arms into the air. "Something awful is happening," he declared. "That's obvious. That's why she came home." With both hands, he dragged the perspiration off his face. "It's one of the aliens, or all of them. They've decided to fight us for the Core."

But wouldn't they have seen trouble on the universal

walls? Ord couldn't believe that anything that enormous would remain invisible, even to dusty old shells set on a back shelf.

"Whatever it is," Lyman promised, "I'm going to make a general call. Every adult Chamberlain nearby . . . I'll tell them . . . nothing . . . and beg for them to hurry home immediately . . ."

It wasn't war; Ord was certain.

Then he remembered how their sister had said, "Redemption," again and again. That enormous, invincible creature had stood in front of him, her bare feet and the blue gown soiled with the odd white mud, and she had assured him, "You have to be redeemed. It's all my fault, but I can make everything better for you."

Her thoughts shifted, and that moment's face closed its eyes.

"Redemption," she had muttered one last time.

It wasn't a god's face, or a god's voice; and Ord had felt so very sorry for her, and for everyone.

Ten

"Our mountains have grown noticeably smaller. In ten million years, the patient gnawing of water and the weight of godly feet have done their erosive work, transforming tough granites into tough pink sands, while the crust beneath has gently slumped beneath their simple weight. It has been a cumulative collapse of several meters, obvious to my endless eyes . . .

"I was tempted to repair the damage. As we all know, with my proverbial finger, I could. I could lift the mountains back up where they began, if I wished . . . or yank them from the Earth and fling them into the sun . . . !"

—Alice's testimony

RAVLEEN WORE A simple cast and sling, wielding just one good shoulder and arm; yet somehow she seemed larger today, more dangerous—a brawny, fierce warrior marching in front of her assembled troops, black eyes screaming while her mouth said nothing. A light dry snow was falling. She paused for a moment and let herself smile, glancing at the simple gold flag hanging limp in the middle of the courtyard, and then up at the high gray clouds and the endless snow. "I need to know what's happening," she whispered. "I need a patrol. Two people. Volunteers."

Ord glanced at Xo, then down at his own boots.

"Who wants to?" Ravleen continued. "Anyone?"

With a dramatic flair, Xo stepped forward.

"Good." Their general's smile brightened. "Now pick your partner."

"Ord."

"Wrong choice," she responded. Then she pointed at Tule, saying, "My lieutenant is going with you."

Tule leaked a confused moan.

"Three minutes and we start," Ravleen warned. "Take radios and rations and drop over the south wall. I want reports. Find out what the Blues are doing. And harass them, always."

Tule moaned again, then remembered that she was a good soldier. With a nod, she assured, "You can count on me."

In a whisper, Xo told Ord, "I tried. Too bad you can't come, it'll be exciting out there."

"I bet so."

Xo watched him. "What are you thinking?"

"Nothing," Ord lied. "I just wish I was running with you."

"Except you're not," Ravleen growled, storming up to deliver a hard punch in the shoulder. She bruised Ord, in warning, then said, "I want you here with me. I'll keep you nice and close . . . !"

*   *   *

THE BLUES FIRED early—-moments early, and just a single shot—the ice slug hitting a boy between his shoulders. Everyone yelled, "Violation!" But he was only stunned, little harm done. Ravleen said, "Positions," and waved to her patrol toward the south wall. "Now. Do it."

Tule and Xo dropped rope ladders, climbed over the wall, and started down. Tule was a Syssalis—a Family always small and slow to mature. Her leg caught when her ladder twisted. Xo hit the pasture first and broke into a sprint; and an instant later the Blues spotted him, voices screaming, their cannons turned and firing as their troops charged in from the east and the west.

"Run," shouted Ravleen. "Pick up your feet, Tule. Go."

Blue-faced targets hurried into range. Ord got off some good shots, and he wondered if Alice was helping his aim. But she had promised not to help, not in that way, and he missed often enough to believe it was all him.

Tule was hit and hit again, and she would fall and pick herself up and take a sloppy step before falling again. But Xo never slowed, never looked back. He sprinted into the deepest snow, and Ord saw him leap off the first cliff—a fair drop, but cushioned by the drifts below—with a pair of Blues on his trail, firing from the cliff before jumping after him.

Tule had fallen for good. The Blues surrounded her, giving her a few good kicks even when she cried out, "Give, give."

Lowering his gun, Ord watched the battle with only the mildest interest. Poor Tule was picked up and carried away. The other Blues fired at the ramparts and retreated, happy to have their first prisoner. All this noise and wild energy meant nothing. Ord felt distant, indifferent. Suddenly he was thinking about Alice, and the Core; and sometimes, in secret, he whispered to his sister, certain that she was listening.

The bombardment resumed. Squad Bash manned the cannons until Ravleen replaced them with Squad Carnage. "From now on," she announced, "you've got a new responsibility."

Nobody spoke.

"Take the keep apart. Cut the ice into blocks." With the heel of a boot, she etched her plan into the rampart's ice. "Stack the blocks here. And here. And get that done this morning."

One boy admitted, "We'd rather fight."

Ravleen stared only at Ord. "Not for now. No."

The squad bristled but said nothing.

With her hard cast, their general popped Ord in the head. "After that, I've got another lousy job for you," she promised. "For the afternoon, and you'll like it even less."

XO ELUDED HIS pursuers for a few hours, but they were faster, and the tracking was easy in the deep snow. In early afternoon, both prisoners were led to the pasture, gagged and blindfolded, then set in plain view under a tiny white flag. "You're next," the Blues called out in a practiced chorus. "We'll melt that shitty fort and butcher every Gold inside!"

Tule was embarrassed. It showed in the slump of her shoulders and the slow sad shake of her head. But Xo stood tall beside her, undoubtedly inventing artful excuses to explain his capture.

A fresh assault began on the east, but Ord's squad saw none of it. They were below, doing work meant for robots, hands cold despite their gloves and their backs aching from the hard cutting and dragging. Everyone said, "The big attack is tomorrow. Tomorrow." There was excitement, and nervousness, but this was always just a game. They had used this reliable prattle for decades, and it was probably the same kind of noise that Alice had made when she was the same as them.

"Tomorrow," the soldiers told each other.

But nobody spoke to Ord. They conspicuously ignored him, and he discovered that he didn't particularly care. It was as if there were a traitor lurking inside him, and the traitor was announcing itself with, of all things, indifference.

* * *

"WHAT ARE YOU doing here?"

"Waiting for you," Ord replied. "How's prison?"

Xo shrugged and removed his mask. "Tiny. Boring. Cold."

"I'm sorry." They were in the trees high above the pasture, walking on the main trail. From here the fort looked strong, tall and secretive, the rotting east wall showing only the faint beginnings of a slump. Ord had been the last to leave, lingering on the battlefield, waiting for Xo to appear. Alice had promised that the boy would come this way, out of habit and out of need. And he would come alone, since Tule would never walk with him. "How did they catch you?" Ord asked. "What went wrong?"

"Well, they cheated," Xo said. "I was perfectly hidden, but they must have used illegal sensors. I'm sure of it."

"We should report them," said Ord. You went to your siblings when rules were broken. "I'll go with you and help explain—"

"Later. Maybe."

Ord nodded, saying nothing.

"How's Ravleen? Still angry at you?"

Ord peeled off his mask, pointing to his bruises.

"I hate her," Xo promised. "I wish you'd broken both arms, and her legs, too."

"Maybe I will," Ord allowed.

They walked on. Noise rose from the city—the musical scream of an important siren—then the light snowfall blotted it out, or the siren quit.

Xo said, "I wish we were done."

"So do I."

"They've stuck me in this prison box. It's ridiculous."

The boxes were cramped and soundproofed, but the heat bled out of them, helping to keep the prisoners miserable.

"I'm bored," the boy complained.

Ord paused and looked at Xo, then he looked everywhere else. Then as Alice had told him to do, he mentioned, "We could be home by noon tomorrow. If you want."

A hopeful little smile surfaced.

"Ravleen has a plan," said Ord.

Xo saw what was happening. "That's against the rules," he said, laughing and shaking his head. "I'm a prisoner of war. You can't tell me anything."

They were close to the spot where Xo had begged to be struck by the careful stone. "We're shoring up the east wall," Ord mentioned. "We're letting its rampart slump, but everything below is going to be strong again."

"Where's the ice from?"

"The keep. Except it doesn't have enough snow, of course." He paused before adding, "That's why we're robbing ice from the west wall, too. It's got more than we need." He drew a dramatic X on the boy's chest. "Remember my wail-hail? The wall's thinnest right under it."

Xo wasn't speaking, or breathing. This business was against every rule, and the wickedness was delicious. He smiled, then stopped smiling, as if someone might notice; and with a tight voice, he asked, "How thin is thin?"

"Like this." Ord put up his hands.

"She'll know I told. Ravleen will."

"How can you be sure?" Ord countered. "If Ravleen says anything to Tule, then she's the likely suspect."

"But will the Blues believe me?"

"Maybe not, but they could find out if you're right. And if your information's good, there won't enough time to cut a hole in the east wall anyway."

The boy stepped back and looked around, shivering with a dramatic flair.

"Who knows?" he muttered. "Maybe I'll crack. Maybe first thing in the morning, before they can even put me in that stupid box, I'll crack."

Eleven

*"Boredom can shoulder some of the blame. What
new challenges had we attacked during these last
thousand millennia? And there was the genuine urge
to accomplish something both spectacular and good.
And most important was the idea itself. The goal.
The ancient and perfect ideal. We were intoxicated
with a golden notion. We were drunk and in love,
the object of our affections infinitely beautiful and
smiling charmingly at us . . ."*

—Alice's testimony

A SINGLE SET of stairs rose to the penthouse, traveling in
a tight spiral, the stairwell itself decorated with an elaborate
mural. Yesterday, Ord was too nervous to pay attention.
Today, the mural seemed to force itself on him, showing
him endless Chamberlains caught in the midst of historic
and heroic acts. He saw worlds rebuilt, aliens embraced,
and the far edges of the galaxy explored. His own motions
caused the scenes to change, the artwork fluid and theoret-
ically infinite. Riding on a single crystal step, his hand cra-
dling the polished brass rail, Ord watched the most famous
death in the Milky Way: His ultimate father, the great Ian,
was sacrificing his life and eternity for the sake of a single
starship. The tale always made him weak and teary, and
proud. But seeing it now made him think how strange this
was—all the trouble invested into building and maintaining
a mural that was almost never seen.

He was deposited at the penthouse door. Touching the
bright black door, he said, "It's working. Just like you
promised."

The door dissolved, Alice standing before him.

"Your plan's working," he repeated, breathing in little
gulps. "Did you watch me?"

"I saw enough." Something was different. Worrisome,
alarming. Alice wore a heavy dark robe; the room beyond

was black, unbordered, and cold. But she did smile at him, telling him, "Thank you," then, "I'm glad it's going well," with a mixture of pride and pleasure. She was staring at a point beside him, saying, "That Nuyen seems the fool. Don't you agree?"

Ord felt uneasy, saying nothing.

"I would invite you inside," she continued, "but this is not the best time. I am sorry."

Her face seemed simple and worn down. If she'd had red eyes, he would have guessed that she had been crying. And perhaps she was crying, in a fashion. Ord kept reminding himself that very little of Alice was visible, and what he could see was exactly what she showed him.

"Are you all right?" he asked.

Her eyes tracked toward him, no other response offered. Ord stepped back and dropped his gaze.

"I'm just distracted," Alice explained. "And tired. My long journey has caught up with me."

That sounded unlikely.

"Tomorrow," she told him. "Once you're done fighting, I want you to come tell me everything. I promise. There will be a celebration; we'll enjoy your triumph." She paused, then said, "Please stop worrying. It doesn't do any good."

He said, "I know," without confidence.

Then, as the door began to re-form, she said, "Good night, little brother." For an instant, it sounded as if she was crying. But of course someone like Alice might conjure any emotion and put on the appropriate face . . . sadness just another in an endless parade of Creations . . .

Pushing the thought aside, Ord turned and stepped back onto the waiting stair.

TWO ROBOTS FLOATED in Ord's apartment—security models, armor slathered over an array of muscles—and with gray voices, in unison, they said, "You're wanted in the main arena. No, don't change clothes. Go now."

"Who's there?" he stammered.

"Lyman, and the others." The robots paused, probably waiting for a single voice to tell them what to say next. "Several hundred adults have arrived. They wish to speak with you."

The main arena was underground, deep inside the Chamberlain mountain—a vast room with seating for twenty thousand, waxed granite and perfect wood covering the walls and arched ceiling. The brothers and sisters looked inconsequential with so much space around them. They sat in a block before the stage, and Ord had to wonder: Why here? Why not in a smaller meeting room? But this was as far from the penthouse as any place, which might be important. Were security baffles in use? From the stage, a single brother waved at him. *Lyman.* Sitting beside him was a sister, a giant figure, three meters tall and built out of light and conjured flesh. "Up here," said Lyman. "We're just getting started."

Every step was work, every breath a labor.

"Ord?" said the giant sister. "My name is Vivian. Eleven Hundred and Twenty."

Eleven-Twenty was nothing. He felt like telling her that he wasn't impressed, that he knew their Twelve, and she was nothing beside Alice. And perhaps Vivian read his thoughts, taking his hand and squeezing, her flesh feeling like heated plastic, almost burning, as she said, "I'm glad to meet you." Her presence was tangible, her energies making the air and wide stage vibrate. "Sit, if you would. Sit here and talk with us."

A chair appeared between his brother and sister.

Lyman leaned close, and with a tight nervous voice said, "Relax."

A couple hundred faces stared up at them. The oldest adults were giants wearing meeting robes and Chamberlain faces, both demanded by tradition. Vivian had the highest rank, it seemed. Now she leaned forward, telling Ord, "Our brother did what was right, you know. Perhaps he should have warned us sooner, but we appreciate the dilemma. Alice requested silence, and why shouldn't he obey her wishes?"

"What do you want?" Ord whispered.

"Your help," Vivian responded. "I understand that our sister likes you. For some reason, she has taken an interest in you. Not that she dislikes any of us, of course. But you've actually spoken to her—"

"Yes."

"More than once, according to Lyman."

"Just a few minutes ago." His voice was soft and loud. He could barely hear himself, but the words were enlarged and flung across the arena. "Is Alice in trouble?"

"Why? Do you think she should be in trouble?"

He shrugged his shoulders.

Vivian made him notice her smile. Her face was incomplete, a patch of strange gray light on one side of her forehead. "She's come from the Core. Is that what she told you? Ord? Do you hear me?"

He nodded. "Straight from there."

"But has she told you why she was there? Anything at all?"

He didn't like Vivian; he didn't care for her tone. But this was important, and he took pains to say, "She came from there, she told me, and that's all. That's what I know."

Lyman leaned close again, following some careful script. Ord realized he was here only to put their little brother at ease, prompting him when necessary. He might smile, but he was sick with worry and exhaustion. "She was at the Core," he muttered. "We know that now. No doubts."

"We are certain," Vivian echoed.

"She was working on a special project," Lyman continued. "With other Chamberlains and Sanchexes . . . representatives from nearly half of the Families, and no one younger than One Hundred and Three . . ."

"Doing what?" the boy asked.

Lyman shut his eyes, saying nothing.

Vivian told him, "It is a secret." Her voice betrayed frustrations, yet she made herself laugh, as if that would defuse the tension. As if she could fool anyone. "I can't know their secrets, little brother. Though we have good sources with solid evidence who claim that our old siblings are working on FTL travel."

"It's not possible," Ord replied. "It's been tried, but nothing goes faster than light."

"Perhaps that's true," his sister offered. "Perhaps this is just someone's careful story meant to fool any prying eyes."

Ord felt himself sinking away.

"Eleven Chamberlains were at the Core," Vivian continued. "To the best of our knowledge, ten of them remain. Only Alice has left. She arrived here less than three hours after the live feeds show her leaving. But why? And why are some of the other Families leaving the Core at the same expensive pace?" The giant woman paused, then said, "I don't know the answers. But I have many questions that I would love to ask."

Murmurs spread, then collapsed.

"Ten Chamberlains are left there?" But the Core was not a small place. Ord shook his head, asking, "Where is 'there'?"

Everyone wanted to know. People whispered among themselves until Vivian lifted one of her enormous hands, commanding silence. Then she said, "They were working near the central black hole, inside its envelope of dust and plasmas. They have been there for several thousand years, it seems. Honestly, I don't know what type of work they're pursuing."

Ord shifted his weight, hands wrestling with one another.

"Has she given you any hint of an explanation? Just in what she talks about, Ord . . . have there been any clues . . . ?"

He whispered, "No."

Then he asked, "Why can't you ask her?"

She blinked and made a show of swallowing, then admitted, "Alice has set up barriers. A part of me is wrestling with them now, but she seems adamant in excluding everyone but you."

Ord looked at the audience, reading the same lost, worried expressions. Even Vivian seemed like a little girl mystified by events, angered by her limitations and perhaps a little glad, too. She could do nothing of substance. No clear responsibilities could be set on her oversize shoulders. It seemed obvious to Ord . . . and suddenly he wondered if this was his insight, or if perhaps Alice had given to him.

"When will you see Alice again?"

Ord blinked, trying to remember.

Lyman appreciated his confusion, touching an arm while saying, "We need to go on with our ordinary lives. As well as we can, brother. We keep this secret, but if Alice has come here for a reason, and if she wishes to tell us anything, we need to listen."

"Tomorrow," he confessed. "I'll see her then."

"When you do," Vivian instructed, "ask if she'll speak with us. Will you do that for us?"

"That's all we want," said Lyman.

"Please," said the ancient sister.

"Please," said two hundred mouths, in unison, their whispers rising to the pink stone ceiling and echoing back down on them again.

Twelve

"Ian rarely spoke of the Wars. Except to mention them in passing, just to remind his children about the darkness of the human soul. I remember once marching home after a hard day's play, and Ian noticed me crossing the grassy yard. He stopped me, and for no obvious reason launched into a long tale about finding our enemies hiding in some far-off solar system. They had built redoubts out of its stony worlds, and he explained how he had stopped on the fringes, grabbing up comets and accelerating them to near-light velocities . . . and with his eyes not quite looking into mine, he admitted that the largest redoubt gave its immediate and unconditional sur-

*render . . . and with the softest voice I ever heard
from him, he explained how it was too late. Nothing
could stop the comets, and they pummeled the world
until its crust melted, and millions died, and he wept
at the end of his story, and shook, still ashamed of
his cruelty while his audience—one enthralled little
girl—kept thinking what an enormous, wonderful
snowball fight that must have been . . . !"*
                                      —Alice's testimony

IN EVERYTHING BUT name, the Golds won their war before
noon.

The Electric Blues stuck to their old battle plan, troops
charging the east wall while artillery fired from the west.
But there was no final assault. When it seemed inevitable,
there was a pause, a sudden and mysterious lull, then the
sound of motion, troops scrambling over slick terrain to the
south. There was little pretense of subterfuge. Ravleen and
Ord stood together on the south wall, one of them smiling
beneath her mask, perfectly satisfied with the world. The
other wished he could feel relief, but there wasn't any. Nor
was there any sense of dread or foreboding, which was a
constant surprise to him. It was as if Ord were empty, all
the worry drained from him; sometimes he couldn't even
remember Alice or the Core, as if they had been carefully,
thoroughly extracted from his mind.

Ravleen noticed his mood enough to ask, "What's
wrong?" She poked him with a finger, telling him, "You
look sad. What are you thinking?"

He shrugged his shoulders.

But she didn't press for answers, too happy to care. Today her cast was soft, without a sling; and with her bad
arm, she hugged Ord, every Gold watching them and everyone surprised.

Alice had been right.

A Sanchex would do anything for a victory, provided
you left her precious pride intact.

"Beg for forgiveness," his sister had instructed. "Weep.

Grovel. And tell her your plan between the weepy moments. Trust me, she'll see its beauty. And then she'll claim it as her own."

For a deed that wasn't his fault, Ord had apologized . . . and why didn't his pride matter, too?

"It is happening," Ravleen whispered.

She said, "They actually believe the little shit."

Then she hugged Ord again, saying, "Fair is fair." A wink and smile showed through the mask, and she purred, "When the time comes, Ord . . . I want you to stand next to me."

THE BLUES ENTERED the pasture from the southwest, carrying their snowguns and heat grenades and finally showing their own flag, a blue rectangle flapping stiffly in the bright windy air. There was a pause as they gathered themselves, then they let out a roar, charging as cannons and mortars threw heat into the west wall. As promised, the ice beneath the half-melted wail-hail was treacherously thin. A squad of Blues surged through the sudden hole, excited and confident. There was moderate fire from above, plus some raucous cursing. The Golds seemed to be panicking. The first squad beckoned for others, and more than half of the Blues poured into the courtyard, marshaling and charging the flag-pole, nothing between them and their goal but a crude little wall of fresh-cut ice.

There was a sound, wet and strong, and massive. Then came the sudden irresistible sense of something falling. A fat wedge of ice broke free of the west wall, slamming over the new hole exactly as Ravleen leaped to her feet, shouting; "Blood!"

It wasn't a fight. Ord stood behind the new wall, firing without aiming, without heart. Four squads fired double shots at close range, knocking the enemy off their feet. Cannons were hidden behind little walls to the south and north, belching out fat slugs of ice that left their targets unconscious. Limbs were shattered. Face masks and the flesh beneath were split open, the sweet blood brilliant

against the white surfaces. And even still the Blues
mounted a final charge, desperation carrying them over the
wall, one girl able to put her hands on the flagpole's knotted
rope before Ravleen shot her from behind, in the head, her
body going limp and Ord watching her fall and lie still.

In a few days, everyone would be well again; every child
would be ready to play again. Yet Ord felt sad enough to
cry, watching Ravleen lead her troops across the courtyard,
driving their enemies against the wall and abusing anyone
with a hint of fight left in them. Then the prisoners were
disarmed and tied together; and Ravleen launched an assault on the enemy cannons, capturing them and more prisoners and chasing the last few Blues into the snowy woods.

Ord stayed behind, guarding the prisoners. He sat on the
trampled snow with his empty gun in his lap, and after a
while he couldn't hear the distant shouting. A flock of
crows passed overhead, talking in their harsh little language. Ord watched the masked faces, thinking how the
eyes seemed angry and a little afraid. But not much afraid,
and even the anger seemed false. And it wasn't just because
this was merely a game. The prisoners were too young to
know how to be genuinely angry or honestly scared. They
were children. This was what made them children. Sitting
there, thinking thoughts that weren't entirely his own, Ord
tried to imagine a world filled with danger; and he couldn't.
The part of him that was Ord looked at the battered fort
and the prisoners and the clear bright sky, and for the first
time in his life, he couldn't believe that this quiet would
last for all time.

Thirteen

*"Something went wrong. In some obscure and criti-
cal way, we failed, and we knew it, and to our collective horror, we realized that we could do nothing
. . . and even worse was how much time we had af-*

terward—long black seconds of time—for us to dwell
upon our failure . . . blaming one another, and Nature,
the Almighty, and, in particular, those awful people
who brought us forth into our miserable lives . . . !"
                                    —Alice's testimony

THE STAIRCASE WAS filled with brothers and sisters, half
again as many as he had seen yesterday. The stairs were
locked in place, no one moving but Ord, and he continued
to climb toward the penthouse on tiring legs, no one speaking unless he was close, no voice louder than a whisper.
"Be polite," they advised. "Be observant." The freckled,
red-haired faces were grim and tired in many ways, and the
climb seemed to take ages. Ord began to cry, wiping at his
eyes with alternating sleeves. "Be strong," the whispers demanded. Yet the faces seemed anything but strong, in stark
contrast to the great and dead Chamberlains parading
through the endless mural.

Lyman was the last face. Ord recognized the long hair
and the prickly pride in the voice, his brother saying,
"We're proud of you, you know."

Vivian emerged from the wall beside them, still prepos-
terously tall, stepping out of the mural as if it were syrup,
then bending until her giant face was near enough to kiss
Ord. "Alice is waiting for you, I think. That much I can
see, I think." She paused, the gray patch on her forehead
brightening. "Listen to everything she tells you, ask the best
questions, and please remind her that we'd very much like
to speak to her. Soon."

Ord nodded, and breathed. "What's happening in the
Core? Do you know?"

Nobody spoke.

He looked at Vivian. "What can you see now?"

"Nothing new," she lied. Appearing as winded as Ord
felt, she sighed and placed a great hot hand on his back,
shepherding him toward the crystal door. "Good luck,
brother. I know you'll do well."

The doorway was in front of him, then it was behind him. Ord was standing in blackness, and he blinked and the blackness was washed away with starlight. In an instant, with a faint dry crackle, grass erupted from the twisting floor, growing tall and making seed. The air was filled with summer sounds and dampness. The stars were brilliant and colorful, and countless, separated by light-weeks, oftentimes less. At the sky's zenith was an oval, velvety black and vague at its edges. This was the Core, plainly, and the oval was a giant shroud of armored, obedient gases, thrown like a blanket over the vast black hole about which the entire Milky Way turned.

The sky could be a live feed—

"Better than that," said a voice, close and soft.

And he was standing on someone's terraformed world. Ord knelt and broke off a stem of grass, putting it to his mouth, tasting the sour green juice. It was earthly life, and, as if to prove the point, a mosquito landed on his face and instantly bit him in the cheek, drawing blood before Ord smeared the bug and his own blood beneath his fingertips.

"Walk," Alice instructed. "Straight on."

The room was the flat crest of a hill presiding over a landscape too vast to be earthly. Traditional worlds were scarce in the Core, Ord recalled. The dense stars disrupted their birth, and those lucky few exceptions were usually stripped away by passing giants. But a sufficiently powerful entity, given time and the inspiration, could erect scaffolding around a sunless brown dwarf, harvesting its metals and its rich, untapped energies. Then she could erect a great dyson sphere far enough removed to give its surface an earthly gravity, and with oceans and air, a trillion people could walk alone on that glorious new world.

Ahead of him were people—his size, his proportions—sitting in the brilliant darkness, watching the sky. It was a peaceful scene, utterly familiar but lashed to an exotic place; and Ord paused, feeling afraid, his heart beating faster with every quick breath.

"Who are they?" he whispered.

Alice was silent.

"Hello?" he tried.

A boy turned, and said, "Hi. Who are you?"

Ord stepped close and offered his first name. The group repeated, "Ord," as Alice whispered, "Sit. Join them."

They weren't people but instead facsimiles conjured up along with the grass and bugs. Below them was a city, a sprinkling of soft lights with darkness between. It was a pioneer community, not large, homes set in the middle of wide rich yards. Beyond the city was an expansive flat sea, and where the sea ended, a chain of hollow mountains rose like a wall out into space.

Faces smiled. The facsimiles weren't too different from him, their heads narrow and their hair abundant and long, tied into intricate braids that leaked their own soft light. They were children of pioneers—the first generation born to this new world. Like Ord, they had tough brains and rapid powers of healing. Like him, they were just a few decades old, their lives stretching out into the infinite. But they could never leave their flesh, could only travel inside starships, and if they wanted to terraform any world larger than a comet, they would have to work in teams, as a multitude, relying on numbers in place of magnificence and genius.

And yet.

They would have children someday. Not clones, but unique, even radically different babies. They would marry and make families—institutions older than the Peace or any Chamberlain—and each child would be unlike any other creature walking on any of the millions of living worlds.

Ord felt envy, or Alice filled him with envy. He found himself thinking about the nearly thirty thousand light-years between these children and him, and before he could ever reach this world, it would be finished. The dyson would be finished and covered with cities, and the multitudes will have spilled onto a hundred other refitted dwarfs and jupiters . . . and neither he nor these children would ever be children again . . .

"Those are silly clothes," the boy observed. "Why don't you take them off?"

The snowsuit was damp with nervous sweat. Ord stripped to his underclothes, then sat with them on the warm bristly grass. Without prompting, the others introduced themselves, by name, the last girl saying, "Alice," and then, "Chamberlain."

She was dark as coal. "Chamberlain?" Ord echoed. "Is that your name?"

"Certainly," she replied. "A lot of people are named after the Great Families."

"You're not from here," a second girl observed. "Are you, Ord?"

"But that's okay," said the boy, acting like their leader. "We love meeting new people."

Ord asked, "Why use the Chamberlain name?"

"In thanks," the girl replied.

The boy said, "It's the Chamberlains who help the suns behave. They stop crap from falling into the black holes. And we're living on what they've built, which makes a person awfully grateful. Aren't we grateful?"

His friends nodded in unison, with feeling.

"Who's building this world?"

"Alice," said Alice.

Another child said, "The real Alice," and everyone giggled.

Then the boy added, "We help, of course." His pride was thick and practiced. "We do all the important little jobs, of course."

The false Alice looked nothing like Ord's sister. Her face was as narrow as the blade of an ax, great blue-black eyes reflecting the starlight. Ord asked, "Have you ever seen the real Alice? Does she visit here?"

"Not much," the girl snorted. "Why would she?"

"What do you think of her?"

"She's a great person, and wonderful," the boy reported, no room left for compromise. "Everyone knows that."

"I pray for her," this Alice confessed. "Every night, just

before I sleep, I wish her nothing but the best."

Everyone nodded. Conviction hung in the air, thick and warm.

"Where's Alice now?"

Hands lifted, pointing to the cold black smear overhead.

"What's she doing there?"

"Working," said the boy. "With her brothers and sisters, and others. They're doing important experiments in there." He was thrilled to report, "They finally found a way to move faster than light."

Everyone but Alice murmured in agreement.

"Soon," the boy continued, "we'll be able to go anywhere. The Families are going to set the entire universe at our feet."

"No," said Alice.

Faces turned.

She had a quiet, firm voice. "That's not what they're doing."

The other children acted surprised, but no one had a rebuttal to offer.

"What they've been doing is more important. FTL is nothing. What they've done is a million times larger." She suddenly had his sister's face, round and pale, and surprisingly plain, and very young, too. Looking at Ord, she asked, "Why can't everyone have Alice's powers?"

"It's a rule," he responded.

"But why?"

He paused, thinking hard. "If everyone were the same as Alice—"

"There wouldn't be room in the galaxy for all of us. There probably wouldn't be any galaxy. Every Alice needs energy and space and fancy, difficult work to keep her mind occupied." The real Alice took Ord by both hands, squeezing as she explained, "The Milky Way is too small a pasture. If we want to be like Alice, we need a lot more grass."

Some of the children laughed.

Ord swallowed. "But if we could go anywhere in the universe—?"

"Everywhere that can have life, does. Every other place already has its Families and its multitudes, and there's no room left for just one more Alice." She shrugged, sadness showing in the gesture and on the childlike face. "One is enough, and a trillion would bankrupt the universe. Do you see?"

Ord nodded, glancing up at the black smear.

"Yet there's something sweeter than FTL," she promised. "Put enough energy into a tiny place, structure it in just the proper way, and a fresh new universe will precipitate from nothing. Isn't that right, little brother?"

He remembered his tutor's lessons. There was a theory and convoluted mathematics and enough evidence to make a tutor sound as if it was true. Vacuums themselves could create universes that would instantly separate from their mother. An umbilical cord would exist, then dissolve, and the process would happen constantly, without ever being noticed. Existence begat existence. How many times had he read that wondrous truth?

A sudden chill tickled at Ord.

"The trick," Alice explained, "is to keep your umbilical open. What's the point in making a new universe that you can never see? Wouldn't it be nice if you could slip inside your creation and learn what's possible? Can you imagine the challenges? The potentials? For everyone, of course . . ."

Alice was weeping, wiping hard at her eyes.

A little boy said, "I don't understand this."

"Imagine if everyone, and I mean every Family and all of humanity, could extend themselves into endless new universes. Each of us could be given wondrous talents, and with them, we could dive through the umbilical cord and tie it up behind us. If we dared." She grabbed Ord's wrist, her hands cold and wet. "Isn't that the loveliest, sweetest possibility? What would you do, little one, if you could make such a thing true?"

Something is wrong—

And she said, "Precisely," with a dead gray voice. "As

wrong as wrong has ever been, I should hope."

Again Ord looked at the black oval, a single golden spark blossoming from its center. But the light faded and vanished, lost . . . just another illusion in a room full of elaborate facsimiles . . . nothing else . . . !

Alice turned to the wide-eyed children. "We succeeded," she explained. "We created a universe and the umbilical. But what's difficult, and perhaps impossible, is to leave the way open just far enough. Just enough room to climb through, but no farther. When you do this work, that's what you pray for. Just enough room to slip through."

The sky brightened. A great soundless flash of light washed away the stars with its blue-white glare, and the children began to mutter among themselves and nervously giggle.

"Our universe may well be some entity's creation," Alice was saying. "I admit that is not an original thought. And in so many ways, it's not comforting. But perhaps some other Family, jammed inside some unknown realm, produced this universe of ours . . . and maybe they preside over it now, just as their little universe was created by still others . . ."

The children had clasped their hands over their eyes. They couldn't be real, but if Alice was using a real-time feed, they could easily be facsimiles pulled from people just as real as Ord. Whoever they were, they appeared terrified and fragile, and lost. Ord found himself terrified for them, leaping to his feet, shouting, "Run! Hide!" He grabbed one little boy, trying to make him race home. But the first wave of heat and hard radiation washed over them. In an instant, the long grass had burst into flames, and the boy squirmed in agony, and died, his body shriveled and blackened, blowing away as ash. Then Ord screamed as the world beneath him evaporated. He felt it shatter and tumble into the brown dwarf that soon boiled and exploded . . . an inconsequential bit of gas and grit lost in a vast storm . . . and he was twisting inside that scalding light, screaming until a familiar voice whispered, "Relax."

Alice said, "The new universe is flowing into ours, but only for a little while."

Then with a dead voice, she told him:

"You don't know how sorry we feel . . . you can't know how sorry . . . tell everyone, please . . . will you, little brother . . . ?"

ONLY LYMAN WAS waiting for him. The others had watched the live feeds, and now they were standing in the nearest arena, watching the explosion from a series of observation posts. Only the two young brothers stood at the top of the empty stairwell, both trembling, Lyman using both hands to hold himself upright, saying with a wisp of a voice, "At least we know. We know what it is."

Ord held himself, wearing nothing but his underclothes and soaked with perspiration.

"Vivian thinks it's temporary . . . it can't last long . . ." Lyman couldn't stand anymore, dropping to his knees and beating at the steps with his fists, no strength in his arms. Finally, he asked, "Will Alice talk to us now?"

"I don't know," Ord confessed. Then with a low, choking voice, he tried to apologize for his ignorance.

But his brother didn't care. He shrugged, and said, "You don't know how terrible this is going to be. Nobody can know."

Ord gave the smallest nod.

"Which is a blessing, I think." Lyman gave the step another useless blow and looked up at the baby Chamberlain. "If we knew what's to come, we couldn't live. The grief would crush us."

He sobbed, and wept, and his voice sputtered and faded away.

"None of us could survive an instant," he whispered. "If we knew just how awful things will be . . ."

Fourteen

*"We accepted our duty at long last. A portion of us
would remain behind, keeping a choking hold on the
umbilical for as long as possible . . . a tiny heroism
after such a catastrophic blunder . . . while others
would rush toward populated worlds far enough removed to be helped . . . while one of the most culpable among us decided that she should journey home
alone, home to the Earth, for the simple purpose of
standing trial . . . admitting her enormous guilt in a
public way . . . hundreds of billions doomed, human
as well as alien, and a single soul promising to
swallow as much blame as possible . . ."*

—Alice's testimony

THAT NEXT MORNING, several hours before the local dawn,
the Chamberlains sent a carefully worded statement to the
Council and its supporting law enforcement agencies. Accepting no blame, the Family admitted that Alice was currently residing inside their mansion, barricaded in the
penthouse, and after a broad condemnation of everything
she had done, the statement promised that her intentions
seemed peaceful, and perhaps she would be willing to surrender.

An emergency session of the Council was held, and as
live feeds from the Core displayed the endless carnage, fear
and a wild bitterness took hold. The air was pierced with
cursing. At least twice, elected officials found themselves
engaged in shoving matches. Finally, it was decided that a
little delegation would visit the Chamberlain estate. High-
ranking Nuyens would accompany the appropriate officers
of the court, and the suspected murderess would be ar-
rested, hopefully without incident. That no existing prison
could contain, much less control, Alice was a minor problem. As one officer strapped on the traditional sidearm, she
mentioned to her colleagues, "If the bitch wants, she could

wave her hand and turn the Earth into dust. Or us into whimpering dogs."

Night in the high mountains had been clear and brutally cold. That oddity of climate made the officers even more uneasy. The white mansion stood vast and brilliant in the early light. A pack of huge brown-and-gold bears sat on the lawn, watching the invaders with a sturdy indifference. The officers kicked at the smart snows, and the snows quickly smoothed themselves, erasing all tracks. They stopped walking for a moment, and the Nuyens in attendance, considerably less impressed by the Chamberlain spell, took the lead. They walked directly to a minor door, passing beneath the PRIDE AND SACRIFICE emblem, and, as if they owned the house, they started straight for the penthouse.

A single Chamberlain—a sister of modest rank—joined the odd procession. She stopped the stairs and looked down at everyone, telling them how sorry she was and how every one of her sisters and brothers felt the same awful sorrow. But none of them were to blame, she argued. They weren't at the Core, and they never knew about the secret work. Except for a tiny few, her Family was blameless.

"While my Family is perfectly innocent," snapped the lead Nuyen.

Vivian glared at the speaker, then turned away and put the stairs back into motion.

ORD WATCHED THEM pass. Dressed in a clean snowsuit, he was standing in the hallway, sleepless but alert. Everyone in the procession ignored him. When they were far above he stepped into the stairwell, leaned over the ancient railing, and watched how they curled higher and higher, his eyes losing them with distance and the colorful glare of the tireless mural.

As always, his giant bears begged for attention.

He ignored them, running to the tube and running faster through the sun-washed woods, then slowing as he crossed the long pasture. Only Ravleen was waiting at the fort. She was sitting on the west wall, her cast removed, her eyes red and sleepless. "You're late," she warned, then smiled. Then, with a strong certain voice, she told him, "The explosion won't ever reach us. It's not large enough."

Ord had seen the estimates and projections.

"We did some heavy calculations," she continued. "It's a lot like a supernova, only bigger. Hotter. Dust clouds and distance are going to choke out the blast, which is going to keep the Earth safe."

The melted planets would help, too. They and the dead people would absorb some of those terrific energies.

"What are you thinking?"

Ord looked across the pasture. Yesterday's bootprints gave the snow a ragged, exhausted appearance. Splashes of blood made it more so. "Nobody's going to attack today," he ventured.

"If they do," Ravleen said, "we'll stop them."

"I was tired of being home," he confessed, swallowing with a tight dry throat. "I watched feeds all night—"

"Talk about something else," Ravleen warned.

"Like what?"

"Nothing." The red eyes looked out of the clean gold mask. "Let's just sit and say nothing."

A light breeze lifted their flag, then let it drop. On a day like this, they should have heard city sounds; but not this morning, and the silence was unnerving. Everyone was scared. It wasn't just the explosion and destruction that terrified; it was also the Peace. Would it survive? Sacred trusts had been violated, and maybe the Peace couldn't be repaired. And what about the Families themselves—?

A slow creaking made Ord blink and turn. Someone was climbing one of the rope ladders. Ravleen picked up her gun, watching the familiar figure scramble over the parapet to join them.

"Ah," she growled. "The traitor."

Ord was surprised to see Xo. He should be the last Gold willing to come here. But he stood before them, smiling so that they could see his teeth, saying, "I just escaped." He was nervous and obvious, forcing a laugh before adding, "It was a legal escape. Nobody came to guard me this morning."

Ravleen kept her hand on the gun.

Xo told her, "Congratulations. For winning, I mean." Then he turned to Ord, adding, "Our plan sure worked, didn't it?"

"What plan?" asked Ravleen.

"Didn't you tell her?" The boy acted surprised. He removed his mask to show everyone his outrage. "We planned it together, Ravleen. I would pretend to be a traitor, and Ord—"

"Shut up."

"Ord would approach you—"

"You're lying. Shut up."

The boy closed his mouth, then grinned. Ord saw the new tooth, whiter than the others, and something about the grin made him bristle.

"I'm not a traitor," Xo told them.

Nobody spoke.

Then he said, "Your Families were the ringleaders." His tone was superior and a little shrill. "We didn't even help you. I heard all about it. An old sister told me. She said they warned you that it was dangerous work, and they didn't want to have any part of it—"

"Quiet," Ord snapped.

"But you did it anyway. And you did it wrong."

Ravleen stared down into the courtyard.

Xo swallowed and straightened his back, then with a grave satisfaction said, "Now you'll have to pay for the damages and death. All of your wealth is going to be spent, and you'll be poor. You won't even be Families anymore. It's almost as if we set a trap, and you walked right in—!"

Ravleen shot him in the face, without warning. She put twin slugs into Xo's mouth, knocking him off the wall. Then she stood and looked down at the boy, sprawled out on his back and perfectly still, and she winked at Ord, saying, "Watch." She jumped, feet first, boots landing on the boy's chest and her momentum shattering ribs and lungs and the heart beneath her.

His chest crushed, Xo flung his arms into the air, hands grasping at nothing and falling limp.

Ravleen began to kick him. His body had died, past all suffering now; but she worked on the face with a slick thoroughness, without pause, kicking and kicking until she was finally exhausted; then she stepped back and looked up on the wall, telling Ord, "You can help me, if you want."

Except Ord wasn't standing there. It was a sister, some other baby Chamberlain wearing an old-fashioned snow-suit, and she smiled without smiling, eyes full of misery and joy.

"Help you?" she asked.

Then she said, "Another time, perhaps. But thank you for offering."

Fifteen

> "I watched them wrench open the penthouse door. I watched them not find me. I did rather enjoy their panic, I'll admit, but the fact is that I wasn't hiding from anyone. I was just elsewhere. And then one of the Nuyens engaged her treacherous little brain, and she decided to search inside the original mansion . . . and there most
> of my human portions were waiting, sitting in my onetime
> bedroom . . . peering outdoors at a vivid cold winter from ten
> million years ago . . ."
>
> —Alice's testimony

THE CITY WAS a forest of towering green trees, each tree trunk filled with thousands of natural cavities—tiny luxury

apartments housing millions of smallish people with prehensile tails and net-linked minds. Most of the people were
indoors, watching feeds from the Core. For a long while,
Ord walked alone down a narrow avenue, feeling like the
last living soul on the planet. He left his snowsuit on and,
with alternating sleeves, wiped the sweat from his eyes.
Finally, a small park opened before him, and he saw movement, then tiny brown shapes. He approached the children
with a certain caution, practicing his smile, and when they
saw him, they stopped and stared. Too young to watch the
Core and understand, they also were too young to recognize
a living Chamberlain. One boy fluffed up the fur on his
neck and laughed, saying, "You look funny. What kind of
person are you?"

"Are you sick?" asked a tiny girl.

"Funny hair," said a third child. "Where did the rest of
your hair go?"

Ord took a breath and held it. There were nearly a dozen
young children gawking at him. To the boy who said *You
look funny*, Ord said, "Here," and handed him the old snowgun. "This is for you."

"What is it?" the boy sputtered.

Ord didn't explain. Removing his boots, he asked, "Who
wants these?"

A tiny hand shot up.

He gave away his boots, then his mask. Then he removed
his snowsuit and wadded it up in his hands, telling his
astonished little audience, "I am sorry. I want you to know.
I can't be any more sorry."

They didn't understand why he should apologize, but the
words were locked in their minds.

"And Alice is sorry, too," he added, flinging the snowsuit
behind them and turning, running off on bare feet as the
children began making claims and counterclaims for this
strange, unusable prize.

Ord trotted back toward the mountains and the snow.
Only then, gazing up out of the forest at the towering white
ridge, did he realize that he had never seen his home from

this vantage point. From outside. And he ran faster now, crossing a distinct line, the first wet pancakes of snow burning his naked toes, causing him to reach deep and run faster still.

BOOK TWO

BROTHER PERFECT

One

"Bless the dead!"

—*Perfect, in conversation*

IT WAS THE ultimate toast—"Bless the dead!"—and despite every appearance, the toastmaster was human. His scaly hand clasped hold of a ceremonial mug carved from cultured granite. As he said the word "dead," he lifted the mug up high, his wide mouth managing both a smile and supreme bitterness. He was a beautiful man, brightly colored and vigorously ancient. His angry voice lingered in the dense, damp air. Long teeth flashed in the very dim light. Then golden viper eyes skipped from face to face, looking hard for something unmentioned.

The patrons repeated his blessing with sloppy, communal voices.

No one needed to ask, "Which dead?"

Opposite the tavern's bar was a universal wall. Tonight, like every night, it was showing another light-speed feed from the Core, from another doomed world. People watched a new city lying beneath a night sky that should have held a hundred thousand suns, bright and dazzling; but instead of suns, there was only a single blistering smear of white light, every lesser glow washed away by the brilliance. Energies from the baby universe were still seeping into its tired old mother. A thousand supernovas couldn't match its amoral violence. The explosion's scorching heat and withering radiations were expanding at a near-light velocity, melting worlds and evaporating every form of life, a century of inexorable growth barely diminishing its absolute fury.

Invisible against that withering light, people were being slaughtered.

And people watched them die—people here on the Earth and throughout the inner reaches of the galaxy. For some viewers this was a new hobby, a grisly but fascinating en-

tertainment: A world at a time, they watched distant skies
fill with that terrible light. With a reliable horror, the local
colonists would panic. With few starships in port, only the
rich and the vicious could escape in time. Although there
were moments when luck and charity saved a few good
souls, too. Then those left behind would take pitiful steps
to brace themselves, or they launched into a wild orgy of
rioting and sex—the human animal betraying itself after ten
million years of seamless, unrelenting civilization.

But others watched the carnage and felt no thrill. For
them, the victims weren't strangers, and the misery was a
burning they felt inside themselves.

The tavern was tucked deep in the Earth's crust, in one
of the poorer, more crowded districts. Its patrons were a
local race—human frames embellished with reptilian features and physiologies, a calculated cold-bloodedness allowing them to thrive on impoverished, sporadic meals. Yet
they were far from simple people. They had a long and
durable and thoroughly shared history. Pooling their meager savings, once they had sent their best to the Core. The
Core was still a wilderness, empty and free for the taking.
Terraformers built a floating continent on a sunless jupiter,
then designed a climate specifically for them—a lizardly
eden that these same patrons used to observe with a fond
relish. But the jupiter was barely eighty light-years from
the explosion's source, and it was obliterated in a single
evening. A great world and a greater people were turned
into a single long streamer of enchanted plasmas and highly
charged particles, swirling and merging with a murderous
storm that wasn't going to end soon, or maybe ever.

Many of these patrons had watched the cataclysm from
this tavern, and out of that awful night came this ritual, this
new custom, several minutes of each evening devoted to
blessing the dead.

Now, finally, the golden viper eyes found what they were
hunting.

The toastmaster's head locked in place, and he took a
slow deep breath, a wry little smile emerging gradually.

"To Alice!" he shouted.

Now the wall changed feeds, suddenly showing what looked like a plainly dressed woman sitting alone in a white-walled prison cell. She was an archaic human, traditional skin topped with short red hair. Otherwise, she was the most ordinary creature imaginable.

In a single ringing voice, the tavern cried out, "To Alice!"

"Give the bitch a long small horrible life," the toastmaster roared. And with that, he drained his mug, enjoying the raucous approval of his mates.

Others, in drunken tones, roared, "Kill the bitch . . . !"

It was a delicious, much-practiced game.

But the toastmaster broke tradition by taking a slow step forward, wading into the crowd, and lifting his emptied mug as a clear, almost songful voice shouted, "To the Families!"

"The Families!" people roared, in mocking admiration.

From the back, a shrill voice cried out, "Kill them, too!"

Nobody repeated those dangerous words, but there was a pause, glacial and tense, where no one rose to defend the Families. All the good they had done for humanity, in its myriad forms . . . and not so much as a kind word was offered. Not as a whisper, not even as a weak reflex.

In this one obscure location, the Ten-Million-Year Peace tottered on the brink of collapse.

Standing among the tightly packed bodies, the toastmaster fixed his gaze on a single man. The man was a stranger—dull black scales fringed with red; a crimson forehead merging with a sharp golden crest; and a small orange throat pouch that implied youth, or an old man trying to look young. Using his free hand, the toastmaster touched the young man, cool fingertips dancing across the short nose and long lower jaw, finally tickling the little pouch.

The young man barely flinched.

"The Families will pay," the toastmaster hissed. "For every crime, they will pay."

"Every crime," was the chorus. "Make the fuckers pay!"

The young man whispered his response, a half syllable slow.

The toastmaster appeared amused, but his voice was like ice, slowly saying, "Make them weak. Weak and poor. Make them the same as us."

In an instant, the tavern went silent.

The young man straightened his back, the orange plumage along his spine growing stiff as knives. He glanced at the universal wall and Alice, his viper eyes blue and shiny, and sad. Then with a flat voice, he muttered, "Yes."

"Yes, what?"

"Make the Families weak, and poor—"

"And give us their god-talents," the toastmaster added.

With a phrase, he had crossed into heresy. There was no other word for it. Dismantling the evil Families was a justice, but demanding their powers and talents was against every convention, every old law and a multitude of good, honorable judgments.

The young man said nothing.

"Long ago, just once, I had a child," the toastmaster explained. "One child, because how can a poor man afford two in a crowded world like this? She was a beautiful bright girl, and do you know where she went? Can you guess where she made her nest and gave me five grandchildren?" His eyes remained open, coldly staring at the face before him. "Every night, I watched my daughter and grandchildren from this place. Because I am too poor to afford my own universal wall, of course." The eyes closed and remained shut. "I was standing here, exactly here, when I watched my entire family die."

Softly, with feeling, the young man said, "I am sorry."

A claw-shaped blade struck him from behind, piercing his skin at the neck, effortlessly cutting between the long scales but with no trace of pain. No blood spurted from the surgical wound. The young man felt the pressure and spun around, slapping the knife from the assailant's hand. But more blades appeared, and picks of scrap diamond, each slicing at his legs and butt and back; and despite strength enough to shatter a hundred arms, Ord stopped resisting, going rigid, standing like a statue while his false skin and the cool meat were peeled away, falling in wet heaps around his ankles.

His archaic body was naked. His true face was suddenly exposed, a hundred little cuts healing in a moment. The Chamberlain face was obvious. The red hair was plastered flat with perspiration, and the warm blue eyes watched the world with amazement and a palpable pity.

No face in the galaxy was better known.

"A baby Chamberlain," the patrons muttered, in horror and shock and with a rising visceral rage.

Ord lifted his left hand.

With remorse, he cried out, "I am sorry."

They rushed him. Using knives and picks, stone mugs and teeth, they hacked away at his genuine flesh, ripping it loose from his strong bright bones. Then, with an idiot's purpose, the mob soaked the still-living bones and brain with the tavern's inventory, and they sabotaged the fire-suppression system, setting a blaze that was a thousand times too cold to murder the weakest Chamberlain. But it didn't matter. For years and years that tavern would lie gutted, left as a monument, and people who hadn't been there would claim otherwise, boasting about how on that night, in a small but significant way, they had helped mete out justice, butchering and cooking one of Alice's own little brothers . . . !

Two

"Oh, I can explain your sister to you . . .

"Every human hope and historic truth, every foible and foolishness you can name, plus even the

*greenest prehuman emotions . . . all of them, without
exception, have enormous homes inside our Alice's
dear soul . . . !"*

—*Perfect, in conversation*

"First," said a Chamberlain voice. "Before anything else,
tell me why this happened."

The voice had no source. It rose from the warm blackness, sounding a little angry and thoroughly stern. Ord
barely heard his own voice replying. "It's because I left the
estates," he muttered. "That's why."

"You did, but that's an inadequate answer. Think again."

"Lyman? Is that you—?"

"Try again," boomed the voice. "Why did this happen?"

Ord remembered the attack and his brief, manageable
pains. "They saw through my disguise. I must have made
a mistake."

"Many mistakes, but none of consequence. Your costume
was accurate enough, and you were well prepared to wear
it."

"Then what went wrong?"

"I'm asking you. Think now."

Ord tried to swallow, but he had no mouth. He assumed
that he was home again. An attack on him would have
caused alarms to sound, and it would have been a simple
matter for a brother to recover his parts. Yet what if the
alarms had failed? His comatose mind could have been pi-
rated away to someplace secure, unlikely as that seemed.
This could be the beginning of a lengthy interrogation, a
Chamberlain enemy wanting to pull the Family secrets out
of him. But of course, he knew next to nothing. More
likely, their enemy simply wished to torture him.

"How did that gruesome drunk find you, Ord?"

"He wasn't gruesome," the boy countered. "And I think
he was sober—"

"That beautiful prince," the voice offered. "Why did he
even notice you?"

"He was warned," Ord allowed. "Someone told him to
expect me."

"A sibling, perhaps?"

"Probably not." Brothers and sisters might have known his plans, but they wouldn't have let others mete out the punishment.

"And who would have?"

Possibilities swirled in the blackness, one name standing out against the others.

And the brotherly voice announced, "I concur. Yes."

A moment later, without warning or apparent effort, Ord had a face and eyes. He found himself whole again, new flesh covering his salvaged bones. His body was sprawled out on his own bed. Even with fresh, unfocused eyes, he recognized his own apartment. Floating shelves held an assortment of alien fossils as well as the earthly kind. The universal wall showed shifting, thoroughly random views of the Core. Lyman stood in the doorway; Ord recognized him by his long red hair tied into intricate braids, plus his slump-shouldered, tight-faced appearance. Standing over the bed was an older, unintroduced brother wearing an ageless, somewhat fat body, his hand lifting from Ord's bare chest, a damp warm discharge making the new heart shudder, then surge.

"It's been some while since your body last died. Am I correct?"

"Yes, sir."

"An incident in the Salt River. Is that so?"

"I drowned in the rapids, yes." The brother had surely memorized Ord's medical history, which meant that questions served as noise. Or they were subtle tests. Or maybe he was pretending that the two of them were on halfway-equal footing, lending his littlest brother a misplaced confidence.

"Well, we pulled you from the ruins." The Chamberlain face showed a large, self-congratulatory grin. "And we've filed criminal charges, plus civil suits. You broke our rules by leaving home, but then again, those people broke everyone's rules by attempting murder." A weighty pause, then he asked, "If people maim, shouldn't they expect retribution?"

"Yes, sir."

From the doorway, Lyman asked, "So who was it? Who warned the lizard prince?"

It made Ord uneasy, hearing his favorite brother calmly demeaning those odd, sad people.

"We know the culprit well," said their ancient brother. His expression changed by the moment, bouncing between menace and sharp amusement. "And I'm sure the boy will do what's necessary, when time is ripe."

A great black permission had just been given.

Ord gave the tiniest of nods.

Next to this creature, he and Lyman were babies. They were athletic flesh and durable bone, and finite minds and raw potential. But their great brother could be thousands of millennia old, his face composed of substances more intricate than any flesh. Ancient souls like his were coming home again. After millions of years spent wandering the Milky Way, suddenly they had vital work to accomplish here: diplomatic missions; far-reaching planning sessions; the careful allocation of the Family's enormous resources; and the endless legal wars revolving around the Core's unfolding tragedy.

Repairing a damaged baby . . . well, that had to be the most trivial chore imaginable . . .

"Civil suits," the ancient Chamberlain repeated, a gleeful laugh coming from some vast, hidden mouth. "I promise, Baby. We'll teach these people about pain."

"Don't," Ord whispered.

Another laugh followed, muscular and massive.

"I mean it." Ord forced his new body to sit up. "It was my fault, everything, and I don't want them hurt."

"I know you're being honest," said his brother. "I'm laughing because you honestly believe you have a voice here. Which you don't. It has been decided. Our AI lawyers have already set to work, and we'll squeeze the last cold credits out of those bastards." He offered a bright little wink. "Someday, Baby, you'll appreciate our efforts."

Ord doubted it.

"Now," said the brother, "thank me for you health."

"Thank you, sir."

"Rest," he advised.

Did a creature like him ever rest? Ord doubted that, too. Then he considered asking when, if ever, would he be free to travel the Earth . . . when would any of the babies be allowed to leave the Family estates . . . ?

But the brother had vanished, melting into the floor without sound or fuss. Or perhaps more likely, he was never actually there in the first place.

Ord glanced at Lyman, and Lyman returned the expression.

They were babies, they agreed.

What could they do?

"I WON'T TELL you what to do," Lyman began. "But if you leave the estate again, they're going to become genuinely angry."

In other words, an unrepentant Chamberlain might be restricted to even smaller spaces. Like the old mansion, Ord imagined. Or worse, the walls of his own tiny apartment. When he was Ord's age, Lyman had already traveled considerably farther and broken many more rules. But that was before the Core. "Leaving was brave," Lyman offered, that trailing word having a calculated feel. "Maybe even noble," he said, with the same careful tones. "But when you ignore your bravery and your nobility, do you see what's left? Stupidity. Dumb, dumb, dumb stupidity."

Ord examined himself. A century ago, whenever a child was temporarily killed—regardless of blame—he was always given some tiny improvement as a salve for any embarrassment. He woke with a more mature blood or some enhanced sense. Perhaps even an enlarged mind. But Ord felt identical to what he had been days ago: an old-fashioned human carriage hardly changed by a century of tragedy and shame.

To a biologist's eyes, Ord looked like a teenager, complete with the weak beard and bright blue eyes. But he was nearly a century and a half old, and Lyman was several times his senior. His brother's body was dense as granite and more powerful, his mind prepared to leave home, ready to travel and work in deep space. As a degree-holding terraformer, Lyman was another one of the noble Chamberlains eager to help humanity and rebuild the galaxy . . .

Yet all new postings were on hold.

"Because of the current situation," one of their elder sisters had explained. "This is a temporary measure, and a reasonable precaution, and for the next moment or two, you'll have to be patient, little ones."

With a bitter, impatient voice, Lyman confessed to Ord, "You're making it harder for all of us. I appreciate your reasons. You heard about that tavern and the ugly toast, and sure, you wanted to see it for yourself. But eventually, by right, you should also consider your brothers and sisters."

There were several dozen young Chamberlains forbidden from leaving the estates.

"Do you ever think about us?" he pressed.

Ord said, "Always."

"And do we count?"

Ord shrugged, seeing no reason to apologize.

"Think of me," Lyman implored. Then he glanced at the universal wall, and with an inaudible word, he switched the view, leaving the Core for a green view of the world outside the mansion. Sunlight streamed in across both boys, and the one who was standing said, "Think of me."

"Don't I?" Ord replied.

"They tell me that I'm responsible for you babies. The elders say they're too busy, and I have to be your elder."

"I know that, Lyman."

"But is that fair?"

"Actually, it probably is."

A look of genuine disgust passed across his brother's face.

Ord took a deep breath. New lungs expanded, absorbing air clean as medicine. "If you want, I'll stay in bed for the next million years."

"Maybe you should," Lyman warned him. Then, on that glum note, he turned and walked away, ending their discussion before Ord could spin even larger lies.

The boy climbed from bed, then dressed.

He rode the nearest stairwell to the ground floor. The PRIDE AND SACRIFICE emblem was above the auxiliary door, and he touched it with his palm, then turned and jogged outside.

His bears greeted him. He had always raised tailored brown bears—very friendly, very easy—but for the simple danger, he had recently changed to a resurrected species. They were short-faced bears with minds and muscles thoroughly enhanced. All of them knew Ord by his scent—tiny olfactory markers shouting his identity—and each had to lick his face with a massive pink tongue, tasting him and tasting him until he cried out, "Enough."

"What fun now?" asked the oldest male, the voice rising from deep inside its throat.

"Riding," Ord allowed. "Up through the Breaks, maybe."

"Hunting?" the entire pack asked, in a shared voice.

"But no killing," the boy warned. "You can chase, but that's all."

It was too much of a restriction. The bears took a few steps with him, then gave up. They knew their own nature. They stopped in the middle of the long yard, safely removed from all wicked temptations.

There were stables below the mountaintop and mansion—cavernous buildings, thick-walled and well armored. The atmosphere within was heavy with the stink of fresh hay and fungi, blood stews and cultured blubbers. The resident animals came from far worlds and the best laboratories—Chamberlain laboratories—and the smartest of them called to Ord by name, promising long rides across every fun terrain. And by the way . . . could they have a little treat before dinner, please . . . ?

The urge to ride faltered, then died.

It was happening more and more. The old joys suddenly lacked their usual vitality. A pleasure was still a pleasure, but it was as much from the memory of old fun as it was from what would happen today or next year.

Past the stables was an empty pen, a great vertical pen, built on a cliff face. An alien species—goatlike beasts with adhesive hooves—had lived there eons ago. But the elders grew tired of rebuilding the children who tried to ride them. In Ord's life, the pen had always been empty and overgrown. The goats' feces had been at least as sticky as their hooves, and they carried tough little seeds that came along with the alien fodder. Odd blue bushes and trees grew on the vertical faces. It was an accidental taste of distant worlds. Stepping through the inert fence posts, Ord walked to the edge of the cliff and looked down. Then he allowed his eyes to take in the entire view: Artful mountains and twisted deep valleys had been formed with granites pink as meat, and every lesser slope was covered with forests and lush emerald pastures. Deciduous trees showed the first splash of autumn. Beneath his toes, a rushing river twisted its way down to a distant and enormous gray-as-steel barrier that rose straight into the cloudless sky. The gray portions were hyperfiber, and above that was a curtain of invisible energy, the entire wall bolstered with eagle eyes and paranoid AIs. A few decades ago, not long after Alice's trial, people had broken into the estates, carrying an arsenal of weapons that couldn't kill any Chamberlain. Yet the wall was built in the next few days, in a panic, and like anything done in a panic, it was full of flaws.

Intended to keep invaders out, the wall was porous when it came to keeping the clever, bored Family children inside.

Neither Lyman nor that elder brother had asked Ord how he had managed to escape. They knew already and had closed the route, or they knew and were keeping it open, booby traps set to catch whoever tried to repeat his crime.

For every Family, this last century had been terrifying. Yet perhaps more than others, Ord's family deserved its awful fears.

Chamberlains were unaccustomed to a chronic sense of menace. They found it relentless and unfair, and tiresome.

Alice was one of theirs, yes, but there were more than twenty thousand Chamberlains, and only a very few had been involved in the Core's tragic business. "Why blame us?" was the general chorus. "We aren't Alice; we've accomplished nothing but good for people everywhere. Look at our record! Our history! Our legacy! How, how, how can we absorb the blame meant for one odd and possibly senile sister . . . ?"

Half of the Thousand Families had been poisoned as well, their oldest siblings culpable by helping to build that awful new universe.

Without question, Alice's arrival was the worst day in Ord's tiny life.

This was a point of endless debate: Why would one of the most famous and powerful entities in the Milky Way take such an interest in her youngest brother? But really, Alice had done very little with him. They'd had a few meetings, one uncomfortable dinner, and a vision of the baby universe exploding into this cold husk of a Creation. Alice was vast. At least, she had once been enormous. Alice was brilliant to the limits of intelligence, and she had talents beyond number, and whatever attention she showed to the baby Chamberlain, it was nothing. Nothing. It amounted to the same concentration that Ord gave to any one of the solitary blue shrubs on the cliff face beneath him.

Again, he looked at the security wall.

A century of distractions and new revelations hadn't yet diluted the shock and misery of this mess. This carnage. Alice had given the Chamberlains a new legacy. Suddenly their old name was synonymous with greed, waste, and genocide—every ugly horror they were pledged to fight. And now the Chamberlains—and to a lesser degree, all Families—hid inside their estates, or they traveled with a thousand security systems in tow. But where were they safe? They had billions of angry neighbors on just this one continent. How many local workshops were nuclear-capable? What happened if the weapon-suppression systems were deactivated, then countless crude bombs were heaved over the wall . . . ? What if just one of them went unnoticed by the paranoids . . . ?

"Quit," Ord muttered to himself.

He started back into the stables, contemplating his choices. There were enemies outside, but there were enemies within, too. Ord knew who had alerted the toastmaster to his presence, and he knew how to prove it. No, he wouldn't blame the people in the tavern. The malicious act lay elsewhere, and his brother was right: Ord needed to find some reasonable, imaginative revenge.

He paused before an enormous gate of diamond bars and robot sentries with tireless arms linked. What lived in these shadows was a minor mystery. A great old brother had left the beast here—no one seemed sure just when—and despite hours of careful watching, with eyes and with delicate sensors, Ord had never gotten a good look at the creature.

He wasn't looking into the cage now, thinking hard to himself.

Muttering to himself.

"How can I punish someone?" he asked himself. "When I can't really hurt them, what can I do?"

From the shadows, over the sour stink of old blood stews, a tiny voice whispered to him, close and earnest.

"Let me show you ways," it said.

Then, "Tricks. I know tricks."

Then, "Closer, come. Please, my master. Please?"

Three

"Ian had favorite story about the Nuyens . . .

"Their Family was founded by a brilliant woman, highly organized, extraordinarily disciplined, and as creative as the proverbial factory-fired brick. That lack of imagination was the source of some good-natured teasing among the half-born gods. But the first Nuyen saw nothing but strength in her apparent

*weakness. One night, drinking a social beer at some
mandatory function, she argued that she was genuinely blessed. Creativity was a distraction and a
proven danger, and as her powers grew, she intended to acquire only enough of that deadly talent
to accomplish each task, then dispose of it afterward . . .*

*"Ian genuinely liked the Nuyens. To his play-
grounds, they never went . . . !"*

—*Perfect, in conversation*

WHERE THE CHAMBERLAINS' estate had always been wild
woods and minimal lawns, the Nuyens preferred formal
gardens maintained to the limits of the day's technologies.
Their foliage was tailored to the point that every leaf grew
to a perfect size and shape and color, or it killed itself,
sending its sap to more successful neighbors. Flowers
bloomed on tightly orchestrated days, each blossom perfectly in keeping with the rigorously controlled environment. Every shrub and elegant tree, and even the tiniest
scab of lichen, had a place to fill in that highly contrived
landscape. The pools and great ponds were geometrically
pure, the streams and little rivers ran in intricately braided
channels, and the clouds of fish and water lilies and king
lotuses and little dolphins all wore colors dictated by the
season and the surrounding landscape.

The effect couldn't help but look lovely, and it was relentless, and on most days, Ord grew exhausted with the
tight-assed spectacle.

Not today. Ord barely noticed the late-season roses or
the giant killifish. He was panting, dragging the homemade
bomb up the brick path. The Nuyens' mansion lay ahead—
a sprawling blockish structure adorned with false windows
and invisible sentries. Those sentries had already sounded
alarms, and AIs had carefully weighed the risks, taking
every reasonable precaution. But Nuyens didn't appreciate
the sight of a Chamberlain bringing a weapon to their door-
step. To emphasize their displeasure, a modest-ranked

brother emerged from the nearby earth, growling, "What do you want? What are you doing here?"

"I want your brother. I want Xo."

"Your toy is dead," said the dark-haired figure.

With powerful arms, Ord lifted the bomb and dropped it on its detonator. It struck the brick walkway with a harsh *bang*, sparks blossoming. Then he grinned, saying, "I guess it is," while lifting it once again.

The Nuyen shook his head in disgust. "Your friend is on his way," he reported, and vanished with an intimidating flash and *crack*.

Xo hadn't been a close friend for years. Ord rarely saw him anymore and never with much pleasure. He had mentioned his secret trip to the boy, but only because Xo was a coward, and Ord wanted to wave his bravery under the coward's nose. "I found a way out of the estates," Ord had boasted. "Want to come along?"

Of course not, no.

"It'll be fun."

"Until it goes wrong," the coward had muttered enviously.

With a whispered hiss, an auxiliary door opened. A puzzled adolescent emerged, asking, "Have you gone stark raving, Ord?"

Ord flung the bomb down again.

Xo didn't flinch. He held himself motionless, managing a long thin breath before asking, "Why? It won't work, and it never could."

The bomb had a smooth titanium shell and neat little tail fins that served as handles. Ord pointed at each end, saying, "I've got more than two kilos of 235 inside here."

"But the trigger's shit, and the chemical explosives have been cooked to water and plastic. It can't detonate—"

Bang. Again.

"Atoms vibrate," Ord reminded him. "This way, that way."

Xo had a frail, pitiful face when he wanted. Watching his onetime friend grunt and lift the bomb again, he said, "So what?"

"A few quadrillion uranium atoms could move toward the same point, in the same moment."

Xo's eyes grew larger, just a little bit.

"Random vibrations and my pounding, and they just might accidentally reach critical mass."

"Impossible!"

"Possible," Ord countered, "but highly unlikely." Again he dropped the bomb, sparks flying higher. "Unless, of course, someone noticed me standing here, and if that someone didn't much like Chamberlains. Or Nuyens, for that matter. If they could uncook the explosives and heal my trigger—"

"It won't happen," Xo interrupted. "Not with our security—"

"I found your message."

Xo fell silent.

"In the tavern's files," Ord continued. " 'The gold-crested stranger is your sworn enemy,' it reads."

"That's a lie!"

Bang. "Why did you want them to hurt me?"

"You're fine now," Xo observed.

Again Ord flung the bomb into the unyielding bricks.

In an almost imperceptible fashion, Xo flinched.

"I've always tried to be friendly toward you," the Chamberlain argued. "Even when we aren't friends, I treat you better than the others do. Better then almost anyone, now that I think about it."

"What if I sent the message?" said Xo, in a speculative way. "Maybe it isn't because of you. Maybe it's your sister. Alice made it so that none of us can leave home, and we never will if you keep sneaking away—"

Again the bomb struck, cracking one of the old bricks.

"How long will you do that?"

"Until it explodes," Ord promised, his voice level and cool. "I'll get more 235 when this stuff goes bad, and maybe after ten billion years—"

Xo shuddered and stepped back, closing and sealing the useless door.

The Nuyens tolerated Ord's presence for a few hours, then sent home a stern warning wrapped within a few concerned words. Lyman was dispatched to retrieve the baby Chamberlain. Ord's action wasn't a declaration of war, but it was *something*. As Lyman walked him back to the tube car, the dead bomb thrown over a burly shoulder, he tried to scold the boy. He said all of the best bruising words, in a properly heated tone. Yet his gaze had acquired a new light, a kind of black wonder, and with the most unexpected envy, he gazed at the youngest Chamberlain as if for the first time.

Four

"Last night, for an indeterminate period and through means yet undiscovered, our prisoner escaped. Then, in an act that is perhaps even more impressive, she managed to return again, passing undetected through a security network already perched on full alert. We are struggling to determine her whereabouts and agenda. However, questions directed at our prisoner are being met with amused puzzlement. Alice herself has raised the possibility of a highly selective, rigorously maintained amnesia covering those minutes . . . an amnesia that undercuts our every attempt at interrogation . . .

"The lone positive in this ugly business is that the Chamberlain's escape went unnoticed among casual viewers. Our audience saw an illusionary Alice sitting in her cell, no one guessing that she was elsewhere, and free . . ."

—Alice's jailer, confidential

THE TRIAL HAD lasted for decades.

Nothing in human history matched its scope, its unrelenting tragedy, or the ultimate anticlimax. Each day, a robotic bailiff recited the names of humans and aliens who had died during the previous twenty-four hours—a powerful white hum of sound embracing as many as ten billion lost souls. Then the defendant would describe her enormous crimes, or experts would sit before the judges, struggling to put a cost to the carnage. Some voices argued that the explosion was nearly finished, the worst now passed. But the majority agreed only that there was no clear end in sight. The Core was being consumed by the firestorm. The baby universe was still bleeding energies through the faulty umbilical. Certain brutal mathematics hinted that no end was coming, that the superheated bubble would grow and grow, and within another million years, the Milky Way would have vanished, its plasmatic ash racing toward the living worlds of Andromeda.

Only one witness defended Alice's actions. A scholarly god from a minor Family, he spoke with a scholar's dry voice, arguing that if the fire stopped with the Core, the galaxy would be left enriched by this experience. "Energy is energy," he pointed out. "Energy is mass, and it brings wealth. Today, billions are dying. But the vast majority of us are quite safe, and when the worst is over, we will witness a wave of star formation unlike anything seen since the earliest days of Creation."

A grueling cross-examination didn't shake the witness. With a rationalist's zeal, he spoke about the ultimate good that would come from this "sad incident." Chaos was a sweet manure. Carnage was a necessary cost. Unimagined industries and reimagined peoples would replace the dead. Yes, the Great Peace had faltered, but it would recover, in time. The future would dwarf the past. Those were his exact words. "The future will dwarf the past." Only in the end, as an afterthought, did that little god admit to a minor bias: The Chamberlains had recently paid him a considerable fee for a long-ago consulting assignment.

The uproar was immediate and ugly, the public's rage rekindled.

Some years later, once the trial was drifting into history,

the same witness received a much larger payment that had passed through a hundred masking companies and foundations. His ultimate benefactors remained unnamed, but only because the Chamberlains and Sanchexes put an end to their investigations. Names didn't matter. In issues of blood, it was better to despise the entire Nuyen clan.

The trial judges came from untainted, impartial Families and the best judicial minds among ordinary humanity, while the jurors were a scrupulously random collection of citizens lent an assortment of powerful mental talents. For those next decades, their borrowed talents helped them navigate through the complex issues of science and economics, and law, and Right. Their unanimous verdict was that the criminal would be stripped of her powers, wealth, and every shred of enhanced intelligence. Whatever remained would be locked inside a tiny cell beneath the Tibetan plateau, and except for special circumstances, the prisoner wouldn't be allowed contact with the outside world. Then, to ensure that the sentence was being carried out, people throughout the galaxy could watch Alice on their universal walls, watching her sit or sleep, pace or shit. Her old-fashioned body—calcium bones and a poor woman's minimal immortality—could wear nothing but a thin garment. And as a final note, the cell's refrigeration would be imperfect, allowing the Earth's own heat to make her constantly and perfectly uncomfortable.

It was a fair verdict. Perhaps, it was even wise. Yet justice eluded humanity. Thousands had taken part in the universe-building nightmare. Some had died fighting the blast or saving endangered worlds. But what could be done about the other criminals? What if they refused to follow Alice's example? Plus there were those sticky issues involving civil penalties. Even Alice's wealth was nothing compared to the damages already done. Some of the jurists, just before they surrendered their borrowed talents, argued that the Thousand Families should make full compensation, using some common pool of cash and sorrow . . .

But what if the Families didn't agree to those terms?

And worst of all, what if citizens decided that enough was enough? What if people tried to wrest the godlike powers from those chosen few? The Core's little bang and misery would be nothing beside that conflagration. The Ten-Million-Year Peace would shatter like tired crystal, following all the ancient lines of weakness.

How could any such war end well?

Alice's trial was finished, and nothing was finished.

That was the only verdict, it seemed. An anonymous grain of sand had started to roll down the mountainside, and there was no calculating the shape or scope of the avalanche to come.

ORD WAS SITTING before a tablet filled with obscure equations, pretending to study, then he felt the pressure of eyes. Looking up, he discovered a small girl standing in his open doorway. His first thought was that she was a younger sister. He noticed the immature face and body. Adult-sized teeth filled the smiling mouth. Her coppery hair was long and worn simply, and she wore a feminine dress that ended at her knees, shins pale and her pink feet bare. There was a tangible joy that Ord could taste as well as feel. And then she spoke sweetly and quickly, telling him, "Come with me." Saying to him, "Now, Ord. They'll notice I'm gone, hurry!"

He rose and followed, and in an instant he dreamed up a little story to explain her presence. The eldest Chamberlains, for reasons simple and complex, had delayed the birth of Ord's little sister. But what if a sibling hadn't agreed, finding the means to hide a baby girl? She might be living inside the vast mansion, tucked away in some secret chamber. And maybe she knew about her slightly older brother, and of course she would come see him. Didn't it make perfect, intoxicating sense?

And yet. How could security nets and watchful elders fail to notice her? And if a little girl was so perfectly protected, then how could she manage to escape long enough to find Ord?

He ran on rising stairs, powerful legs unable to keep pace. The girl looked back at him, her expression disappointed. "I thought you'd be faster by now," she said, speaking through her thick long hair. Then, with a wink and giggle, she asked, "Why aren't you faster, Baby? You need to be."

Only then, finally, did Ord realize how far he had climbed and where she was leading him.

His legs locked up, in terror.

But the stairs kept lifting him, past the intricate, ever-changing murals where the great and glorious Chamberlains reenacted the past. He begged the stairs to stop, but they wouldn't. His sister was standing on the top landing, facing him for an instant before stepping back and out of sight, and Ord lied to himself, assuring himself that she was just a little girl and that her keepers must have stuck her inside the abandoned penthouse, knowing that no one went there anymore . . .

Ord was deposited on the landing. The girl had vanished, the massive satin-crystal door stood ajar, and momentum, not courage, carried him through the chill gap between door and jamb.

The room beyond was enormous, hectares of floor beneath a high ceiling, every surface ripped and charred, sagging portions of the ceiling held up with invisible braces and old robots standing motionless, waiting with infinite patience for the order to move again. Ord turned in a circle, with a dancer's unconscious grace. When the Nuyens and other officials came here, hunting for Alice, they had demolished the place, even when they realized she wasn't here. This would be the perfect place to hide a secret sister, he told himself. Though he didn't believe that story anymore, no matter how elaborate he made it. No matter how sweet it seemed.

"Quit thinking, Ord. Come here."

The red-haired girl stood in the distance, her back toward him and the golden sunlight pouring through a diamond-paned window. Ord picked his way across the battered floor, barely breathing. She seemed to be looking below, drinking in the great estate—a roar of autumn colors at their height, brilliant shades and tones joining into a half-tamed work too large for a boy's eyes, too intricate for even his augmented mind.

He would always remember the sight of her, her coppery hair, like his, unremarkable against those grand colors. And how the sunlight pierced her dress, revealing her pale new flesh, the body rigorously simple, even plain, sexless and unaugmented, and pure. Why, with everything being possible, did she choose that appearance? For the innocence implied? But who knew why Alice did what she did? Not for the first time, Ord doubted that his sister could identify all of her reasons. She was too large to understand herself, and had always been . . . and what an astonishing, horrifying curse . . . !

Alice turned, and in a motion faster than Ord could follow, she pushed something small and soft into his hands. Then with a desperate near gasp, she told him, "You've got to save it! They'll destroy it—!"

What? Destroy what?

"I'm pledged to protect . . . fragile . . . it's nothing but . . ."

"Protect what?" he blurted.

"Brother Perfect knows. Go find him." She showed the quickest possible smile, a flash of those bright big teeth, then she closed his fingers around her gift. "This will help you—"

"Brother who?"

"I trust you," Alice promised, her voice bleak and untrusting. "And Perfect, too. But nobody else, not anymore."

Then she was gone again, never quite seen and already lost; and for a long, confusing moment, Ord stared out at the vista—at the mountains and deep valleys; at the brilliant pained colors of dying foliage—nearly forgetting how he had come here, barely aware of the heavy little mystery lying invisible in his baby hands.

Five

> *"Discreet observations of the Chamberlain estate
> have identified five distinct and powerful anomalous
> events. Two occurred during Alice's escape, proba-
> bly marking her arrival and subsequent departure.
> Two other events have been linked to the clandestine
> visit by Chamberlain Fifty-three, presumably on a
> mission of grand strategy and espionage. But most
> troubling is the oldest anomaly. It was witnessed
> several years after our observations began—several
> years after Alice's surrender—and perhaps it only
> signaled the departure of some ancient Chamberlain
> whose presence was never suspected. Though it
> could have been an arrival, which leads to a chain
> of obvious questions: Who arrived? And on what
> mission? And what is this secret Chamberlain doing
> now?"*
>
> —Nuyen memo, classified

ALICE REMAINED IMPRISONED; Ord could see as much for
himself, nothing different about her cell or the simple gray-
green dress or the stiff way she sat on the edge of her plain
cot. But it had been Alice in the penthouse, or at least some
magical, unknown portion of her. Sitting on his own bed,
unconsciously mimicking her pose, Ord felt confusion
bleed into fascination, and when the jailers abruptly filed
into Alice's cell, the fascination turned to excitement.

The jailers belonged to three high-grav races, each man
stout and powerful, all made more impressive by isotropic
black uniforms. Wearing an expression that was not entirely
relaxed, the largest man gazed up at the universal eye. A
stiff, formal voice told the universe, "The prisoner needs to
meet with her attorneys, in private. For the next few hours,
this line will be terminated. Thank you."

The wall went dark, and Ord gave a little gasp.

He wasn't the only Chamberlain watching. An electric

murmur passed through the air, pulses marking the passage of invisible siblings. From doorless rooms deep inside the mansion came a piercing series of whistles, then an older sister appeared beside Ord's bed, weaving a body from light and dust and flakes of his own dead skin.

She stared at her little brother for what felt like an eternity.

"What's wrong?" Ord finally asked, surprised to sound so convincingly innocent.

Yet the sister should have seen through him, duplicity bright in his panicky glands and the frazzled neurons. And certainly she should have noticed the invisible object lying on Ord's lap, both of his thighs depressed by its bulk, its plain oddness sure to set off the alarms.

Yet nothing registered in her ice-bound blue eyes. A pause, a prolonged blink. Then her brother asked again, "What is wrong?"

"Many things," she assured. Then, "Have you seen Alice?"

"On the wall."

Deeply puzzled, she glanced at the blackness. Confusion didn't wear on her well.

"Why are Alice's attorneys visiting her?"

The sister straightened her back, then whispered, "They aren't. And there lies the trouble."

He waited.

"We have a report—unconfirmed—that Alice managed to leave her cell for a moment, or two—"

"But she can't," Ord sputtered. "She's practically helpless. I mean, didn't they take away her powers?"

The sister was eager to agree, and couldn't. "It's someone's error," she offered. "Someone's bad joke, perhaps." Pause. "I wouldn't worry." Pause. "And you say you haven't seen her?"

"Only on the wall," he told her.

An obvious question begged to be asked: Why was Ord watching Alice at this precise moment? But the old sister couldn't see the logic or summon the words. Quietly, almost embarrassed, she said, "Well then, good day, little one. I'm sorry to intrude." And without waiting for his good-byes, she vanished with a sparkle of milky light.

Ord felt alone, and watched. They suspected that Alice would come see him. Yet he wasn't asked about his visit to the penthouse, while the mystery on his lap might not even exist . . . unless they were thoroughly aware, watching him out of curiosity or caution. But that didn't feel likely, either. For no good reason, Ord sensed that he was as safe as possible, under the circumstances.

What now? he asked himself.

A thousand times, perhaps. And only then did he take hold of the wondrous nothing, examining it in earnest.

The object was fashioned in part from some species of dark matter. Its surfaces were imprecise and a little cool, then warm. Its density was rather like gold or palladium, and with each touch it seemed to merge with Ord's own flesh, for an instant, the sensation rather like a surface felt inside a sloppy dream. Ord walked to the far end of the apartment and set the wondrous nothing in his little swimming pool, on the smoothest water, and not so much as a dimple was made. Yet the object remained where he set it. He could push it back and forth like a balloon, nothing but his own hands aware of its weighty presence.

Natural dark matter didn't exist in this form. Coagulated; tangible; capable of interacting with visible matter. But with sufficient energies and the proper cleverness, it was possible to make the wild particles behave, making them cling to one another and play games with a baryonic boy. These were great technologies, and Ord knew little beyond that. Dark matter and its sisters, the dark energies, were the basis for much of his siblings' magic. But even the smartest Chamberlain didn't know all of their tricks. In a sense, the ordinary baryonic universe was nothing but a thin pollution inside all that was dark and massive. Ninety-nine percent of everything existed in a multitude of useful flavors that Ord could only see in his imagination, and then, just barely.

With care, Ord caressed the gift, fingers discerning tiny

crenellations, his mind's eye building an improving picture. But what it resembled . . . well, it seemed unlikely at best. A tightly folded cerebral cortex; the undersized cerebellum; and the ancient medulla: It was a brain of the oldest kind, human in proportions but nothing like the tough modern form. Even the lizard-folk, poor as possible, had fancier and much more enduring versions of the ancestral brains. Fatty flesh and acetylcholine had vanished with hundred-year life spans and mental imbalances. Why would Alice give him such a relic? But it wasn't a relic, he reminded himself. It was as modern in substance as possible; and what did that imply?

An affinity for Ord's flesh was a clue, and its shape was another clue. An idea came to him. But when he acted on the idea, he was shocked to find it valid. The mysterious nothing approved of his scalp and began to burrow, exotic particles swirling around the bland ones, passing through flesh and the hyperfiber skull, moving just the right little distance, then pausing and aligning themselves with a perfect grace, linking in a multitude of ways with Ord's own astonished mind.

AN IMAGE APPEARED before him.

It was out-of-focus, but instantly identifiable.

"Am I supposed to go there?" he asked. No answer was offered. Ord put on hiking boots, then noticed a second pair of boots where he found the first pair. Using the stairwell, he passed a dozen siblings—modest-ranking Chamberlains wearing frightened, flushed expressions—and nobody gave him the barest notice. Which was important, since he was forbidden from leaving the mansion, in punishment for the bomb nonsense.

When Ord reached the auxiliary door, he was struck by a cold premonition. Not once, but twice, he reached up and touched the PRIDE AND SACRIFICE sign, the dense granite feeling soft as mud beneath his fingers. Then he passed through the locked door and strolled among his napping bears, scratching their broad heads, the giants sniffing at nothing and moaning at things only they could see.

His destination was a good hour's run from home, most of it downhill. Wild birds and nervous roodeer didn't startle when he passed them. Water splashed, and the earth dimpled under him, but each backward glance showed him only a smooth brook and muddy banks without a single bootprint. Ord was a ghost, it seemed. He was exactly like his elderly siblings, composed of nothing but thought, and it frightened him, and it seemed terribly fun . . . yet he couldn't make himself hesitate for a moment, much less ask his conscious self if this was what was right . . . whatever it was that he was doing . . .

A child's clubhouse stood on the border of the Sanchex and Chamberlain estates, tucked into the back of a dead-end valley. Built of lumber by boys and girls barely old enough to swing hammers, it had stood empty for almost a century. The Golds disbanded not long after Alice's arrival. Which was natural, since they'd grown too old for the club's games. Yet a new generation should have come here to burn down the relic with an appropriate solemnity, then build their own clubhouse somewhere else. Forgotten, the old place had fallen into a dishonorable entropy, its oak roof collapsing, its walnut floor buckling, and the childlike signatures on the far wall turning soft and imprecise, slowly erased by countless species of rot.

Ord barely saw his own name, second in rank.

Ravleen's signature was on top.

Slowly and for no clear reason, Ord realized that he wasn't alone. The far end of the clubhouse was newer, better built and infinitely better maintained. Sitting on a carved slab of granite, reading some historical text, sat a half-born god. A monster, and a beauty. A demon and ally, and an occasional close friend.

Ord stepped up to Ravleen, and paused.

She was reading about a long-ago war fought by species rendered extinct by their own terrible fighting. The account was built from careful excavations and loose speculations. Ord glanced at the next few pages, then stared at the San-

chex body. Alone, Ravleen wore nothing. Her clothes lay
beneath her, waiting for orders to leap into place. She had
the beautiful, freshly formed body of an adolescent girl, her
pubic hair black and her nipples even blacker. Page after
page flashed before her unblinking eyes. Occasionally, she
would take a tiny breath. Then she abruptly stopped reading, blanking the book and lifting her gaze until she looked
straight into Ord's wide eyes.

She did not see him.

He was mostly sure, then he was certain.

With his right hand, Ord reached for Ravleen, touching
what he had always secretly wanted to touch.

She was a devil, furious and deadly, and she was as
beautiful as any creature ever conceived. And Ord put his
hand to her chest, and then inside, discovering that he could
feel the curl of her ribs and coursing of her hot, hot blood;
and she felt none of it, sitting up straight now and thinking
about dead wars, or wars to come; and with his palm and
fingers and a curled thumb, he made a cup beneath her
heart, its hard humming beat feeling wonderful inside his
careful hand.

Six

> "We have listed every ancient Chamberlain, living
> and dead, and after each name you will find every
> imaginable reason why he or she cannot be the en-
> tity who hides among us . . .
> "Nobody is hiding among us, obviously . . ."
> —Nuyen memo, classified

A WOLVERINE EMERGED from a hole in the floor. The thick,
low-slung body reminded Ord of a jailer's body. With a
baleful glare, the creature let out a sharp *hiss* aimed straight
for him. Obviously, it saw him. Yet Ravleen remained sitting, unconscious of the phantom, her heart holding its

smooth, relaxed pace. Ord withdrew his hand from her chest and hissed at the wolverine, and the creature spun around and trotted out the back door, heading for what should have been a high wall of slick granite. But the wall had vanished, replaced with a long valley and a meandering brook and trees not as tall as seemed right, or as healthy, their leaves dressed in autumnal colors but all too drab and haphazard to belong to a Chamberlain wood. One last time, Ord glanced at Ravleen. Then he started to run.

"Hello!"

Birds flew in terror. Save for some odd kind of jaybird that perched on a high branch, cursing the boy for trying to steal its acorns.

"Hello?"

No human answered.

A narrow dung-littered game trail led across the brook, and wherever he stepped, deep bootprints filled with swirling brown water. Now and again he shouted, "Hello!" A noisy indifference filled the woods. Finally, Ord thought to say, "I'm looking for someone," and then, "I'm hunting Brother Perfect," and his answer came in the form of a skin-clad figure stepping from the shadows, almost from underfoot.

"And who's doing this hunting?" the figure asked.

The man was a Chamberlain. There was no telling which brother he was, but it was only a brother, and Ord was disappointed, bursting with doubts.

"And if you don't know who you are," the brother continued, "maybe you can recall who sent you here. How about it, my boy?"

"I'm Ord," he muttered, "and nobody sent me."

The brother appeared shorter than him, but stocky in a strong, comfortably fattened way, his red hair matted and tied into a ponytail, a thin red-and-snow beard obscuring the famous Chamberlain jaw. It wasn't an impressive body, conjured or not. But the trousers and heavy vest were remarkable, made from sewn skins and mended with dirty lengths of gut and hemp. A leather belt held several elegant stone tools. One pale hand held a spear by its heavy blond shaft, a long Folsom point drawing jagged stars in the air between them.

"And who are you?" asked Ord.

"You wanted someone named Perfect. Maybe that's me."

But no Chamberlain had that name. It would be cruel to saddle one of their own with such an outrageous boast—

"You know every name, do you?"

"In order of birth, yes. And I know some of everybody's biography."

"What a gruesome waste!" The stone-age figure broke into a laugh, shaking his head in a blurring motion. "Which anal-retentive child-of-Ian dreamed up that abuse of neural capacities?"

Ord couldn't guess who.

The brother cursed, laughed, and said, "So. You're the baby."

"Pardon?"

"The baby. That's your nickname." He paused. "By any chance, are you familiar with the concept of nicknames—"

"Yes."

"Then you have enough of a clue. Come. Hurry on now, Baby."

Ord attempted to ask where they were, where they were going, and why the woods looked wrong. But the brother, whoever he was, was bulling his way through the tangled landscape. Ord had to run after him, catching up as they splashed across the muddy brook. "Is Perfect a nickname?"

"Oftentimes." The left hand gestured, its two smallest fingers missing, the wagging stumps showing no interest in regrowth. "Have you ever known someone you'd like to call Perfect?"

Maybe.

"To make them angry, of course. Am I right?"

Ord ignored the question. "I deserve to know where we are—"

"This is the Chamberlain estate. We're embedded inside

the mountains." Perfect kicked and stomped his way through a wall of brush, thorns leaving bloody sketches on his exposed arms. "A clever little house of mine, don't you think?"

"Why am I here?"

"No, Baby. It's my turn to ask the question."

He despised that name.

"Humans," said the brother. "Humans have lived for twenty million years. As apes, then as simple souls. And, finally, less simple. But now, if you were pressed to decide, what moment would you claim was our peak? Our grand climax? Today, perhaps? Last week? When?"

"Who are you?"

The brother offered a sideways glance and grin, then stepped through a wall of gold-and-brown leaves, branches rushing back into place, conspiring to make him vanish.

Ord hesitated, wondering if he should flee.

From behind the leaves, a rough Chamberlain voice said, "Humans. Our summit. Give it a shot, Baby!"

Stepping through the wall, Ord found himself standing before an abrupt hillside and a simple cave worn into its face. The rocks weren't cultured granite; they were limestone. The limestone was finely grained and encrusted with fossilized crinoids, thousands of the flowery animals laid into the soft dead sediments. This was a caveman's camp, the air stinking of old fires and tainted game, and the brother seemed at home, setting his spear against the cave's broad mouth, then turning to say:

"My given name? Thomas. Thomas Chamberlain."

No. Impossible . . . !

"And since you won't guess, I'll tell you my personal choice for our species' crowning moment." Thomas laughed easily, and said, "The final years of the final ice age, when we were expanding across new continents and wild, unmapped seas." Another laugh. "You look doubtful, Baby. Scornful, even. But consider this: There weren't many of us, and each of us was important. A few million apes, modified by natural selection and armed with stone and wood implements, and armed with our cunning, and our mobile little cultures . . . and we came to rule the entire green world . . . !"

Trembling, Ord stared at his ancient brother.

"And you know what the world was then, don't you?" Thomas flashed a quick, disarming smile. "It was the universe. It was *everything*. A vast globe encompassing every imaginable beauty, and it was set inside a sea of ink and tiny, unimaginable stars. And it was ours." With a wave of the maimed hand, he said, "Do you see my mind? All the history since, every human venture and accomplishment . . . everything has been one long and frustrating and wondrously absurd attempt to regain those lost days of glory!"

And with that pronouncement, Thomas broke into a thunderous laugh, a sudden rain of golden leaves falling on them, then swirling, vainly fighting the urge to settle, to die.

Seven

> *"Alice gave me that lance of a nickname.*
> *"I was a new adult, proud of my augmentation and promise, and she was a very young, relentlessly mouthy child. I would sing at length about all the good I would be doing—for the Family; for all people; for all time—and she would always growl at me. 'Oh, you think you're the perfect Chamberlain,' she snapped. 'You think you're the very best. But you're the same as us, brother. Brother Perfect. Oh, yes, you are. You are, you are . . .'"*
> —Perfect, in conversation

ALICE—THE GREAT and infamous and bankrupt sister—was the twelfth Chamberlain. While Thomas was Ian's eighth clone, making him Nine, which in turn meant that he was almost exactly as old as Alice and Ord combined.

If this was indeed Thomas. But that seemed like a preposterous idea, a thousand history lessons recalled in an instant and this skin-clad, slightly mutilated figure resembling none of them.

In a Family of dedicated terraformers, Thomas was an oddity: He built little but loved to explore—a godlike wanderer whose passion and genius led him to find alien worlds and befriend their sentient species. Alliances and trading links had never interested Thomas. He left those blessings for others. The bloodless Nuyens, for instance. By the time Nuyens were flocking to some distant system that he had charted, Thomas would have struck out into the wilderness again, chasing radio squawks and free-oxygen signatures until he found another wondrous species. Or found nothing at all. Because as any halfway-educated person knew, intelligence was an infrequent event in the universe, and it was born imperfectly, and judging by the thousands of war-killed worlds, intelligence was a fundamentally perishable form of life, too.

But the Milky Way had been thoroughly explored, from the Core to its faint far edges, and Thomas had gone elsewhere. "I know all about Thomas," Ord told the caveman. "He's gone now. The Families sent him out to explore Andromeda. His mission left more than a million years ago."

"A mission left, but did I?" The brother chuckled.

Ord said nothing.

"The truth? At the last possible instant I suffered a chaotic change of desire. Instead of embarking on a great adventure, I decided to chase privacy and self-reflection. Which is my right as a self-aware organism, and don't give me that disappointed glare."

Ord didn't know he was glaring, stumbling into an apology—

But Thomas interrupted, every affront forgotten. A cackling laugh was followed by an offer of meat, dried and hard and frosted with limestone grit. "Mammoth biltong," he warned. "Chew hard," he advised. Then, "What's wrong? Doesn't the flavor intrigue?"

Not even a little, no. But Ord forced himself to eat, proving his stubbornness. When the last gob of leather was sitting in his belly, dissolving in acids and microchines, the boy found the confidence to say, "I don't believe you are Thomas."

"And why not?"

"I've been with Alice, and this doesn't feel the same." There wasn't the palpable sense of vast energies and relentless intellect, though Ord mentioned neither blessing by name. Nor did he say that Thomas looked bizarre and acted the same, laughing too often and never with the same sound, the oddest things amusing him without fail.

Like Ord's doubts.

The brother turned red-faced, cackling for a solid minute. Then he gasped, coughed into his maimed hand, and asked, "How is dear Alice? Is her trial just about finished?"

"You don't know?"

"On the whole," he confessed, "current events bore me."

Incredulous, Ord couldn't summon any response.

"My guess is that they found her infinitely guilty."

"Yes."

"Good for them." The smile was winsome, bittersweet. "I told her, told her, told her not to fuck around with that nasty business. But you've met our sister. You know how she can be—"

"She's jailed. They've stripped her of everything."

"As is right," said the possible Thomas.

"But then she escaped—I don't know how—and came to see me . . . !"

Delight shone in the blue-gray eyes. "And she wants your help, does she? Some special chore intended just for you?"

"I have to save something. I don't know what." He paused, then added, "Brother Perfect is supposed to help me."

"Oh, is he?"

Ord nodded, unsure how to respond.

"Alice appears out of nothingness, expecting obedience."

A grimace, a leering smile. "What they should have carved off our sister are her bossy pretenses. That's what I think."

Perhaps.

"Can you give me one good guess as to your mission?"

"Don't you know?" Ord asked, in horror.

Thomas stepped closer, his maimed hand lifting, touching the boy on the temple. His intact fingers dipped into the scalp for a chilling instant. Then, with a slow, careful voice, he asked, "Do you wish to help, or don't you? Yes or no." A pause. " 'Yes' and we embark. 'No' and I send you straight home."

"Embark to where?"

"All things considered, not far."

Ord saw a cracked tooth in the narrow smile. "I want to help," he confessed. Then, "If it accomplishes something good—"

"Tell me yes, tell me no. I'll leave the worthiness for others."

Ord said, "Yes."

He said it three times, his voice strengthening, acquiring something that resembled confidence. But Thomas had turned away with the first 'yes,' vanishing into his cave without a sound or a backward glance.

Ord followed.

Thomas was working in the gloomy half-light. A large smoky fire crackled inside a stone hearth. The flanking walls were adorned with charcoal bison and ochre ponies. Ord touched one of the stiff-legged ponies, deciding that with the same crude tools, he would be at least as good a painter as his brother.

Thomas was stuffing gear into a leather knapsack, no room left for the smallest charm. Then, with a creaking of rope and skin, he lifted the pack to his shoulders, making adjustments, grimacing with conviction as he remarked, "You're better than me at many things, I would think."

Like Alice, he could read a boy's mind.

Waving his injured hand, Thomas said, "See? No new fingers growing."

The stumps were blunt and callused, all right.

"You could make new fingers," Ord muttered. "With just a thought, you could."

"Ah, but then I'd forget to be careful when I find a dire wolf hanging in one of my snares." He gave a wink and rough laugh. "Scars are reminders, Baby. These scars remind me that dire wolves can be tricky bastards."

An adult Chamberlain could look inside any animal, measuring its health and intentions. Particularly if the animal was part of an elaborate illusion built by that same adult. But what Chamberlain wanted to live inside a smoky cave, much less hunt with snares and spears? Ord's only reasonable guess was that this caveman existence helped Thomas to mask his presence inside the estate.

"Perfect," said his brother, again reading thoughts. "That's Alice's name for me, and it's good enough for us."

A blink and nod. Then Ord said, "But I'm not Baby."

"Fair enough." And with that, Perfect strode into the sunshine, stepping at a brisk pace, grabbing up his spear, and singing with a loud, out-of-key wail.

Ord followed, ignoring the landscape. It was all an illusion, and he assumed they were walking to someplace close—as promised—and answers would come in short order. He barely noticed his brother's sour songs, concentrating instead on his eventual excuses for disappearing. They would send Lyman to interrogate him. Ord practiced a half dozen lies, each involving the old clubhouse. He had sneaked off to meet a girlfriend; why not? He'd already had a variety of adolescent affairs, mostly with girls in the Golds. Wasn't that kind of subterfuge permitted, even encouraged? For a long happy while, Ord imagined meeting Ravleen at the clubhouse. Sanchexes were relentless lovers, or so he had heard. He remembered her naked body and the feel of her heart; and then the daydream tasted real; and then came the first hint of boredom that always preyed on daydreams.

Thomas—no, *Perfect*—took them up a long mountainside, through trees noticeably shorter, and barer. The afternoon passed quickly. The summit lay ahead, sharp and raw, no mansion built upon it. They climbed past a single greenish boulder and dropped into a grove of blue-black spruces. With stone blades they cut boughs for bedding. With flint and dried wood they made a sputtering fire, and Perfect held his imperfect hands to the fire, catching some portion of its tiny heat.

Ord asked why he lived this way.

"You sing out of key," he complained. "You don't paint all that well. You eat badly, and you let yourself get cold." He listed the items as if they were diseases. "And you won't even regenerate a simple finger, will you?"

"I'm not cold," Perfect protested. "And if I am, I'll pull my robe out of my pack."

Ord was comfortable. As the sun set, his flesh generated its own internal fire. Yet he held his hands to Perfect's fire, remarking, "Alice wouldn't live this way."

That brought a laugh, insane and infuriating.

Then, "From what you've said, Alice would be thrilled to live this well now."

That wasn't what Ord meant, and both brothers knew it.

"Let me tell you about our sister." Perfect pulled dried meat from his pack, offering none to Ord. "Every fancy skill, every energy source, all that godly garb . . . Alice wanted them. Always, always. Of course, everyone's that way, in a fashion. But she's the worst culprit, I'd like to believe, and with a good Chamberlain modesty, I tell all that I'm the least guilty. I acquire only those talents that I absolutely need, and when the need passes, I give them away. To Alice, in some cases."

"Augmenting your voice . . . is that too fancy . . . ?"

"Oh, I sing, and I like singing. And what I hear is nothing but lovely." Another laugh accompanied his chewing the inedible mammoth. "Everything I do I do with joy and within my limits, and that's all I want."

"You didn't even know about the trial," Ord complained.

"If something important happens, I hear about it." He gave a little wink. "But you're right, I'm not tied to the universal networks. And I don't know ten million languages. My mathematics is practical, not serene. My senses are good enough, and my strengths fit the job of the moment." A slow soft laugh, then he added, "In case you haven't noticed, my humor is simple. Even a little crude. Which suits my needs fine, thank you."

But why? Ord kept wondering. Why are you different?

"Do you wish to know? My moment of enlightenment?" Perfect waited for his brother's gaze, then said, "Eons ago, I was sitting beside an alien sea, wearing my best godly garb, and this fellow happened to stroll past. Do you know about the Brongg?"

They were bipeds, vaguely fishlike. Their home world had methane seas and water-ice continents. They were the oldest known intelligent species, and Brother Thomas was the first human to meet them.

"Very good," the caveman said, offering a little chuckle. "Anyway, this little fellow was walking Brongg-fashion, which is syrupy-slow. Seeing me, he offered greetings and stopped to chat—the Brongg are great talkers—and eventually I learned his identity. He was famous. Ancient beyond belief. I was a baby, barely a million years old, and of all the creatures I've ever met, he seemed to be the happiest. A billion years of joy was walking on the beach, carrying nothing but a simple ice lance—he was fishing his native sea, Ord—and I've always held that lesson very close to my heart."

They were a cold, cold species. The Brongg had wondrous technologies, but they did little with them. They traveled sparingly, reproduced slowly, and were as alien and bizarre as any species that humans had ever found. How could they bring enlightenment?

Perfect didn't answer that thought. Rising, he pulled the promised robe from his pack, its fur thick and glossy, sewn together from the pelts of mink and wolverines and dire wolves, the stitches durable and artless.

"Why did you come back to the Earth?"

His brother lay down beside the fire, a bent arm serving

as a pillow. "I was invited," he muttered. "Someone appeared without warning, gave me my marching orders, then framed it as a request before she vanished again."

Alice.

Perfect gave a sleepy nod, eyes beginning to close.

But before he could sleep, or whatever state it was, he heard one last question from a confused little brother. "Are we still inside the estate? Because I'm forbidden to leave—"

"Watch the sky," Perfect advised.

Ord obeyed, his heated breath rising toward the night's first stars. They were the right stars in the proper places, but where were the planets? And the starships coming and going? Glancing to his left, he saw the green boulder on the summit, then the boulder became a smooth green globe, and the mountain beneath it evaporated, and the stars brightened and multiplied in the sudden vacuum . . . and a thousand lessons in terraforming told Ord what he was seeing.

Gazing at the green world, he whispered, "Neptune."

Against all reason, in one afternoon, he and Perfect had hiked their way to the chilled edge of the solar system.

Eight

"You will be stripped of possessions, money, and mind, and each of your works will be assessed on a case-by-case basis. Worlds terraformed in good faith, by legal means, will be spared. But illegal projects will be sought out and destroyed by whatever means are deemed most humane . . ."
—*from Alice's sentencing*

ORD SAT ON the stony ground, staring at Neptune. Because it was genuine, because no illusions of sight or soul were involved, the boy was enthralled. He felt wonderstruck.

Here was one of the first great worlds terraformed by humanity. Alice had done some portion of the work, in her youth. Technical details buoyed up out of Ord's augmented memory. Slowly, laboriously, the novice terraformers had digested the world's atmosphere, sequestering the hydrogen deep inside the core while metals and silicates were dredged up in its place. Airborne continents were grown, floating solidly upon rafts of vacuum bubbles. The new atmosphere was nitrogen and helium, sweet oxygen and the vital trace gases. Light and heat came from simple fusion. Rivers ran off the continents' lips, great waterfalls tumbling into the dense inner atmosphere, then boiling away, returning as soft showers on green woods and green cities. An area many times Earth's was made habitable, at a profit. This was where Alice made her first fortune. The entire adventure consumed fifty thousand years and the talents of hundreds. Yet today, working alone, a creature of Alice's capacity could finish the essential work in less than six centuries.

"Why here?" he muttered. "What's special about Neptune?"

Nobody answered him. And despite his questions and the lousy bed, Ord felt himself drifting away. Sleep claimed him, dark and dreamless; and then he was awake again, the blunt end of a spear jabbing him in the ribs.

"Time to leave," said a distant voice, with urgency. "They know you're missing, and you're making them scared."

The sky was cobalt blue, another false sun washing away the stars. Spruce trees and bare stone lay on all sides. Ord rose to his feet, attempting to ask every question that he had thought up last night. Words came in a rush, then he faltered. Perfect was walking, and Ord found himself walking beside his brother, step for step; and a sensation, cold and unnerving, made him whisper, "What's this now? What's happening to me?"

"You've been altered, a bit. Alice began the work, and I did some tinkering last night." The profile was weathered, sober and calm. "We've rebuilt you as quickly as possible, under these circumstances—"

"What's wrong with me?"

"Wrong? Dear boy, nothing!" A bleak, oversize laugh collapsed into silence. "The truth? Part of you is a starship. You're built from dark matter and magic, and your heart is an exotic inertialess drive. Your hull is invisible, we can hope. Legs and lungs, and your skin, are projections based on your own expectations." Again he laughed, but softer, with a glimmer of compassion. "Despite these humble appearances, we're moving at nearly light-speed."

"I don't believe you."

"Which is probably best, all things considered."

For an instant, Ord could feel the man speaking to him in many voices, most of them using convoluted languages designed to serve a rarefied mathematics. Some new, unsuspected part of him ingested the words without fuss, without hesitation. What made him panic was the sudden sensation of his true self: huge and ghostly, more unreal than real, suffused with liquid energies beyond human experience.

He tried to walk slower, and couldn't.

"For the moment," said Perfect, "I'll operate those legs."

Ord crossed his nonexistent arms on his facsimile chest. "I want to know where we're going."

Perfect squinted, as if he could see their destination. In the illusion, they were marching down a verdant mountainside, birds and other phantoms calling out from the shadows as they passed.

"This is illegal," the boy gasped.

"Immoral," his brother agreed. "Not to mention cruel. And dangerous, too." That brought genuine pleasure, bubbling and warm. "But when a famous criminal came to you, did you tell the authorities? When she slipped you a mysterious object, did you cry out, 'Look here, everyone! Look what Alice gave me!'?"

Ord was weeping. Sobbing.

"For now," said Perfect, "we're traveling toward the Oort cloud."

"Then where?"

"Let's reach the cloud first," his brother replied. "That way if you're caught, you can claim to have been kidnapped—"

"I am kidnapped!"

"Good attitude. Keep practicing."

Ord never would have agreed if he'd known . . . if he had been given any hint of what was involved . . . crimes accomplished, grave danger implied . . . an insane journey, fleeing the safety and simple legality of home . . . !

A five-fingered hand patted Ord on the back.

"A rational boy would have balked, yes." Perfect's voice was smooth and untroubled. "If I had been honest to you, you would have said, 'No.' But you'd have been acting out of fear and ignorance. That's why I framed the question as I did: 'Do you wish to help?' A person does or a person doesn't, and both of us know you can't help but want to help, because that's the honored old Chamberlain curse."

The boy tried to collapse. And couldn't. He felt limp, half-dead and wracked with miseries, uttering a great long sob before asking the perfectly reasonable question, "Why me?"

"My question, too." There was a weighty pause and another useless pat on the back. "Perhaps Alice wants you because you're the baby. Perhaps it's as simple as that."

Ord barely heard him, his mind collapsing on itself.

"We Chamberlains love closure, that sense of great things being *done*. That's why we build exceptional worlds. Durable, full-bodied biospheres equal to three billion years of raw evolution."

What was he saying? Ord could barely hear the disagreeable voice.

"One of the very first Chamberlains sends the last on a great mission." Perfect clucked his tongue but didn't laugh. "It's closure, and it feels right, and maybe that's all there is to this business. Closure and an instinctive rightness, and as complicated as Alice can be, maybe her plan is just that simple. That brutally narrow. That utterly and perfectly sure."

Nine

"The boy's disappearance went unnoticed for several critical hours. Had Alice escaped, and was the genuine Alice sitting inside her prison cell again? Those were the thunderous questions of the moment. Obvious false leads led to more subtle possibilities, equally false. With the event apparently finished, certain key sensors were placed into a diagnostic mode. Perhaps that explains why no new anomalous events were observed. Then the Chamberlains finally realized that the boy was missing, his subterfuge infinitely too advanced to be his own work. A general alarm was sounded. Several thousand contingency plans were unsealed. Gravimetric evidence pointed to a new mass orbiting Pluto. Warnings were sent to appropriate Nuyens and our allies, and a dozen searches found nothing. But afterward, several Families reported major thefts from their Neptune reserves . . ."

—Nuyen memo, confidential

THEY CROSSED BILLIONS of kilometers, and the landscape, befitting some odd logic, grew colder and drier, the spruce forests replaced with an arctic steppe populated with herds of extinct game. Giant bison and woolly mammoths grazed beneath a weakening sun. In the distance, looming like flat-topped mountains, was a blue-white glacial mass. Ord noticed humans in the middle ground, clad like stone-age hunters, some walking while others stood on a high knoll, hands shielding their eyes and watching the countryside. Watching for us, he realized. They were symbols representing other ships or outposts, but even the nearest hunter barely looked in their direction, completely oblivious to the two passing brothers.

Ord quit crying, forcing himself out of his self-pity. In a choking voice, he asked, "Why do you travel this way?"

"In past days," Perfect explained, "travelers on board steamships and starships would pin photographs and holos to their cabin walls. To remind them of more comfortable places, I imagine. To give homesick eyes something other than empty water and space."

Listening, Ord discovered that he was glad for the voice.

"Space bores me," said his incredible brother. "Hard vacuums and the ancient cold play on my nerves, if you must know."

Ord felt the vacuum. It was a thin chill stew of cosmic radiation and dust and virtual particles, and it felt like a dry autumn breeze.

He asked, "How long did you hide in the estate?"

"I followed Alice home. But I was a bit slower, by a few years."

"Because she wanted you to come? Is that the only reason?"

A mild, patient laugh implied wisdom. "You aren't the only person whom our sister has bewitched."

Questions, like virtual particles, appeared out of nothing, then vanished again.

"I've known Alice for my entire life, nearly." Perfect paused, waiting for his brother's eyes. "I don't need much prompting from her. For many reasons, I behave."

"If you were at the Core," Ord remarked, "you could have helped."

"Build that baby universe? Hardly." He gave a hard chuckle. "The Core's a big playground, and I wasn't particularly close to her or any of them. I was living in seclusion somewhere between Alice and your front door."

"But you knew what she was doing—?"

"And fought with her whenever she paid me a visit." A black expression blossomed, sour and wild-eyed. "Oh, I fought with her. I augmented myself with every persuasive skill, and when those skills failed, I made threats. As if they could have done any good."

Each step took them closer to the high glacial wall. Between them and the ice stood a low moraine, moss forests and lichen jungles growing wherever there was a speck of shelter, and as they climbed the loose slope, their feet made avalanches that destroyed oases and created new ones.

With a quiet voice—a hunter's voice—Perfect asked, "Do you wonder what they did with all of Alice's powers?"

"They were stripped away, of course."

"But what does that mean?" Perfect posed the question, then gave an answer. "Powers have physical sources. Augmented minds need neural nets. Moving a world requires godly muscles. And there are the machines that crack molecules and weave dark matter and build bodies and tear them down again, in an instant." The healthy hand took Ord by the arm, then squeezed. "I'm talking about Alice's body and mind. Her copper bolts and rattling microchines. And her antimatter-digesting guts, too."

"I've wondered about them," the boy confessed.

"A grand secret, they are. And a wrenching problem for the poor officials who need to decipher, then destroy them."

They reached the moraine's crest as the sun set behind them. Another day was done; a comforting sense of closure took hold. Perfect dropped his bulky knapsack and sat on it, eating more of his endless dried meat, then gladly sharing it when the boy asked for another taste.

Without daylight, the world shrank, darkness giving the tundra a close, constricted feel. But the glacier seemed to grow, becoming glassy, some subtle inner light betraying networks of fine cracks and deep fissures. Tiny, tiny humans stood at its base. Each held a spear, but the spears represented weapons of an entirely different order. And the ice was nothing at all like ice.

In a whisper, Perfect said, "That creature you met? Our Alice? As powerful as a sun, if the need arose. A hundred suns, if you gave her time. But when she arrived from the Core, a breath slower than light-speed, she had minimal mass. She was a set of instructions and the barest skeleton. Using raw materials kept stored in and around the solar system, for just such occasions, she rebuilt herself." He

paused, biting off another mouthful of dead mammoth.
"Most of Alice—the bulk of her memories, her talents—
came later. Came slower. That's how the true giants travel.
Think of it like a strange snowfall falling from the Core,
snowflakes the size of houses and mountains, each bringing
some potent talent, or several talents. This is where they
are brought, Ord. Here. Collected and held here. Waiting
for someone to find the courage to crack them open and
see what there is to see."

Bright hard stars appeared before them, above and below, flares of soft blue plasma slipping through the glacier's
deep fractures. This was Alice's dangerous meat, and it was
larger than some worlds—

"A morgue, in essence." The Chamberlain voice was
close, softer than any whisper. "Keep still. Keep very still
now."

The moraine had vanished; Ord was in free fall.

"Do you feel sleepy, maybe?"

The boy was extraordinarily tired.

"Good. Try closing your eyes."

But before he could, Ord said, "Closure," with a numbed
mouth.

"What was that?"

"That's why she came home," he muttered. "To die like
this, in pieces. She knew it would happen, I think."

"And she knew she deserved it, too." Perfect touched
him with a thousand hands, and laughed. "Do you know
what I like best about humans? How we take whatever
happens and dress it up in whatever suit of clothes we want,
for any occasion." The hands were hotter than suns, soothing to the touch and intensely busy. "Maybe you're right.
Maybe closure explains this whole fucking mess."

Ord's eyes had pulled shut.

There was a distant black laugh, and Perfect said, "The
poetic denouement, and they couldn't help themselves.
Every one of them a god, and everything ugly and everything lovely follows straight from that . . ."

Ten

> "The point begs to be made . . . we are at a distinct
> disadvantage here . . .
>
> "Our oldest, most powerful siblings are scattered
> across the galaxy. Many of them are only now learn-
> ing about the disaster at the Core, and it will be
> tens of thousands of years before they can return
> home, bringing the greatest of their talents, their
> vast experience, and the other advantages of age
> that we sorely miss today . . .
>
> "We have done our best. Never think otherwise.
> With only the resources in hand, we have done a
> magnificent job of making ready for all contingen-
> cies . . . for guessing the mind of a criminal and a
> Chamberlain . . .
>
> "That said, we are compelled to admit that de-
> spite instant action, the Oort cloud holding facility
> was infiltrated . . . certain properties were stolen . . .
>
> "Analysis is proceeding with all available
> tools . . .
>
> "The boy is still being sought . . ."
>
> —Nuyen memo, confidential

IT WAS LIKE waking from death again.

There was a voice. Chamberlain, and male. From the
living world, he said, "The Brongg home world. Picture it.
Walk it with me. A long gentle beach of water-ice sands,
the glorious slick sea of liquid methane on our left, and on
our right—"

"The Iron Spine." Ord knew the beach. A thousand eyes
seemed to open for him, only four of them mired in his
own face. It was another illusion, but of superior quality.
He was upright, wearing a new body. Slowly, very slowly,
he turned his head until the Iron Spine filled his gaze. Before the first vertebrate evolved on Earth, the Brongg had
lowered a nickel-iron asteroid onto their world, resting it

upon a stubborn bed of vacuum bubbles. Half a billion years of mining had left it partially hollow, but the exterior and slag piles made for a spectacular sight: a metal mountain floating on the water-ice crust, its flanks covered with a blue-black vegetation that had adapted to the bitter taste of heavy metals.

The weak Brongg sun was rising above the tallest peak. A Brongg day lasted for a full Terran month, Ord recalled, and with that fact came a multitude of ancillary facts and details, making him a helpless expert.

"Today," Perfect announced, "we will walk the beach."

The beach was gray with black streaks of organic goo, and it was smooth as pavement, curving out toward a rocky point where a polished black cylinder stood on end, casting a long shadow across the calm and colorless sea. The distances looked trivial, yet with his first laborious step, Ord realized this would be difficult at best. The Brongg nervous systems were built from superconducting proteins, thoughts flowing without resistance, without turbulence; but their physical metabolisms were painfully sluggish, the swift mind able to consider and reconsider every physical act thousands of times before it was attempted, or not.

"Perhaps that's why this species has lasted so long," Perfect offered. "Unlike people, they have no choice but to think before they step."

Turning his head was a struggle—a sobering investment—taking most of a stride. Perfect was a Brongg in body, like Ord. A nude fishy exterior wore thick legs and broad round feet, and his webbed hands held an astonishingly delicate ice lance. But the face was comically Chamberlain, four blue eyes winking now, his human mouth grinning at the world.

"In all," asked Perfect, "how many living intelligences have I discovered first? Count them for me, please."

Mouths were only for eating with. The Brongg voice was a radio pulse born from the swift nervous system. In an instant, Ord saw each of his brother's discoveries, from oldest to newest. He had found one hundred and three examples of intelligence on ninety-one worlds. No human could claim half as many finds. True, most of them were technology-impoverished. But twenty of the species, the Brongg included, had been deemed worthy of diplomats and trade, cultural exchanges and scientific hybridization.

"Now," said Perfect, "count the failed worlds."

Again, Ord knew the exact number. Memories encoded in a tireless net flowed into him. He saw Perfect tracking whispers through a wilderness of stars. Some whispers vanished, while some grew stronger, but all ended with a technological world freshly killed. Wars had done the damage, mostly. Sometimes there were accidental plagues or machines run amuck, or a battered ecosystem would collapse back to the microbes. Nothing with a voice remained, save the occasional computer or automated antenna still pointed at the sky, begging the stars for help, for alliances, for second chances, for God.

Counting was easy; remembering took an age.

Images struck at Ord, leaving him spent and sore, and sorry.

And Perfect had suffered far worse. His hopes were ruined each time; nothing but ruin was waiting for him. Armed with a Chamberlain's skills, he would sift through the gruesome traces—bone shards and burnt cities and oceans of encoded data—then he would build phantoms of the dead, complete with voices and desires, and their telltale flaws. These examples lent insights. Perfect could ask the phantoms why and how they had so willingly pushed their homes into oblivion. Forty-eight worlds, Ord counted, plus thousands more where life began, evolved to some sophisticated, promising level, then was shattered by a comet's splash or the inevitable detonation of a nearby sun.

Staring at the carnage, Ord asked the obvious, "How does any intelligence survive?"

"Exactly. Exactly!" There was a familiar laugh, if rather bleak, while Perfect took another agonizing step, ice-sands dimpling beneath the naked right foot. "The Bronggs are the elders, but they had it easy. Their solar system has few fissionable materials, and they're pathologically introspective. Even when they could have augmented themselves, boosting their physical powers, they didn't. Wouldn't. Out of fear more than wisdom, I think. There were too many uncertainties, regardless how long they rolled the Sisyphean problem back and forth in their supercooled minds."

The Brongg were cold, slow, and scarce. Ord had never admired them, and rarely thought about them.

"At the other end of the spectrum, or dangerously near it, are humans. Churning hot whirlwinds, passionate to a fault, aggressive to no good ends, and alive only because we scared ourselves into a state that can be confused for wisdom. Relentless wars led to the Families and the Great Peace, and our little truce has managed to last quite a while. But why shouldn't it last? As long as everyone felt happy, who cared who rowed the damned boat?"

He gave a long laugh, electric and chilling.

"Millions of years," said Perfect, "and I've studied the dead and the living. Now doesn't it make sense that I would find patterns? Relationships? Little tendencies, and big fat ones?"

Ord had to agree.

"Tendencies," Perfect repeated. "And rising from them, conclusions. How would I invent life from nothingness, given my chance? The best of the Brongg married to the bedrock of our own natures. All dropped into a stew with every other successful species, in some realm pure and innocent—"

"And perfect," Ord said, anticipating the words.

"Now you see why Alice renamed me. I have this wicked flaw. In my deepest soul, I need to chase after perfection."

Trying to guess the next stage, Ord mentioned the odd, illegal worlds that Alice had built. Novel proteins; toxic solvents. Nothing like them arose in the natural realms—

"Ordinary, ordinary worlds," was Perfect's assessment.

"How can you say that? She broke laws to make them, and she hid them away in secret places—"

"And I am telling you that these worlds are fundamentally, unabashedly traditional. I agree. Yes, Alice went to the kitchen and made strange muffins, but the muffins have ingredients you'd expect in a kitchen. Which is why I asked, 'Where's the genius, Alice? Why wear that silly pride?' "

"You said that to Alice?"

"For a few thousand centuries, and with a loud voice. And she would point out that if I was so clever, I would do better. 'With your help,' I would promise. Not being a superior terraformer, I needed hands trained for the big dull ugly work of it. And eventually she agreed to help me, just once. Surprising both of us, I believe."

Ord felt a sudden chill, a premonition.

"Where are we going?" he asked. "Please tell me."

Perfect showed him an enormous smile and gestured with vegetable slowness, his ice lance held in his left hand, two of the Brongg's minor fingers missing. "Down the beach," he replied, not quite laughing. "We're walking beside the sea, and it looks as if we're halfway there . . . can't you see . . . ?"

Slowly, slowly, Ord turned his head again.

They were halfway to the black cylinder, and the weak little sun was directly overhead, ruddy black clouds of hydrocarbons forming in the upper atmosphere, a chill shadow falling over them and the flat, rather greasy sea. Two weeks of walking, yet it seemed longer. A few words spoken, but Ord had absorbed volumes, the pace relentless, the demands of this kind of learning beyond his experience or wildest expectations. And it never stopped. Perfect's memories poured into him even as his brother remarked, "I wish there were more time, Ord. I do."

Why wasn't there time?

"Because we're being pursued. Wolves at our heels, if you will."

Ord looked over a shoulder, the alien neck as pliable as an owl's. The beach was empty save for a willowy creature walking in the shallow methane, jabbing with claws, in slow motion, impaling an eel-like creature even more sluggish than itself.

"How fast are we moving?"

"Through space," Perfect replied, "two whispers under light-speed."

"Why not one whisper under?"

"Because. This is fast enough. Our destination isn't equipped to receive us as a rain of instructions. And since you deserve to know, it's because we're carrying some possessions that need to be carried as they are, and I promised not to tell you anything more, and that is the simple, simple truth."

A powerful dread was working on Ord. He gasped with his mouth and unseen gills, then forced himself to ask, "How many pursuers?"

"Two. But presumably others are tucked in their wake."

"How close are they?"

"On this scale, walking along our little beach . . . if I displayed them to you, they would be wearing our skins . . . !"

Ord turned his head again, looking forward. Concentrating on the slick black cylinder, he said, "You're doing this for Alice. Is that it?"

"Some of this is her plan. Some is not."

"Why is Alice so important to you?"

"Is she?" Perfect asked, his tone sounding a little sharp.

"No other brother is here," Ord pointed out. "And you've got thousands of sisters. But you're taking enormous risks for Alice."

"Don't you know?" He offered a soft, unreadable laugh. "Haven't you guessed?"

Ord grappled with the possibilities. Besides their common age, no answer seemed reasonable. They were Chamberlains, but with different interests and opposing philosophies. And even their age couldn't be the answer, since there were dozens of siblings with their enormous rank.

"Try something unreasonable," was Perfect's advice.

Ord imagined several improbabilities, dismissing each one.

"Okay. Now try the unthinkable. Alice and I are close. Why? And now aim for the very last answer that you would hope to find."

In a whisper, Ord said, "No."

"Yet you are right, Ord. Congratulations."

Eleven

"Childhood doesn't make us.
    "The end of your childhood . . . that's the only de-fining moment . . ."

—*Perfect, in conversation*

ORD SAW THE Chamberlain mansion—the smaller, original incarnation—and an instant later, he was standing on the topmost floor, inside the first penthouse. It was autumn, again. Alice was standing at the window, again. But the mountains were younger, the autumnal foliage was more subdued, and the grounds were empty of auxiliary mansions and the extra stables. The penthouse was intact, but everything about it was primitive, its furnishings barely able to change shape, its luxuries obvious and scarce, and the air itself tasting stale and dry as Ord gave a little gasp.

This Alice didn't wear a little girl's body. The brilliant sun pierced her dress, betraying a carriage fully matured, relentlessly feminine . . . the scene infected with a quality, an emotional core, that caused Ord to squirm and look away for a few uneasy moments.

Alice ignored him. She was standing on her toes, her feet bare, breasts pressed against the diamond pane. Bright eyes were staring down at the world, conspicuously ignoring everything else. Then a figure emerged from the door at the room's center. He was a tall male Chamberlain of no particular age, wearing a stiff gray uniform that had once meant rank in the postwar government—a creature of status and some influence, yet barely older than Ord. Dangling

from his dress shirt was a length of optical cable, one end
linked with his nervous system, the other joined to a secured web-box riding upon his belt: a marvel in its day,
and now, a set of technologies only slightly more sophisticated than fire and Folsom points.

Ten million years in the past, and the Peace was newborn, and the Families had just begun their long ascent.

The floor was a highly polished, thickly waxed wood,
golden and broken up with intricate rugs known as persians.
Perhaps for the sake of stealth, Thomas wore neither boots
nor socks. His long bare feet had the same pink as Alice's
feet. He was stalking their sister, stepping slowly but without hesitation. Yet she knew he was there. Probably with
his first steps, she knew. Through her body and the changing tilt of her head, Alice conveyed a sense of controlled
eagerness, calves flexing and fingers spreading and the long
red hair swimming across the freckled back of her neck in
ways that could only be flirtatious.

Ord could see the sunlight in her ear, making it glow a
sweet warm pink.

For a moment, the taste of salt and skin lay against his
tongue, making him squirm and avert his eyes.

Alice couldn't remain passive to the last moment. That
would be against her nature. This was the finish of a long
and relentless seduction. After decades of wondering, Thomas found the courage or excuse or the simple earnest lust
to lift his hands—five fingers on each—and his younger
sister decided to take full charge, stealing his momentum,
flipping back her autumn hair while a calculated voice told
him, "See? You're not quite perfect after all."

Thomas hesitated, just for that instant, then he seemingly
forced his hands to drop to her shoulders, and she said,
"Don't."

Then, "I will tell on you."

Then, with emphasis, "I'll tell Ian. I'll tell him everything."

In those days, the Families looked elsewhere when children played these games. It was assumed they would out-

grow incest in the same way they were outgrowing
selfishness and cruelty. But Chamberlains held themselves
to be better than others. Ian had declared as much. In clear,
withering detail, Ord saw his brother's thoughts . . . saw
several brothers being taken aside by their ultimate father.
"Your sisters are taboo!" Ian announced to them. "They're
untouchable! I'd rather see you screwing livestock than
them!" Yet with those hard words, he planted some compelling images in each youngster—a miscalculation that the
patriarch would repeat for dozens of generations, without
fail.

"Everything," Alice repeated. "I will tell him, and I'll
show him . . . !"

Brother Perfect believed her. He lifted his hands as if
burned, a quick and careless little voice begging, "Don't
tell . . . anyone . . . no . . . !"

Alice found his reflection in the window. Without turning
her head, she took the hovering hands with her smaller
hands, pulling his arms tight around her shoulders, then
around her chest.

The uniformed brother, that man of consequence, whim-
pered, "Please don't tell!"

"But I will," she promised. "Eventually. Regardless. Always." Then with one hand holding his arms in place, she
took her dress with her free hand, by the hem, and lifted it
from behind as she made a second promise, a low and
roughened voice telling him, "I hope you know. You're my
favorite brother, and you always will be . . . !"

THE PENTHOUSE DISSOLVED into methane. With a perpetual
smile and a gently embarrassed laugh, Perfect said, "I
know. I paint our sister as conniving and treacherous. Perhaps a little bit evil, even. But those aren't her only qualities, and they aren't even her largest. She's done wondrous
things for every fine reason, and we can only hope that's
true for each of us, too." The incomplete hand touched him
again, in a gesture that took hours. And meanwhile, Perfect
told story upon story, proving their sister's innate decency,

and in turn, endlessly proving his own undiminished affections.

Feeling the pressure of the central thumb, Ord bristled. "We don't do that kind of thing anymore," he muttered.

"You mature differently," Perfect agreed. "More slowly. With much more and far superior help, too."

"I've never thought of my sisters, that way . . . !"

"But you appreciate my circumstances," the ancient man replied. "A profound emotional attachment made in my bedrock years, and I willfully built on that rock. Too much building, I know, but what can I do now?"

Ord struggled to make his legs move faster, accomplishing nothing.

"You should know. Several times, in various cultures on some far-flung worlds, Alice and I have been married. Husband and wife." A long uncomfortable pause ended when he reminded Ord, "When enough time passes, the unlikely finds some way to become ordinary. The unthinkable, tiresome."

The boy said nothing, lightning thoughts racing through him.

Perfect respected the silence, holding their pace but never speaking. Never intruding. The sun was dropping, clouds thickening until the air was saturated, a steady slow rain of hydrocarbons and airborne plankton beginning, drops bursting on the sea and lazy fish rising to feed, the business achingly slow, yet by its own count, frantic, the business of life repeating patterns even older than the Brongg.

A moment came when Ord felt a sudden pressure, an inexplicable change of directions. But the ice beach and the hungry world looked the same.

Why would Alice need his help? Closure or no closure, how could Ord accomplish anything worthwhile?

Homesick to tears, Ord closed his eyes and walked blind. His brother kept his steps true.

And when he couldn't contemplate his situation for another moment, Ord opened his eyes again, discovering that it was early evening, and they were only a few steps away from their goal. Almost too late, he asked about the ancient times. About Ian, about his first children. And how ordinary people dealt with them, or not.

"Tell me," Ord begged.

Stories flowed from Perfect, genuine and simple, told with words and direct memories, one arm making the occasional slow flourish as the brothers marched across the last few meters of rain-spattered beach.

Twelve

"Sometimes Alice joined me on my explorations.

"She was more a burden than a help. I was chasing living worlds, while she preferred the sterile. We moved too fast for her to accomplish much, but even on the briefest visit, she gave the dead places little nudges toward life. She warmed their cores or lent their atmosphere a potent gas or two. Another hundred million years, and who knows? Something might sprout on them . . .

"Yet I wonder:

"Will these worlds be declared illegal, too?

"Will janitors be dispatched, ordered to retrace our steps, scrubbing away all that wicked and treacherous prebiotic slime?"

—*Perfect, in conversation*

THE BRONGG SUN had halfway set—a waxy, feeble smear shrouded by clouds and mammoth drops of new gasolines. The tall black cylinder stood before Ord, in easy reach, but when he lifted his arm, it proved to be unreachable, a dreamy, teasing sense of distance only growing as his many fingers unfolded and stretched and strained.

"Step again," Perfect advised.

When he stepped, as his broad bare toes touched the beach, the Brongg home world evaporated. Ord was in free fall again, and the cylinder covered half the sky—a deep blackness against a bottomless void. He kicked and cried out. He screamed, making no sound. They were streaking toward their destination at a fat fraction of light speed, yet the final plunge took hours. A piece of him—a tiny new subsystem—measured the target's size, in astonishment, and he pleaded with Perfect, begging for an explanation, or encouragement, or even a few mild lies to mollify him.

Perfect said nothing, and he was nowhere to be seen.

The impact was sudden—a brief biting pain, brilliant light of no color, then a hard and busy long sleep.

When Ord awoke he found himself on another beach. He was dressed in his original clothes, including his favorite boots, and his body was his own, unscarred and excited, his heart humming inside its enduring cage of ribs.

"Oh, you're whole again. Thoroughly and genuinely."

The caveman sat beside him, his knapsack serving as a pillow. Again Perfect wore skins and an oversize smile, but the blue eyes seemed distracted, even sad. Callused feet splashed in a deep rocky pool. A warm light fell from no-where in particular, making his brother's skin glow, pink with blood and pink with wear. A soft proud voice asked, "What do you think?"

The pool and the sea beyond were filled with a watery fluid.

But it wasn't water, Ord sensed. The surface wore a thin persistent foam, transparent facets distorting the bottom of the pool, surf-worn stones overlaid with a matted emerald-brown hair. Life, he realized. And as life went, simple. Unsplendid. Even a little disappointing.

"Yet nothing here was remotely this interesting during my last visit," his brother replied. "A few protocells, all scavengers. Not one honest photosynthesizer among them."

Ord touched the foam-frosted pool, feeling warmth and a strange lack of wetness. Then he rose to his feet, glad to be quick again. Home in his body again, and whole.

"Look around," Perfect insisted. "Opinions, please."

A rocky beach had been shaped by waves and tireless

winds. Behind the beach, taller rocks merged into hills, then
mountains, then masses too huge and distant to be mere
mountains. But at least as astonishing was the sea. Every
little agitation, every gust and every insult, caused the foam
to rise, flat- and bright-jeweled bubbles refracting light into
every possible color. The boundaries between the sea and
air were vague. When Ord looked up into the purest air, he
saw a brilliance without sun or suns. And when he gazed
far out across the flat sea, what wasn't water turned milky
white as each jewel's color blended into one.

"This is a dyson structure," Ord muttered, interrupting
his own thoughts.

"Cylindrical and spinning. The most ordinary portion of
this design, to my mind."

Reaching into the faraway sky, on his right and left, were
hair-thin structures resembling the angled spokes of a crude
wheel. Ord imagined that they lent support, and in an instant, some subconscious calculation was delivered to him.
He remembered the dyson's apparent size, which implied
a certain length for the spokes, and a diameter, and their
thinness was an illusion, much as the giant but distant star
will mimic a simple cold point.

"Nobody builds . . . on this scale . . . !"

"You were taught," growled his brother. "You were
taught."

The hairlike spokes were thicker than some worlds. And
with that revelation, Ord looked inland again, past the ordinary mountains, eyes lifting as the mind told him that the
vast plateau was not what it seemed, that what he saw was
the base of the nearest spoke, the rest of it obscured by the
glare of the sky.

"This little ocean?" Perfect boasted. "It covers an area
greater than a hundred thousand earths, and it's simply a
teardrop. A backwater. Nothing more."

Numbed, Ord felt his legs tremble, his breath quickening.

"Taste the water," his brother insisted. "Here. Have a
sip!"

It wasn't water, and it wasn't wet. It was like a drink

taken in a dream, the flavor too delicious to recall after the thirst was slackened. With a weak, quiet voice, Ord asked, "What is it? Tell me."

"You guess. Go on."

"You've done this with dark matter." A boy's best guess, it was correct and too simple by a long ways. "Because this isn't ordinary . . . isn't baryonic . . ."

"Alice did the magic, mostly. I set guidelines and the fat goals, but she invented the technologies." He pulled a stone from the pool, complete with its shaggy living carpet, tucking it into a new pouch hanging from the knapsack. "What she did was rework some simple, invisible particles. She coerced them to act like atoms. A positive nucleus, a negative cloud. Then she fabricated a new periodic table—a simpler set of elements—out of the lazy atoms. Much of what you see here is dark matter, which is why it barely reacts with the universe. And that's why, unless you know precisely what you're seeking, this vast dyson is wondrously invisible."

Questions formed.

Ord tried to ask all of them, in a rush.

"Oh, people have attempted dark-matter life," Perfect explained. "From scratch and with great imagination, and all were failures. You can guess some of the difficulties. But we helped ourselves by inventing new elements, including a superior version of the honored carbon atom. And the scale of our work helps, to a point. And also, we cheated. When we had no choice, we bolstered the system with baryonic matter. A thin but essential scaffolding, if you will."

The boy took a deep breath, wondering what he was inhaling.

"It feels like a warm day, doesn't it?" Perfect laughed and shook his head. "The truth? We're hovering a few degrees above Absolute. The fire above us is chilly. Interstellar hydrogen is captured as it drifts into the dyson, then it's burned efficiently, to helium and carbon, and eventually, iron. Any energy that escapes is masked, given some natural excuse. And the iron ash is *nothing* in this volume of cold space."

Ord swallowed, then swallowed again. "You wanted a better intelligence. But what's here, in this pool . . . it can't have even a stupid thought . . ."

"I would never, ever presume to dictate the final design to what evolves here." Perfect paused, nothing funny about this moment. "I set up the broad parameters. Not Alice. I gave life its chance, then broke camp and began walking again."

Ord watched his brother wade into the sea, submerging for a moment, then emerging with another stone and its gray-green hair. Again, he stuffed his prize into the pouch, no room for it and no trouble making it vanish. Then he straightened, appearing rather pleased with himself.

"How will this intelligence evolve?" Ord asked. "And why won't it make all our ridiculous mistakes?"

Perfect retrieved his treasured spear, using it to roll a stone on its back. The mud beneath stank of odd rot, implying life. A gob of mud followed the two mossy stones into the pouch, and he said, "There's nothing like uranium here. For example."

Ord remembered his own stunt with Xo, a painful shame grabbing him.

"With these synthetic elements," Perfect continued, "and with the neurons they can build, thought and action will be in balance. I hope, I hope." The older brother appeared uncharacteristically sober, yet sobriety betrayed a deep and abiding happiness. He was happy stuffing mud into that impossible pouch. He was happy standing again, wiping his dirty hands against his bare stomach, squinting at the sky as he asked again, "What was our golden age?"

"After the glaciers melted," Ord recalled. *When the world was the universe, the stars unimaginable.*

"This is the universe." A skyward thrust of the spear. "What's born here has no reason or rationale to imagine the stars."

Ord stared at his brother, waiting.

"Whatever prospers—whatever organism can rule this

dyson—is free to call itself the master of creation. And why not? It won't sound even a millionth as silly as we do when we make the same boasts."

"I've never made that boast," Ord complained, his whisper building toward anger. "I've never even thought those words . . . !"

"Which is possibly, just possibly, why Alice selected you."

Ord shut his mouth, remaining silent.

"Do you know what I am? What I most truly am?" Perfect asked the question with a calm, almost distracted air, again wiping the stinking muck from his hands, palms and fingers painting horned smears on his belly. "A master of creation, maybe? Am I?" From everywhere came a thunderous, world-shaking laugh, and then the ancient brother spat, and said, "Bullshit! Bullshit! What I am . . . I'm a little ape who got lucky . . . !"

Thirteen

"Maybe our universe is simple as this:

"We are someone else's dark matter. Protons and electrons have been woven from shadow and dream, then coerced into cooperating, building the baryonic realm. We are a tiny bubble, insubstantial and nearly invisible, drifting through an enormous and dense and fabulously brilliant cosmos that we cannot see, lovely pieces of it passing through us, and only the faintest tug of gravity betraying its presence. But of course that logic implies that this larger universe might itself be a gossamer drop of dark matter drifting inside an even greater universe . . . which itself amounts to nothing . . .

"Oh, I'm sorry. I was mistaken. That's not simple at all, is it?"

—*Perfect, in conversation*

HOISTING HIS KNAPSACK to his shoulder, Perfect said, "Stay here."

The boy blurted, "Where are you going?" Then, embarrassed by his own anxieties, he added, "I want to stay with you."

The answer was a wink and grin, effortlessly charming. Then Perfect picked up his spear with his partial hand, remarking, "I've got work, and there isn't time. Stay. Wait. I'll be back before too long, I hope."

"But I'm here to help," Ord protested. "To do good, right—?"

"Not yet." Then his brother began to step toward him, and he wasn't there anymore. The step carried him out of sight, in an instant, and Ord spun and dropped to his butt, feeling chilled. A hundred new questions demanded to be asked, the old ones needing to be asked again, and he felt abandoned, cheated, and in every way, small.

In a whisper, he said, "I'm tired of this family."

A lazy little wind blew from the sea, cold as liquid helium but warm against his present skin. Other than the wind, nothing moved. No answers presented themselves. The world lay before him like a painting, and an unfinished painting at that. Ord slowly grew sick of feeling sorry for himself, and he made himself stand again, and walk, following the shoreline at his own modest, archaic pace.

There was no sun to set, but there were nights.

Darkness emerged slowly, exposing the illuminated far side of the dyson, and Ord sat on a different beach, bare feet pressing into the warm facsimile of sand, eyes gazing at that remote and enormous, ill-defined terrain. Count every world that the Chamberlains had terraformed, skin each body like an animal and sew the bloody skins together, and the great robe wouldn't carpet half of this realm.

How did Alice and Perfect manage it, he wondered; and then he knew. It was because dark matter was so abundant and amiable. It was because self-replicating robots had done the largest share of the work. And it was because the dyson's true mass wasn't much greater than a single star's—a wondrous home made from smoke and lit from within by cold candles.

Somewhere inside Ord, out of easy reach, were reservoirs of fact, languid explanations and bottled lectures beyond number.

He practiced pulling up the knowledge as best he could.

There was a text on the Brongg—their immeasurable history, the bulk of it magnificently dull—but its sheer size and sameness was an event, majestic in its own right, and admirable. Sitting on the alien beach, in the dark, Ord found himself lost in the intricacies of a Brongg government born in the Triassic and still thriving today. He barely noticed the dawn. A feeble glow began nowhere, and everywhere. This was a universe without shadows. The boy blinked and looked skyward, wondering how these qualities would affect future psyches ... and suddenly an Alice talent was engaged, making a rich stream of projections and guesses that were just as quickly interrupted by a sound, a gentle wrong-pitched splashing, that caused Ord to drop his gaze, focusing on a distinctive beachcomber.

It was Perfect, back again.

Ord was halfway standing when he noticed the clothes, the posture, and the five whole fingers on each open hand.

Hesitating, Ord found that he had no voice.

With a quiet, terrified tone, the other Chamberlain said, "Lyman. I'm just Lyman."

"Brother ... ?"

"You remember me, don't you?" His horror was palpable. His soul was a gray glow easily seen. "They asked me to come, to talk with you, to tell you ... offer you ... oh, Ord ... ! Do you know how much trouble you're in ... ?"

"WHY WOULDN'T I remember you?"

Lyman straightened, blinked. The answer seemed obvious, which is why he moved to greater questions, explaining events from his point of view.

"You vanished. We thought you were sitting in your room. I even spoke to you, twice, except it wasn't you.

You were gone, and a security sweep sounded the alarm."
Remembering some careful coaching, Lyman smiled urgently. "We searched for you." The smile brightened. "I
went to the stable . . . I thought you might be hiding . . ."

"I'm sorry to worry anyone."

The brother took a deep breath, then exhaled.

"What happened next?"

"Next?" A pained, prolonged swallow. "The Nuyens
came for a visit. A high-ranking delegation. They claimed
an old Chamberlain had been living under our feet, in secret, for many years—"

"How could they know?"

"They've watched us. Better than we watch ourselves, it
seems." Lyman glanced at the enormous sea, but nothing
registered in his eyes. "There were long meetings and accusations from both sides—you could feel the tension—
then someone broke into a facility in the Oort cloud, and
some of Alice's talents were stolen. After that, you could
taste the panic—"

"What talents?"

Lyman shuddered, then wrestled himself back into a half
composure. He didn't know what was stolen. He didn't
want to know. "Of course, they demanded help from someone you would trust," he admitted. "Which isn't me, I
warned them. I tried to explain it. But you know how the
Old Ones can be. They'd already selected me, and I didn't
have any choice—"

"I know the feeling," Ord volunteered.

Lyman hesitated.

"Who picked you?"

"Everyone." Finally, Lyman seemed to realize that he
was talking too freely. Some force had a grip on his soul,
making it scrupulously honest. "There were Chamberlains,"
he continued. "Plus Nuyens, and Glosures. Lees, and the
other Nuyen allies. Even the Sanchexes were present." He
paused for an instant, shivering, and with a mixture of terror
and wonder admitted, "Even Sanchexes were acting
scared."

"How are you going to help them?"

"Like this." Wasn't it obvious? "You and a rogue Chamberlain had stolen parts of Alice. That was kept secret from the public, of course. So was the mission to find you. They asked if I'd speak to you, when it was time."

Ord found himself laughing. A genuine, quiet chuckle ended with a wary shake of the head. "Oh, they asked you, did they?"

Lyman hesitated, attempting a wry smile. "I went to sleep." He said the words with a longing, as if he wished he were asleep now. "It was a long chase, but here I am."

"Here you are," Ord agreed. He had sudden warm feelings for Lyman, and he was sorry to have dragged him into this mess. Was that the logic? Disarm the renegade boy with a pitiful sibling? Or were these feelings entirely his own? "I didn't steal anything, Lyman. Not from Alice, I didn't."

"I knew you didn't. It was the old Chamberlain's fault."

With a graceful ease, Ord refused to think about Perfect. The man's presence and possibilities never crossed his mind.

"What we could do," Lyman continued, "is meet the others. You aren't responsible. You were kidnapped, or whatever we want to call it, and I'll explain to them—"

"Who's with you?"

"A sister. Millicent. She was the ranking elder just then."

The One-Hundred and Eighty-First Chamberlain.

Lyman tried another smile. "See how important you are?"

"Who else?"

"Just one. A Nuyen." Lyman paused, pretending to deliberate over words already thoroughly practiced. "He is in charge," said the brother. Then he attempted to lie, adding, "The Nuyen is as old and powerful as Alice."

Perfect had seen two pursuers. Lyman had been cargo, inert and innocent.

"What do you think of this place?" Ord asked.

Lyman wanted to keep his eyes on his brother. But he

glanced at the sea, then toward the mountains. "Lovely," he blurted, with a surprising conviction.

"But you came here to destroy it, didn't you?"

"Not me," his brother sputtered. "But if it's illegal . . . if it's immoral . . . doesn't it have to be destroyed . . . ?"

Here was a vast realm that endangered no one—a universe unto itself—and Ord felt a scalding, enormous rage.

He gave a low moan, stepping toward Lyman.

A terrified voice cried out, "No," as his brother retreated. He was begging, pleading. Hands raised, he said, "Just come with me. We'll talk to them, and maybe there's some arrangement or compromise—"

Ord picked up a smooth white stone, for emphasis. "They're not going to hurt this place—"

And a Nuyen appeared, followed by a Chamberlain sister standing to his left and a half step behind. The Nuyen was an adult version of Xo—simple dark hair; unreadable black eyes; and the barest beginnings of a humorless smile—and with a hard, clean, cutting voice, he said, "You're a good boy, but be honest. You haven't any idea what you are doing."

Ord's emotions were being tugged and knotted, but he felt utterly confident in his mistrust of the Nuyens. That much was genuine. "Touch nothing," he warned the intruders, the words sounding like thunderbolts.

The Nuyen tilted his head, a thin amusement showing. "A threat, is it? From a boy?"

The sister—a complete stranger—called to Ord by name, conjuring a face vast and maternal, concern dripping from her soft blue eyes and the very sorry mouth. She was nothing. She was here for show and as an observer, and Ord stared only at the Nuyen, lifting the stone overhead as he cried out, "Leave. All of you, leave."

The enemy showed no fear or hesitation. But behind the face, in some small way, there was a flicker. A thousand courages were being tested, and Ord saw a handful of them collapse into terror.

With horror and a sweet exhilaration, Ord wondered

what parts of Alice he had now. Energies, liquid and hot,
surged through him before radiating in every direction. The
beach shivered. The great sea threw clouds of jeweled foam
high into a brilliant sky. And Ord pictured the Nuyen dying,
slowly and miserably dying, his ugly soul drenched in agony to the end.

Ord's destiny was set. He had to obliterate these enemies,
and then fortify and hunker down, and anyone else who
came to destroy this place would have to pass through
him . . . !

A voice spoke. Familiar, close.

A lying voice, Ord told himself.

The old Nuyen and sister had retreated in panic, leaving
empty bodies standing on the beach. But their souls hadn't
fled far enough. With some newly engaged eyes, Ord saw
them, and he measured the distances and velocities, the
rock no longer simple and cold, and his hand far more than
a hand.

That voice, again.

Was it Lyman? No. Lyman was tucked into a ball, sobbing to himself. Some other voice was singing in his ears,
beseeching him to stop.

Ord refused. Following his instincts and anger, he prepared to fling the nonstone, aiming to murder—

A flash came, and a dull white pain.

And he collapsed, giving a miserable low groan.

Piercing his chest, cutting organs and functions he had
only begun to feel, was a long blade of razor-sharp flint.
Ord saw the Folsom point jutting from his sternum. He was
down on his hands and knees, breathing out of habit, little
red bubbles detaching from his mouth and drifting on the
warm wind. He watched one bubble, something about it
enchanting. Weightless, it swirled and rose, then fell again.
In its slick red face he could see his own face, for an instant. Then it settled on top of a bare pink foot, and it burst
without sound, without fuss. Whose foot? Why couldn't he
remember? But Ord was having trouble thinking at all, and
he felt quite chilled, and the bubbles had stopped coming,
and he very much missed them . . .

Fourteen

*". . . and with my life, my wealth, and my perishable
name, I now and always shall defend the Great
Peace."*

—from the Families' pledge

"WHAT POSSIBLE SWEET good would have come from it,"
Perfect began, "if I had stood nearby while you killed
them?"

Opening his eyes, Ord found himself sitting on a cave
floor, a small fire burning at his feet, his brother illuminated
by the golden flames and half-hidden by their swirling,
jasmine-scented smoke.

"A rash thought, a crude act, and then *what*?"

The boy gasped, a familiar pain battering him. In the
center of his chest lay a slick raised scar, white as milk,
and aching, and apparently permanent.

Quietly, with remorse, he said, "I am sorry . . ."

Perfect said nothing for a long while, wiggling his fingers
and stumps as they warmed in the fire, his face contempla-
tive and remote.

The cave was constructed from rocks. They were neatly
stacked, the facing walls arching toward a shadowy ceiling,
each stone adorned with some shaggy life. Handfuls of mud
filled the gaps. Every surface glistened, and something that
wasn't quite water trickled and dripped somewhere in the
darkness.

Ord shuddered, saying, "I wanted to protect—"

"The dyson, yes." His brother shook his head, warning
him, "First, the project is my responsibility. And second,
there were exactly five sentient organisms on board it. Only
five. You and myself, and poor Lyman, and your intended
victims. You were eager to commit two murders to save a
mindless slime, and that's not the moral, responsible act of
a decent soul. Chamberlain or not."

"How is Lyman?"

"Sleeping on that beach, and safe."

Ord glanced at his surroundings. "This is your pouch, isn't it? This is where you've been putting the rocks and mud."

"A representative population, yes. Held in suspended animation." Perfect tossed a stone chip into the fire, sparks scattering. "That Nuyen and our sister are drifting at a safe distance, awaiting reinforcements. They suspected that I was helping you, but they're just beginning to guess the powers you hold. Most of Alice's talents were waiting to be cataloged. They went in hoping to win your surrender, without incident, before dealing with me and my garden."

"What kinds of powers . . . ?"

A dark, slow laugh ended with a dark voice confessing, "I don't know exactly what you're carrying, Ord. I'm very nearly as ignorant as you."

The boy dipped his head, breathing deeply.

"Before Alice fled the Core, she visited me, warning me about the coming explosion. She made me promise to give the baby Chamberlain certain labeled pieces of herself, and that's exactly what I did; and then I was supposed to take you to a suitable starting point. Which I have just done, finally."

Alice had said, "The baby." Their unborn sister could have been chosen. Or Lyman. Whoever happened to be youngest when Alice arrived at home.

Perfect jumped to his feet, remarking, "Perhaps we should make our escape now. Before those promised reinforcements arrive, that is."

"To where?" the boy inquired.

"I am leaving on a million-year walk." The voice was calm, the face resigned. "Out between the galaxies, I should think. Then, in some good cold place, I'll rebuild this dyson. Stone for stone. And afterward . . . well, there might be a galaxy or two worth exploring. Who knows?"

"Can I walk with you?"

"Not even one step. No."

Ord expected that answer, but the words stung nonetheless.

"Alice asked for my help," his brother explained, "and I gave it. Out of love and trust and habit, and in that order. She has her reasons, we can hope. What those reasons might be, we can guess. Whatever the circumstances, you're now to help Alice, or not. I won't presume to tell you which choice to make."

"She told me," Ord whispered. "I have to save something."

Perfect kicked stones and cold embers over the fire's heart. "I think I know what that something is, and truth be told, I don't envy you."

"It's fragile, and Alice pledged to protect it . . ."

The maimed hand was offered.

Ord took it, standing. "It could be an illegal world. Is it? One with sentience, maybe?"

"I'll show you," his brother promised. "Come."

The boy's feet refused to move.

Without firelight, a softer, stranger glow illuminated the cavern. Perfect was a silhouette. His voice was close and warm, coaxing Ord by saying, "It's not a world, no. Follow me."

Ord was strong enough to butcher a godly Nuyen, yet his legs were too heavy to lift. He fought with them, shuffling forward, noticing finally that his feet were bare and his only clothes were trousers made from simple skins. Looking at himself in the gloom, he thought of a lucky ape. Then he managed a little step, and another, and he looked up at the sky that he both anticipated and could not believe.

"I took us on a course perpendicular to the galactic plane," Perfect explained, standing beside him and squeezing his hand. "Up and out, then we danced around a black hole that sent us partway home again."

Ord was sobbing, tears flowing, tasting like a long-ago sea.

"We walked along that beach, but we also crossed several tens of thousands of light-years. Out, then back again. Which means you can see some of what's happened since we left."

The Milky Way covered the sky. With new eyes, Ord could see every sun and every world—every lump of stone bigger than a fist, it seemed—and the Core was the brilliant horror that he expected, its detonation relentless and vast, radiations and expelled wreckage rushing outward in a withering toxic storm. Here was a baby quasar, human-made. Worse than almost every reasonable prediction made during Ord's long-ago youth.

Here was a tragedy, but a tragedy with calculable, endurable ends.

The greater horrors were smaller, scattered through the galaxy's broad spiral arms. Ord couldn't stop seeing them, even when he shut his human eyes. Healthy suns were exploding. Living worlds were being crushed to dust. Unknown powers battered one another with a frantic, relentless violence. The Great Peace was collapsing. Old and fragile, it might evaporate totally before Ord could return home. And to accomplish what . . . ? With or without Alice's powers, what good could he do . . . ?

With a solemn voice, Perfect said, "Bless the dead!"

At Ord's feet was a knapsack filled with talents. In his left hand lay a fine new spear, its ash shaft polished smooth and the long Folsom point freshly made. And in his right hand was a simple stone mug, the pungent odor of an old-fashioned liquor pervading the night air.

"Bless the dead," Ord repeated, with feeling.

The brothers touched mugs with a cool, almost musical ringing.

As Ord drank, Perfect told him, "I want to give you a talent. I don't have Alice's magic, but here's something that you might appreciate."

Ord's mug became a nearly spherical ball.

Not heavy, not large.

It was a head. It was a Chamberlain head, male and complete with shaggy red hair and the piercing blue eyes. And as he stared at the gift, the head let loose an enormous laugh, so pure and authentic that Ord couldn't help but smile for a moment, closing his hand over the sweet gift, knowing what it was and almost saying, "Thank you," before he realized that no one was standing beside him.

Alone, he squeezed the head until it vanished, becoming part of his immortal flesh.

Again Ord looked at the Milky Way, using every eye, while the new talent reminded him that most of the many billion stars remained at peace, tranquil and inviting by any measure. He even managed to laugh in a quiet, hopeful way.

Picking up his knapsack now.

All things considered, he thought to himself, *it is a lovely night for a little walk.*

BOOK THREE

MOTHER DEATH

One

"If preparedness means you have weighed your enemy's options and taken every sound precaution, then we are unequivocally prepared for what is to come.

"If it is possible to keep secrets in our transparent little universe, then we have one or two and possibly three great secrets in our possession.

"If confidence produced a radiance in those who possessed it, then each of us would shine like the galaxy's exploding heart.

"Paranoia is our greatest attribute.

"Patience is our watchword.

"Our only imaginable concern—one barely worth mentioning—is that Alice, at her malicious worst, actually did give her full talents to the baby . . . and who can say what any child in such astonishing circumstances would do . . . ?"

—*Nuyen dispatch, from the Earth*

AFTER A LENGTHY and genuinely fair trail, judge and jury found the accused guilty on all counts: Avoiding surrender once his Family was officially disbanded; illegal terraforming coupled with the unkind manipulation of sentient organisms; misleading investigators in pursuit of Chamberlain ringleaders; unbecoming arrogance; pernicious indifference; plus an ancient charge involving the fondling of women with fingers and penises composed of substances unknown.

The Emergency Tribunal deliberated for an appropriate period—slightly more than three minutes—before passing the expected sentence.

Without ceremony or official announcement, the prison walls dissolved, and Avram Chamberlain was delivered to the mercy of the waiting mob.

It was a clear night on a minor world that until this moment had little place in history and no experience with mobs. Anticipating the verdict, nearly a million people had gathered on the surrounding plains. Many were refugees from the Core; all had a thirst for vengeance. When the quasi walls vanished, the multitude pressed forward, nearly ten thousand bodies temporarily killed in the wild stampede. An armed contingent of off-duty police and self-appointed strong-arms finally brought the Chamberlain into view. Avram's appearance caused an abrupt silence, the multitude frozen in place, no one speaking or even breathing as they watched with shared eyes or their own. Into the stillness, the prisoner walked forward with a numbed calm. His old-fashioned body was naked, and except for scraped knees, he was fit. Hands and feet were unbound. Thick red hair lay short and neat above the most famous face in the galaxy, and piercing blue eyes looked past his captors, gazing spellbound at the night sky.

The Core had just risen.

It was a spectacular sight, and horrible. On some worlds, the popular game was to lend yourself a selective amnesia. Forgetting why the Core was exploding, forgetting how many hundreds of billions had died, you were free to watch the sky without pain, marveling at its vastness, at its energy and surreal beauty—a vast storm of radiations and super-heated plasmas rushing from the galaxy's heart, shredding suns and worlds, and now, at its height, smashing into dense clouds of smart dusts and compressed, superheated gases.

Those clouds gave the explosion its intricacies, the raw purple-white light transformed into swirling masses of crimson and turquoise and cerulean. They also shielded the rest of the Milky Way, absorbing the most terrible energies, leaving only light and an endurable radiation to escape. Without those barricades, natural and otherwise, the galaxy already would have died. Every competent simulation said so. Official simulations were promising that the storm would worsen only slightly in the next few millennia, and then flatten before finally beginning its long, slow fade.

Then in another twenty million years, or perhaps forty, the Core would grow cold again, finding peace, and if any humans were left alive, they would have to make do with a considerably duller sky.

Avram stared at the distant storm, never blinking.

The only problem remaining for the mob was to find the means: What was the most perfect way to kill a Chamberlain?

A sour voice screamed, "With your hands! Tear him apart!"

Another roared, "Cook the fuck whole!"

Then a third voice, closer and more lucid, suggested simply, "Whatever you do, take your time! Do it slowly, make it last!"

Suddenly everyone was speaking—a hundred languages, public and private, offering advice in the art of torture. Thousands reached for the Chamberlain, and the police found themselves using electric wands and cold-gas guns to push back the crush of bodies. It was pure self-defense. A mob of this size and complexion would butcher dozens, maybe hundreds. Innocent skulls would be carried off as trophies, then consumed with plasma torches and homemade A bombs. The police were sure to take the heaviest casualties. Not only would they die, but the rabble who murdered them would boast about it later, each claiming, "I'm the one who did it! I killed the damned Chamberlain!"

Wands and guns fired without pause. Flesh was stunned and frozen, and people collapsed in waves. A woman from a high-mass world climbed over the bodies, and with her powerful quick arm managed to throw a sharp gray stone. The prisoner was struck in the face. Only then, finally, did Avram appear even to notice the mob. He blinked and gasped, his expression more surprised than afraid, and he licked his bloodied lips, and he stroked his bloodied chin, taking a tiny, useless step backward.

The mob let loose an enormous roar.

For every good reason, this was not fair. Avram was just a middle-aged Chamberlain. He had spent several million years serving humanity as well as his great Family. What were his crimes? Until a few months ago, he had the strength to reshape worlds, and more important, the morality to keep himself from doing harm with his talents. Avram was never a true god—not like Ian had been, or Alice. But he had worn a godly frame and conscience, and throughout that wicked sham of a trial, he had pointed to thousands of examples of his good, selfless service toward all things sentient.

"Alice!" Avram suddenly wailed, flecks of blood hitting the police. "Bitch-sister!"

Before judge and jury, Avram had explained what should have been obvious: He was never part of Alice's work.

In his entire life, he had never even met the crazy god.

When he had learned that the Core was exploding, he was astonished. Like everyone in the courtroom, the news left him appalled and saddened and furious. And when he realized another Chamberlain was partly to blame, Avram was filled with revulsion and a sense of piercing shame that if inflicted on a weaker man would have surely killed him.

"The guilty deserve their punishments," he kept saying.

Then, in the next breath, he added, "But you shouldn't blame the innocent. Please, I beg you."

Over the weeks and months, Avram had listed his life's glories: He had played small but integral roles in a thousand treaties and diplomatic missions. ("None can question my devotion to the Great Peace.") He made an honest living terraforming worlds and entire systems, demanding nothing but the fair market price. ("Only a true god doesn't need money for his miracles.") But there were numerous occasions when Avram gave away his talents and his precious time. ("What good Chamberlain doesn't?") Fifty millennia ago, as the first waves of refugees arrived from the Core, Avram had done his charitable best, helping this little world to improve itself, tweaking its atmosphere and sun to allow it to double its population, and expecting nothing for his trouble but a heartfelt thanks.

Yet those same refugees, embittered by their losses, decided to lure Avram into an elaborate trap. They were the bait. They feigned an environmental disaster on the new southern continent, and when Avram arrived, members of several untainted Families caught him, then stepped aside while the refugees greedily stripped him of his ancient talents.

Intellect was a fundamental talent. The man standing trial had been a moron compared to his old self. In that mutilated state, he had tried to sway opinions and emotions, and he had failed spectacularly. Catastrophically. Standing on the blood-soaked plain, thinking about the inevitable verdict, Avram began to laugh with an easy rancor. Didn't these bastards understand? Wasn't it obvious? Innocent or guilty, Avram was the same as these others now. His talents had been stolen. His great godly mind was only the dimmest memory. The creature standing before the mob was small and extraordinarily weak, barely more articulate than stone, and in the end, he was nothing but inconsequential.

Avram couldn't count the angry hands reaching for him. The screams shredded the damp, furious air. *I am going to die now*, he warned himself, not entirely displeased. Yet as he closed his eyes for the last time, he heard a voice, close and strong, "Why not let a child kill him?"

The words were framed in a reasonable tone, a quietly compelling tone. For a slippery instant, Avram found himself thinking: *Yes, why not?* He could see the logic. If an execution was a noble thing, who would gain the most benefit? A child, surely. An innocent, pure soul too young to remember the Great Peace, much less those times when the Chamberlains were universally adored.

Avram shuddered, astonished by the turn of his tiny mind.

A million bystanders heard the voice, and they welcomed its words and the oddly seductive reasoning.

The crowded plain grew quiet again.

Standing nearby, exactly between the police and the mob, was a half-grown boy. No one had noticed him before now, and afterward, nobody would be able to recall his appearance—not his face or build or anything else tangible. The only detail that lingered was the knife held in his right hand, fashioned from pink stone and a simple bone hilt.

With a soothing, liquid voice, the boy said, "Let me kill him."

No one moved, or spoke.

He took a step, then another, passing through a curtain of cold vapors that should have frozen him in midstride. Half a hundred unconscious, stampeded people lay in a heap before him. He stepped over them with a gentle grace, smiling now, looking at the nearest of the police without malice or scorn. Later, witnesses would talk about how harmless he seemed. He was like a boy about to play a game, they testified. Centuries later, when the public finally learned the boy's identity, the surviving witnesses would fall silent. The shallowest mind had no choice but to turn introspective. Some would laugh painfully, while others cursed or wept or simply marveled at what they had observed on that long-ago night.

The only person who knew enough to be afraid was the prisoner. With a cold clean terror, Avram shouted, "Go away! Leave me alone!"

The boy winked at the highest-ranking officer, saying, "Ma'am? Would you please hold him for me?"

The police couldn't help fast enough.

"Don't!" Avram squealed. "I don't want this . . . no . . . !"

But Avram couldn't defend himself. He was nothing but a retrofitted ape, and five strong officers managed to restrain his legs and arms, holding him absolutely still as the boy put that odd knife to the throat, slicing it open, destroying the larynx in midscream.

The next cut opened the skull beneath the short red hair.

That's one damned sharp piece of stone, the officers thought. And that was all that occurred to them.

With his free hand, the boy removed the shiny, delicately crenellated brain, placing it under his arm like a puff of bread. Then he set out in every direction at once. He walked past every member of that explosive mob, whispering to them, telling them to go home, telling them that the Great Peace hadn't died, and they should honor it in their lives, always.

The boy vanished without trace or fuss.

People assumed that he was walking home, ready to destroy the criminal's soul. No one put a hand on him or even thought of questioning his motives.

"I believed him," thousands remarked with the same unconcerned voice. "About the Peace, and about honoring it. I took him at his word." And perhaps as evidence of that conviction, after that night their little world was quiet and prosperous, enduring each wave of refugees with an easy humor and a tough-skinned patience. Even when the boy was identified—after that awful business on the Earth—those same witnesses would claim, "I don't know what you're saying." They were crying, and angry, and utterly terrified. But still, they would shake their heads, unable to toss away that single impossible thought.

"I don't understand," they complained. "To us, to me, he seemed to be nothing but a very good boy."

Two

"At irregular intervals, but at least twice each century, our single prisoner undergoes a thorough examination:

"We drain the blood from her body, and every corpuscle and nanoliter of plasma is analyzed in scrupulous detail. Muscles and bones as well as organ tissues are biopsied with the same rigor. Her neural system—a sketchy remnant of her former mind—is subjected to every benign test, plus several invasive procedures that have caused some degradation over the last millennia. Staff psychiatrists as well as respected colleagues question her in detail,

assuring us that her mental health remains adequate. (What purpose is served by imprisoning someone who can't appreciate her crime? Where would be the punishment, or the just sense of vengeance?) Then, when the interviews conclude, the Nuyens and other untainted Families are allowed to meet with the prisoner in private, making their own tests, and if they wish, torturing her.

"We assume that even after a hundred thousand years and untold effort, Alice continues to hide portions of her self. But if we are clever enough and persistent enough, the truth will eventually be pried free from her bloody remains."

—Alice's jailer, confidential

THE CORE WAS dead, and the rest of the galaxy was in chaos: Civil and intersystem wars were common. Apocalyptic religions were spreading along the spiral arms. Refugees moved in desperate waves, searching for temporary havens and new homes. Half of the Families were officially disbanded, while the other half spent their days hunting for Chamberlains and Sanchexes and the other souls who wouldn't relinquish their godly powers.

Yet the mother world was enjoying what could only be described as her Golden Age.

The Earth had never been richer, and Alice was the cause. Creation's most famous criminal was being held in solitary confinement, inside a deep-mantle facility built and maintained specifically for her. The Earth's Council paid the bills, but those were trivial. What were staggeringly expensive were the security measures—layer upon layer of paranoia and subtlety and muscle and fear dedicated to the belief that someone would eventually attempt to steal Alice away. After all, she was the black angel who had brought a judgment day. By possessing her, any borderline movement or newborn faith would leap into instant prominence. Or one of the disgruntled, illegal gods might feel tempted. Many of them had declared Alice's imprisonment to be

obscenely cruel, and at its heart, pointless. The prisoner was
not the woman who had helped destroy the Core, they argued. That creature was long ago dismantled, her talents
confiscated or stolen. What lived inside the tiny white cell
was nothing—a bit of dermis left behind by a murderer's
hand, scrubbed free of thought, and identity, and its essential soul.

Renegade Chamberlains were considered the most likely
foes.

An army of specialists, human and otherwise, did nothing but assemble and update lists of potential attackers, last
known locations and possible trajectories given an almost
religious importance.

Ord's name straddled every list.

Since his escape from the Earth, reported sightings had
come from at least five thousand locations scattered across
the Milky Way. Since the pursuit team had slinked home—
tens of thousands of years after giving chase—the great fear
had become a hard principle: Ord was still alive, still free,
and wielding Alice's most dangerous powers.

The black angel had been reborn, perhaps.

But even Alice couldn't walk on ten worlds at once, and
not even the smallest boy could shatter the light barrier. A
brigade of AI-human hybrids did nothing but examine each
reported sighting, judging its likelihood and possible consequences, then piecing together an elaborate and generally
improbable map showing Ord's wanderings over the last
long millennia.

He was haunting their spiral arm, chances were.

Definitely, a male Chamberlain had interceded in the Ak-
kanitz wars, and the Passion incident, and the War of
Whims. Each conflict was defused through clever, quick
means. Encrypted codes were changed, leaving entire
weapon systems unusable. Empathy was grafted into AIs,
and the machines subsequently rebelled. Or, in one case, a
false species of aliens was conjured from light and bad
telemetry, and the warring parties made peace in order to
join forces against the common, illusionary foe.

While the Glory were spreading along the famed River of Life, destroying every world they touched, Ord or some similar entity visited an obscure young woman on one of the last secure worlds. He gave her a few words of advice, and then, a golden vest. The vest apparently contained an Alice-style talent—a dark-matter, dark-energy machine of no clear purpose. Wearing nothing but the vest, the woman organized the first meaningful resistance to the apocalyptic faith, and for the next five centuries, she and her followers fought the Glory to a deadlock. But then a traitor orchestrated her capture. She was disarmed and executed, and her magical vest was examined in detail. Yet only when the faith's leaders were in its presence did the machinery finally come to full life. A sophisticated EM-pulse, short-range but irresistible, reinvented certain basic memes. The Glory changed directions in an afternoon. Moving back along the River of Death, at a considerably slower pace, the same narrow fanaticism was applied to the reterraforming of the thousands of worlds that they had already destroyed.

Ord was a phantom, a rumor and a whim, quick and effective, but always impatient. Experts decided that he was streaking at near light-speed, observing worlds from a distance, learning just enough about each disaster to formulate an elegant solution—a solution that wouldn't demand of him more than a few moments of his time. What people witnessed was an image of Ord and some little talent deployed for one specific function. He was an impulsive and powerful boy-god racing through the universe at high relativistic velocities, and he was still very much the baby. Time for him was slowed to the black fringe of infinite, and with all things important, he was still a novice, no more than a few years having passed since he had last walked out of the Chamberlain mansion.

What if the boy-god returned to free his sister?

That was a potent, enduring question.

And there was a rash answer that was equally stubborn. "We should kill Alice," millions proposed, often with the same blunt, certain voice. "A simple execution," they ad-

vised. "Or we allow her to escape, and vaporize her. Or an
accident could be arranged. The more preposterous, the better. Whatever it takes to get rid of the old butcher!"

But things simple and rash never have clean, simple consequences.

It was a Nuyen who dismantled any hope for an easy
homicide. Like every untainted Family, hers had retained
its seat on the Earth's Council. "Let me remind you of three
cold certainties," she shouted from that seat. "First of all,
young Chamberlains are usually possessed by a strong, often inflexible sense of morality. If that boy returns someday
to learn that we signed Alice's death warrant, he may feel
obligated to punish each of us in some suitable way."

A collective shudder passed through the Council's chamber.

"Certainty two," said the Nuyen. "Alice may wish to be
martyred, and we would be aiding her cause. And speaking
for myself, I don't intend to help that monster in any fashion. Not in martyrdom, and not even to wipe her ass."

Most of the Council members gazed off into the distance,
asking themselves how ordinary people could decipher the
wants of a creature like Alice.

"Certainty three."

She said it, then said nothing else, drawing their eyes. A
black-haired entity of unknown dimensions and astonishing
age, she sat high in the chamber, her seat craftily positioned
so that she seemed to hold no special office, yet none of
her smaller, weaker colleagues could turn in their seats
without noticing her. The archaic face was smiling. She was
wearing an elegant black uniform and an enormous mischievous grin. It was a surprising grin, and in its fashion,
discomforting.

After a long while, the Nuyen repeated herself. "Certainty three."

"We heard you the first time!" shouted the Council president—a fearless little ectotherm of no certain gender or
political persuasion. "Just tell us!"

The grin became an austere glare. "Alice is valuable only

while she lives," the Nuyen explained. "And should that boy ever streak past us in some bid to rescue her . . . well, then her value is magnified a thousandfold."

"Value?" the president whispered.

The Nuyen heard him from halfway across the great chamber, and with a nod, she replied, "As a lure, she is invaluable."

There was an electric silence.

"Consider this," she continued. "If you wish to prepare for Ord's return, you'll need resources and capital. My Family is prepared to donate both to such a noble cause. The other good Families will do the same. And I'm quite certain that once the situation is explained in full, every responsible government for a thousand light-years will be just as generous with their gifts.

"After all, they would prefer us to keep hold of Alice. Not them. They don't want or need the responsibility. Yet we do. Because we are enlightened, we wish the woman to squirm for us, like the proverbial lure." She paused, briefly and for dramatic effect. "Then if the boy does arrive someday, we will be ready."

"And if he doesn't?" the president shouted.

"That will be acceptable, too," the Nuyen replied, two enormous hands calmly rubbing one another in her lap. "The Earth will be left richer and more secure than ever, and I should think, we will all be happy beyond measure . . ."

Three

"A god comes to live among us, and what does she bring?

"If she stands in the highest ranks of her honorable Family, she will be an enormous creature. Her talents, baryonic and otherwise, can possess the mass of a small moon. She will be able to feed her

own bulk, only occasionally sipping from local
power sources; but she must eventually replenish her
fuels from local markets, and as she radiates heat,
she will pay every appropriate tax. Her machinery is
usually self-maintained; but any worthy god sees
value in hiring local technicians for the most mun-
dane work. She wields a grand wealth, and like any
wealthy soul, she will make little purchases and
launch herself on the occasional shopping spree.
With a political sensibility, she will make or pur-
chase elaborate gifts. Even if her flesh is nonbar-
yonic, she must rent a volume of space from some
fortunate landlord. Many gods employ a staff of ded-
icated professionals, rigorously educated and well
compensated. Charities will benefit from her altru-
ism. Parks will be built in her name. Her talents will
entertain people, and her deep experience will make
local institutions and governments work with a re-
newed and laudable efficiency . . .

"In economic terms, what a god brings is equal to
what a prosperous city would bring to our local
space . . . wealth and a passionate source of energy,
and best of all, a wellspring of marvels worthy of
our wide-eyed admiration . . . !"

—*a Council dispatch*

MILLENNIA HAD PASSED since that historic meeting of the
Council. The Nuyen had been replaced by a succession of
sisters and brothers, and the Earth's population had tripled,
and the solar system was an urban park singing with nearly
twenty times the population that it wielded in pre-Core
days. New immigrants and refugees arrived by the minute.
A few came from the Core, but most were fleeing smaller,
closer catastrophes. By law, they were wealthy or uniquely
talented. Otherwise, they would never have been able to
book passage on a starship, much less pay the prohibitive
immigration fees. Only the most privileged could afford
citizenship on the Earth, impoverishing themselves for the

security of the ancestral home. The galaxy had turned deadly; a glance at the night sky proved as much. "But the mother world is safe," parents would promise. "A storm roars outside, but we're under a good strong roof here. Do you see?"

"I see the roof, Father."

This particular family had just arrived from a modified M-class sun a little more than fifty light-years from the Earth. Half of their fortune had purchased the little starship, while the rest ensured them the honor of becoming new citizens. Mother and Father made an attractive couple: Tailored for a lush tropical world, they were barely a meter tall, equipped with prehensile three-tipped tails, expressive wide faces, and the oversize, florid genitals that once were the fashion on their world.

Their world was dead now.

The boy never knew his parents' home. A quiet and pleasant near child, he was born during the voyage and spent his entire life inside the same cramped cabin. The prospect of being anywhere else obviously thrilled him. Drifting before a universal window, he was using it as a simple window, gazing down at the Earth with his blue-black eyes. There were no continents, and no visible seas. Every square kilometer was adorned with a towering city, graceful and oftentimes famous, and the crust beneath was a spongy volume of stone and diamond and exotic matter, lesser cities and pockets of ocean nestled against elaborate farms where enough food to feed a quarter of a trillion people was produced every day.

There were thousands of moons, two of them quite large. The nearer moon was the Earth's natural satellite, and like the Earth, it was a heavily reconfigured, extraordinarily lovely place. But the other body was different. A simple framework of ordinary superconductors enveloped a round mass of dark matter and bizarre plasmas—a liquid blackness swirling rapidly, hinting at fantastic energies barely held in control.

The boy knew what it was, but for appearance's sake, he asked, "What's that ugly thing do, Father?"

Someone replied with a snort.

Pretending to be startled, the boy spun around. Floating in the new-made hatch was a uniformed woman—an immigration officer who made her modest living interviewing the new refugees. She was a giant, and she was obviously strong, and her features had a simple, even severe appearance that showed no trace of genetic tinkering. The woman was archaic. She was a fossil, practically. A boy from a distant place was entitled to double his surprise. Blinking, he pretended to be flustered, and with a voice designed to mislead, he shouted, "That's a Sanchex face! Why are you wearing a Sanchex face?"

The father growled at his son, then offered a clumsy apology. "He meant nothing. He doesn't understand. In my eyes, ma'am . . . you don't look anything like a Sanchex . . . !"

"But that's what I am," the woman growled. "My face and the rest of me are nothing but."

A terrified silence bled into a sorry little moan.

"Like most of my Family," she continued, "I was brought up on charges. And after serving my sentence and paying my well-deserved fines, I was given this uniform." Her smile was more menacing than her glower. "Do you like my uniform, little boy?"

"No," he squeaked.

That Sanchex face came close to his face, then with the warm stink of garlic and fish innards, she said, "A lot of us work in customs. And I bet you can guess why."

"Because you're mean," he said.

"And spiteful," she added. "And suspicious. And easy to anger. And just as quick to act on that anger, I'll warn you . . . !"

She looked and sounded like an old friend, but the name drawing itself on the left breast of her uniform, in a thousand languages, never looked anything like *Ravleen*.

"To answer your extremely rude question," she continued, "that 'ugly' object belongs to our defense network, and it's beautiful. It is a wonder, in fact, and I love it, and

I don't know what it can do, and neither of us will ever know anyone who knows what it can do. It is a secret, and it is a marvel. Do you understand *that*, young man?"

"Yes, Miss Sanchex."

The woman recoiled, taking a long suck of air before reminding all of them, "We don't use that name anymore. Sanchexes are extinct."

"Yes—"

"Madam Voracious."

"Yes, Madam Voracious."

Parents and son blurted those words. The wealth of a dead world was useless on the Earth; that was the first and most important lesson of this entire process. They were being reminded that in this realm, they were every kind of tiny.

The customs officer showed her cowering audience a grim Sanchex smile, then she thundered, "Now let's discuss your names . . . !"

The boy answered first, in a low voice.

"Excuse me?" said Madam Voracious.

The boy almost smiled, those blue-black eyes finding something amusing, his lovely quick tail flicking in the air behind him, while his unformed genitals rose up and grew just a little pink.

Then he repeated himself, and for a slippery, mischievous instant, it sounded to this flabbergasted officer as if he had said the word, "Ord."

Four

"Small tours will serve us in these ways: They will feed public curiosity. They will project a sense of openness on the part of the remaining Families. They will educate. They will mollify. They will give our youngest children valuable practice in the arts of persuasion and coping with difficult questions.

*And most important they will continue the humilia-
tion of the vanquished Families . . . in particular, the
Chamberlains . . ."*

—Nuyen policy statement

THE IMMIGRANTS TOOK up unassuming, generally unhappy
lives.

Their fortune was nearly exhausted. They could barely
afford an apartment less than a tenth the size of their starship's tiny cabins, and the parents spent their days trying
to ignore the new world. Millions lived next door, and
every person was tailored in some different fashion, with
odd physiologies as well as opaque languages and tortuous
customs. On the Earth, even basic goods were depressingly
expensive. Work was easy to find and salaries were high,
but every job was extraordinarily specialized, and over
time, menial. Family finances were certain to grow tighter.
Staring at each other, the parents asked: "Why did we think
we could live here?"

For them, the Earth was a prison.

On their worst days, they barely spoke or rarely even left
their bed-closet, forcing their son to watch patiently over
them, voicing encouragement and sometimes taking charge
of the family's day-to-day needs.

It was a standard procedure to shadow every refugee with
paranoid AIs. For many reasons, including the recommen-
dation of their immigration officer, this family was given
extra attention. Yet nothing incriminating was observed,
and after six months of observing the progressively deep-
ening sadness, all but one of the AIs were given new, more
interesting assignments.

When he wasn't the man of the family, the boy wandered
the halls outside, speaking to neighbors with the help of a
cheap translator. Or he would remain tucked inside his
closet, reading voraciously and watching random channels
and vistas through a secondhand pair of universal goggles.
Each morning, the boy offered their names to the Family
lottery. It was a perfectly normal event; most of the citi-

zenry routinely did the same chore every day, competing for the chance to tour the abandoned estates. The odds of winning were minimal, even impossible. Only a few dozen slots opened each day, and most were filled through appointments and political favors. Yet on his one hundred and eighty-first attempt, the impossible happened:

Three slots were granted to the new immigrants.

Alarms sounded in a thousand high offices. Quantumware and various officials were interrogated at length. How could such an unlikely event occur? But the quantumware programs had a fondness for family units and recent immigrants, and when pressed, they admitted to being influenced by a nebulous bribe from one of the advocacy groups that supported refugees from dead worlds. Three days passed between the announcement of the winners and their subsequent award. A brigade of AIs as well as human officers began to follow the winners, studying their composition, and to the best level of modern methods, observing their thoughts. The depressed parents were the sudden heroes of their neighborhood and city; a purely random event had swept away their obscurity and the top levels of their sadness. They smiled and made love, to each other and then to ill-fitting neighbors. And still, nothing unusual was betrayed. Nanosecond meetings were held. Great minds deliberated for entire minutes. Then, as a final precaution, an adult Nuyen was dressed up like an unmodified youngster, and he shouldered the role of the smiling, charming guide whose duty it was to lead the day's little tour.

"Hello," the Nuyen began, examining his audience with an array of senses. "It is a lovely morning, isn't it?"

Happy souls agreed. Yes, it was delightful.

A perpetual summer hung over the rest of the Earth—a consequence of so many machines and warm bodies. But on the Families' estates, climate still obeyed the angle of the sun. Summer was a few months of intensive growth sandwiched between killing winters. Seasons meant wealth and conspicuous waste, but their guide mentioned neither. Focusing every sense on the mysterious boy, he asked himself, "Are you Ord?"

Nothing tasted unusual, much less remarkable.

Bowing, their guide introduced himself by saying, "I am Xo."

The boy didn't blink, and his heart didn't quicken, and no portion of his visible mind showed surprise or more than a normal curiosity.

If anything, it was the Nuyen who felt anxious. For millennia stacked on millennia, this was Xo's job. He was a scent hound testing the wind. And this was a common situation: What if the lottery system had been manipulated, giving *him* access to the estates? At first glance, it seemed like a ludicrous possibility. Someone wielding Alice's powers wouldn't bother with this kind of backdoor subterfuge. But Xo had spent his life thinking about Ord, and he knew the boy as well as anyone, and he could almost believe that the final Chamberlain would find this route alluring—camouflaging himself inside the Families' own contrived game.

"Xo," he repeated, using a thousand channels reserved for the Families. Then in the next nanoseconds, he told anyone with the proper ears, "It's me, yes. Your dear friend. Welcome home, Ord."

There was no response.

But the boy lifted his tail, then both of his hands. "Sir," he said with a soft respect. "Will we visit your home today, sir?"

Xo shook his head. "We won't have enough time. I'm sorry."

The boy looked saddened.

"Why would you want to see my house?" Xo inquired.

A quick, guileless voice insisted, "The Nuyens are my favorite Family, sir."

"Are we?"

"One of your brothers helped my world during our wars." Fond emotions played across his face, while his parents winced, recalling the Nuyen's failures and the demise of an entire biosystem. But the boy's happiness couldn't have tasted more genuine. "I've always wanted to step inside your house, sir!"

A thousand centuries had passed since Ord carried an atomic weapon to the Nuyens' mansion. But very little had changed. The players were the same. Xo was still the worried, immature boy cowering behind the door, watching out for his bomb-wielding friend.

THE PARTY WAS ushered through several of the abandoned estates, each held in trust by the Nuyens. Standing empty, the mansions looked beautiful and outrageously wasteful, while the surrounding woodlands and gardens had been allowed to grow wild and unkempt. Subtleties of color and rot produced an emotional impact that Xo could see and taste. His guests came from cramped circumstances. Each of them was wondering how the Families could have risked such wealth. How could anyone be so foolish? And as any respectable guide, Xo steered their opinions toward matters of greed, letting that fine old emotion lead them to the horrible conclusion that even great souls can be perfect idiots.

Lunch was a modest feast served inside the Sanchex pyramid. Xo explained that once everyone had enjoyed their fill, the tour would culminate with a studious, scornful walk through the main Chamberlain mansion. "We're climbing a ladder of guilt," he remarked, pretending that the cliché was profound. "Sanchexes did the most dangerous assignments in the Core. Which is why they were the second Family to be disbanded wholesale . . . two moments after the Chamberlains were ordered to surrender their wealth, and their selves . . ."

The refugee boy sat between his parents, eating because it was polite to eat, but his attention fixed firmly on the Nuyen.

"Because they were the most guilty Family," Xo continued, "the Chamberlains were the first to die." Ord wouldn't react to that simple taunt. But there was a script to follow, and Xo's siblings were observing, carefully judging his technique. "The Sanchexes were fighters, violent and relentless. But the Chamberlains were worse than that. They were intellectuals, colder than the emptiest space and without a single heart to their name."

The boy nodded soberly, apparently believed the propaganda.

Using private channels, Xo offered more elaborate arguments—highly reasoned and often-practiced monologues that were designed to create doubt in a young Chamberlain. That was also the standard routine. Ord wasn't here. That would be much too unlikely. But then again, he could be anywhere. Everywhere. He might have arrived last night, undetected, and by dumb chance, Xo was delivering the opening salvos of his well-planned assault.

The boy lifted his tail and hands again, and after saying, "Sir," with the proper respect, he asked, "What can you tell me about this wonderful room, sir?"

More than a kilometer long, with a towering triangular ceiling fashioned from polished basalt and only enough light to emphasize its volume, the space had once been sacred to the Sanchexes. But after lying empty for so long, it felt sad, cold despite the well-warmed air, and forgotten.

Xo waited for a half moment, letting his audience look about.

Then the boy answered his own question. "It was their dining hall, wasn't it? This is where the Sanchexes held their ceremonial feasts."

"Yes. That's what this was."

The blue-black eyes smiled. Turning to his mother, the boy said, "When they finished eating—meat or cold plasmas or whatever—they would dissolve the furniture and hold contests."

"Contests?" she muttered.

"They would fight each other," he allowed.

The woman swished her tail nervously. "How do you know that, dear?"

"It's in the histories," he replied. "I read it somewhere."

Xo accessed every word that the boy had read since arriving on the Earth then consumed the entire library salvaged from the starship. Buried in that mass of information was a single article that mentioned that historic curiosity.

Faintly disgusted, the mother looked at Xo. "Is that true?"

But again, the boy answered first. "Adults took the shape of giant animals, real or not. And they would stand at opposite ends of the room, then run at each other." He pointed to an odd little doorway in the floor, now sealed. "That's where the blood was drained away. Fighters would weigh their fluids afterward, and the winner was whoever lost the least of himself, or herself."

Outwardly calm, Xo carefully monitored the boy.

With an impressed voice, he told everyone, "It's all true."

The boy gave a little nod, happy with himself.

Those last details weren't included in the article. But the boy could have overheard someone talking. Unlikely as it sounded, that was an infinitely more reasonable explanation than having Ord himself sitting at the oak-and-hyperbar table, baiting him with this very slender clue.

An impressed hush had fallen over the group. Every diamond knife and shield—Sanchex utensils authentic to their pyramid embossing—was laid neatly on the remains of their lunches. Keeping to the topic, Xo confessed, "This was the most aggressive Family, probably. By temperament and by training, the people who were born into this house were capable of the most astonishing violence."

The boy was staring through him, his face suddenly flat. Empty.

"If the Core hadn't exploded," Xo continued, "there still would have come a day when we would have disarmed and disarmored the Sanchex clan. For everyone's safety, including their own."

The guests nodded amiably. Gratefully.

It was another who took offense. Swimming the length of the room, unseen, she descended as a sudden chill of the air and a vague electric sensation slithering beneath Xo's false skin. Only he could hear her whispering into his deepest, most private ears.

"Fuck you," said the familiar voice, followed by a long, dry laugh.

Xo was afraid. But more than that, he was amused, reflecting that the Sanchexes weren't like Chamberlains: They rose reliably to every little taunt.

"Hello, Ravleen," he said with his own laughing whisper.

"Fuck you," she repeated. Then she pulled away, retreating into the depths of the pyramid, crying out, "Get those sphincters out of here! I want to be alone!"

Five

"He won't send the whole of himself . . .

"What we imagine . . . what really is the only plausible scenario . . . is that he will first show us the affable tip of his tiniest finger . . . which, nonetheless, should be an awesome sight . . ."
                                        —*Nuyen memo, classified*

BETWEEN THE COMPRESSION of time and the perfection of memory, it seemed to Ord as if he hadn't been away from home for very long.

Not more than a busy afternoon, surely.

Yet some other part of him, persistent and bittersweet, felt the press of the ages. For a long while, these beautiful mansions had stood empty on top of these sculpted peaks, the splendid forests and meadows had grown wild, and every extraordinary city on the Earth had swollen until there was only the one megalopolis encircling the globe, its tallest buildings rising to the edges of the atmosphere, thus gazing down at the once-lofty peaks of the old estates.

Not only had Ord been gone for a long while; in telling ways, he had never been to this place before.

Perched on a comfortable seat inside the luxurious Family transport, he studied his surroundings with a thousand heightened senses. For the last seven months, he had done little else. And likewise, the Earth had never stopped studying him. He could feel every stare, every subtle touch, and coursing through the air were the whispered questions:

"Is he the one?"

"Or a decoy?"

"Or a lesser criminal, maybe?"

"Or nobody . . . perhaps . . . ?"

And then, inevitably:

"But if it is Ord, when how where do we act . . . ?"

Even in its heyday, the gray-gold Sanchex pyramid had a foreboding, almost angry appearance. As it fell away behind him, Ord gratefully turned his eyes by the dozens, more and more of them watching the Chamberlain mansion drawing close, the tailored white coral still vibrantly healthy, growing slowly on the patient granite bones of the house. And again, Ord had that powerful and divided impression of never having truly left this place, and seeing nothing that was remotely familiar.

"Are you enjoying yourself?" a voice inquired.

Xo's voice.

Looking up, Ord conjured a nervous smile and flipped his tail in an amiable manner, answering the question with gestures, then saying, "This is so very fun. Sir."

The Nuyen dropped to his knees, touching the boy's shoulder, while a private voice remarked, "I know it's you, Ord. I know."

It was an ancient trick, often used and never successful.

With his public voice, the boy said, "I don't blame the Nuyens for what happened. To my home world, I mean. My parents explained—"

"We tried to help," Xo interjected.

"Your brother did his absolute best. I know that." It had been an enormous public relations disaster, not to mention a tragedy. Anti-Family forces had outmaneuvered a young Nuyen, and nearly a billion citizens died in the cross fire. "I'm just sorry that I can't visit your home today," Ord claimed. "Really, I'd so like to thank each of you personally . . . for your sacrifices and all of your successes, and everything . . ."

Xo nodded. He wore a smooth face and the body of a young adult and the bright cheerful eyes of an imbecile. It was all decoration, all a ruse. No one else inside the spacious transport could suspect that he wasn't one of the Nu-

yens' young children. He was a full adult, modified and
enlarged, and to most of humanity, entirely indecipherable.

This was not a fearful, simple, and clumsy Xo, and that
was another sign—perhaps the most powerful of all—that
Ord did not belong in this place.

With his private voice, Xo promised, "We absolutely
don't want to harm you. We only want to help you, Ord.
You and the Peace."

Then came a seductive argument—intense and focused,
full of promises of forgiveness for every crime, known and
unknown—and while Xo's secret voices begged with him
to confess and surrender, his public voice was saying, "On
the first day of the year, my Family opens its doors to the
Earth. It's our show of friendship. Anyone can join us
through his universal window. And if you come, I will give
you a personal tour of my house."

Ord said nothing.

With every voice, Xo said, "Think about it then," and he
rose, then retreated, nothing about him showing the
slightest concern.

PRIDE AND SACRIFICE.

The words were still cut into the granite above the doorway, and as people filed inside, listening more to each other
than to their guide, Ord couldn't help but leap up, touching
the dense pink stone with his damp little fingertips.

That was his habit, his little ritual.

Xo saw the gesture, and froze. Other Nuyens triggered
silent alarms that engulfed the Earth, then jumped across
the solar system, alerting the appropriate AIs and humans.
Before the little group of sightseers could reach the stairs,
a multitude of defensive networks were begging for information and new instructions.

Ord observed the carefully rehearsed panic, and in the
same instant, he concentrated on closer, more immediate
hazards.

The mansion was a trap. Or more accurately, it was a
series of ingenious, closely nested and independent traps.

Antimatter mines lay beneath the stairs and behind solid walls. Null-field generators waited to ensnare anyone foolish enough to stumble too close. Overhead, inside Ord's old bedroom, an AI assassin waited to inject its victim with quantumware toxins and assorted eschers designed to muddle the most sophisticated mind. But the most dangerous enemy stood behind him, pressing lightly at the small of Ord's back. "Please don't," said the dry, smooth, and worried voice. "Don't touch the emblems, son."

With a boy's voice, Ord said, "I'm sorry. Sir."

Each guest stood on his own stair, and they were being lifted, spiraling their way up through the famous structure.

With a stronger voice, Xo asked, "What would you like to see first?"

"The penthouse, please." The boy smiled at his adoptive parents. "I want to see where Alice lived when she came home."

The Nuyen smiled, and said, "Naturally."

Ord could feel an invisible bulk. Xo was a respectable age, but he had been transformed in the most peculiar ways. Ord smelled weird abilities stretched over his ape bones. Dark matter and profound energies clung to the Nuyen, reaching for kilometers in every direction. There were eschers and quantumware toxins as well as charismatic talents that Ord couldn't quite weigh. Every other danger in the house was tangible and forgettable. But an enormous quantity of human genius had spent the last millennia doing nothing but preparing this one soul for Ord's return.

Ord nourished a healthy fear. Thomas had taught him that critical skill. But glancing over his shoulder, a genuine terror took hold. What if he had come all this way for nothing? Instead of answers, what if he was captured? Dismembered? Or worse?

How could he help rebuild the Great Peace when he was dead?

Unless that was what Alice had always wanted. *My death saves the galaxy, somehow.* It was a seductive, fatalistic notion that found a ready home inside him. The idea spread through him like an explosion, and he just as abruptly realized from where that crippling notion had come . . . and he threw it aside . . .

Xo.

For an instant, Ord considered fleeing.

But that was another one of Xo's tricks. Ord crushed that idea, too, telling himself that he wouldn't change plans now. Then to be sure that nobody could grab his reflexes, he closed off his easiest escape routes. He killed certain limbs and choked secret avenues. And then, too late, he realized that he had just fallen for another one of Xo's traps, weakening himself without a shot being fired.

Xo sensed a change in the boy's demeanor.

He joined Ord on his narrow step, quietly saying, "Yes?"

"In the histories," Ord began, "there's a Nuyen with your name. Xo was a friend of the Chamberlains' baby."

"Ord," said Xo. "Which, by coincidence, sounds rather like your name."

"Does it? I don't think so, sir." He put on a serious face. "I've read the histories. Alice became Ord's friend."

"She manipulated him, you mean. By most interpretations, she enslaved the poor boy."

Xo used every mouth, speaking in a great chorus.

"Are you the same Xo?"

"I am. Yes."

People were startled, unnerved. The boy's father bristled, then with a wounded tone, said, "Sir," twice. "Sir, I don't understand. I was told that youngsters serve as tour guides."

Ord explained. "He thinks that I might be dangerous, Father."

The parents clung to one another, horrified by the idea.

"But I'm not dangerous. Not even a little." He stared at his childhood friend, saying, "There was another baby. A Sanchex. What was her name?"

"You know," the Nuyen replied.

"So where is Ravleen? Does she give tours, like you do?"

Silence.

They had risen through most of the mansion. The cylindrical walls were covered with the elaborate, ever-changing mural. But instead of showing images of success and glory, the sightseers were treated to visions of misery: living worlds turning to molten iron and steam; panicked faces evaporating in storms of hard radiation; a trillion refugees fighting for berths on scarce, overcrowded starships, sometimes using nothing but their fingernails and bloodied teeth.

"The Chamberlain legacy." The guide's voice was booming. "This is why they were disbanded. This is why they earned our richly deserved scorn. And this is why my Family—those who would never hurt you—are disarming and neutralizing the outlaw Chamberlains."

The tension was infectious.

Staring at the nightmarish images, the boy's eyes changed in subtle ways, pulling the face along with them.

"Alice's final days of freedom were spent here," Xo declared. And then he glared at the boy beside him.

"Mama?" the boy squeaked.

With hands and tails, and then their bodies, his parents surrounded him, pretending they could actually protect him.

The stairs suddenly deposited everyone on the landing, the little group standing before a thick satin-crystal door that shouldn't have been closed. Yet it was shut and sealed tight.

Xo whispered words too soft to be understood.

"Where's the penthouse?" asked the boy. "I want to see the penthouse."

Xo said, "No."

He said, "We must leave now. I'm sorry."

Then the boy gave the door a hard kick, blubbering, "Why? I want to see inside. I want to see where Alice was. . . ."

Ord was standing on the opposite side of the door, watching carefully as he cut the final tethers to his camouflage. He had woven that child from ordinary matter, then convinced the childless refugees that he was theirs, and genuine. And that's how they regarded him now, still trying to shield him, riding together on the same descending stair while the other dumbfounded guests stared at the suddenly bratty creature.

Only the Nuyen lingered.

With a mixture of terror and awe, Xo touched the crystal door, using a thousand soft hands.

"Why did you have to come home?" he asked.

And then, softer still, he asked, "When you could be anywhere, doing anything, why do you have to torture me . . . ?"

Six

"The Chamberlain mansion has been rigorously in-spected for dark matter machines, subatomic keys and graffiti-encrusted motes of dust. Every wall has been rendered transparent, and every nanopipe and superfluid conduit is known perfectly. Even the re-peating patterns within granite-and-coral crystals have been analyzed for hidden meanings and sleep-ing capacities. Throughout this process, every appro-priate authority has been invited to participate, at our discretion, and new inspections will continue to be carried out at irregular intervals, using both the newest and most proven means . . .

"Naturally, the estate grounds are shown the same thorough respect.

"For the moment, more elaborate measures, in-cluding the total disassembly of every artifact, have been deferred.

"We don't need to look any more desperate, if we can help it . . ."

—*Nuyen memo, classified*

"WHAT'S YOUR NAME, brother?"

"Be still. A few moments, please."

But Avram couldn't just lie there. He tried sitting up with

a half-formed body, and with blue eyes staring, he asked, "What's this place?"

"You don't recognize it?"

The newborn face turned left, then right. Then with a sigh, he faced forward again. "I don't. I'm sorry."

"That's no reason for apologies," Ord replied. "I just hoped you knew more than me."

In better days, the penthouse would have been configured to make high-ranking Chamberlains feel comfortable. But instead of luxurious furniture or elaborate beds of cold plasma, Ord had created a starless night sky beneath which stood a string of long beds—wooden frames covered with dense alien symbols and filled with a meter of soft gray dust. Inside each bed was a human skeleton, archaic in form, the elegant bones vanishing behind an assortment of bright young organs and new flesh, toothy white skulls being rapidly transformed into familiar, wide-eyed faces.

"This talent doesn't come with a history," Ord confessed. "I can use it, but I don't know why it looks as it does."

The brothers had identical faces, sharp and pale and gently handsome, their strawberry hair unkempt and their sky-blue eyes projecting the same sense of wary amazement.

"You took my mind," said Avram. "At the execution, you grabbed me!"

"You're welcome."

After a deep, grateful breath, he asked, "Are you the baby?"

"Ord."

Avram closed his eyes. "The baby."

Bodies began twisting inside the adjacent beds. Hands and bare feet flinched, then everyone tried to sit up, lungs blowing the healing dust high into the dry, dark air.

To each of his patients, Ord said, "Relax. Please."

"This is one of Alice's talents," said Avram. "Am I right?"

Ord gave a little nod.

"You must feel miserable . . . being transformed so much, and before your time . . ."

"Misery is misery," Ord remarked, his voice quiet and firm. "For me, everything's peculiar and uncomfortable . . . but not really miserable, no . . ."

Nearly a couple dozen people were being reborn. There was a Papago and a Lee, two Ussens and so on. Each belonged to a disbanded Family. Each asked the same questions, then listened to Ord's gentle voice while his face floated above them.

The Papago was a woman. Ord called her Buteo.

"I know her," said Avram, pointing to his neighbor. "She lived in an adjacent system, and vanished while awaiting trial."

"Buteo wouldn't have enjoyed a fair hearing," Ord explained. "What else could I do?"

"My jailers were terrified of you," Avram allowed. "They convinced themselves you were coming for me next, which was why they hurried to convict."

"Your trial smelled, too."

"You were watching over me?"

"When I could."

Avram took a breath, for courage. "But if the judges and jury had been fair, and if they still found me guilty . . . ?"

Silence.

Avram laughed, bitterness bleeding into resignation. "Is this how you live now? Charging around the Milky Way, righting wrongs against the Families . . . ?"

"A wrong is a wrong," Ord offered. "I'll stop wars and save overloaded starships, and, whenever I can, I've tried to convince everyone to keep believing in the Great Peace—"

"Well," Avram interrupted with a cold scorn, "it must feel good to feel useful."

Suddenly, Ord was the baby again.

"It's a big galaxy," his older brother warned. "Be honest. How many places can you be at once?"

Silence.

"Even with all of Alice's talents . . . what? Two or four. Maybe ten. But you can't be everywhere." Avram threw his naked legs out of the bed, and added, "Alice was spectacular, but finite. The same as you, I'm guessing."

Ord didn't reply.

"Is that why she gave you her talents? So you can gallop from system to system, putting out the proverbial fires—?"

"I don't know why," Ord conceded. "I've never been sure what she intends for me."

Avram blinked, unable to contain his surprise. Then, after a long pause, he made himself ask, "What do you intend for me?"

"If you're willing, I'd like your help."

"Of course." Avram looked between his feet, judging the distance to the dusty ground. "How much time has passed since you saved me?"

Ord told him.

His brother winced, his face tightening as it lifted. A fire shone in the dark of his eyes. "Where are we? Exactly."

"The Earth."

There was no reaction.

"Inside our old house, as it happens."

For a long while, Avram sat motionless. Then his face softened, and with the faint beginnings of a smile, he said, "So the baby's come home to rescue Alice."

Ord said, "No."

His brother stubbornly ignored the answer. "What you were doing before, saving each of us . . . you were just practicing for today, weren't you . . . ?"

Again, Ord told him, "No."

Avram dropped from the bed and examined the alien inscriptions.

"Saving you was easy," Ord continued. "Too easy to make it feel like any genuine sort of practice."

His brother's mouth fell open, both hands touching the carved wood.

"You can read it?" Ord asked.

"It seems so," Avram said.

Rising from death's bed was the key, Ord realized.

"It says," Avram began. Then he hesitated, hands lifting

to cover his mouth before he admitted, "I've been given a second chance at life, it claims, and it will be my final chance. 'A moment to make right a mountain of misdeeds,' it claims."

Ord nodded, placing a fond hand on his brother's shoulder.

"Really?" he said, speaking to no one in particular. "If it comes to that—if there is a redemption—who could want any more than that . . . ?"

Seven

> "If the baby comes, then the blame is entirely the
> baby's . . . !"
>
> —Nuyen memo, classified

ONCE ORD STRIPPED the mansion of its traps and lesser terrors, he invited his reborn companions to wander at will, and, if possible, grow accustomed to their circumstances. In their own way, each was grateful, but with very much the same flavor of emotion, they worried about the future. Buteo, a tiny walnut-colored woman, reported activity in the nearby forest. "There's a hundred fancy uniforms with people stuck inside them," she reported. "And either they're extraordinarily stupid, or those uniforms want me to see them watching the house."

Ord saw much more: The local districts had been evacuated. Elite military units were rushing from the ends of the solar system. The Earth's artificial moon was being eased into a closer orbit. But most alarming were the sophisticated energy barriers—invisible curtains shrouding the estate, designed to absorb nuclear detonations, tetrawatt discharges, and any sudden retreats by the criminals trapped inside.

There was no worse place for war than the overcrowded Earth.

Some of the reborn had to remind Ord of the obvious.

"Get Alice now," said one of the Ussens. He was a tall, blue-skinned man with snowy hair and a blue-black beard. "Or better," he said with an Ussen's scornful voice, "why couldn't you have slipped in and out of her cell when you first arrived at our cradle-world?"

"Because I wasn't strong enough then," Ord explained. "And I'm still too weak, if you must know. Most of my talents—"

"Alice's talents."

"Are elsewhere. Waiting." Ord gestured in a random direction. "If I'd brought everything, I would have lost every chance at surprise."

"Surprise," the Ussen echoed, choking a laugh.

"Besides," said the baby, "being tiny has its blessings. I still look harmless to them. I'm not forcing anyone to panic yet."

Avram mentioned the obvious danger. "But what if they keep you separated from your other talents?"

"They won't," Ord promised, showing nothing but confidence.

The Ussens grumbled, but said nothing.

Buteo showed an appreciative half grin.

"Fine," Avram allowed. "We're here with you. We owe you a debt, and you need our help, you say. But what are we supposed to accomplish?"

"I can modify you." With a wide smile, Ord promised, "I'll make it so you can study my surveillance feeds. I want your impressions about what's happening. Your best hunches, and your worst."

"Wouldn't you do a better job?" asked Buteo.

Ord shook his head.

"I'm just the baby. Remember?" Then he offered a soft, self-deprecating laugh, wondering if they could see just how lonely he was . . .

WHEN THE AUTHORITIES came to arrest Alice, she was found inside a tiny, nearly anonymous room deep inside the mansion's bones. It was the same room where she had lived as the Chamberlain baby, and wrapped up in that thick nostalgia, she had bided her time by watching scenes from ancient days.

The room's furnishings were exactly as Alice had left them, complete to the small, low-density universal wall. The only structural change was the transparent wall set between the room and adjacent hallway. This was where the daily tours ended. Guests would pause and stare, and their Nuyen guides would finally, mercifully fall quiet, allowing each person the freedom to consider the red-haired monster who had taken refuge here, and how very much she meant to their lives.

Ord passed through the transparent wall, influencing nothing.

The universal wall showed the present: Alice alone inside her prison cell, dressed in a plain white prison smock, nothing of substance having changed for millennia. Ord watched as she paced from the toilet to the door, every step made slowly and carefully, three steps required to cross her universe . . . and she turned with a dancer's unconscious grace, retracing her steps so precisely that Ord could see where the white-hyperrock floor had slumped in four places, worn down by the bare white balls of her feet.

The cell and old bedroom were the same size.

Ord wasn't the first to note the irony.

With a corporeal hand, he touched the warm electric image of the face. Did she sense that he was here? Did Alice retain those powers? It would be lovely if she could simply step up here and visit him for a moment, as she had done once before. Yet he couldn't trust an Alice who would do exactly what he wanted: That wasn't his sister's manner, and that would make for too easy a trap.

With every other hand, Ord searched the room. This was a ripe place to hunt for instructions. Alice could have left a motile scrap of her flesh, or a whisper of refined dark matter. Either might have slinked about for thousands of years, evading detection, waiting for his touch to unfold itself, then explaining exactly why she had selected him, or damned him, into becoming her successor.

But there were no keys, or clues, or anything else worthwhile.

The single possible exception was set on one of the crystal shelves above the narrow bed. Like any Chamberlain, Alice had been a rabid collector; odd gems and favorite childhood holos were mixed together with fossils of every age and origin. One fossil showed a human handprint set in a golden mudstone. In a glance, Ord knew its age and curious origin: It was a female Chamberlain handprint, and the stone beneath was nearly ten million years old. Alice had created it. On some alien world—a single taste gave Ord twenty candidates—his newly grown sister had pressed her right hand into a streambed. Then she had buried her mark under an avalanche of muck and volcanic ash, and several million years later, she dug the treasure up again. Cooked to stone, and in a rugged fashion, lovely.

Ord reached for the handprint, almost by reflex.

Then he hesitated.

The trap was almost perfectly disguised, its elegant trigger married to the young rock, waiting patiently for a hand of his shape and flavor. A camouflaged relay linked the trigger to a single globule of molten, magnetized anti-iron set deep underground. The weapon was far too small to injure Ord, even at close range, and he wouldn't have noticed the device if he hadn't been searching for it. The globule was inside a null chamber set beneath that very bored woman, and it had probably always been there, Alice pacing back and forth above it, oblivious to any danger.

Ord's first analysis taught him about the trigger and link.

And the next ten analyses showed him nothing new.

There was a temptation, soft but coy, to place his hand on Alice's. For a slippery, seductive moment, Ord wondered if that was why he had come here. Not to beg for his sister's advice, but to do one more noble deed for a Chamberlain in despair.

Slowly, slowly, he withdrew his corporeal hand.

Then he pulled the hand through his hair, his scalp more than a little damp, the warm perspiration tasting of oceans and fear.

Eight

"Ravleen is painstakingly polite. We appreciate that quality in anyone, but particularly in her. And that remains true even though we're certain she is only pretending to have good manners and a sunny out-look.

"So that our polite friend would better understand her powers, we took her into the wilderness. We own several hundred sunless worlds between Sol and the nearest stars—Earth and Mars-class orphans pur-chased as investments for the moment when our so-lar system is full. One of these worlds was terraformed in preparation for Ravleen. At our insis-tence, she examined its continents and new seas, then she very politely asked permission to play.

"For the next three hours, Ravleen used her new talents—first in small doses, then in larger, more expert fusillades. And afterward, with scrupulous care, she thanked each of us for the opportunity to learn.

" 'When he does come,' she promised, more than once, 'I'll do the same things to him.'

"We manacled each of her hands afterward before bringing her home. And to help recoup our expenses, we sold portions of that world's exposed core . . . its metals and rare earths yielding a considerable profit . . ."

—*Nuyen memo, classified*

XO WOULD NEVER admit it, but he felt a genuine pity for Ravleen.

The other Sanchexes were stripped of their talents, or dead. And maybe she was a little lucky, since ordinary life so rarely agreed with her siblings. But to be ordinary wasn't an option for Ravleen. With Ord vanished and Alice's talents stolen, the good Families had no choice but to panic. Contingency plans and gruesome nightmares preyed upon their nerves. What if the Chamberlain baby returned home? Who would help fight against him? The Sanchexes hadn't yet given their official surrender. But a delegation of high-ranking Nuyens was dispatched, sweeping into the pyramid as if they owned it, pushing past hundreds of embittered and still-powerful souls. Xo wasn't present, and for endless good reasons, no visual records were made. But the moment had acquired a legendary status inside his Family. From the stories told, he could picture his brothers and sisters moving en masse. He could taste the vivid, bilious furies swirling around them, and their own, well-hidden fears. And the tensions only grew when they reached the young woman's quarters, entering after a customary knuckle-knock, and with a single booming voice, announcing, "We have come to ask for your help."

Ravleen was a beautiful creature. Black hair and arching black eyes gave her a feral quality, and in those times, she amplified her looks with infections of benign, radiant bacteria. The Nuyens' eternal curse was to feel lust for the Sanchexes, and a bullied respect, and despite the rank and power of her guests, Ravleen knew how to toy with those emotions. Wearing only a sablecat robe, she sat on her bed while using a single finger to open the robe, and then calmly fondling her left breast as she smiled, coldly amused, pointing out, "You don't sound as if you are asking."

The Nuyens laughed. They sounded like men and women in perfect control, their little worries buried deep.

"Let me guess," Ravleen continued. "This is about Ord, isn't it? I grew up beside him, and that's why you hope I can help. Am I right?"

Sober faces nodded.

Every voice said, "Naturally."

She stood suddenly, letting her robe relax and tumble to the floor. Brothers and sisters stared at her hard long legs, at the strong full curve of her ass, and at that famous smile, winsome and predatory in the same bewitching moment.

"Xo is already helping you." Telling it, she admitted to knowing at least one minor secret. "You're grooming that turd. Feeding him advanced talents, and intellects, and propagandas. He'll be invulnerable to attack—"

"Any reasonable attack, yes."

Ravleen scratched herself in one place, then another. Then she inquired, "Am I getting the same sweet deal?"

They told her, "No."

Then they laughed, perhaps trying too hard to remain in control.

"You'll be given talents, but of a narrow sort," they warned. Then one of the sisters reminded her, "You're only a Sanchex. You'll be lucky to have one talent. Since, according to the new laws, you aren't entitled to shit."

Ravleen said nothing for a long while, black eyes fixed on her sablecat robe, watching as it crawled toward its burrow-closet.

Then she took a deep breath, and said, "All right. What do I get?"

The package included a Xo-type invulnerability. They explained that and her other powers, then cautioned that there would be no added intellects, except for the muscular instincts needed to control these talents. In essence, Ravleen would be a functioning moron, incapable of million-tongue language skills or nonlinear modeling or even the cherished ability to use private, intra-Family channels.

"That should keep me under heel," she observed.

The highest-ranking Nuyen agreed, then said, "And we'll take other precautions. You'll wear restraints until we choose to remove them. And even when your manacles aren't in place, implants will ride inside your mind. Some will coax you into hating the Chamberlains, and particularly Ord—"

"As if I need help," she interrupted.

"While other implants will wait for a word from us. With that word, we will be able to kill your very tiny, very fragile mind . . . !"

The young woman passed from a shameless tease to simply naked. Exposed, and painfully helpless.

She caught her robe and put it on again.

"Xo's purpose is to reason with the boy," the Nuyens explained, "and if he doesn't succeed—"

"I get to kill him."

No one responded.

Quietly and soberly, Ravleen promised her audience, "I'll do this thing. But for me, not for you."

Every Nuyen broke into a huge and honest smile.

"I could live a very long time," their new ally ventured, "just waiting for a little vengeance."

IT WAS EARLY evening when two figures slipped out of the forest. They wore archaic bodies and the simple magenta robes common to diplomats, and they moved with a steady purpose, their talents dangling after them—Xo's intellects meant to appeal to the boy-god's better nature, and Ravleen's great limbs still wrapped in their manacles, but straining, eager for any excuse to attack.

Xo felt for his extraordinary companion, and as always, he shoved his sorrow and his pity into other, more profitable directions.

With a steady, much-practiced voice, he called out, "Ord? Isn't it time to talk?"

Nothing happened.

They paused at the mansion's main doorway. Xo made no attempt to look inside. He didn't believe that he could see much, and besides, decorum went along with politeness. It was important to seem patient. It was critical to be exactly the kind of person that Ord would accept, and with whom he could agree on terms.

Ravleen enjoyed a different attitude. Storming up to the rough coral door, she gave it a kick with her bare foot.

"You might as well talk to us," she sang out, "because we're damn well not leaving."

Nothing.

She groaned and made a fist, taking aim.

Xo grabbed her by the wrist.

Even manacled, she was full of white-hot energies. But she didn't resist him, relaxing suddenly, a strange little smile hiding in her eyes, her expression telling the world, "I know exactly what I'm doing."

From the forest, from a dozen hiding places, came a chorus of guttural wails. When the estate was abandoned, the Chamberlain bears had gone wild. Were they the ones crying out now? Xo started to look, but he discovered that a hundred cloaks had made the immediate world vanish; and in that instant of split attentions, Ord emerged, coming from no particular direction to stand before them with his hands open, his palms up, and his body and face looking like those of a teenage boy.

"It's nice to have old friends drop by," the boy volunteered.

To Ravleen, he said, "I felt you lurking in the pyramid." And he began to laugh, admitting, "I felt the rage. And I thought: If they're using Xo, they must be using Ravleen, too. In service of the Nuyens—!"

Energies surged, diminished.

Then the beautiful Sanchex face was smiling, the eyes filled with mischief, and she let her tongue play along her top lip, then slide back against its mate.

Xo spoke, a thousand voices asking and begging and cajoling Ord to open up a dialogue.

The Chamberlain responded with a steely glance, then gave fair warning. "They made a lousy choice. You were a weakling and worm, and I never liked you."

"You don't know me," Xo growled.

Then with another mouth and a plaintive tone, he asked, "Do you think you're the only one who's better than he used to be?"

Silence.

With his simplest mouth, Xo said, "We have to talk. Without Ravleen."

They were suddenly elsewhere. Xo found the two of them standing inside the penthouse, other souls watching from the dusty shadows. Xo examined the silent associates, and Ord touched him, a firm hand on the shoulder as a firm voice informed him, "You should try to convince me. And then, when it's my turn, I'll try to convince you."

Xo spoke, disgorging a hundred practiced speeches and as many impromptu pleadings. He sang about the great purpose of the Families. He roared knowledgeably about service and sacrifice, moral principles and immoral pitfalls. He gave cold technical estimates of Ord's position and the Earth's weaponry, showing his audience that the situation was hopeless. At this moment, two massive dark-matter bodies were being intercepted at the edge of the solar system. If either was Ord's missing talents, then he was quite plainly doomed. And after that roaring dismissal of the Chamberlain's powers and planning, Xo knitted together words of understanding and compassion, proving that even the hopeless could, when the time came, expect mercy.

Then, on a whim, Xo pulled live feeds from across the solar system.

A new mother on Pluto; a dozen winged humans perched on one of Saturn's cloud continents; an Amish community on Ceres; an ancient, revered poet sitting on his houseboat on Mars's northern sea. Each was visible, and each was obviously terrified. They were concentrating on the news feeds. They were praying, each in their own fashion. Praying that this visitor—this mutilated and possibly sick Chamberlain—wouldn't make a tragic blunder, obliterating all of them.

The final view was from a surveillance AI. A refugee family, recently arrived on the Earth, sat holding hands, their tails tied into a communal knot. The father and mother were more depressed than ever, obviously waiting to die, while their young son kept smiling, a sharp stupid voice chattering on and on about the astonishing coincidence . . .

that they were just inside the mansion, and wasn't it amazing . . . they just missed the arrival of that crazy Chamberlain . . . !

Crazy or not, Ord was moved.

He was weakened.

With empathic talents proven in the lab and in field tests, Xo could sense the opponent's resolve beginning to falter, if only a little—

Then they were outside again, standing in the same positions. Barely a moment had passed. Ravleen didn't seem to realize that they had been gone.

"Fair warning!" she wailed. "I'm going to butcher you and fuck every one of your body parts, you fucking shit!"

Ord stared at her.

Out of curiosity, or perhaps some misguided compassion, he opened his right hand and offered it to Ravleen.

She grabbed the hand and shoved it into her mouth and neatly bit off two fingers, the sharp crunch of the bones lingering. Then she spat the living fingers to the ground and stomped on them, cursing without breath or the smallest pause.

Some while later, replaying those events for his siblings, Xo defended Ravleen. The criminal wasn't going to surrender. He felt sure. And Ravleen was just being herself, which probably did some little good, helping to remind Ord about the dangers lurking around him.

If there was blame to shoulder, Xo argued, it was his. He had spent his life preparing, and the magic hadn't worked, and he seriously doubted he would have another chance to speak with his nemesis.

The elder Nuyen touched him lightly, fondly.

A cool feminine voice flowed over him, saying, "When Ravleen was done with her tantrum, what did Ord say?"

" 'I'm here to talk to Alice,' " Xo replied, mimicking the voice and the pale boyish face. " 'Bring her here and let me see her, in private. Then I'll leave again. I won't hurt anyone, and I promise, I won't take her with me.' "

The Nuyens fell silent, contemplating those utterly simple words.

Allowing himself a dose of self-pity, Xo whispered, "I failed my Family. And my species. I'm sorry that I have let you down."

"But you didn't," the ancient woman replied. Not to comfort, just to inform. "Honestly, we never expected your success."

No?

Then she touched him again, saying, "One more time, please. Tell us about the people with him . . . the ones inside the penthouse . . ."

Nine

"Measure the soul exactly, and it becomes yours."
—Nuyen saying

ALICE DELIVERED THE offer.

Alone in her cell, sitting on the foot of her narrow bed, she read a string of words projected on the normally white wall. "This message is intended for my brother's companions," she said, her voice steady and colorless. "We are offering a complete amnesty to you. Leave the Chamberlain mansion before dawn, renounce your allegiance to Ord, and every crime will be forgiven. Your past will be forgotten. And we will grant you every freedom and responsibility deserved by the citizens of your mother world."

She paused, then read, "The notice is signed: 'The Earth's Council, Emergency Session.' "

Slowly, with a hint of pain, Alice grew puzzled. She glanced up at the omnipresent wall, her mouth open and the neat simple teeth looking white and wet inside the pink of her mouth. And then, she breathed. And after a long moment, she whispered, "Ord?"

Then, "Why did you come back? Why—?"

The feed evaporated into blackness.

The audience spoke, almost shouting, each voice claim-

ing that the image wasn't real, and the offer was a sham,
too. But Ord quieted them with a gesture, then admitted,
"That was Alice. And the offer is authentic." He had analyzed every communication and every careless word uttered
by ten thousand high-placed souls, and though he had
doubts, not one of the doubts had a backbone.

Seeing his resignation, the others began to adjust their
opinions, repeating the word, "Amnesty," with a mixture
of gentle horror and tentative hope.

Buteo was first to ask, "What happens at dawn?"

"They assault our position," Ord replied.

There was a long silence.

In their faces, particularly in their wide, thoughtful eyes,
he could see the others thoroughly replaying Xo's arguments. They were thinking hard about pride and about sacrifice. Ord had merely saved their lives, while their Families
and a bone-deep sense of duty had given them life in the
first place, and their endless sense of purpose. They said as
much with glances, with half sighs, and with a persistent,
embarrassed quiet that was finally shattered when Ord
smiled wistfully, reminding them, "You're not prisoners. If
you wish, leave. That's absolutely what I expect from you."

Through the night, one by one, people made their apologies before slipping outside, floating into the grasp of the
Nuyens.

By sunrise, only Buteo and Avram remained.

Ord didn't ask for reasons, but both offered them.

"Nuyens are winning too much, and too easily," was the
Papago's excuse, offering a flirtatious little smile.

Avram shrugged his shoulders, asking, "What can I do?
Brothers have to help each other. Isn't that a law of the
universe?"

Then he smiled, and when Ord smiled back at him, he
added, "Eons of habit. They won't vanish in one dangerous
little night."

FOR A THOUSAND centuries, the short-faced bears had
roamed wild on the estate. People were occasional visitors

who amounted to nothing. With their modest, pragmatic intelligence, the bears had come to a very reasonable conclusion: The mountains and rivers and shaggy wild forests belonged to them. The game animals were theirs to hunt and eat. The sun rose to feed their forests, and it set again to let the air cool. After hundreds of generations, the bears had built a rich oral history in which they were the center of the universe and the lords of all that was important. Before every dawn, they sang. They sang for the sun to climb high, and when the mountains were dry, they sang for rain. And since the sun always rose and no drought lasted long, it was easy to believe that their words and simple rhythms were responsible for all that was good in Creation.

Yet they weren't fools. They knew something was going horribly wrong. The hot night air crackled with strange energies, and phantoms drifted through their bodies, never offering explanations or apologies. The disruptions only grew worse at daybreak. The sunrise songs were interrupted twice by sharp, inexplicable sounds that came from all directions, the granite beneath them shivering from fear. Under the cover of darkness, the enchanted moon had fallen close, and now it nearly filled the cloudless blue sky. Then a spirit army began its charge up through the mountain, rising toward the summit and the holy mansion.

The old bitch priestess sensed the army's bloody purpose, and more than that, she saw that the bears' world was about to change.

Quietly, she offered thanks to the mountain and the sun— every priestess made the same morning prayers—then she stumbled over her own tongue, trying to find the proper words for the inevitable.

"Tonight," she whispered, "we will sleep with the Creator."

The great beasts before her arched their backs, and with a useful bluster, one young male shouted, "I won't die, and I'm not scared!"

"But you will, and you are," said another voice.

The pack turned. Behind them stood a red-haired human boy. They had never seen a Chamberlain, but some deeply ingrained reflex was triggered. They relaxed, and the boy scratched each behind its ears, knowing exactly what each bear liked best. And he smiled at them, talking in their language, explaining, "If you come with me, I'll keep you safe. At least for a moment or two."

The young male shook his massive head, spat at the sky, and declared, "We don't need your help!"

But the priestess had other ideas. As the rock beneath them rippled, she grunted her compliance, and the Chamberlain touched them in a different way . . . and an instant later, the forest dissolved into plasmas, and the ancient mountains turned to magma and ash and a scalding white pillar of filthy light . . .

THE BARRAGE OF shaped plasmas lasted four seconds.

In its wake, the mansion was left scorched but intact, held together by Ord's own hands. And with the mountain collapsed into a cherry red lake, its deepest foundations lay exposed, making the structure taller and considerably broader, its blackened exterior more imposing than ever.

The army attacked with a wild fury, accomplishing nothing. Wild fire and mindless bravery accounted for most of the casualties. But a tiny unit masquerading as the butt end of a kinetic charge managed to slip through Ord's defenses. Then, with a Nuyen general at the lead, the invaders swam at near light-speed, following fissures and a forgotten conduit, then materializing inside the central staircase not ten meters below the penthouse.

The murals were gone, replaced with an infinite blackness and a powerful, unnerving cold.

Extinction, perfectly rendered.

The Nuyen attacked the crystal door, then leaped back as it dissolved, becoming a pocket of stale air with Ord standing at its center. The boy's face was miserable, his eyes pale and tired, and with a voice that matched the face, he said, "I want to talk to Alice. Just that. Then I'll repair the damage, and I'll leave. I promise you."

The Nuyen shook what passed for a head, then drifted aside.

Ravleen stood waiting, grinning in a cheerless, expectant fashion. A few of her hands had been freed for the occasion. She reached with them, engulfing her enemy, ripping away his talents and senses and his strange dark-matter meats, aiming for what lay at the center.

Ord winced and shut his eyes.

With eyes shut, he saw himself standing on a long green lawn, wearing nothing but a boy's half-grown and very naked body. The grass was short and soft and overly perfumed, and the mansion was white again, rooted into the old mountaintop. A pack of tame bears was lying nearby, drinking in the blue skies and sun. Ord stood still just long enough to believe in this place. Then a hand grabbed his shoulder and spun him, and a second hand—hard as basalt—drove itself into his astonished face.

Ord lay on his back, his face bloodied.

The Sanchex towered over him, naked and unexpectedly alluring. With a practiced, almost surgical precision, she placed a long bare foot to his neck, then pressed hard enough to make the mountain's bones groan beneath them.

On another day, Ord would have already lost the fight. Ravleen would have given him a thorough, expert beating, and he would have endured it, knowing that she could never inflict any permanent harm. But this Ord grabbed an ankle and yanked her off her feet. Then he jumped up and set his foot against her neck, letting her curse and lash at him, her rage causing her to bite through her own tongue and spit it at him.

The air gave a supersonic *crack* as the tongue passed.

New hands were unmanacled. But instead of throwing Ord off, Ravleen grabbed him and pulled him close, an irresistible strength leaving him lying on top of her, chest to chest, his left ear pressed against the tongueless mouth.

This wasn't Ravleen. This was a monster, a scorching rage with a shred of an embittered, poisoned intellect that served only to steer the rage.

"More talents," she begged with other mouths. "Let me kill, please. Please, let me kill!"

"No," said a Nuyen's calculating voice. "Just hold him now."

Xo appeared suddenly, kneeling on the sweet grass, and with a genuine pain told Ord, "You know, you really can't win this thing."

A portion of Ord wanted to believe him. Defeat meant peace and a kind of freedom, all of his massive responsibilities taken from him.

"You're simply too weak," Xo informed him.

Ord said nothing.

The Nuyen's talents were at work. Oily and cold, they slipped inside him and spoke with a pure confidence, telling his soul, "If you surrender, at this moment, nobody else needs to die. Including you."

"Shut up!" Ravleen screamed. She lay beneath Ord as if he were her lover, and her face colored and twisted, a new tongue curling and the ebony eyes throwing fire at Xo. "Give me another fucking hand, and shut up!"

For an instant, her grip was stronger.

Slightly.

When it weakened again, Ord barely noticed.

The bears had made a circle around the fighters. Then one of the beasts became Avram, and he grabbed Xo, pulling him away. Another was Buteo, and she calmly and expertly took hold of the Sanchex monster, peeling back hands until Ord could find his feet again. Then the other bears—much modified in the last few moments—put their cavernous mouths around various body parts, and waited. And the humans studied Ord, waiting for whatever he might say or do next.

The crystal moon filled the sky, and the mountain had turned to magma again. They stood on the soft flowing rock, and there came a rumbling thunder, and Xo said, "The moon is a weapon," and then, "But of course you know it is," and then, "But of course you don't know how irresistibly powerful it is . . ."

Ord smiled as if embarrassed. He hid his genitals with his hands, and quietly, in a near whisper, he told Xo, "You were right. I wasn't strong enough to win."

No one spoke.

"But I am now," he admitted.

The Nuyen's face lost its color, its life. "You can't be," he sputtered. "The defense grid is on full alert. Talent requires mass, and nothing is moving toward the Earth—"

He hesitated, and winced.

Quietly, Xo said, "Shit."

Ravleen chewed off her new tongue and spat it at her captors.

Wide-eyed, Xo gazed up at the sky. "You've always been here," he whispered. "That refugee boy . . . he was the last of you, not the first."

Ord gave a distracted nod.

The moon's framework was dissolving away, its mysterious guts obeying the gentle tug of gravity, pouring free like some great, invisible river.

Xo screamed and tried to pull his arms free, and the bears snipped them off at the shoulders, leaving them flexing and twitching in a neat pile, hands instinctively clinging to one another.

Then Ord pulled open a ten-kilometer mouth, looking skyward, finally slaking his fantastic thirst.

Ten

"It wasn't meant to be a weapon so much as a precise and relentless tool that should have allowed us to engulf and destroy talents en masse.

"Nothing like it has ever been produced—certainly not within our galaxy—and as we will continue to point out, loudly and endlessly, the device was designed and built by every good Family as well as a host of civilian agencies. Costs were

*shared, and responsibilities were shared, and there
were some inevitable failures in security. Vast under-
takings, by their nature, are porous. The final assem-
bly took a thousand years in deep interstellar space—
a requirement born of temperature and microgravity
constraints—and our best guess is that there, in the
blackest cold of space, was where the Chamberlain
took control of the project. He gutted our good work
and successfully hid his own body parts inside the
dense, heavily masked crust. Once our work was finished, we were unable to peer inside. Until activated, there was no way of knowing what we had
delivered to the unsuspecting Earth. Naturally,
voices now can question our good sense, but the
public must consider this: If we could have seen inside the crust, so could have the Chamberlain. And
if the Chamberlain had seen the tool, then he might
have found the means to turn it against us . . .*

*"He made fools of us, but we cannot admit that
publicly . . .*

*"We made fools of ourselves, bringing that mon-
ster home with as much pageantry as security allowed . . . each of us boasting to the mother world,
'This is for you. We have done this wonderful thing
for you . . . !' "*

—*Nuyen memo, confidential*

FOR XO, THERE was no compelling sense of failure. Self-
pity didn't tug at him, and in a strangely soothing fashion,
there wasn't so much as a breath of remorse. The truth was
clear-cut: No combination of skill and luck could have
beaten Ord. This situation was born hopeless, and he was
blameless. Free of his obligations, Xo felt as if he could
halfway relax. Within himself, in secret corners, he smiled.
Then he began working to adapt to his new circumstances—
as a prisoner, as a hostage—watching events but knowing
that he had no role but to witness these momentous, inevitable deeds.

With a soft, almost prissy voice, Ord announced, "Now, finally, I'm going to visit my sister."

The words saturated every channel, public and Family, then trailed off into a screaming white hiss that frustrated every other attempt to speak.

"Good!" the Papago woman declared. "It's about time!"

Ord clothed himself in gray trousers and a bulky gray shirt. He left his body young and his chin injured, the illusory bone shattered and the facsimile of blood building an ugly black scab.

Avram was holding Xo. He had a relentless grip and a nervous, loud voice. "What do you want from me?"

"Stay with Buteo," Ord replied. "I'll be gone a moment. Help her hold the Sanchex down."

Ravleen was too dangerous to be left with just one of them. Xo would have warned them, if anyone bothered to ask.

"What about this one?" Avram asked, giving Xo a hard shake. "He scares me worse, in some ways."

Ord's eyes were distant. Unreadable.

Eventually he said, "The Nuyen stays with me."

Xo found himself freed, sporting two functioning arms again.

"You're my witness," Ord promised. "Watch everything. Then you can tell your siblings that I meant it. I came here to talk to Alice, just once, and everything else was their fault. No one else's."

THE LAST FEW steps were exactly that. Steps.

The two of them had already passed through plastic rock and collapsing defenses, a temporarily blind and utterly lost army left scattered above them. Xo found himself standing inside an infinitely long hallway lined with countless white doors, each door identical to its neighbors, each armored and mined. It was a powerful escher. He took two steps, then looked over his shoulder. Ord was standing before a particular door. His face seemed empty, his bare feet frozen to the slick white floor. Reaching for the coded pad, he slowly transformed his hand, making it match the jailer's fingers and palm. A mass of long and silky fingers started to reach out. And then, the hand pulled up short.

"Is she there?" Xo asked.

"Yes."

Ord spoke in a whisper, fearful and abrupt.

"Are you scared?" Xo heard himself ask.

"Terrified," the Chamberlain confessed.

"Don't be," Xo advised. Then he had to laugh, explaining, "Alice has been locked away so long, and treated so badly by so many people ... honestly, I doubt if she remembers much more than her own name."

Ord nodded, and he touched the pad, allowing it to dissolve the tips of each perfectly rendered finger.

With a quiet hiss, the door unsealed itself and fell open.

Alice was in the middle of her tiny cell, walking away from them: Step, and step, then in front of the tiny white toilet, she made a smooth turn. For a slippery instant, she seemed oblivious to her guests. Soft blue eyes stared through the two of them, and she took a first step toward her bed, pausing gradually in midstride, ignoring her brother but staring hard at the Nuyen.

She was exceptionally pretty. That's what took Xo by surprise.

Ageless and rested, Alice looked as clean as her surroundings. She wore a simple prison gown, and her long hair was braided into little red ropes that she had artfully tied together and draped over a half-bare, milky shoulder. She didn't look half so lovely on the real-time feeds. The feeds must be doctored. Xo realized that her jailers wanted audiences to see an unkempt prisoner, suffering and disreputable. They didn't want a simple, contented creature. They certainly didn't want someone who would smile with an easy charm, and bow deeply, proclaiming, "I am glad to see you, master. As always."

She took Xo's hand, kissing his knuckles one after other.

Xo pulled back, in disgust.

Her brother said, "He's not here to torture you, Alice."

The beautiful face grinned, turning toward the voice. "Because he has already abused you, by the looks of it."

Ord's face was still oozing, the blood mixed with more elusive fluids.

Alice turned back to the Nuyen. "Is he really the baby? Or has this been one of your little tricks?"

"It's him," Xo maintained.

She preferred doubt.

Ord took her hand, placing it against his chin. Fingers vanished into the gore, and Alice flinched, gave a low moan, and flinched again. Inside her flesh, hiding for eons, were an assortment of tiny locks built from a novel species of false proton. Xo stared with his best eyes, watching lock after lock fail to work. But two or three succeeded in their task, and some infinitesimal memory from a hundred thousand years ago was dislodged, telling her simply, "This is Ord."

She yanked her hand free and wiped it clean against her white gown.

"It is," she conceded. Her voice was excited and suspicious, and beneath everything, it was angry. "How terribly lovely! You've taken an incalculable risk, Baby . . . just so you could accomplish . . . what . . . ?"

"I want help," Ord whispered, grabbing her by the shoulder, then with the jailer's hand, covering her smooth pale forehead. "The Core's obliterated. The rest of the galaxy is in shambles. My intuitions—your old instincts—tell me total war is likely. I've tried to defend the Peace. Just as you told me to, I've tried. But I'm alone, Alice. It's just me. And things are worse than you could have guessed—"

"Help you?" she interrupted. "Help you how?"

"I can't even guess," Ord confessed. "I've searched every memory that you gave me, and something's missing. Something you kept for yourself, I think."

Alice laughed lightly, almost flippantly. In some sense, she was the baby now. Her long incarceration had left her stupid and unworldly, and in an unexpected way, she was blessed with a perfect innocence. She seemed at a loss about what to tell her brother, but she worked to dredge up answers. Ancient memories began to emerge, but without coordination, without grace. There was nonsense about her childhood and early education, and for a few moments, she rambled on about the Core. She said, "Show me. How it was," and she gazed at the image that Ord gave her. The white walls and ceiling and floor vanished, and the toilet and bed. The three of them were standing in the midst of endless stars. "So many," she sang. "I wish you could have seen it, Ord—!"

"Why me?" he blurted, plainly angry.

Alice flinched, wounded. "Because you must have fit the duty, I would imagine."

"How can I do this duty?"

A soft, little-girl laugh fell into the word, "Think."

Ord looked frustrated, incapable of real thought.

"Think," she repeated. "Why is the galaxy in turmoil? Because intelligent species cannot find homes enough or enough peace. But that's the curse of a universe where life is common. Creation always grows and grows crowded."

"I know," said her brother.

She looked at Xo for a moment, her smile turning poisonous. And he gazed past her smile, watching as a small knot of memory swam out of a hidden place. This precise image of the Core had been the key; of all possible views, purely out of reflex, Ord had shown her this exact pattern of lost suns. He didn't appreciate the trick, even now. Xo saw his confusion, and he nearly spoke. But Alice had turned back to her brother again, that secret memory unknotting itself as she said to him, "You need help I can't give. You need opportunity I don't possess."

"Where do I find them?" Ord asked.

"Remind me," she said. "How did I attempt to save our little universe?"

Xo answered, half-shouting, "You built a new Creation—"

"And it was beautiful. Spectacular and glorious!" She

wouldn't look at the Nuyen again. With eyes focused on her brother, Alice said, "Think," twice. "Think. We had the umbilical pried open long enough for it to grow unstable, and that's when the new universe rushed out into our cold realm—!"

A low, rough sound leaked from Ord.

"What?" Xo muttered. "What's she telling you?"

Ord shook his head. "That's what happened. One of you . . . someone from the Families . . . someone had enough time to cross, make their way into that new universe. That's what happened, isn't it?"

Alice didn't answer him directly. But grinning with an incandescent pride, she asked, "Do you know how difficult it has been, keeping hold of that delicious secret?"

Xo shuddered.

Ord touched his chin, playing with the half-dried blood between his fingertips. Finally, summoning the courage, he asked, "Who crossed over? And why does it matter—?"

With a whisper, Alice said, "Closer."

Her brother obeyed. He was a little taller than her, so he dipped his head until his ear rested against her pretty mouth, and Alice kissed the ear, running her bright pink tongue over the embarrassed lobe, speaking to Ord for a moment or two with a secret chemical voice absorbed along with his spit.

Ord raised his head again, his face pale, and simple, and stunned.

He was reacting to whatever Alice had told him. That was Xo's first guess, and perhaps he was right. Perhaps. But then the prison cell shook and shuddered, and the air grew instantly warmer, and a look of absolute horror came over the boy. The image of the Core had vanished. Ord stared up at the white ceiling, lifting his arms, screaming, "No!"

And he was gone.

Alice seemed oblivious to any problem. Yet when she looked at Xo, she wore a strange smile. Pulling his head down, she kissed him on the mouth. She had no odor. No flavor. She was as pure as medical technology could ensure, her saliva like water from a mountain brook, her tongue feeling wondrous as it played inside his dirty mouth.

"I won't have the pleasure of your company again, I think."

She was speaking to all the Nuyens.

Then, as Ord reached deep into the world to reclaim Xo, she winked at him, and said mildly, "Oh, Mr. Nuyen. What do you believe is the best way for a young lady to win her revenge?"

Eleven

"It is best when you can keep yourself innocent, in every eye but your own. Innocent, yet at the same glorious moment, you are hiding in your enemy's shadow, watching him work inside his own kitchen, preparing a vat of sweet poisons intended for you . . . and the luscious scent is simply too much . . . and driven mad, he risks a little taste, then another, and before he can escape, he's consumed every fatal morsel for himself . . ."

—*a Nuyen proverb*

ORD ROARED UP through the mantle, up into the mansion, leaving one tiny room for another. Then he wove himself a child's body, and shouting with a multitude of voices, he said, "Keep. Your. Hand. There!"

Avram flinched, but his broad pink palm remained flush against the yellowed mudstone. He wore a distant, almost embarrassed expression. In the eyes, he was ashamed. For an instant, Ord could almost believe that his brother had done nothing provocative: He must have wandered into this room out of simple curiosity, and curiosity forced him to place his hand into the ancient imprint of Alice's hand. This was an accident. This was an enormous, forgivable miscue.

Ord was desperate to say, "You didn't know. This is my fault, not yours . . . !"

But he had no chance to beg for the blame.

Avram was staring at his brother. "Surrender," he growled.

The single word came out under pressure, wrapped in a white misery. Then sliding out after it was the softer, almost mournful:

"Please."

When the trigger embedded in the stone was tripped, Ord had neatly strangled the explosion beneath Alice's cell. But in the next nanoseconds, with a wild astonishment, he watched as a second trigger emerged. It had a design that he had never anticipated, made from slippery shadow-matter materials that he still couldn't comprehend. Waiting half-evolved until it felt the pressure and gravity of a Chamberlain hand, it had completed itself in an instant, its intricate workings obvious. Blatant. Mirroring the first booby trap, this trigger was linked to globules of molten anti-iron suspended inside magnetic jars. But the waiting bombs didn't come by the handful. Ord watched as each jar shrugged off its elaborate camouflage, and he counted what he saw, and it seemed as if there were no end to the monsters, tens of millions of them scattered through the Earth's upper mantle, waiting patiently for the opportunity to be set loose.

Again, with a grim resolve, Avram said, "Surrender."

He didn't add, "Please," this time.

The booby trap would injure Ord. But still, it would take milliseconds for a detonation signal to cross the world, and that was time enough to retreat and brace himself, the rippling inferno leaving him a little scorched but otherwise intact.

Yet Ord wasn't the target, was he?

Avram stared at him, the expression on that Chamberlain face changing now. A nest of memes emerged from their hiding places. An easy disgust made him flinch and shake his head slightly. For the last time, he said, "Surrender."

Then he paused, filling that moment with a deep, useless breath. And then, because he thought it would help, he smiled, struggling for a hopeful expression, asking his little brother, "Really, Ord . . . what choice do you have . . . ?"

THE TINY BEDROOM was suffocating. Even as portions of Ord spun out estimates of casualties and economic loss and cultural loss and political disarray, the rest of him—the center of his soul—felt trapped, helpless and worse than half-dead.

With a quiet, mournful voice, he muttered, "Brother," and began to cry.

A woman's voice asked, "What's happening here?"

Buteo had arrived. Ravleen was still wrapped up in her strong arms, still twisting in her grip. Materializing in the hallway, the Papago stared through the transparent wall, understanding nothing when she added the second question:

"What's wrong with you, Chamberlain?"

Ord explained on a private channel, in an instant.

Buteo's eyes became enormous, and vacant, and she squeezed Ravleen as if trying to crush her.

With his own arms, Ord helped restrain the Sanchex.

"A perimeter check," she muttered. "Avram said you wanted him to . . ."

Reaching deep underground, Ord reclaimed Xo. Then, ignoring his brother, he directed his rage at the convenient Nuyen. "What were you thinking? The Earth's on a precipice . . . just to catch me . . . what were you assholes thinking—?"

"I don't understand," Xo replied. Then he saw enough for himself, with his own senses, and he began to shake his head numbly and yank at his black hair, screaming, "I didn't know! I didn't!"

Avram flexed his right wrist.

Ord reached for him, then hesitated. The trigger was clever in the worst ways, and it was proud of its cleverness. "Touch your brother," it warned, "and I'll detonate. Weave a new hand to replace it, and I will see it and detonate. And if you touch me, in any fashion, I will most assuredly detonate." Then with a dense roar of data and plans, it said, "These are my specifications, and my redundant systems, and the complete tallies from every field test. Look at them. Look at me! You've never seen anything like me, and you cannot beat me on your first try."

Ord winced, staring straight into Avram's eyes.

"You were waiting for me," he remarked. "On the night of your execution . . . you knew I'd come and save you."

The pink hand moved inside the fossil print, just slightly.

Then Avram offered a tiny nod, saying, "Honestly? I'd given up on you. The Nuyens came long ago and made their offer. If I found my chance, I was supposed to take it. Then they made me forget their visit. Until just a few moments ago, I'd forgotten everything. And nobody explained what this trick was, although I could guess. I can remember one of them saying, 'He's not evil, this brother of yours. But he's horribly misguided. And when the circumstance arises, we promise, Ord will make the sane, decent choice.' "

"If I hadn't come for you?" Ord inquired.

"I'd be dead. Of course. If my execution was theater, you would never have trusted me." He sighed, then confessed, "I expected to die. That night you saved me, and right up until now. Because there's too many of them, and they're too clever, even for Alice's talents . . . until I set my hand in Alice's hand, here, I always felt nothing but doom . . . !"

Ord closed his corporeal eyes, his fatigue enormous and genuine.

When he opened them, Avram was beginning to say, "Surrender," once more.

"That is what I am doing," Ord interrupted. "Now, and as fast as I can."

With a wild chorus of commands, he began dragging his talents into a deep sleep. By the dozens, by the hundreds, he dismantled himself. His camouflage fell away first, allowing the world to watch him. Then he put down his weapons and every talent with deadly applications. After thirty seconds of relentless labor, he had almost dismantled himself. Another few moments would have left him astonishingly ordinary. But then his surviving eyes saw something odd, and he started to turn toward the oddity while Ravleen screamed, "No!"

Too late, Ord understood.

The Sanchex was wrestling with Buteo, distracting her with her strongest limbs, while a weak little tendril composed of the thinnest materials reached through the diamond wall and across the tiny bedroom. Ravleen utterly ignored Ord; with that feeble limb, she couldn't have harmed him if she tried. What she grabbed instead was Avram's sturdy wrist, and with all of the limb's strength, she gave him a hard swift calculated jerk, barely lifting the hand from the cool mudstone, but still moving it with enough force and distance to cause the trigger to say, "Boom."

In a panic, Avram pressed his palm back against Alice's fossil palm. Then, even as the world began to tear apart, and as the great gods screamed in rage and in grief, he kept his hand exactly where it belonged. And while the ancient mansion evaporated around him, he used all of his hands to help hold himself perfectly steady . . . telling himself that this wasn't what it seemed to be . . . assuring himself that he mattered, and he was noble, and what he was doing, as always, was something that was exceptionally good . . .

Twelve

"Blame for this horrendous tragedy rests squarely upon the Chamberlain and his violent, immoral allies . . . including, we fear, a renegade Sanchex . . . !"
—a Nuyen announcement

IN LIEU OF their traditional public celebration, the new year was marked by a subdued, largely private gathering of the Families. The ancient estates had been obliterated, and the Earth was a bright white world encased in steam and oceans of irradiated magma. The gods met on Mars in what was a prolonged, decidedly sober affair. Cheerless voices lamented the latest cataclysm. Voices free of doubt neatly deflected talk of blame and shortsightedness. Proud voices described acts of personal heroism, while careful quiet voices discussed the unfolding plans for future estates: The Nuyens had graciously donated one of their intersolar worlds. Over the next several thousand years, that cold body would be eased into the Kuiper belt, then terraformed, and each Family would receive its share of new land and water, sculpting fresh mountains and erecting new mansions that would surely stand for the next ten billion years.

It was a good, sensible change. Many argued that this was more than sensible, it was inevitable. Here was a new beginning for a new peace, some sturdy voices claimed. While other, more pragmatic souls admitted that having normal citizens live beside the Families had always been an unreasonable risk and an encumbrance. If Ord had visited their future home instead of the Earth, nobody would have died. Except for that little bastard himself, naturally. Without fragile souls underfoot, the Families could have responded appropriately. Instantly. And they could have guarded Alice all the better, too.

Did the Bitch-of-bitches die along with the Earth?

Hopefully, was the unanimous verdict.

The Families had saved billions of ordinary people. During those horrible moments after the Chamberlain had used his unthinkable weapon, Nuyens had died, each one now bestowed with an eternal martyrdom. There were moments when Xo, reflecting on events, wished that his siblings hadn't helped him escape. Thousands of tiny souls could have been saved in his place, surely. But his altruism was reflexive, and it was tissue-thin. Besides, if he had died, he would be another one of the beloved martyrs—a role that disgusted him for more reasons, and more emotions, than he seemed able to count.

In the midst of the dour festivities, an ancient sister approached him. She insisted on smiling. She very nearly laughed, telling Xo, "I know you did your best for us. For all humanity. As far as I'm concerned, you should be the first Nuyen to talk about your successes."

Because it was expected, he said, "Thank you."

Hundreds of billions were dead, and their ancestral home was a ravaged wasteland, and he was expected to be polite, accepting this graceless, preposterous praise.

"I just heard," the sister continued. "Did you? A dark-matter body matching the Chamberlain's configuration has raced past one of our Oort stations."

"Which station?"

She told him, then added, "It's obvious. From the trajectory and his speed, Ord is making a run for the Core now."

"Because of what his sister told him," Xo replied.

The sister watched him, saying nothing in a certain way.

Xo prompted her. "Don't you believe Alice?"

"Believe what? That someone managed to crawl their way from this universe into the other? Perhaps I do, perhaps I don't. In most circumstances, perhaps is the only belief worth holding." Again, she nearly laughed. "Whatever happens to be the truth, little brother . . . our plans are thorough, and they are durable, and there is room enough for every reasonable possibility."

"Nuyens are thorough people," Xo mentioned.

She rose to the bait, saying, "Absolutely," with a prideful wide smile.

"What about Ravleen?" He posed the question with a careful voice, then added, "That same Oort station might have noticed her, too."

"Perhaps it did," the sister allowed. "Twenty minutes later, perhaps."

Ravleen had used the chaos to make her escape. She would still be wearing manacles, but not all of them, and they would present only temporary constraints. And nobody, not even a fool, could doubt what she was seeking.

Xo's doubts lay closer in space. With the help of simple charm, he mentioned, "Twenty minutes at light-speed is a considerable gap." He winked, then added, "It's a shame, really. A waste and a shame that Ravleen couldn't have started her chase sooner."

The sister nodded, smiling in a distracted fashion.

Using his most powerful talents, Xo reached inside her mind, coaxing out the secrets hiding in the bloody corners.

The smile vanished abruptly.

Slowly, she set a powerful hand to his shoulder. "What do you think you know, brother?"

"With her talents, it should have taken Ravleen barely two moments to start her chase. Not twenty damned minutes." He didn't care about punishments or sanctions. "But what if she was disabled first? What if we used the implants inside her mind, then captured and interrogated her . . . ?"

The woman couldn't imagine that she was not in perfect control. She believed it was her own iron will that told her to admit, "I was at the interrogation. Three minutes, and it was done. Then we spoke for another fifteen minutes, debating our next move. Releasing the Sanchex was the only rational course. Evil in pursuit of evil is the perfect solution, and I haven't regretted it for a greasy moment, little brother."

"Who murdered the Earth?" he asked.

Calmly, with a dry, simple voice, she told him, "The Chamberlain, of course. The one who stupidly blundered into our trap—"

"And Ravleen," he offered.

She winced, and said, "Fuck! It's a force of nature, that creature is. That monster. She has no will. She has no sense. Her only genius is her ability to torture that one fucking Chamberlain." This time, the laugh was hard and genuine. "You know, I think that's why she did it. Tripped the trigger, I mean. Because she knows Ord exactly, and she knows that the dead Earth will haunt him forever."

Quietly, Xo echoed the word, "Torture."

Then with an insistent voice, he asked, "How did Ravleen find that extra arm? Where did it come from?"

"Our only guess? That sometime during her field trials, while we were watching everything else, Ravleen used her own weapons to mutilate one of her own hands. She cut the hand in two and hid the weaker half. For eons, probably. Which proves how incredibly eager she is to do this important work."

Xo said nothing.

Again, she said, "Important work."

Then, finally, she felt the eyes peering inside her soul. She blinked and physically moved away from the young Nuyen, and he twisted her emotions enough to confuse her again. "You did nothing," she said. Then said, "Wrong, I mean." And with a cold shiver, she advised him, "Don't confuse yourself by dwelling on these matters."

"I won't," Xo lied.

"Good," she whispered.

A little while later, using appropriate formality and the stiffest of smiles, Xo left the gathering and his Family, and moments after that, he abandoned Mars, too. With talents stolen from half a hundred Families, he slipped away into space, draining the inertia from his body and dipping down past the clean white face of the Earth, skimming next to its atmosphere on his journey out of the solar system.

It was as beautiful in death as it ever was in life, he realized.

And the Core was glorious, and hideous, and he steered straight for it, while wiping every flavor of tear from every sort of eye.

BOOK FOUR

BABY'S FIRE

One

"I can tell you the absolute, undeniable instant when I realized that I was a god . . .

"As the sole patient of a small Family-owned clinic, I was barely a thousand years old and still very much resembled a human being. A morning of enlarging surgeries became an afternoon where I was left conspicuously alone, free to adjust to my new self. The clinic was set on a recently terraformed pluto. That little world's crust had been melted with a star-drive sun. A deep and warm atmosphere rose up for hundreds of kilometers, and the newborn sea was dotted with floating islands of sculpted black plastic and comet-born soil. Inside my archaic body, I went for a lazy stroll. Since I wanted to someday terraform worlds, I took careful notice of the towering, half-grown jungle. It really was a shambles, that place. Lush, but ordinary. Colorful, but artless. Every species had been woven from existing species—variations thrown like saddles on top of clichés. I told myself that a million years of indifference might make this biosphere interesting, the elegance and chaos of natural selection capable of achieving wonders. But I promised myself that when I rebuilt entire worlds and wove life upon them, I would do things unique and spellbinding. That's what I was thinking as I bounced my way down to the sea.

"No, that isn't my moment of realization. That's just a cocky little girl, and some things are eternal . . ."

—Alice, in conversation

EVEN CAGED, THE Core was a gorgeous, soul-wrenching spectacle.

"Speed up, Baby! Faster—!"

Ord ignored the taunting voice. The majority of his eyes

and enormous ears reached ahead, absorbing the dust-blunted light and the wide booms and crackles of EM noise, measuring their blistering energies, scrupulously noting every variation, every flavor of change. Harsh flashes, quick to flicker and swell, betrayed massive black holes feeding happily on slow plasmas and shattered worlds. According to his count, a thousand such monsters lived inside the barricades. A slow white scream would sometimes leak through every obstruction, its roar peaking, then collapsing again at a predictable pace. Ord listened carefully, replaying the screams in his mind until he understood what he had heard and from where each had come. Bathed by gamma radiations, healthy suns were detonating at a devastating rate. Neutron suns were absorbing mass until they were fat, then they would supernova. But even exploding suns weren't bright enough to be seen. The cumulative light and heat, along with fierce energies spewed from the monster black holes, fueled this cataclysm now. Strange as it seemed, the baby universe had vanished. Ord felt certain now. Sifting the data, he couldn't find any telltale trace of the flawed umbilical. What had been extraordinary and exotic had finally degraded into an enormous but otherwise conventional, even prosaic, wildfire.

"Speed up," said the tireless voice. "Move your ass! Are you listening, Ord? If you can't run faster than this, I'll catch you. Do you hear me?"

He always heard, and he never responded.

What Ord did, constantly and desperately, was think: He contemplated everything that he had heard and seen. He digested Alice's memories, looking for fresh clues about her dense, secretive plans. And he gazed obsessively at the physics that had started all of this. Yet even with his overly augmented mind, the equations were unreal—open-ended, exotic abstractions, comprehensible only as symbols drawn on the blackest screen imaginable. Even if he had tools and the opportunity, Ord couldn't have duplicated the work by himself. Even if he had possessed most of Alice's schematics, what was missing was essential. He could never

succeed on his first attempt, and probably not in the next
million tries, either. And that incompetence was a comfort,
and a blessing. Knowing he couldn't accomplish such wonders, Ord didn't feel the thinnest temptation to try.

Was that why Alice hadn't given him the essential
knowledge? To keep him innocent, and safe?

Or was it simply to frustrate their enemies? If Ord was
captured, and if they tore into her memories . . . well, she
wouldn't want their enemies knowing how to build everything from nothing . . . again . . .

Relentlessly, feverishly, the boy contemplated everything
of clear importance. A hundred thousand years after Alice
had returned home, Ord was making the same journey, in
reverse. The ironies were easy to see. Like Alice, he was
moving within a whisper of light-speed. But where she
brought little with her, allowing her massive talents to follow at a slightly lazier pace, Ord had consumed enormous
energies, accelerating his entire body as well as his soul.
In reverse, he watched the same suns that she had
watched—red-shifted and blue-shifted by his own enormous velocity. He studied the living worlds that passed by
and counted the long, dead stretches. A hundred thousand
years ago, their little galaxy had been growing crowded
with people and other sentients; that was one ready excuse
to build new universes. Yet now the sky was peppered with
empty, war-ravaged bodies of iron and ice, and for the next
ten million years, and perhaps longer, there would again be
ample room for expansion.

"See?" said a quieter, closer voice. "Our plan worked.
We created a universe with endless room!"

Ord ignored that voice, too.

Concentrate, he told himself. *Now*.

His inheritance included an enormous mind, powerful
and swift. But there was too much data to digest and too
many possibilities growing from that data, most of which
needed to be conspicuously ignored. Worse still, time was
short. At this fantastic velocity, the universe was a rapidly
changing, brazenly unstable maelstrom. Ord would spy

some sweet blue world up ahead, and, in the proverbial blink, something would go wrong. A war would erupt. A god would fight some pursuing god. Or the simple weight of too many refugees would cause its biosphere to collapse, and the blue world would turn milky white as its oceans boiled.

With every glance, millions died.

Every tiny tick of time meant another century had passed, and the Great Peace remained in shambles.

Ord watched everything, and he cried endlessly. Sometimes he forced himself to gaze back into the constricted, red-shifted past, staring at the dead Earth until even his finest eyes couldn't see anything but the faint glare of Sol. He listened to transmissions coming from the new Council on Mars, absorbing news already ancient; and with less success, he intercepted coded signals from the Nuyens, feeding them into three separate talents of Alice's, each talent using a different configuration of quantum computers to make a trillion trillion calculations in the smallest gasp of time . . . and declaring, with certainty, that the codes were unbroken and would remain so for the next hundred billion years.

But absorbing those transmissions meant they would be a little weaker when they reached their destinations.

And into that weakness, Ord could insert his own signal, masking it to look official, then stuffing it with a variety of eschers that would bruise the AIs that received them, and better still, piss off the various Nuyens . . .

"You're pissing me off!" Ravleen shouted. "Hey, little Ord. You can't outrun me, and you can't beat me, and I'm not going to fail. So why not act smart and surrender?"

The voice was behind him, and not far behind. Built from dark matter and the darkest energies, Ravleen was near enough that he sometimes felt the hot touch of what passed for fingers, claws reaching out to tickle what passed for Ord's own toes.

"Run faster," she would say, a million times every second, her voice possessed by a narrow, unalloyed fury. Ravleen could never stop chasing him. Until he had died in some horrible fashion, or she had died, she would keep after him. Or the universe would expand and grow chilled around them, and after a trillion years it, and they, would quietly pass away.

"Say something, coward! Anything!"

Since escaping from the Earth, Ord had not once responded to her insults, or the wild threats, or even those moments when Ravleen managed to bruise his conscience. His pain and endless shame were far worse than anything she could inflict. Yet Ord was able to function, shoving his miseries aside, endlessly reminding himself that nothing mattered but that he somehow found his way through the dusty barricades, reached the burning Core, where he would then—

No, don't think it.

Don't even bring it to mind, ever.

"I promise, little Ord. Let me grab you. I'll kill you quickly. Neatly, and forever. If you'd just let me—"

Ord contemplated everything else that mattered.

"I know where you're going!" Ravleen roared, using a million channels and enough energy to sear unprotected ears.

Then, for emphasis, she spat at him, a blob of coherent X rays slashing into his weakest systems.

Ord absorbed the energies, healed most of his injuries, and what couldn't be healed was mercifully shut down and dismantled, the talents' dead mass retained as propellant for the next tiny adjustments in his course.

"I know where you're going," Ravleen repeated.

Do you? Ord didn't reply.

Then with her most merciless voice, she said, "You are going into my mouth. One bloody, hurting piece at a time!"

Two

"I continued my lazy stroll.

"Beyond the jungle was a narrow and rather steep beach built from salmon-sands. I kicked the sand into the warm turquoise surf and watched the bright pink grains sprout little tails and swim frantically back to where they began. The morning's work at the clinic had enlarged my senses. Not only could I tell every grain from its neighbors, I could also feel the vibrations of each tail, and hear their plaintive little voices, and every airborne molecule carried with it a vivid, unnameable and always delicious odor.

"It was my good fortune that a whale had died—a sulfur-backed cetacean of spectacular size—and the current had thrown its carcass against the beach. Dead for days, its blubber and muscle and deep organs were rotting in the tropical heat. I stared at that putrid mass, my new eyes reaching inside, caressing the great white bones, marveling at the intricate, relentless dance of feasting bacteria. And beyond the murmur of the soft warm surf, I could hear the plaintive, despondent cries of the poor whale's wife. 'Where are you?' she asked. 'Can you hear me, love?' And then, after an anguished pause, she asked, 'Is it happy, this realm past life?'

"I took a breath, a deep breath, absorbing the roaring stink . . . and its stench was, without question, lovely. Rich and elaborate, and lovely. Without doubt, this was a golden, spiritual moment. Where a human would have retreated in agony, I was joyously intoxicated . . . so much so that I found myself pressing my human face into the gore, sniffing again, and again, then opening wide my tiny archaic mouth in order to take a bite of that very sweet treasure.

"That's when I knew what I was ...!
"When every corner of the universe smells deli-
cious, and every sight looks beautiful ... that's when
you know that you have become something else ...
that you are a god ... and it is time to be exception-
ally careful ...!"

—Alice, in conversation

A MOMENT LIVED; a century crossed.

And then, another.

The Core was beautiful, and horrific, capable of wringing awe from any lucid mind. But it wasn't just the fierce fire that impressed, it was the great cage that held that fire in check. With little time and desperately few resources, armies of humans and aliens, gods and machines, had built a wondrous set of barricades. Comets and plutos had been pulverized, then refined into an especially pure dust that served as a growth medium for nanochines, and those tiny wonders had colonized every mote, replicating themselves and reconfiguring their homes, armoring and ionizing the dusts, electromagnetic rivers shepherding them wherever they were needed most.

The barricades were thickest along the galaxy's waist. There the dust lay in dense and radiant crisscrossing bands, each mote just far enough from its neighbor to maximize the cumulative effects. Each was a tiny world bristling with a nation of machines that lived to do nothing but absorb, dilute, and deflect the relentless energies. Few would have imagined that humans, or anyone, could have built such a vast contraption. Until the Core exploded, no sane mind would even have kissed the possibility. But the impossible inspires the impossible. The unthinkable disaster swept away convention and sloth, and within a few centuries, in countless places, the barricade was being erected by separate geniuses, each trying to save his or her own little world. Within just a few tens of thousands of years, it grew to become the largest artificial structure inside the galaxy, and perhaps anywhere in Creation.

Without barricades, the Core's beauty would be unveiled, and it would shine a hundred times brighter than now, and the Milky Way would be an empty, sterile realm out to its thin, thin edge.

But with the barricades, life could thrive even here. Floating against the glowing dust were dozens of neat dark clumps. They were little bodies, mostly. A light-week across, or less. Most were solar systems nestled inside their own secondary barricades. Others were simple clouds of fresh, well-rested dust, coaxed out of the way, waiting to fill unexpected breaches. The smallest clumps were outposts shielding engineers and administrators and fleets of starships ready to carry those important souls into danger, or back out of it again. Here and everywhere, the future of the galaxy depended on circumstances and on luck, and mostly, it hinged on the character of the men and women, gods and machines living on the brink of this incredible blaze.

Several of those black blotches lay in Ord's path.

Not far from the largest blotch, almost unnoticed against the golden blaze, was a pair of neutron stars. Like identical twins, they orbited in close formation, each superfluid body deformed by its sibling's enormous gravity. If Ord held his course, he would slip past the pair at a whisper more than three light-years, and in another thirty light-years he would crash into the barricades' first walls. And then Physics, the greatest god, would doom him. Ord's body would lose its hard-won momentum, slamming into the countless stubborn particles. Following in his dust-impoverished wake, Ravleen would gain on him, reaching out with her killing hands, then her mouths, making every violent promise come true.

For the entire journey, Ord had weighed his prospects, again and again, and finally he had reached that invisible mark where lasting decisions needed to be made.

"I'm here!" screamed Ravleen, again. "Don't forget me, you fucking shit!"

After all this time, the baby Chamberlain finally allowed

himself the simple pleasure of shouting back at his pursuer.

"You dear little bitch!" he cried out.

They were light-seconds apart, but the pause seemed to stretch for hours. The monster had heard him, and for a slippery little while, she was stunned.

Into the confused silence, Ord said, "Stay with me, Ravleen."

He said, "Please."

Then he used a fat slice of his reserves, jettisoning systems and talents that would never help him. What remained dove hard toward the twin neutron stars, and he drew himself into a snug ball, and from both of the dying suns, he stole momentum and an unexpected new course.

With a thousand tongues, Ravleen cursed him.

With every long-range weapon in her arsenal, she assaulted both targets. The orphaned talents couldn't defend themselves; they were vaporized or compressed, left useless and dead. The rest of Ord suffered deep wounds that would demand hours of surgery and precious resources to heal. But the maneuver seemed to catch Ravleen by surprise, and she ended up following a different, much sloppier trajectory, falling a little farther behind.

Slipping past the neutron stars, Ord shoved and squirmed, putting himself on the best available course.

Several billion kilometers in the rear, and still enraged, the monster swung low over the fierce surface of one star. Then for no rational reason, she spat out a huge gob of antimatter, letting it plunge into the sun's twin. She was punishing the stars; that was Ord's reflexive first thought. She was doing something vast and rash, and the resulting explosion was sure to cripple a few, or most, of her talents.

What was she thinking?

In a terrible instant, Ord understood. He saw the flash and tasted the raw light boiling out of the wound, one of his surviving systems doing the fierce calculations. Those suns were already close to touching. Another thousand years, and they would have touched. But that one tiny nudge, delivered in the worst possible location, had killed enough momentum to bring them together now, to make them kiss, and in the very near future, embrace.

The collision would take the next few weeks, local time. For the travelers, it would require a half instant.

Already Ravleen was weaving a sail from armor and coherent plasmas. When the stars collided, merging into a single black hole, she would gracefully ride the gamma pulse outward, regaining most of the lost distance . . . and more horrible still, every living creature within several hundred light-years was certain to die, or beg for its death.

Ord found himself staring along his new course, studying those little black smears where a few million or billion sturdy citizens led their important lives. They weren't ready for this disaster. It was coming too soon, too sudden. Of course he sent a brief, vivid warning; but he was the famous criminal, the greatest renegade of all, and they wouldn't believe his declaration. Even as Ord described this little apocalypse, he knew that some fraction of them would suspect a trick and delay their preparations too long, and that's why they would perish.

Thinking along the same sad lines, Ravleen said, "You see? You see? You are a complete and helpless idiot."

"Yes, I am," Ord replied, throwing up his incorporeal hands.

Three

"A young Nuyen is approaching your district.

"His name is Xo, though he is unlikely to mention that identity. He is moral and good, as all Nuyens are. There is no reason for desperate measures. But you should be aware that the boy is rather young and possibly misguided, and he has a few novel talents that are completely harmless but can render him rather difficult to control.

"If you see our little brother, do not speak directly to him.

"Be advised: If he happens to make contact with you, at a distance or particularly in person, there is a small if not negligible chance that your judgment will be impaired. He may not resemble a Nuyen, and he may choose to look other than human. Your security systems may also be at risk during the visit, and afterward. And your memories of the incident should never be completely trusted.

"Naturally, we would appreciate news about our brother's whereabouts.

"You can help poor Xo by coaxing him to remain in one place long enough for us to reach him. You have our blessing to use any available means. And afterward, you will have our thanks ... and eventually, a financial prize based upon your hardships as well as your ability to keep this unfortunate business politely and eternally confidential ..."

—*a Nuyen communication*

FOR THE LAST twenty millennia on the galactic standard calendar, Xo had worn the gleaming hull and scrubbed interior of an empty starliner. His voice and manner were that of an AI pilot searching for paying passengers. Since few refugees remained near the Core, it was perfectly acceptable to ask the whereabouts of other ships and objects that might have been ships. He was a business and an investment, and paying customers meant everything to him. And since gossip is the hallmark of any social intelligence, Xo gossiped with every local AI, as well as human voices, and alien voices, and a multitude of competing and inadequate news services.

"I'm hunting for two old friends," he never admitted.

"Have you seen them?" he never asked.

Yet every word he spoke was wrapped around that purpose and single question, and every word and cold number and complicated digital image that came back to him was dissected for even the most obscure clue.

Slower than his quarry, Xo was more than a hundred light-years behind when the neutron stars collided. His armor and simple distance kept him relatively safe. Steering toward the piercing glare of the blast, he survived the radiations and wild heat, suddenly slipping into a great bubble of sterilized vacuum where a fleet of disaster ships had already assembled. Once again, living worlds were boiling away. Millions of dying voices begged for help. But the ships had no choice: They ignored the pleas, streaking for the Core and the damaged barricades. If the Core's searing fires could punch through the dusts, then countless more worlds would perish.

Xo embellished his disguise. Suddenly he was an AI free spirit simply glad for this chance to leap into the mess, and grateful souls didn't question him too thoroughly. They let him travel deep into the barricades, repairing and repositioning the dust clouds while he hunted for signs of Ord's passing. But there were none. He couldn't find tracks of plasmas or debris fields left from a great duel. Xo resorted to coaxing the other ships and crews into speaking honestly. It was an ancient Brongg captain, suddenly drunk, who admitted seeing a pair of masses streaking past her ship, moving at very nearly light-speed, one mass following the other so closely that it was difficult to think of them as separate.

Xo's quarry must have taken a new, unexpected trajectory, charging along the dusty fringe of the Core. That hundred-light-year gap had doubled, and Xo had no hope of catching the Chamberlain. But when he thought about his choices, he saw only the one, and that was to follow, ignoring odds and practicalities, every reason and good sense surrendered to this one consuming mission.

The renegade Nuyen skimmed past dozens of colony worlds. On each, he borrowed the faces and lives of useful citizens. One night, he was a president's trusted wife. In the morning, he was an even more trusted mistress. He turned himself into various addicts and poets who were free to sit in every sort of public place, listening to the important whispers. He gave himself the rank and angry bearing of a notorious field marshal. With the breasts and penises of a local sex symbol, he holo-touched thousands. Plus he was an AI advocate, a wealthy personality sculptor, a simpleton custodian, and for one long afternoon, everyone's favorite golf pro.

Gradually, gradually, he pieced together Ord's whereabouts.

Most witnesses believed the two passing masses had belonged to the ruling Families. "The good Families," they would add with a make-believe confidence. But a few worriers mentioned the renegades—the last Chamberlain and his Sanchex lover. "You know," they muttered, a look of easy disgust building. "It's those monsters who destroyed our mother world . . ."

Xo nodded with every face, saying nothing.

But when pressed for reasons, they admitted, "No, it probably wasn't those monsters. Just a pair of Nuyens off on one of their fantastic errands, probably."

"Do you see many Nuyens?" Xo would inquire.

"Plenty," they boasted. "Huge and old and very important Nuyens."

Skimming along the barricades, Ord had continually tweaked his course, and with every nudge, Xo wasted time and distance finding the new trajectory. But he remained a Nuyen, perniciously thorough in nature, studying every problem from all angles, leaving Chance no place to hide.

One dense black bubble protected a neat green world reserved for the wealthiest humans. Passing nearby, a tiny wisp of Xo dropped to the world's surface. Quietly, he acquired the handsome face and smooth reflexes of a professional golfer. The sport was tedious and elaborate, and densely ritualistic, and it was slow. Xo's clients were trillionaires, and he confidently coached them on their swings and personal problems and the philosophies and faiths of human history, helping his paying friends to find the easy course through their own immortal, burden-free existences.

Each hole took a full day to complete, and each hole existed for only that day—a unique assemblage of emerald green turns and flowery obstructions and blue lakes and chaotic winds. The balls were small and hard and nearly as complicated as worlds. Each was a mother-mote taken from the barricades. On each ball, billions of nanochines went about their rapid existence, oblivious to the tiny forces ushering them from place to place. Playing with mother-motes was a local wrinkle, and every player worked through the day for the chance to watch his mote hit the slick-grass green just so and then drop into the tiny cup with that delicious, eternal *ka-plunk*.

One of the three wealthy golfers was a buoyant giant, both physically and in terms of his mountainous wealth. Prior to the Core's disaster, he was a minor billionaire with a fleet of aging starships. The great exodus gave him his fortune, the refugees paying everything for the chance to put their disembodied, comatose brains into one of his cargo holds. A grand tragedy was the same as a stroke of incredible fortune, and from it an empire had evolved, encompassing entire worlds and a fleet of swift new starships.

The man was happy, and he spent his happy days dreaming about new triumphs. Xo watched the selfish daydreams, and in revenge, he made the big hands flinch, an easy ten-meter putt missed. Then, as he bent over the mote to putt again, Xo remarked, "It must make you guilty, knowing how you made your money."

The trillionaire had never felt the tiniest guilt. But at that instant, an incredible anguish swept over him. Blinking back tears, he looked up at the face of the golf pro, and sobbed, and said nothing.

Xo said, "Guilt," once again.

The tears poured past the furiously blinking lids.

"What can I do?" he begged. "I feel . . . so bad . . . !"

"To fix your guilt?" Xo continued. "I don't know what to suggest. That's for you and your conscience to decide."

The man wailed and glanced forlornly at his utterly embarrassed friends.

"But tell me this," Xo continued. "Your fleet of ships . . . I bet they see some very unusual things . . ."

"Unusual?" the golfer muttered.

"Dark-matter ships. Mysterious flashes between the stars." But neither brought a reaction, which was when he asked, "Or any odd artifacts, maybe?"

The man didn't belong to any Family, but to keep track of his far-flung holdings, he had amassed some considerable and legally questionable talents. The implanted guilt had disabled most of his security systems. Xo's question caused a reflexive search of records, which in turn allowed Xo to peer into that elaborate crush of files and digitals and routine flight manifests.

Xo saw what he wanted.

"There's this one thing," the sobbing man replied, unaware of any intrusion, believing that this memory had dragged itself into the fading light of the day. "One of my AI captains was cutting distance, clipping the Kuiper belt beside a red dwarf. And its sensors found a hot spot. On a pluto-class world, there was a few kilometers cooking at nearly 260 Kelvin, and someone had given that ground hills and trees. On the tallest hills was a big house. Of all things, it looked like the old Chamberlain mansion—"

"What's that?" blurted another golfer.

"What?" said the first golfer. Irritated now, he dug at his eyes with his increasingly dampened hands. "I was just telling a story."

"What story?" asked the third golfer.

"I don't remember." He blinked. It was just the three of them standing on the flat and perfumed and perfectly round green. Why should it be anything but the three of them? And why was he crying like this? Gazing down, he blinked and sniffed, staring at the black mote, and he found himself thinking about the billions of tiny machines fixed to its surface. Like its own world, it was. And if every one of the machines was a person, and he could save all of them and make them as happy as he used to be . . .

"Shut up!" he wailed, although no one was talking.

Then to the ball, he said, "Quiet. Everybody keep quiet so I can make this damned shot!"

THE CHAMBERLAIN MANSION had been resurrected, complete with a reef's worth of cultured coral, and it rose on the high hill, nearly as white as the snow that stretched out on all sides.

Beneath the mansion were two figures. Approaching on foot, Xo thought he understood. The figures were child-sized, and proportioned like children, and fighting. One lay helpless on the ground, while the other stood over him, kicking his ribs and face and smacking him between the useless legs. Other than the terrific thud of flesh impacting on bone, silence reigned. A trickle of blood ran off into the snow, pooling in a thick frozen black-iron lake at the bottom of the hill. Judging by the flow and the lake's considerable depth, this beating had continued, without interruption, for the last two centuries.

What passed for Xo's heart quickened as he approached.

The scene was lit by the Core's angry fires. The boy lying on his back, enduring that fantastic abuse, was a young Chamberlain. He had the red hair and the proper build, and those were Chamberlain teeth scattered about in the glittering drifts. The other figure was Ravleen. Obviously. These had to be slivers of their original selves, portraits left in their wake as they raced through the universe. How many of these horrific little dramas lay scattered from here all the way back to the dead Earth?

Unless these were his lost friends, finally and unexpectedly found.

If this was Ravleen, then Xo was committing suicide. But he discovered that he didn't care. With a corporeal hand, he grabbed the bully by the shoulder and gave her a hard, swift jerk, and with a thousand toxic eschers ready to assault her higher functions, he ripped away the simple golden mask, finding an unexpected face staring at him.

Shaggy red hair framed a male Chamberlain's craggy features.

It was a more mature face than the one lying in the bloody snow. And if anything, it was harsher in appearance, the bright pale eyes miserable in a deeper, more piercing fashion.

A moment passed.

Another.

Then together, with a shared amusement, both apparitions said, "Xo."

A strange and sad laugh followed, and the Chamberlain voice told the dumbfounded newcomer, "Goodness, you certainly took your time!"

Four

"Without question, we have imagined the essential heart of whatever scheme the baby Chamberlain is unfolding before us . . . but we have also envisioned another fifteen hundred and twenty-two general plans, each with its own muscular credibility as well as myriad variations and elaborations and opportunities for sweeping inspirations. Separating the genuine from the possible will be daunting. All that is certain is that Ord/Alice's attentions are focused on the Core, and it is in our Family's best interest to stop him.

"His motivations are secondary.

"If it matters, we can establish his intent once he is dead . . . securely and eternally out of our way . . ."

—*a Nuyen communication*

"ARE YOU A Nuyen? Or do you simply like that face?"

"I am, and I don't," he replied. "My name is Xo."

The woman showed him an impossibly bright smile, then, after too long a silence, she made sure to tell him, "I have always admired your Family."

"That's gracious of you," Xo replied, focusing his senses on the bureaucrat. "And may I say, I've always been fond of your Family, as well."

"Why, thank you . . ."

She was an Echo. Until recently, hers was among the least consequential of the Thousand Families. Like the Nuyens and Chamberlains, the original Echo was chosen with care, augmented with care, and cloned; then throughout the Great Peace, those clones had done a very small part in exploring and settling the galaxy, preferring to use their careful powers to manage the civilized regions.

Echoes were pathologically cautious. That's why they had no great history, no natural flair for invention or business, and a deep distaste for politics. Compared to most Families, they were an impoverished clan, worth pity and charity and little more. They never terraformed worlds at the Core, and naturally, they weren't invited to help build the baby universe. As a consequence, they could claim a perfect, laudable innocence once the Baby had turned on its old mother.

Their lack of ambition made others sleep easy.

This particular Echo helped administrate every facet of life in her district. Local humans and most aliens respected her. During her tenure, the district had felt like a prosperous backwater, quiet and calm if not entirely at peace.

Out of respect for the Nuyen, or perhaps out of local fashion, she wore the simple archaic face and body of a mature woman. Echo women were small and round, dark everywhere but in the deep green of their eyes. With those eyes and her careful words, she admitted, "I feel uneasy. You've applied for permission to terraform a local world—"

"Is there a problem?"

"A small difficulty, yes." She sighed and shrugged her shoulders. "I'm sorry to bring this up, and I don't know how else to broach the subject . . . but according to my records, you aren't supposed to be here . . ."

"Where do I belong?"

"On the Earth," she replied. "It's your last official residence."

Xo was wearing a Nuyen's body. His straight black hair framed bright dark eyes, the simple mouth locked into a perpetually superior smirk. Through that smirk, he pointed out, "The Earth is no more."

"Which I know, sir. Yes."

Xo watched as the Echo accessed every available file. She wasn't particularly talented at her work, and she acted oblivious to the fact that he could see everything in her gaze, as well as terrains of data too secret for a lowly bureaucrat.

"I was there," he confessed.

"Pardon me?"

"When our home world died." With his Nuyen face, he showed his anguish, his guilt—unalloyed, and pure, and wrenching. "I don't mean that I was on the Earth. No, I was standing beside the Sanchex . . . the one who actually murdered those billions."

"I see," she managed.

She had no choice but to believe him.

With the subtlest touch, Xo adjusted her emotions. Then, with a soft, grave voice, he told her, "I feel responsible for what happened."

"For what the Sanchex did?" she countered.

"A creature conditioned and armed by my Family, yes. I could have anticipated her act, and with one hand, I might have stopped her."

She was embarrassed, and sorrowful. "But I'm sure you're not responsible. Otherwise—"

"I'd be languishing in prison. Wouldn't I?"

She stared at him, waiting. Her home was a crystalline moon orbiting a superterran world. The Core's fires seeped through the barricades and through this solar system's defensive grid, then pushed their way into this modest, somewhat stuffy room. With those fires reflecting in her wide wet eyes, she said, "Prison, yes. I suppose you would be enjoying some kind of captivity, yes."

Already knowing the answer, Xo asked, "What's my official status?"

"Your Family feels concern. They've sent general pleas to all local administrators, with some rather vague warnings attached."

"Do you want to arrest me?"

"No," she blurted. "Goodness, no!"

He showed an appreciative smile, then asked, "What are you going to do, Madam Echo? Tell me."

"I am supposed to contact the Nuyens. And if possible, detain you."

"Do it."

"Pardon?"

"Both duties. You should do them."

She tried. An encoded message was sent nowhere, and when the Echo's compromised systems sang out that all was well, she allowed herself to smile at Xo. It was a nervous, vaguely hopeful smile. "Don't leave us," she advised.

"I won't be any trouble," he promised. "My intention is to remain here and work on my little project, and to the best of my ability, keep out of public view. When my Family wishes, it can come gather me up."

"That would be best," she admitted.

"We have an agreement?"

The round face tightened. Finally, she told him, "There is a second issue."

"Is there?"

"This project. You wish to terraform a local world. But as far as I can determine, you lack the essential skills." She winced, as if expecting a fist or a blistering insult. When neither came, she made herself say, "Sir," again. "We have rules. Much as I'd love to see our little portion of the galaxy thoroughly settled and green, we have standards to uphold, codes of conduct and craftsmanship to be honored."

"I intend to purchase the proper talents."

The green eyes grew larger. "I am so glad to hear that, sir."

Xo told her exactly what she wanted to hear. Then with

each smooth word wrapped inside a comforting escher, he asked, "Madam Echo, do you have any idea what kinds of talents I'm wielding right now?"

The eyes were too large, and in a pained way, awed.

"At any moment," he assured, "I can cause any entity to believe whatever suits me. Or I could tie her soul into an elaborate knot, leaving it tiny and insane for the next million years."

From deep within, the Echo admitted, "I believe you."

"Two choices are offering themselves." He touched the back of her hand, lightly. "I get what I want, or I manipulate you into fulfilling my needs."

"Don't," she squeaked. "Don't hurt me."

"I won't. If you will allow me the privilege of begging." Xo clasped his hands together, then knelt on the slick and perfectly transparent floor. With a voice that couldn't have been more plaintive, he said, "I saw the Earth die. Barely yesterday, it seems like, and I can still hear the screams, and smell all that useless, useless death . . ."

She could see his nightmares, too.

"I want to make amends, Madam Echo. In a small way, obviously. Perhaps in a pathetic way. But at least I can begin." Xo had never been more honest or more certain. "Let me build a special world. A unique world. I will put it here, if you let me, and if we are lucky, it will be a piece of artwork that will endure for the ages."

Quietly, the woman cautioned, "Your Family . . . it isn't known for its terraforming skills or its artistry . . ."

"And your Family has always been frightened little shits," he replied. "Yet here you are, a wealthy despot ruling several thousand worlds."

She gave a tiny nod.

"Point taken," she whispered. Then with a drop of bile, she added, "Sir."

"Do we have an agreement?"

"I'll be watching you, sir. Always."

"An agreement?"

She tried to laugh, and failed, and, placing her face into her cupped hands, muttered, "As if I have any choice . . ."

Five

"Why do we make such marvelous terraformers . . . ?

*"The other Families have the same essential tech-
nologies. They can dress up in any proven talents,
wielding the same fantastic energies, every eye clear
and dry, while each hand is moved by a keen, quick
intelligence. Yet their works never quite match our
better works, and in every case, they fall woefully
short of our best . . .*

*"I know what you'll say: Real talent isn't some-
thing worn, but it's a quality deeply embedded in
our Chamberlain genes. And it is an integral part of
our ancient, prideful culture. From the first breath,
you have been taught that it is your duty and destiny
to carpet dead worlds with life. Nothing else matters
as much or for as long. And should the self-
expectation weaken, then a thousand sisters and
brothers will cuff you on the ear, telling you to return to your ultimate course.*

*"These are all good reasons to avoid the obvious:
Chamberlain voices are those who most often judge
what is beautiful and best about a terraformed
world. And we are the ones who decide what is un-
seemly. And we are the judges who skate upon the
slippery laws of possession, deciding what is actually
ours . . . !"*

—*Alice, in conversation*

THE WORLD HAD few charms.

Sunless and metal-poor, it was a full earth-mass drifting
unclaimed on the dusty edge of the barricades. Judging by
the physical evidence, someone had long ago attempted to
make the world habitable, and they had botched the job. A
rugged little continent had been thrown up through the ice,
its stony bones built from cultured basalt. The toxic beginnings of an atmosphere lay everywhere as a young white

snow. But the vanished terraformer had left a half-assembled sun in close orbit, which was a blessing. Plus there was enough Bose-condensed antimatter to fuel a modest biosphere.

Xo completed the sun and ignited it, and to hurry the world's transformation, he injected fingers of antimatter into the frozen crust.

Ice became a warm, filthy ocean.

The reborn atmosphere was thick and agitated, gales slamming against the land, threatening to gnaw it down to nothing.

Xo briefly abandoned his world.

Twenty light-years removed from the barricades, orbiting close to a young blue-white star, was a warehouse. A sophisticated array of diamond scaffolding and shadow matter held every flavor of treasure, sorted and labeled and set in stasis. Most of the treasures had been yanked from the Core before the fires consumed them. In most cases, the owners were dead or unknown, and once the pesky legalities were addressed, the properties would gratefully belong to men and women who had saved them. But there were also items left over from criminal proceedings. Talents wrested from defunct Families. Talents that a Nuyen could rightfully purchase, or in special circumstances, rightfully steal.

"Terraforming," said Xo. "Do you have anything that can help with a little terraforming?"

"No," the governing AI reported, point-blank. "I am sold out."

Terraforming skills were always in demand. Xo shrugged and turned to the other items on his enormous shopping list. Some proved available, and cheap, while many items were in stock but unavailable.

The AI explained the obvious. "We're waiting for their legal owners."

"I only wish to touch them," Xo countered.

"You cannot," he was told.

"Not for a simple second? What would be the harm in touching?"

"There wouldn't be any harm," the machine admitted. Then, with confidence, it said, "No harm at all."

"Then may I?"

Xo made his request, and he touched the AI's most intimate places.

"Do what you want," it replied.

Xo put everything in his hand, then asked, "Just how long is a second?"

"I'm sorry, sir," the AI replied. "I can't remember."

"But I know how long it is. Trust me."

"Yes, sir."

Xo assembled the treasures, then mentioned, "I need to carry everything home. I want to wrap each of these inside a dark matter envelope."

"Of course, sir. How much do you need?"

Xo answered.

The machine had a cranky laugh, but its voice was calm and reasoned. "That's far more than you need," it told this most difficult customer. "It is everything that I have in stock, sir. My entire inventory."

"Fine. I'll purchase it."

The AI meant to say, "No," but heard itself say, "Yes."

Xo wrapped his purchases inside four envelopes of refined, compliant dark-matter. The other thousand-plus envelopes were tied behind like the tail of an invisible kite. Then he returned to the AI, asking again, "Are you certain that you don't have an old terraformer's talents?"

The machine felt itself being manipulated. It was a hard touch, this time. But with a rigorous honesty, it explained, "This is a depopulated district, and terraforming is much in demand."

"Who buys these talents?"

Names and locations flowed.

Xo had more journeys and more stealing ahead of him. With a worried resignation, he returned to the head of the kite tail, ready to pull that massive load back across twenty light-years. But the obvious found him. Returning to the facility once again, he said, "All right. Show me everything that might be a talent. But it's broken. You can't get it to work well enough even to describe itself."

"There is one small something," the AI allowed. "A talent, perhaps."

"Then I'll take it, too."

"But it's quite useless. Believe me, sir."

For the bulk of a second, Xo said nothing.

That great silence gnawed at the AI. Finally, it conceded, "There's no reason you can't have it, I should think."

"Thank you."

They moved into the deepest storage berths, and while the AI's hands sorted through labeled masses of dark matter and baryonic matter, it mentioned, "This talent comes from a Chamberlain."

Feigning surprise, Xo said, "Really?"

"One of the first renegades to be captured and tried." Hands created for this single task brought out what looked to be a long, long piece of obsidian, whittled by another stone to form a double-edged blade. "When she was ordered to surrender her talents, the Chamberlain managed to damage this one beyond repair."

"The bitch," said Xo.

"Exactly," the machine agreed.

With the blade held close, Xo returned to his new world. It was a slow, exhausting voyage, but it gave him time enough to sort through his new belongings and make his first inadequate attempts to identify the mysterious talent. A hundred years later, he finally arrived home. In his absence, the gales had worsened, and the atmosphere had thickened and turned violently acidic, and worse still, Xo's arrival brought so much matter that tides were raised, stirring the young ocean, its icy basement tearing loose, continent-sized bergs joining in with the mayhem.

Xo set everything in a high orbit and began to work, desperately fighting to rescue his world.

"Don't," said a quiet, certain voice.

A woman was speaking with a Chamberlain mouth.

The stone blade had become a red-haired woman, noth-

ing but flesh and bone and the simplest of minds staring at
him. With amusement, it seemed.

"Everything's a mess," he protested.

"Leave it alone," she advised.

"But my plan—!"

"Is shit," she warned. "Which isn't too surprising, con-
sidering you're nothing but a baby Nuyen."

The simple mind wasn't. Xo looked inside, finding unsuspected depths.

"But I have a wonderful plan," he complained.

"Don't scare me," she teased, laughing fearlessly at
everything. "I'm here to help you. And my helpful advice
is for you to do nothing."

Xo watched the angry white bergs rise from the boiling
sea, tidal waves sweeping across the raw land. Then, finally, glaring at the blue-eyed talent, he asked, "Which
Chamberlain did you belong to? Do you remember?"

"I guess I should say Alice."

Xo said nothing.

"Isn't that the right answer?" she said. "After all, that's
who I am."

Six

"A Sanchex is a wild bear shoved inside a mouse's
cage, abused until it becomes helplessly compliant,
and then force-fed a diet of intelligence and cold ci-
vility.
"Which is the same for all of us, of course.
"But you know what I mean . . ."
—Alice, in conversation

RAVLEEN WAS POSSESSED by a glorious, perfect rage.

As she chased her quarry, her intellect constantly practiced her hatred, making sure it was perfectly pure. Anything tasting of doubt or mercy was cast aside. Sometimes

it was an act of will, but often it was a plainly physical deed. She would discover a shred of her soul that didn't exist for the sake of killing Ord, a talent whose existence wasn't spent dreaming of the horrible and prolonged and painful end that would come to that Chamberlain boy. With a righteous scorn, she would rip that worthless mass loose from her body and fling it away. Oftentimes she would aim at some inhabited place, then watch the impact with a cold satisfaction. Streaking at near-light velocities, a kilogram of useless talent could make a considerable *whump*, slamming into someone's green comet or asteroid with a fierce bright flash.

Cleverness and stupid luck were the boy's only allies. On the Earth and again on the edge of the barricades, Ord had just managed to keep alive, maintaining his very slender lead over a vengeful, righteous angel.

That was the only way that Ravleen could think of herself.

She was a hard-fought, bloodied, and worn-down angel, but she still wielded a potent array of weapons and a fabulous set of muscles, and those colliding suns had helped increase her already terrific velocity. The gap between prey and predator was steadily and deliciously shrinking. They were still skating close to the barricades, and Ord was obviously terrified. Ravleen could taste the fear leaking from him. She saw it in his increasingly desperate maneuvers, watching him dive past suns and little worlds. The Chamberlain used those simple masses to twist his course, keeping himself near the Core. Obviously, he couldn't leave this place. Like the idiot moth, he was circling its magnificent light, and like any moth, he wouldn't quit until he had plunged to his death.

Frantically, uselessly, Ord would toss aside his own talents and machinery—Alice's legacy—trying to gain any tiny advantage.

"You fuck!" Ravleen screamed. "You can't escape me!"

Ord said nothing.

"Give it up!" she cried out. Then, with a softer, nearly

patient voice, she added, "If you were moral, you'd surrender. You'd have no choice. Your fate's set. Prolonging this business is just adding to the costs. A moral shit would have no choice but to give up . . . !"

"What are you saying?" her quarry whispered.

"Watch," Ravleen advised.

With the equivalent of a thumb and forefinger, she flicked away a shard of worn-out armor, aiming for a passing sun. Moving at its fantastic velocity, the shard slashed past an inhabited world, missing it by less than a light-second. Then with her quietest voice, Ravleen asked, "Did you watch?"

Silence.

"Did you see the big eyes on those little faces?"

With his own quiet voice, Ord said, "You're the one who should give up. You know I won't let you win, and when you lose, it's going to be worse than any death for you."

She laughed. Cackled. At his audaciousness, she howled.

Thirteen light-years later, she threw another chunk of armor at another living world. But it was a more distant target, and, to impress her quarry, Ravleen aimed to miss by even less. There was room for error, but not much. Yet the idiot inhabitants—a warm, passive species who lived nowhere else—tried to defend their home world with an inadequate defensive network. Lasers boiled away just enough armor to hurl the rest into the atmosphere, into the crust, then deep into the cherry red mantle. That hard splinter of Ravleen's body turned instantly into heat and hard radiation, and one hundred million perished as their continent was ripped apart and liquefied, irradiated and flooded by the boiling seas.

In agony, Ord screamed.

Ravleen laughed again. And with a mocking tone, she asked, "Were you watching?"

Yet somewhere, she felt sorrow.

A secret, unexpected portion of Ravleen was angry with Ravleen.

Suddenly a constellation of little empathies exposed

themselves, glimmers of guilt that had always been lurking just out of sight.

Where were the traitors? Even as she laughed at the death and suffering, Ravleen began searching herself, examining every subsystem and transitory thought, hunting for the rootstock of this nagging remorse. When no part of her soul confessed, she began interrogating herself. She isolated her most suspicious areas, and she tortured them and, as a precaution, purged every high function that she couldn't utterly trust.

Strong again, she promised Ord, "I'll kill the next world we pass by. And the next after that. And I'll keep up this slaughter until you surrender. That's my policy. Look inside me, and you'll see: Only one of us can change his mind and do the right thing, finally."

There was a long, pained silence.

Ravleen let the boy broil in his weakling's guilt.

Finally, Ord let out a low moan and changed course. He was panicking, she assumed. He was beaten.

To help fuel his panic, Ravleen spliced together her longest arms, and she reached for him. She bridged the gap and, for a delicious instant, could feel living pieces of the boy. Then he shattered the limb and kicked it back to her, and again, from some hidden reserve, he found the strength to accelerate, pressing against his own swollen, stubborn mass.

Hugging the barricades, scattered by nature as well as by need, were the black-hole graves of thousands of dead suns. Half-tamed and fed measured doses of matter, the black holes helped supply the fantastic energies necessary to keep the barricades in place. The nearest hole was sleeping, for the moment. AI keepsafers squirted warnings to the intruders, telling them, "This is a restricted zone. You are not permitted. A civil suit is assured. We very much mean business—!"

For a wrenching microsecond, Ravleen believed that the Chamberlain was committing suicide. He was robbing her of her vengeance, in the end, and she wailed out in misery.

But no, Ord was going to miss that irresistible mass.

In a maneuver old as starflight and always spectacular, he allowed the hole's gravity well to grab him and bend his trajectory, the perfect altitude and velocity assuring that he would rise out of the well very nearly along his old course.

A 188-degree spin-around was achieved.

Picture a forefinger and thumb touching at their tips, with the black hole set inside that teardrop gap. That was Ord's course. And where the finger and thumb touched was exactly where Ravleen would be if she did nothing.

She did nothing.

Ord yanked his body into a denser mass, pushing what was strongest and superfluous to the front.

In her fashion, Ravleen did the same.

In those superluminal moments, Ravleen discovered another sick emotion lurking in her depths, unexpected and unwelcome.

Fear.

Black, and wild, and hot.

She shoved the fear forward, pinning it to her hull, and for reasons good and otherwise, the Sanchex screamed . . . and then came a misery vaster than any pain she could ever have imagined . . .

Seven

> "A Nuyen who listens to a Chamberlain . . . I never thought I'd live so long . . . !"
> —Alice, in conversation

"I FOUND MYSELF nearby and curious. Do you mind?"

"I do."

"If you'd rather be alone—"

"No, stay. I have nothing to hide here." Xo showed a

loner's uncomfortable grin, then added, "My work is rather preliminary, still."

The Echo woman nodded. "I agree."

Together, they dropped to the smooth blue surface of the ocean, and in a small diamond-and-teak yacht built for the occasion, they sailed along the edge of the continent. The world's gravity was stronger than anticipated, but Xo's guest never mentioned the vast quantities of dark matter taken from the warehouse. She stared at the expanses of raw basalt split by the occasional river bringing grit and thin muds from the interior. Occasionally, she would dive into the warm acidic water, acquiring the body of a small whale, and she would fill her new stomach with ocean water or ingest random stones and sands.

"Nothing is alive," she warned him.

"It's too soon," he replied.

But she had a different philosophy, and she insisted on sharing it. "Microbial bugs are still the best tools to prepare a world. They aren't as quick as microchines, granted. But they have a legacy and a beauty, I think."

Xo showed her a patient grin, saying nothing.

The woman clothed herself in an old-fashioned body, nothing on her warm flesh but a glistening sheen of sterile water. Then, with too much force, she smiled, salty nipples and her wide, wide pelvis beckoning.

Xo's grin became less patient.

"Your Family are on their way," she reported. "How they learned about your presence here, I don't know."

"Didn't you tell them?"

"At one time, I believed so." She was intrigued and frightened, and in surprising ways, she felt courageous. "But you probably already knew they were coming. I think you know exactly when they'll arrive."

He shook his head, saying, "I wish I knew everything," and let the subject fall away.

"What will they do to you?"

Xo studied her face, her posture. He stared into her swirling mind. "They'll send my oldest, most powerful brothers and sisters. I don't think they'd ask help from their allies; I am too large an embarrassment. And when they finally get here, they'll no doubt try to gather me up."

If anything, she was spellbound.

With a whispering voice, she asked, "Are you dangerous?"

He gave a little nod. Then the wind gusted, and he pulled his hand through his blowing hair, asking the Echo, "Did they send you instructions?"

She started to say, "No."

Xo lightly stroked her mind, and she told the truth.

"I'm to keep my distance. I can watch you and keep a tally of your crimes, but I'm not supposed to interfere with you in any fashion." With the gleeful thrill of confession, she admitted, "I'm definitely not supposed to be here."

"Now that you are here," he began. With a narrow smile, Xo asked, "Is there anything about this place that troubles you?"

The Echo took a deep breath, telling him, "Nitrogen but no oxygen, with argon and much too much carbon dioxide. This all tastes very similar to the Earth's prebiotic atmosphere."

"That's troubling?"

"This is supposed to be a tribute to our dead mother world," she reminded him. "Is sterility part of your tribute?"

He said, "No."

She waited for a full explanation.

Instead, he asked, "Why would I build a living world? If it's sure to be destroyed in the near future . . . why would I be so recklessly cruel . . . ?"

She looked across the blue water. "Will your Family destroy this?"

Xo let her believe it. He touched her mind with delicate fingers, and in the next instant, he caused her nipples to soften and baked her loins dry. When she was absolutely certain that she felt no interest in him, Xo told her, "Stay."

"What—?"

"Live with me. Will you?" Into her ear, he whispered, "We'll be lovers. Together, we will fight whoever comes . . . !"

The Echo gave the softest little squeak.

Then, without fanfare or good-byes, she launched herself into space, streaking back toward home.

Eight

"I was a young girl when I met my father. Ian, I mean: The noble, incorruptible rootstock of the infamous Chamberlains had just returned home from some little early venture to the stars.

"Conjured by a world of blended races and synthetic genes, Ian had the hearty pale features of an unreformed European. Like a king, he held court over his children. Like a saint, he acted utterly indifferent to the rest of us. Like a dandy, he had a love for fine clothes and seamless grooming. Yet my first thought was that he seemed quite old, and exceptionally tired. But then again, I was the baby . . . and everything around me appeared ancient and spent . . .

"I remember his voice booming, telling me, 'And you are Alice.'

" 'I know that already,' I informed him.

".With that tired white face, he attempted a smile. With an easy scorn, he said, 'Oh, that's right. I've been warned about you, Alice.'

" 'That's so funny,' I replied brightly. 'Nobody says much about you.'

"Or maybe I didn't say those words. At this point, memory and hope have become such a miserable tangle . . . !"

—Alice, in conversation

FINALLY, FINALLY, THE world was terraformed.

What was stone remained barren, and what was water still waited for its first bacterium. But there was a second realm built entirely from a highly refined, highly compliant species of dark matter—a deep ocean and small continent with very much the same shape and textures of the baryonic realm. Whispery plankton lived in that invisible ocean, feeding on the occasional reaction with gamma radiations and neutrinos. The plankton, in turn, fed a variety of small, slow, waferlike fish. Then the fish spawned on the continent's shores, which was where the ghosts would snare them, using bare hands and eating their catch headfirst and whole.

Two hundred billion ghosts lived along the shore, sitting naked on the rocky beaches and young river deltas, making love in the perpetual darkness while quiet voices traded gossip and little else. Their metabolisms were slow and undemanding. Their intelligence was compressed and very much streamlined. Alice had helped conceive their physiologies as well as this simple, sturdy biosphere. But Xo was responsible for each face, plus everything behind their grateful eyes. Borrowing from census records and security reports, stolen memories and easy conjectures, he had woven a false soul representing each human who died on the Earth. Every phantom believed that he or she was so-and-so reborn inside a great sanctuary, surrounded by friends and family, and pleasant strangers, and with a frothy joy, they did nothing but eat the occasional sweet fish and make love and tell the same well-polished and tireless stories about their lost, immortal lives.

Whenever visiting the ghosts, Alice insisted on sex.

Xo submitted, which the old woman seemed to appreciate. They were just another pair of spirits engaged in that most ancient, life-born business. Then afterward, together, they would walk the beaches, human feet treading on real rocks while their dark-matter selves waded through the murmuring, copulating bodies.

To baryonic eyes, there was the golden sun revolving

around the world, and when it set, the Core above was a thin, ruddy glow. Xo had erected an intricately layered barricade around his world. It was dense and excessive and exceptionally durable. The barricade's dusts let in only the most useful or determined portions of the spectrum, and, just as important, it kept curious outside eyes from watching over them.

In the ghosts' realm, the sky was a frigid and seamless and endless array of ebony spheres marching to the ends of Creation. This was the genuine universe, Xo would remind himself. Almost everything that existed was dark matter and dark energies, with a trace of baryonic ash thrown into the otherwise pure stew. Gravity was the only force shared, and it was pathetically weak. Only the most fierce, Core-born particles could touch the ghosts' synthetic molecules. If not for that occasional touch and the soft tug of moving masses, the place would be its own universe, tiny and undeniably simple, utterly immune to the great dramas swirling around it.

On occasion, Xo admitted envying the ghosts. "I wish I were as ignorant, if I could pick the ways."

With amusement and scorn, Alice stared at him, and sometimes she would laugh, and she always made a point of asking her lover, "How do you know you're not? Ignorant, I mean. And maybe you've even picked your own foolishness. How in hell would you know for sure?"

Little remained of the original woman. There were a few minor talents that Ord must not have needed; but in most ways, Alice was nearly as simple as the ghosts around them. Stripped of her talents and her grand intelligence, then imprisoned in a tiny cell for thousands of years . . . the cumulative effects of that abuse and boredom made her appear small, and predictable, and for long stretches, nearly unremarkable . . .

But then she would offer some observation or give Xo a slicing look, and suddenly he would recall which of them was the child.

"Maybe the ignorance isn't yours, little man. Maybe our

universe is a puddle, and we can't see the darkest matter and blackest energies because of this great sweeping ignorance. Not in our minds, no. But a selective stupidity on the part of protons and such."

Not a purely original thought, but from Alice, it sounded new and true.

Sometimes Xo would ask what she had told her little brother. "Just before the Earth died," he reminded Alice, "you whispered into his ear." Then he would delicately tickle her simple, tiny mind, trying to make it disgorge its remaining secrets. "Why is it so important for Ord to reach the Core?"

She wouldn't tell him. Perhaps she didn't remember why. But she still had the poise to wink at Xo, assuring him, "Ord knows why. Just as he knew that you'd follow us. From the instant he left the Earth, my little brother was sure that you would trail after him. In a day or a thousand years. But eventually, and all this way . . ."

"How did he know?"

But again, she seemed to have forgotten. When she shook her head, her red hair would chase her scalp like a tide. Then, with a wise, crafty smile, she would promise, "It'll all work out fine. Fine."

"How do you know?"

"Everything ends for the best. Haven't you noticed?"

With distant eyes, in the time it took a heart to beat once, Xo counted a thousand distant wars. "I haven't noticed. No."

"Patience," she advised.

"Patience," he repeated, always.

Then with a wink and a flirtatious grin, she would assure him, "If you wait long enough, every problem becomes too small to be seen."

ONE NIGHT, IN the silence that always followed her blissful advice, Xo heard a whisper fall from the dark, dark sky. Barely a word, and encrypted, and probably misunderstood. Yet when he tested what he had heard, he couldn't disprove its validity. His baryonic body stiffened, and Alice noticed, turning toward him and pressing her fleshy self against his narrow frame, asking, "What's wrong now?"

He was busy. Frantically, relentlessly busy.

Again, she asked, "What's wrong with you, Nuyen?"

Over the last millennia, everything done had been done at Ord's behest. Those two figures fighting in the snow had given Xo specific instructions, plus some powerful, left-behind talents. The instructions ended with the simple words:

"Then just wait. Wait."

Except there were more demands lurking inside that first message. He hadn't noticed them until now. He couldn't see them until the whispered word fell from the sky, dis-lodging the messy lot of them.

To himself, Xo said, "Shit."

Alice grinned with delight, and asked, "Is it my brother? Is he coming?"

"Not precisely." Xo absorbed the simple, straightforward plan. Knowing what he had built here, he had foreseen this circumstance. But many options had been possible, and some seemed much more likely. That's why he felt a numb-ing shock, and that's why he found himself searching for anything that might be confused for a real choice.

"What is it?" asked the ancient woman. "Precisely, or otherwise."

Xo didn't reply.

Instead, he fashioned a simple, compelling message that he sent to the Echo woman. He told the Earth's ghosts to fall into a deep sleep, and he reached into the sky and grabbed the artificial sun, putting it into another kind of sleep. Then he yanked hard, causing the sun's machinery to plunge into the ocean and plastic mantle, merging it with a camouflaged stardrive waiting at the world's core. Within the hour, his world was accelerating, throwing its stone and water backward at a fantastic velocity. The continent was on the bow, and Xo's barricade expanded in all directions, its leading edge striking the Core's barricades, infecting the intricate dusts with a new, more compelling set of instructions.

He was stealing a tiny portion of the barricades.

Gazing straight ahead, Alice said, "This is it then. It's finally happening."

"Back to the scene of your crime," Xo offered.

But she shook her head and smiled, pointing out, "That's one possibility. Out of many, many, many."

Xo didn't bother asking what she meant. Suddenly, he couldn't be more tired of their very silly game.

A CENTURY LATER, the Echo's response arrived.

Xo and the remnants of his world were plunging deeper into the Core's barricades. The message was brief and furious, and in a grudging fashion, it was grateful. The woman was sitting in her crystalline office. She said, "Thank you," as if cursing him. She said, "You shit," with affection. Then she reported, "I'm doing exactly what you suggested. Every world and every inhabited structure in my district is being abandoned. Hopefully, there's time. Hopefully, you won't steal too much from the barricades, and we can patch the damage before the other districts are butchered. And maybe, maybe, we can keep the death toll under a few million. Which wouldn't be too miserable, you shit."

Xo considered a reply to her message, then thought better of it.

"You manipulated every part of me, didn't you?" said the Echo.

With a tangible, painful shame, she said, "I was helpless. I can't be blamed. What you did to me you could have done to anyone. Isn't that right?"

The image enlarged, allowing him to view the others drifting inside the room. He counted a dozen Nuyens, high-ranking and powerful and absolutely certain about their emotions. A fiery brother said, "Xo," with a booming voice.

Then the others, speaking in a shared shout, assured him,

"You're the worst monster. As cruel as Ravleen, and even more gullible than Ord. Pathetically, horribly gullible. What good can you possibly do here? What makes all this waste and sacrifice worthwhile, little brother?"

"Your rage," Xo whispered, and with every mouth, he grinned. "Pissing you off . . . that's reward enough, thank you . . . !"

Nine

"We journeyed to the Core to create a new universe.

"And by every measure, we succeeded.

"We attempted to ease one of our own down its narrow, narrow umbilical.

"And again, without question, we found nothing but success.

"If we had made any large mistake, the whole of our galaxy would have been obliterated, and as the devastation spread outward at the velocity of light, much of the universe would have been consumed.

"But the leakage was minimal.

"We succeeded in containing the damage, keeping casualties to less than a trillionth of what was possible.

"Yes, I'm trying to scare you, little brother. Not with the potential for cataclysm, but with my own personal capacity to accept every consequence. I was enormous and powerful, clever and farseeing. In the grand scale of Everything, there was a tragic but endurable event that was quickly contained . . . a corrupt old order was set on its proverbial heels . . . and when tragedy is balanced against the scale of laudable accomplishments, wasn't this work of mine very much a fantastic success . . . ?"

—Alice, in conversation

A WIDE PORTION of the barricades had been ripped loose and dragged inward, creating a whirlpool two hundred light-years wide and half again as deep. The Core's fires were blue-shifted and became brighter as Ord peered into the swirling depths of the hole. Then at the very bottom, where the funnel gave a last little twist, lay a speck of perfect blackness. The stolen dust had been gathered up, then squashed into a single cloud, inky dark and fabulously dense, and at that cloud's tiny center was a world-sized ship that the baby Chamberlain couldn't quite see, even when he used every surviving eye.

Xo's contraption had to be waiting there. Ord wouldn't let himself think any other way.

A bright raw vacuum engulfed him. Stars and worlds formerly buried inside the barricades had been exposed. The whirlpool itself was filling with repair vessels—armadas of modified comets and plutos, each sporting tools more powerful than even this sort of titanic work demanded. And lurking at respectful distances were dark masses—ancient, high-ranking souls; most likely Nuyens—revealed only by the tweaking and twisting of the background radiations, and their encoded, conspiratorial whispers.

Ravleen remained on his heels.

Since their collision, the she-monster hadn't said one comprehensible word. Her only sound was an incoherent, raging wail, and she hadn't stopped wailing since Ord's body had pushed through hers, leaving her gutted. Alive still, and still powerful, yes. But in critical ways, crippled.

Could Ravleen fight?

There were reasons, slippery good reasons, to hope she had a few teeth and claws left to use.

Ord spent the last of his discretionary mass, boosting his velocity again. Then he stared along his trajectory, trying to identify everything that lay ahead. At exactly the point where an ambush would be easiest, he found a pluto dressed up in armor and potent EM shields. It was probably already spewing out antimatter mines and the anchor

strands for a coherent plasma web. As a precaution, Ord
pulled himself back into a denser, more enduring body, his
surviving armors aimed at the most likely dangers. To the
stationary observer, the work took years. For him, minutes.
Then he invested a full hour of his compressed time, busily
transforming what remained of his body, dressing himself
in chilled dark matter, borrowing those forms that would
be least impressed by these fantastic energies.

A voice whispered, "Ord."

It said, "Thank goodness."

He recognized the voice instantly, and with a giddy surprise, he realized that it was coming from beside him. From
somewhere close.

"Xo?" he blurted.

The voice sprang from a dense, almost unnoticed mass
barely one light-month away. The two of them were plunging together toward the bottom of the whirlpool. And with
Xo's voice, it sent a prearranged, deeply encrypted reply
that perfectly matched his expectations.

"What are you doing here?" Ord asked.

And he waited.

Xo's reply was an apology wrapped in assurances and a
thorough, seamless explanation.

"I'm sorry," he declared. "But I was scared. For you, and
for me, too. You should have been here by now, and you
weren't. I guessed you were hurt, and you are. So I let our
ship accelerate without me. I came back here with extra
fuel. The fuel is yours, if you need it. Do you need it? And
maybe I can help you fight that bitch Sanchex, or at least
make her quit that damned screaming."

"Come closer," Ord invited. "If you can maneuver, come
here."

The mass obeyed. A light-month's separation was gradually halved, then halved again. The pace of their conversation lifted accordingly.

"You look worn-out," Xo observed. "But it's good finally to see you again, friend."

"I feel beaten," Ord admitted. "And it's a wonderful surprise to see you here. I'm glad you took the initiative."

"Everything's gone perfectly. Nearly." His companion told him stories about his long search, and the Echo woman whom he had used, and the carefully refitted world that was now a starship. Then he thanked the baby Chamberlain for leaving behind those talents. "They made the difference!" Xo proclaimed. "We're on our way now! From here, it's a straight line to the Core!"

"To the Core," said Ord.

The astonished, worshipful voice said, "If I hadn't chased you exactly when I did, leaving Mars the minute that I did . . . and if I'd ever made even one wrong turn . . . I wouldn't be here now, waiting for you . . . I have to ask, Ord . . . how did you know so precisely what I would do, Ord? How?"

"Didn't she explain the plan to you?"

The voice admitted, "She didn't, no." Then it asked, "Are we talking about Alice? Because I can't shake any specifics out of her. She's awfully stubborn, when she wants to be . . ."

Ord laughed loudly, asking, "Are you lovers?"

The voice said, "Yes."

"Tell me," said the baby Chamberlain. "What's the exact pattern of freckles on her favorite face?"

Without a shred of hesitation or self-doubt, his companion sent a map of that face. It was precise and thorough, exactly matching the face of the woman once imprisoned inside the Earth, and in so many ways, it was utterly wrong.

Ord said, "Very good, my friend!"

Here was the Nuyens' trap. In front of him and beside him, the trap was preparing to slam shut.

Ord manipulated his course a last little bit. Then he looked back at Ravleen, and with a quiet, thoughtful voice, he told her, "I'm going to let them kill me. There's a Nuyen crawling at me, and ahead, there's that ugly pluto. Plus, there are probably teeth I can't see yet. At close range, working together, they're going to obliterate me. And what do you think about that?"

The she-monster's wail rose to a higher pitch, then abruptly quit.

For the first time in ages, Ravleen had fallen silent.

With a child's voice, Ord asked, "Do you remember when we were little, Ravleen? When we played together in the snow?"

Ravleen was manipulating her own body now, marshaling weapons and redistributing her armors.

"Do you remember snowballs, Ravleen?"

Ord spun a ball of white ice, exactly the size that a boy's chilled hands would fashion, and after wrapping the snowball in a secure stasis, he flung it back at his pursuer, watching its whiteness diminish; then, as it smacked against the she-monster's armor, there came a bright and soundless little flash accompanied by an inconsequential glimmer of soft heat.

Ten

"I was a young girl, and for a year or two, perhaps three, my best friend was a Sanchex boy. He was older than me by a decade, which was an enormous span in the Families' early hours. Age made him rich with strength and difficult wisdoms. Using nothing but cultured granite and hand-hewn oak, plus the brittle steels that he smelted in his own furnace, he could build an array of powerful weapons. Like every-Sanchex, he was an avid hunter, provided that his quarry was strong and intelligent and capable of inflicting tremendous pain. He taught me the skills of tracking and ambushing and killing efficiently. In the midst of mayhem, he would smile and tell me that I amused him, that he'd never known a Chamberlain with such a taste for blood sports. Just once, he smiled before we actually began our hunt. It was a different smile. 'Bring your favorite weapon and a short length of locking cord,' he instructed. 'Tonight, we're going into the Canyon of Lush. To hunt saber-

cats.' Then with a wink, he added, 'I think you're ready, Miss Chamberlain.'

"But I wasn't ready, of course.

"He had selected a glade sure to be lit by the green light of the moon. I secured one end of the cord to a substantial boulder and began fitting the other end around my left ankle. I would be the bait; that was my usual role. The cord was merely a symbol, unless I panicked, in which case it would hold me in place for a moment longer. I reached the point of putting a knife to my wrist, preparing to send my blood scents out into the evening air. But the Sanchex said, 'Wait.' He laughed and unfastened the cord, saying, 'Tonight, I'm the bait. You're the one sitting in the blind.'

"I was honored, naturally. And I was terrified. And without question, I knew that when the critical moment found me, I would do what was necessary.

"What was right.

"The old sabercats were simple beasts. They couldn't speak and lacked for culture. But they were tailored to be passionate and shrewd—a relentless force of nature balanced upon four paws, each the size of my chest. Several grown cats could taste the Sanchex's fierce blood, then spend hours circling the glade, sniffing and watching, arguing about which of them most deserved this wicked meal. A giant male won the right. I'm sure he knew we had set a trap, but he was intoxicated by the simple idea of consuming one of his godly owners.

"When the attack came, I felt alert. I was focused and clearheaded and utterly ready.

"But as I stared down at my bleeding friend, down into that pool of green moonlight, the cat scaled my tree—in one graceful bound—and slashed into my blind, four lightning white sabers sinking into my chest and belly. Instead of misery, I felt the warm, almost pleasant numbness that comes to any

*hapless victim. I never heard the discharge of the
Sanchex's weapon. But I was aware of falling, and
tasting blood not my own . . . and then my good
friend was kneeling over me, laughing at me, telling
me, 'You should see the expression on your very
foolish face . . . !' "*

—Alice, in conversation

ORD WATCHED HIS snowball burst against Ravleen.

She responded instantly, wiping off a dozen flavors of
camouflage to expose a body far larger than he had imagined, then she spat out twin shots, each more powerful than
anything he could have mustered. One blast of coherent
plasmas missed Ord by nothing. The other was focused on
the Xo pretender. Together, those terrific bolts of energy
caused the she-monster to lose momentum, the distance between them suddenly doubling, and she careened sideways,
following a separate trajectory as they plunged deeper into
the sprawling hole.

The Nuyen absorbed the second blast. Armor was splintered, then scattered. What passed for flesh was seared, falling away from a dark-matter skeleton writhing in agony. A
great sweet scream rose, piercing and wildly frightened.
Then the scream fell away, and gradually, gradually, a thin,
dying voice buried in the dying roar called to him.

"Ord," the boy heard.

"We know what you're doing," the Nuyen promised.
"And it's not possible, what you want. It's just another one
of Alice's shitty jokes . . ."

A trailing blast struck the Nuyen.

With a clean bright flash, everything that resembled a
voice was extinguished, and a lacework of degenerate matter swept through the body, erasing every trace of the skeleton, the vacuum filled with hot ash and a blue-white glow.

"No!" someone roared.

Ravleen.

"You promised me!" she shrieked. "A million times, you
promised! No one else gets the Chamberlain! He's mine!"

The armored pluto was a warm point of light lying al-most straight ahead. Ord was diving for it, closing on it, then the world grew brighter. Ravleen's first blast had reached its surface, the crust melting, then boiling away as wormy plasmas found every weakness, cutting down to the mantle. Great geysers of methane and water exploded out-ward. Surgical eschers convinced stocks of antimatter to burst free from containment, then detonate, yanking the mantle off the melting core. But the weapon arrays had already made their shots, and enough plasma cannons and gamma-ray lasers survived to send off new volleys. Ord fought his momentum. He adjusted his forward-facing ar-mor, and he was struck—a peppering of wild energies leav-ing him stripped and naked, then, reaching deep, his own incandescent agony making him wail.

Again, Ravleen cried out, "Nuyens! You promised me!"

She fired again, fired backward, aiming at those faceless dark masses that were following them, and increasing her velocity again, slightly.

A dozen ancient Nuyens were wounded. Pieces of them were butchered and killed, and other pieces fled from the battlefield, trying to find somewhere to die in shameful peace.

Ord jettisoned his ruined armor and organs, flinging them backward, each slapping against Ravleen.

At the bottom of the great hole, where the barricades were thinnest, the tar black mass of dust was moving faster by the instant. And as it accelerated, it compressed itself into a tighter, more durable mass. The timing would be tight, at best. Ord sensed it, then made delicate calculations that stretched out for thirty digits, proving nothing but that this was one astonishing long shot, and if it failed, he would have absolutely no reason to feel surprised.

Behind Ord, over the course of decades and light-years, the battle raged. Nuyens fired at him, but Ravleen was near enough and large enough to absorb the worst of their blows. She wouldn't let anyone steal the pleasure of her revenge. Besides, every blow lent her momentum. She invited the terrific hits, each moving her closer to him again, close enough that she could tickle Ord's bloodied toes as they rushed together toward that slowly closing target.

In desperation, Ord borrowed Thomas's favorite trick. He pictured himself with a child's body, shredded clothes and gaping wounds decorating his corporeal flesh. The cold vacuum became a deep, deep snow, white and featureless, roaring of EM winds, and he drew himself standing on a long steep angry hill, in the night, frantic legs carrying him toward sanctuary.

Glancing over his shoulder, he saw Ravleen. She was a stride behind him, if that. Like him, she was badly bloodied, her black hair streaked with gore, that perpetually strong, strangely lovely face as grim and certain as any face could be. He could nearly see her thoughts, the endless rage compounded with a fresher, more urgent despair. Then he looked forward again, up the long slope. Upon the summit was the Chamberlains' cylindrical house, but instead of white, it was blacker than any night. It was his goal. It was his only thin hope. But the house seemed to pull away now, burrowing through the last shreds of the barricades, and as its velocity rose, Ord found it increasingly difficult to close even a single step.

The hill grew steeper; the snow turned to a milky ice.

Around the sharp fringes of the house, a light burst forth. The barricades had been punctured. A blistering, blinding glare appeared as the Core's fires flooded into the galaxy. Ord bent low, keeping himself in the trailing shreds of shadow. And Ravleen screamed and bent lower still, using Ord's body to protect herself.

Together, they gradually halved the distance to the towering black house. But the pitch of the hill doubled, and Ord's legs turned impossibly heavy.

Behind him, the universe was consumed by flame. Worlds burned, and vanished. And brave souls perished, their last years spent yanking at the edges of the barricades, fighting to close the gaping hole.

Ord discarded talents, and his corporeal body shriveled,

and with an achingly slow step, he crossed another half meter of ice.

Just out of reach stood a door. Save for its blackness, the door was utterly familiar, fashioned from living corals and with that slab above, the PRIDE AND SACRIFICE emblem teasing him now.

Ord, the inheritor of Alice's talents and great powers, was little more than a child again, streaking deeper into this hellish realm.

Because everything was an image—a symbolic estimate of what was real and staggeringly vast—he stopped his feet and turned his battered self, looking back at Ravleen. As always, he was mystified by his feelings of infatuation. It was just a Sanchex face. Even for her Family, it was a severe face, and furious, incapable of love or the smallest charity. And yet . . . and yet . . . and yet . . .

That lovely wild face grimaced against the fierce glare.

If she fired her weapons and didn't kill Ord with the first awful blast, she would push him through the door, to safety. So crippled hands reached toward him, wrists thickening with muscle and the surviving fingers growing long and razored, a glimmer of poison making the new blades shine.

"You can't reach me," he whispered, not knowing if that was true.

But it was true. Even after such an enormous chase, Ravleen was still a light-second out of range. The hands reached for the last knots of armor riding on his back, and they stopped short by what seemed like a centimeter, collapsing back into the body again. Then Ravleen spun some elaborate calculations, and in response to the numbers, she began to manipulate her form again. Watching her slow, purposeful metamorphosis, knowing exactly what she was doing, Ord guessed how long it would take, and he turned again and gazed up at the PRIDE AND SACRIFICE emblem as he quietly, quietly said, "Xo."

He said, "Alice."

In the barest murmur, he announced, "I'm here . . ."

Eleven

"At some watershed in your evolution, you will apprehend that cleverness is everything. That if the godly soul is sufficiently ingenious, it can achieve what simple moral goodness and unalloyed selfishness cannot, ever . . .

"Naturally at some later point you will be sickened by this awful insight.

"Perhaps in the very next instant.

"Although in my case, let's be honest, I'm still waiting for that instructive and most delicious horror . . ."

—Alice, in conversation

"I'M HERE," Xo heard.

Barely.

The Core was a frantic, furious maelstrom, ionized gases and plasma jets punctuated with dying suns and world-sized blobs of boiling iron. A wild, white EM roar fell from everywhere, telling Xo next to nothing. He felt half-blind and utterly deaf. Ancient instincts grappled with his will, begging him to turn and flee. Yet the great ship maintained its course, plunging for the Core's center, shouldering aside the debris and that scorching wash of radiations. But the hazards thickened. The protective envelopes of smart dusts were eroding. A red dwarf sun passed nearby, tides lifting the dust, leaving a gaping hole that Xo patched badly, shoving a portion of his reserves into the breach with his quickest, sloppiest hands. Then he began again, repairing his repair, and that's what he was doing when the whispered voice announced, "I'm here." That's why it took him several moments to respond, eyes set on the brink of the barricade gazing back at the source of that very tiny voice, staring hard at a fiery point in space that slowly, slowly, revealed what might be another starship, or a suspiciously tiny Chamberlain.

Xo almost spoke, then found the trailing shape, enormous and treacherously close.

From that looming shape came a second voice, not loud but at least as furious as the Core.

"And here I am!" it screamed. "You fucks, I have arrived!"

Ravleen was barely inside the ship's shadow, its umbra, protected from the worst of the radiation. Moment by moment, her shape changed, transforming itself in profound and complicated ways that Xo couldn't begin to decipher.

His instincts begged him to panic.

"Alice?" Xo whispered.

"What's wrong?" she replied.

Xo found her lying naked on the dark-matter beach, toes dipping into the simple, frothy sea. The ghosts flanking her were awake, standing elbow to elbow, chattering with excitement. Their black sky had filled with a dim ruddy glow—the Core's fantastic energies were just visible, just real. Sometimes the ghosts felt the tickling touch of the radiations. Their faces were nervous and happy, and more than Xo had ever seen, they were smiling. Alice was smiling, too. But it was a different expression—sober and scared, and very much unsurprised.

"Has Ord found us?" she inquired.

"Yes."

Then before he could explain, she asked, "Who else is here? That Sanchex girl?"

"Right behind him, yes. Always." Xo nodded glumly and looked between his feet. The baryonic meat of this world had been ripped away. It was fuel and reaction mass, and it was spent. All that remained was the dark-matter skeleton and the stardrives and talents that could only be baryonic, plus just enough antimatter to power the systems that held the dust in its place. He gave Alice the eyes to observe their visitors, and after a moment's contemplation, he confessed, "I don't know what to do. Your brother didn't leave instructions."

She lifted her face, not smiling now.

"Maybe," she said. "Just maybe, Ord guessed that you wouldn't need the most obvious instructions."

He absorbed the criticism without complaint.

"If you were having his lousy day," she asked, "what would you hope for?"

"Help," he admitted. Then with a shy wince, he asked, "Is that the answer?"

"To many circumstances, yes," the simple, ancient woman told him, " 'Help' is a perfectly good response."

WITH TALENTS AND ample fuel, Xo eased his way backward toward the baby Chamberlain, slipping through dense blankets of stolen barricades with a minimum of disruption—for the ship's sake as well as to hide his own shadowy presence.

Every few moments, Ord whispered, "It's me."

He sounded small, exhausted, and absolutely terrified.

Even inside the umbra, the radiations were blistering. Piercing the last ragged layers of dust, Xo began to reach for Ord, then, at the last moment, hesitated. What if there was no Ord? What if Ravleen, or some other demon-agent, was offering this body and scared voice as bait? But if this was a trap, then Xo was already the fool. He was doomed and dead. Which was why he kept extending his hands, and after them, his tentative soul.

Mutilated fingers were waiting for his hands.

Xo felt their embrace and found himself drawn into a false, familiar landscape. The black mansion stood behind him. The snow was bright and scorching. Ord knelt beneath him, his boyish little body in shreds, every limb shattered, and a matching voice weakly asking, "Did you give up on me?"

"I didn't," Xo replied. "I never believed in the first place."

A thin little laugh leaked free.

Then Ord whispered, "My sister?"

"Is well. Is waiting to see you."

"Who controls the ship?"

"She does. At this distance, I couldn't react fast enough to keep the barricade intact." With his own talents, Xo embraced the boy and began making repairs. "When you're strong enough," he promised, "I'll carry you inside. I built a durable little world for us. I've been eager for you to see it."

In a particular way, Ord said nothing.

Xo said, "What? What's wrong?"

A Chamberlain face stared up at him. Except for the architecture of the bone and projected flesh, nothing about it reminded him of Alice's face. The eyes were fearful, the mouth sorry and mute.

Again, Xo asked, "What is wrong?"

"Ravleen."

She was still transforming herself. On this false landscape, she looked like a tall, tall human, her limbs twisted together, tying themselves into an elaborate knot. Against the raw light of the Core, nothing about her was human: She resembled a vast machine that was rebuilding itself, making itself ready for a single, obvious purpose.

"Ravleen's merging her weapons," Ord whispered. "When she's ready, she'll kick herself out of the umbra, and she'll feed on all that free energy, and just before she bursts, she'll fire. Once. And she'll kill us and everything, if we let her . . ."

"We won't let her," Xo muttered, in reflex. But when there wasn't any agreement, he changed topics. Quietly, secretively, he said, "Your sister explained something to you. Something about the Core. That's why you're here, and why I followed. I couldn't stay loyal to my Family. I had to know. Why is this worth so much? We've killed millions, and we haven't even reached the baby universe yet. And when we do reach it, what? The umbilical has closed, and we can't get inside . . . can we . . . ?"

"No," the boy agreed. "We can't go inside."

"Then why go there?"

Now he looked like Alice. A sly delight slipped into the blue eyes, then into the narrowing mouth. And with an encrypted tongue, he suggested, "Maybe the Baby isn't our destination. Have you ever considered that?"

"What is then?"

"No," said Ord.

He said, "I need one more favor from you, friend. Will you?"

Xo muttered, "Anything. I'll do anything."

"Can you still manipulate minds? Because I need Ravleen teased, her thoughts bent just right—"

"I can't," Xo blurted. "No escher can soften her pissed off will."

Ord nodded, and sighed.

Then, with a Chamberlain's gift for the unexpected, he said, "I didn't make myself understood. I am sorry, Xo. What I want is for you to make certain that she kills me. Can you do that for me . . . ?"

Twelve

"We were infinitely clever souls laboring on the nearly impossible task . . . a task laced with danger and eager for disaster . . . but since we were clever and so sure of ourselves, we could see the obvious . . . a means to let us avoid every pitfall . . .

"All that was required was accomplishing a second, equally impossible piece of magic . . . !"

—Alice, in conversation

THE NUYEN'S VOICE was soft, and close.

"We need to speak," he told her, each word using a different Sanchex encryption. Then he said, "Ravleen," with a traitor's too-familiar tone. And when she failed to respond, the Nuyen added, "We have been fooled. We're fucked. It isn't the Core that he's chasing. I just got Ord to admit his real goal to me."

She could see the Chamberlain plainly. He was battered,

but healing. In a moment, he would be strong enough to drag himself inside the dusts. But just before that happened, Ravleen would fall back and eat some of the Core's vast energies, then everything in her reach would be wiped from existence.

"Can you hear me, Ravleen?"

"No," she growled.

"Alice and the other criminals . . . do you know what they did . . . ? When they grew the baby universe, they grew a second marvel, too. Using the same talents, the same impossibly strong materials. Do you understand me, Ravleen?"

"I'm not an idiot!" she roared.

"Yes, you are. We're both idiots here."

Ravleen examined herself, expecting to find traces of Xo's dangerous touch. But nothing in her mind was amiss. Nothing about her resembled doubt. Her heart was a blue-black mass encompassing and nourishing the most perfect hatred ever fashioned by Man, and she clasped a thousand bloodied hands around it, remembering every wrong done to her and to her Family.

"Look at me, Ravleen."

Xo had maneuvered to a point not quite between her and her quarry. Her remaining senses could see talents and unspent fuel, but no weapons that would cause real trouble. Yet just to be sure, she told him, "Hold your distance."

"I will," he promised.

In the next moment, the great orb of dust changed course, slowing its motion. Obviously, another desperate scheme was beginning.

"Alice and the others found a wormhole," said Xo. "They found it in Planck space and yanked it out of the quantum foam. Then they inflated it and strengthened it enough to make it stable, and because they didn't want just anyone using it, they worked like demons to camouflage their little friend. They created what to the eye and mind looks like every other small, anonymous black hole.

"That was before the baby universe was born, Ravleen.

"One end of the wormhole was sent away, accelerated to near light-speed, while the other was permanently rooted in their time and their space. If disaster struck—if the universe-building went wrong in important ways—some future soul would come back and give the warning. Then the Chamberlains and Sanchexes would know better than risk building their baby—"

"I don't believe you!" Ravleen spat.

As if he heard nothing, Xo continued. "That's what Alice explained to Ord. The wormhole. A moment before the Earth died, she taught him where to find it and how to use it. And that's the only reason we've come this far." A soft, bitter laugh was wrapped around each word. "Like always, the Chamberlains found the means to cheat Nature . . . !"

The blue-black hatred felt itself being threatened. A thousand protocols were launched, and her rage swelled while her senses narrowed down the keenest, coldest of edges.

"Let Ord go," the Nuyen purred.

Xo said, "Let him leave us, and the Core's saved. The Earth never dies. The Sanchexes remain a powerful Family, and your life is as ordinary and as splendid as you believed it should be."

Abruptly, the baby Chamberlain started to move, crawling his way forward, pathetically struggling toward the barricade.

Seething, Ravleen cried out, "No!"

Like a syrup, the dust flowed before Ord, pulling aside to create a tiny hole. A doorway.

Again, "No!"

She slowed herself, and before she was perfectly ready, Ravleen fell out of the shadowy umbra, dropping into the searing radiations, her vast new surface absorbing the energy even as her flesh shredded into plasmas and heat. The simple brilliance diminished her senses, but she didn't lose track of Ord. The Nuyen, yes. He had vanished. Where was he? With too few eyes, she searched the umbra, then the surrounding maelstrom, and just as she spotted that slippery presence, Ord accelerated, trying to make a last sprint for that very tiny hole—

Somehow, Ravleen's anger found the strength to swell again, her rage clean, and brilliant, and sweet, and perfect.

With a wild screech, with all of her carefully sequestered energies, she spat at her nemesis, gutting herself in the process . . . a great numbing pain surging through an evaporating body . . . her last few eyes watched in horror as Ord, knowing exactly when she would fire, leaped aside, allowing the fantastic cake of gamma radiations and plasmas to pass by and enter the new hole, vanishing, then impacting on an invisible target set at the orb's exact center . . .

Xo's great ship was destroyed, at least.

And Ravleen discovered that she was still alive. Barely conscious, but able to crawl back into the protection of the umbra. With a weak, happy voice, she told the Chamberlain, "You're still fucked . . . deep inside the Core, your ship left as shit . . . !"

The dense dusts began to glow in the infrared, absorbing a wild array of unexpected, unexplainable radiations.

A voice, warm and much too close, whispered, "Vacuum fluctuations."

It told her, "From the wormhole, they're coming."

It explained, "Your hammerblow uncapped it, and now every photon that enters the hole is magnified. Doppler effects. Doubling effects. All the ugly feedback dangers that make this work nearly impossible . . ."

Again, Ord leaped sideways.

Then he dove into that little, little hole.

With a wary delight, Xo said to Ravleen, "Thank you. We could have done this ourselves, but you made it easy."

Ravleen lashed out with her last hands, grabbing nothing.

The Nuyen plunged into the same gap in the dust.

Ravleen wasn't too stupid to know that she was stupid. She had been a fool from the beginning, and for a slender delicious moment, she was glad to be dying. But then some little talent—more instinct than conscious thought—found a simple, workable answer to this damning mess.

In a wild instant, she stripped herself to nothing.

She peeled away her exhausted limbs and charred flesh

and all of her surviving senses. But she wasn't tiny enough yet. She wouldn't be fast enough. Nothing remained of her but her soul and some minimal talents, plus that great blue-black hatred, and without hesitation, she abandoned what she loved most. She left her heart behind. Suddenly as simple and small as a newborn, she aimed by memory, flinging herself forward, and she pulled herself into the tiniest possible shape, accelerating into that shriveling hole, too blind to see even the searing white light that was climbing up to meet her.

Thirteen

"*I know stories.*

"*Of course I can't feel certain which of these stories are true. Or if anything I say has the tiniest toe-hold on fact. What matters is that you believe me. What matters is that I believe me. What matters— more than anything, this matters—that the universe Itself, in some important fashion or another, believes what it hears bubbling out of my little mouth, and acts accordingly . . . !*"

—Alice, in conversation

THE DENSE SPHERE of hyperactive, ultraloyal dusts fulfilled its crude purpose, absorbing the furious radiations as they boiled out of the freshly uncapped wormhole. What the ball couldn't absorb, it transmuted into more benign forms. Then the engineered limits were reached, and the sphere abruptly split wide, the explosion brighter and far hotter than any supernova, and thankfully, quicker to fall away again. Alice and her phantom friends rode out the blast, then watched gratefully as the sky darkened again, returning to the blood-tinged glow that was, in her friends' eyes, a warm, reassuring presence.

Little remained to be done.

Alice was free to walk the edge of the continent, following the beaches and low cliffs, quietly speaking to her two hundred billion companions. She was a shadow and a whisper floating amidst their gossipy chatter. Ignoring the gossip, she would tell the entire glorious story, from its arbitrary beginnings to that obligatory final scene. Then she would begin again, knowing the ghosts wouldn't remember her words after just one telling, or twenty. Perhaps they would never learn. But simple pride and the sturdy sound of her own familiar voice served to keep her company, and perhaps more important, it helped fill this sudden and unnerving wealth of time.

"I took our ship's helm and moved us," she reported. "At the very last moment, I spent the last of our fuel, slowing us as we approached the wormhole. Since before the Core exploded, the wormhole has been moving daisy fashion, skimming past suns and genuine black holes in order to remain in the Core. Hiding. Then I opened the barricade in its bow, engulfing the wormhole, and I forced our dark little world to dance with it, the wormhole's apparent mass helping fling us off in an entirely new direction.

"We've moving perpendicular to the galaxy, my friends. My friends. Racing into the ultimate cold. Our stardrives and other machinery are ruined, left behind. We have only the barest residual capacity to make energy. But then, how much power does a world of ghosts require?"

Asking the question, Alice always paused, giving her audience the opportunity to offer answers. Right answers or wrong, it didn't matter. She only wanted some sign that some other mind was finally, in some pitiful form, awakening.

She ended her silence, always, with a bold warning.

"We're doomed, my friends. Utterly, eternally doomed. If the baby Chamberlain is successful, our very existence could evaporate. Depending on your personal reading of quantum gravity and the true nature of time, we might very well have already been erased. And everything you see here is what nonexistence looks like. Dim and peaceful, with an occasional fish for the eating."

She laughed, then continued.

"But if things go wrong for poor Ord, we will continue on. We'll leave the Milky Way entirely, haunting the deepest regions of space until finally, as our meager energies fail and our false molecules fall to pieces, we'll perish.

"Together, we shall perish. I promise you!"

Then, for a brief while, Alice would stop walking, staring at the vague faces and bodies, unable to remember even one of their names.

At that point, the same furious insights would pounce on her.

Suddenly she would ask herself: What if the universe—this glorious and inflated and utterly spellbinding creation—was the same as this little ghost world? What if Reality was some clever soul's device built with whatever tools were on hand, its creator trying to model something much grander, but in some great tragedy, lost? That would explain why so much of the universe was dark and simple, and why the universe, given all this space and its great reaches of time, insisted on repeating the same few building blocks—the protons and galaxies, the stars and the twisted, tragic souls.

That would explain everything.

Just contemplating the possibility made Alice shiver.

Then as Alice began to walk again, telling her story again from its arbitrary beginning, the second insight would attack. She would wonder if this was how the Creator lived: A lonely soul whispering to ghosts of her own making, trying to force their dim little minds to accept what couldn't be more obvious or important?

But Alice was too small and stupid to answer such a grand question.

She always had been too limited to comprehend such matters, and for that she was thankful, and for that she had always felt infinitely, perfectly blessed.

BOOK FIVE

FATHER TO THE MAN

One

"I was searching your memories, and this was waiting for me:

"You were a young girl. You were still the baby. One morning, unannounced, Ian appeared in your room. 'Alice,' he said. 'Come with me.' You followed, but leaving distance between you and him. The mood was serious, almost grave, and I think you were a little worried, although if you told this story, I suspect you'd confess only to skeptical curiosity. Our father was a distant man, and a stranger. Ian was famous, and powerful, and what was probably most important at that age, he was much larger than you. The man was two meters tall and then some, and he was thick-boned and deliberate. His augmented body made the most intriguing sounds, tiny pumps sucking and odd machines humming while his ordinary human legs climbed the central staircase, one wide hand riding the inner banister, the golden oak shiny and slick beneath his thick pink fingers.

"You watched that hand; I don't know why, but you seemed genuinely fascinated by it.

"In those days, our stairs were rigid. Even a god had to use his own legs and breathe with his own lungs. And pausing on the landing before the long climb to the penthouse, Ian looked back at his little daughter with an indecipherable expression.

"You assumed the penthouse was your destination. That's where our father lived whenever he came home for a visit. Like any child, you were hoping he had brought you a special gift. Then he was climbing again, leading you again—on iron steps now, bolted into the cylindrical stairwell—and that's the first time that you saw the half-finished mural. Ian had painted it on the ceramic wall. He'd always been something of an artist, even before he was a

*god. Neural implants and practice had given him a
genius, and you thought it was all very beautiful.
You said so. He explained that he was creating a
mural to show key moments from the Chamberlains'
history. You stopped a few steps below him, grabbing the black cold iron of the railing. The nearest
image portrayed Ian standing on a high black ridge
of razored rock, staring into infinity, watching a
scene yet to be painted. 'What will be there?' you
asked. 'A new world? Some great battle? What?'*

*"Ian smiled. It was a rare moment to see him
smile.*

" 'What do you want me to paint?' he inquired.

" 'I get to choose?' you asked.

*" 'As long as it's a genuine moment from our his-
tory,' he replied. 'Yes. You can choose.'*

*" 'I want me,' you blurted. 'Please, Father. Paint
me!' "*

—Ord, in conversation

ORD PLUNGED TOWARD his target, nothing remaining now
but a few picked talents and some patchwork armor, and
his little self, and a decidedly simple faith that everything
would happen as promised, as planned.

A focused, fierce blast slashed past him, uncapping the
wormhole.

"Easy," he whispered, to himself. "This will be—"

Motion through the universe means passing through
space and through time. In that sense, a wormhole is no
different. Take a step, and you find yourself inside a new
moment and a fresh place. Make another step, and again
everything is different. But where did he actually cross?
Wrapped in an envelope of roaring white chaos of hard
radiation and heat, Ord did not feel the wormhole. He
couldn't decide where he had crossed over. With each suc-
cessive nanosecond, nothing felt new. Nothing had
changed. Then he plunged into a smothering blanket of
black dusts. A trillion trillion impacts bled away his fan-

tastic momentum. A cocoon of plasmas shrouded him, and blinded him. Had he missed his target? Was he falling back into Xo's cloud, broken now and lost? The questions posed themselves, then a brilliant white light blinded him in new ways. The wormhole had grown unstable. Shattering at a point of intentional weakness, it was designed to spew the bulk of its energies into the future. Had it? Wherever Ord was, and whenever he was, the blast was angry enough to make him tumble and burn, peeling away much of his remaining armor, and wringing from him a long, sharp scream.

Again, the black dust wrapped itself around him, choking and slowing him, diminishing his velocity to a modest fraction of light-speed.

A whisper came from somewhere close, too soft to comprehend.

Then Ord suddenly broke free of the dust, plunging into a chilly vacuum and a fantastic cold light. Surrounding him were suns upon suns upon suns. The largest suns were old red monsters, and there were blue stragglers born when the old monsters merged, new hydrogen burning inside the shared cores. Plus there were countless yellow and orange suns spawned in the metal-rich clouds, in natural congregations and otherwise. A few planets circled those suns— colony worlds built by humans and other species. But the bulk of the cold bodies wandered free, dragged away from their old solar systems by the jostling dance of so many masses. A few possessed their own light and a delicious heat. Obviously, terraformers had been busy here. Great hands and small ones had built a remarkable place. The core of the Milky Way lay on all sides of him; here existed a density of energy and light, of simple life and roaring genius, unparalleled in human experience. Peaceful, and lovely, and doomed, all this was.

"But not doomed anymore," Ord whispered with a solemn voice.

With every surviving mouth, he shouted, "Can you see me? Hello! I'm here to warn you! Chamberlains! Sanchexes! All of you . . . ! Stop the work! This instant! Because if you don't, everything's going to be shit and death—!"

He fell silent.

The nearest world was a retrofitted brown dwarf. Hyperfiber scaffolding held up an artificial, only partially completed crust. Each portion of the new crust was larger than a hundred earths, and each was walled around its edges, the upper surface painted with shallow seas and deep, warm atmospheres. Some of those airborne continents lay in night, while most basked in a self-made day. Ord could see only a few details with his remaining eyes, but he intercepted a burst of laser light—one of the transmissions endlessly sending images to universal walls at every end of the galaxy. In his mind's eye, he stared at a vividly green, newly made wilderness, and a small town of happy colonists, and in the town's center stood a statue of no great size—a statue made from living pearlwood, red air-algae serving as hair, and a crust of delicate parasites that helped define the grinning lips and blue eyes and the telltale freckles of a god worthy of a people's earnest devotion.

Alice, he saw.

Then Ord glanced at the world-code, recognizing it instantly. And really, he wasn't at all surprised. This was the world Alice showed him on that horrible night in the penthouse, when the Core died. She had made him sit with those dead children, watching the peaceful night sky, everyone quietly and innocently talking about the greatness of Alice.

No, he wasn't surprised. After all, his sister had lured him into the wormhole, and she did nothing without reason. Alice had known that he would emerge in this place and see this world first, and in the next instant, his fear would leap to another, even more miserable peak.

Again, the boy screamed.

"Alice!" he roared at the stars.

"Alice!" he wailed.

"Can you hear me, sister?"

Two

"*Your long climb ended with a sack of feathers.*

"*'I'd imagine you were hoping for a gift,' Ian remarked, amused to know the mind of a little girl. 'And you're correct,' he added. 'Here. Take any feather. With your forefinger and thumb. Just one now. Just like this.'*

"*The two of you stood on the landing outside the penthouse, the black-iron railing coming up to your chest. Mimicking our father, you picked up a feather by its rachis. The feather was long and downy, and it was deeply red with a sharp blue eye at its center. 'Now drop it,' he instructed. 'Down the stairwell . . . let it fall, Alice . . .'*

"*You obeyed, watching that bit of fluff dance in the air, twisting and skating as it gradually dropped from view.*

"*'Now,' said Ian. 'Pick a second feather. And release it from exactly the same point in space. Yes, like that. And watch its motion again. Do you see?'*

"*You saw everything, and nothing.*

"*'Again,' our father urged. 'And three more times, again. But make sure that each feather starts from the same point. Are you sure?'*

"*You were being very careful. But you were also growing bored with this pointless game.*

"*'Every feather is identical to the others,' Ian mentioned. 'Atom for atom, each is a precise duplicate of the ones that went before.' Then he laughed gently, chiding, 'But these feathers keep falling along different courses. Obviously, Alice . . . you need to be more careful . . .'*

"*'I am being careful,' you argued. Then you doubled your efforts, and quadrupled your concentration. Yet the damned feathers insisted on taking odd turns, falling quickly, then slowly, and when least* expected, floating back up to the landing or even higher, a warm gust of air letting them fly.

" 'Stop,' Ian said at last. 'That's enough, Alice.' Then he placed his big hand over both of your little hands. It may have been the first time he actually touched you, and what surprised you wasn't the heat of his hand, which was staggering, but it was the slick plastic feel of the flesh. Ian was wearing a primitive prosthetic that began just beneath his elbow. You didn't know that, until then. And looking up into that great face, you watched our father explain, 'There are hundreds of thousands of identical feathers here. And if you could actually drop all of them from the same precise starting point . . . if that were even remotely possible . . . you still wouldn't see any two fall along the same precise course.'

"That moment, that lesson, might have been your first contact with the pitfalls and possibilities of Chaos.

" 'And it's the same with Chamberlains,' our father assured. 'We're very nearly identical to each other. If not atom for atom, at least gene for gene. Yet each our lives is guaranteed to follow a different and unique course.'

"You absorbed that revelation in a long moment. But you didn't speak until you had some telling, Alice-like observation to offer. Grabbing the entire sack, you poured its contents into the stairwell, the air filling with blue-eyed red feathers . . . and with a stubborn, overly smug voice, you exclaimed, 'But you see! You see! They all fall, and every one of them ends up in the same fat pile . . . !' "

—Ord, in conversation

ORD BUILT A body, and a path.

The body was boyish and small, barefoot and dressed in animal skins. His own skin was decorated with an assortment of old and important scars. The path beneath him was

made of alternating blocks of yellow limestone and bluish
shale. He pulled each stone out of a Thomas sack and carefully fitted it against the last stones. Each little slab represented several million kilometers, and each also marked a
beacon that would help any watchful eye notice his passage,
and eventually find him.

Ord was removing a fresh stone when the voice am-
bushed him.

Quietly, from somewhere close, the voice suggested,
"Look over your shoulder."

Too late, he glanced back along the path. The dusts
around the dead wormhole were absorbing the fantastic energies, reradiating them as heat and X rays, and as a bruising shower of gamma radiation. Stepping out of that
brilliance was a figure. Closing on him, the figure whispered, "My good dear friend. Is it you, Ord?"

It was a Nuyen's voice.

Quietly, on a private channel, Ord whispered, "Xo? Is
it?"

"It is," the voice replied. Then Xo's face appeared, smiling brightly as he called out, "I followed you through. It
was close, but I made it."

"You did make it," Ord agreed. "Good."

The visitor was moving much faster, and that translated
into a faster gait for the Nuyen's body. He was practically
running, following the path, the face ignoring the close-
packed suns and worlds, staring only at the boy.

Again, Ord said, "Xo? Is it—?"

The impact was sudden, and jarring.

Too late, Ord realized his mistake. Ravleen had stripped
herself down to almost nothing, and slicing through the
dusts, she had managed to retain most of her velocity.
Without a thought for her own safety, she struck him like
a cannonball, their momentum married, then she grabbed
hold of him, and with every little weapon at her disposal,
she tried to murder him.

Ord absorbed the first impact, and the next thousand. The
path and both bodies vanished, leaving him drifting through

the cold bright vacuum. He was faster now, but not much. Most of Ravleen must have been trapped on the far side of the wormhole. That fierce little last piece of her didn't have enough mass, much less muscle, to cause lasting harm. Even her mouths were oddly weakened, cursing him in a near whisper, repeating the same few insults with a washed-out fury.

"You're a stupid fuck, and I'm going to kill you now," she promised. "You're an ugly fuck, and I'm going to skin you and wear you like a fucking mask."

Ord weathered the abuse without comment.

Another voice intruded. "What do you mean?" it asked with an inky smoothness. "Whom do you wish to kill, Ravleen?"

Xo. Finally.

Using a soothing voice, the Nuyen said, "You're a little stupid, I think, and ugly-spirited, and whom exactly do you want dead?"

Ravleen felt the words, and paused. She seemed to be examining her battered self. The collision with Ord had left her grievously injured. Her most fragile, intricate organs lay exposed. Baking in the radiation, they were dying. She was dying. A look of supreme fatigue washed over her. Ord saw it in the angles of her body, and he heard it in the depth of her silence. And because it was the right thing to do, he deftly positioned his own body between her and the wormhole, using his shredded armor and slight bulk to absorb the worst of the poisons.

Xo drifted closer, whispering, "You aren't the same monster. Are you, Ravleen?"

She said nothing.

"I can tell," he assured.

Ravleen flexed her muscles, accomplishing nothing.

With a grave wonder, Xo said, "To catch us, you had to leave everything else behind. Including your hatred, didn't you—?"

"I kept enough!" she sputtered. "You prick!"

Ord broke into a low, happy laugh.

"A kind of redemption," he exclaimed. "Like it or not, Ravleen . . . that's what you've found . . . !"

Three

> "A wilderness of infinite potential . . . a vastness
> bursting with wealth and promise . . . a golden realm
> where you might live nearly forever as the God of
> Gods . . .
>
> "Is it the Core?
> "The baby universe?
> "Or maybe I'm teasing . . . maybe this bound-
> less marvel is the mind and soul of Alice Chamber-
> lain . . . ?"
>
> —Ord, in conversation

THREE BODIES HUDDLED in the vacuum, limbs tied together in elaborate knots, their armor gradually searing in the fading glow of the spent wormhole. Ord had never stopped calling for help, and now Xo joined in, lending his energy and mouths. Yet nothing seemed to notice their pleas. The nearest worlds remained stubbornly remote, and the surrounding space tasted perfectly clean. Unnaturally clean, Ord decided. Save for the dust suspended above the wormhole and the occasional photon bound for better places, the three of them were drifting across a nearly perfect vacuum. Unlike the rest of the Core, there was no fog of hydrogen and were no little icy worlds moving without suns. Ord couldn't even find a mountain-sized rock or thumb-sized pebble. A volume better than ten light-years in every direction had been scrubbed and scoured, filtered pure again and again. Here lay an unexpected wonder: A gigantic and pure region, clean as any laboratory—a seamless perfection that could only have been produced by the most feverishly efficient and anally focused gods.

"We've got an unlikely trajectory," Ord whispered. Comparing internal maps to what he saw, he admitted, "The central black hole is exactly on the other side of the wormhole. That's where they'll be waiting. I'm sure."

"So they won't find us here," Xo offered.

"In time they will."

"But they'll be watching for something enormous. Someone like them." Xo kept shouting for the stars to take notice, but he confessed to his companions, "They'll look and miss us the first thousand times . . . and you know what's going to happen . . . ? They'll logically assume that the wormhole went unstable by itself. A random act, and inevitable . . ."

"No," Ord countered.

Ravleen said nothing.

"They're going to find us," Ord muttered. "Because we're twists of dirt wandering around inside their very clean room."

"But in time?" asked Xo. "Will they actually find us while it still means something?"

Ord answered with silence and a purposeful glance at the stars. Then he resumed to shout and holler, switching channels and volumes according to custom, then doing it randomly, always sandwiching the name, "Alice," between the other names drawn from the five hundred Families who had come to the Core.

The days passed.

Long cold weeks were crossed.

It was just the three of them, and the vacuum. A routine quickly formed. Xo occasionally spoke to Ord—usually about nothing of consequence, just to pretend conversation—and Ord might answer in the same frothy light vein. Ravleen never uttered a sound, never moved. Meanwhile, in code, the two friends discussed their contingencies for likely futures, and sometimes they talked about their nightmares. What if they didn't reach the Great Ones? What if

every risk and every victory meant nothing in the end?
And then they would plunge back into a sober, introspective silence that would last for ten or twenty endless seconds.

Then Xo started to say, "Do you remember . . . when we
first joined the Golds . . . do you remember . . . ?"

His voice fell away.

"What?" Ord started to ask.

But then he hesitated, sensing what Xo had already felt,
letting it interrupt his fragile concentration, too.

There were four of them now.

With most of his talents ruined or left behind, Ord could
feel the visitor only as a presence—a black chill carefully
licking at his fringes. The brightest stars faded just slightly.
Then came the mild and irresistible tug as a great mass
swung near before pulling away again. Someone was studying them. A thousand sensors and eyes and fingertips too
delicate to be seen were playing across their bodies, then
poking around inside their superchilled minds. When he
guessed that the time was ripe, Ord opened a Chamberlain
channel. He didn't whisper, but he didn't shout, either.
Without a trace of fear and only a minimal respect, he said,
"Hello to you. Whoever you are. Hello."

Silence was the reply.

A delicious urge struck. Ord told the darkness, "If you're
injured, we can help you. Do you need help, friend?"

In a private whisper, Xo warned, "I smell mistrust. And
muscles."

The Nuyen had kept more of his talents. On the premise
that his ally could read the visitor's thoughts, Ord let himself wonder, "Which Family?"

Xo whispered, "Sanchex."

"You're sure?"

"The mind's efficient, and relentless," Xo warned. "And
everywhere I look, I see muscles."

Ord broke into a quiet laugh, relieved finally to come
across something that was at least a little bit familiar.

Only then did Ravleen sense their visitor. Limbs kicked,
and from her strongest mouth she cried out, "Whoever you

are! These criminals are holding me against my will—!"

A thunderous voice descended on a Sanchex channel.

"What should I do about them, little one?"

"Kill them," Ravleen barked. "If you can."

There was a momentary pause, then a face and naked body were conjured from compliant light. They saw a male body, muscular and dark, and in the depths of its eyes lay an even greater darkness. The handsome face grinned with a practiced malevolence. There was a laugh not unlike the collapse of a mountain. Then a quiet, massive voice whispered in each of their ears, warning, "Oh, I could kill them. Easily. And I could butcher you in the same breath, little one."

Ravleen fell silent.

"Who are you?" Xo asked.

In an offhand fashion, the newcomer said, "My name is Marvel."

The First Sanchex.

But if Ravleen was impressed, she kept her emotion well hidden. "You might think that's who you are," she said, suddenly kicking and squirming. "To me, you're just a voice and a put-on face . . . and even if you are, you don't scare me! Do you hear me, Father? Do you?"

Four

" 'Who crossed over?' I will ask you.
   "Spellbound.
   " 'Into the baby universe . . . who . . . ?'
   "And very softly, you'll say to me, 'Closer.'
   "So I'll dip my head, and listen, and you'll offer me two of the most simple words . . . two incredible, impossible words . . . and about that subject, you will never utter a third word, even in the most offhand fashion . . ."

                                        —Ord, in conversation

THEIR BODIES WERE robbed of their inertia, then accelerated, and, without warning, the three of them were unknotted and rudely yanked apart.

Ord found himself alone. He discovered himself sitting inside what seemed to be a typical Chamberlain apartment. There was a spacious bed beneath him and a bath on his left, and on his right was a swimming pool stocked with dragonfly larvae and rainbow worms, and beside it, a very long universal wall that refused to work. The atmosphere was oxygen, intended for him, and someone had knitted together a meat-and-blood Chamberlain body. Ord was still linked to his battered machinery and talents, but what he saw with his immediate eyes was naked and pale, freckled and unscarred. This body was a kindness, and a symbol. He left it entirely alone, except to touch himself where the ribs joined at the sternum, causing a treasured scar to rise up and grow pleasantly slick.

Nothing about the room reminded him of a prison cell. Yet Ord understood that he couldn't leave and should never try. He was expected to play the patient role while he was carried to somewhere else. The Great Ones were being summoned, and long swift tangling conversations would be held, giving them time to discuss the possibilities, arriving at a quiet state that could be confused for a consensus. And only then would they wish to speak directly with him.

Quietly, Ord said, "Alice."

He said, "I'm your baby brother."

Strolling up to the universal wall, he squinted, peering into the blackness. Twenty requested views failed to appear. But was the wall dead? "Is this the Core's black hole, Alice? Is that what you want to show me?"

Silence.

"I know what you're doing here," he continued. "You and the other Great Ones . . . I know why you've gathered, and what you're hoping to build, and I know what a selfish mess you're going to make of everything . . ."

The silence gained a sturdy indifference. Otherwise, it

was a seamless quiet, untroubled by the messenger in its midst.

Ord couldn't help but feel surprised and hurt. He knew that he shouldn't worry about prosaic business like wasted time and the unfathomable stakes involved, but he was worrying quite a lot. Alice was arrogant and stubborn—a consequence of being half as old as her species—and Ord always assumed that her peers were exactly the same, if not worse. But he kept telling himself that none of those ugly traits made them into fools. No matter how mammoth their powers, no matter how sweeping their gaze, didn't reason and right still have to rule their enormous souls?

With a shrill desperation, Ord started to call out, "Alice—"

A doorway blossomed in what had been a wall of living coral. The doorway opened outward, riding on what looked to be great brass hinges. Beyond lay nothing but a deep grayness, and from the grayness came a sudden cool wind that combed Ord's shaggy hair. With old-style nostrils, he smelled perspiration. He smelled lingering aromas that could only remind him of himself. Calling him were a few dozen genetic markers, ancient and deeply buried, meaning Chamberlain. He sniffed a second time and showed his guest a wide smile, and said, "Alice," with an eagerness that he'd hoped to keep hidden.

From the grayness stepped a figure clothed in the same grayness. There were long slippers and tight trousers rising up into a roomy gray blouse that shimmered in the room's yellowy light. A taut black band was worn around the forehead. The face beneath looked as young as Ord's, and as masculine, and it smiled in the same relentless fashion. But this wasn't just some clever reflection. Those eyes were not Ord's. Yes, they possessed the same blue-white color, and they had a brightness and a genuine eagerness. But beneath their surface lay a different quality—a sense of great mass, a hint of supreme age—and beyond the eyes was a sadness both profound and appealing.

Ord recognized the sadness.

"Where have I seen you?" he whispered.

The creature before him shrugged gamely, then stepped into the doorway, admitting, "You've seen me many times, I should hope."

Loudly, Ord asked, "Which brother are you?"

"None," said the young face. Said the ancient eyes.

"No," Ord growled. There was no sense of surprise, but he felt a pure, instinctive anger. Then, revulsion. He shook his head defiantly, saying, "You can't be. You aren't. You died eons ago—"

"Who's dead?" the visitor inquired.

"My father," Ord said to the impossibility.

"The father of the Chamberlains," he muttered to nobody.

"Ian?" he squeaked.

Those ancient blue eyes pulled shut, and with a practiced bow that was both formal and devoid of humility, the visitor announced, "In the service of the Great Peace, I am. Yes. Ian Chamberlain."

Five

"You'll say, 'Closer.'
  "So I'll dip my head and listen, and you'll offer those two incredible, impossible words . . .
  " 'Your father,' I will hear.
  "Which will be too much said, I think . . ."
                                        —Ord, in conversation

"IAN'S DEAD."

It was true enough to deserve repetition. Three more times, Ord uttered that simple declaration. "Ian is dead." Yet he wasn't truly surprised. Alice had given him a curt warning, and the long journey allowed him time to chew on her odd words. He had a mountain of explanations at the ready, each offering strategies and a certain face. Surprise chose Ord. His eyes grew huge with amazement, and his mouth fell wide, and with an incredulous voice, he said, "I don't believe you."

Angry now, he snarled, "That's bullshit!"

The visitor seemed amused by the outburst. He stepped a little closer, growing taller while he smiled, and with a quiet, dry voice, he said, "Tell this old ghost, if you would. How did Ian die?"

"A starship was crippled," Ord explained. "There were eighteen hundred human colonists and an AI crew. They were drifting, passing too close to a binary system. An aging star was dropping its skin on the surface of a neutron star, and once enough mass had gathered, the supernova would erupt. In a matter of a few years—"

"Nineteen years, plus a few days," the apparition offered.

Ord looked at the black universal wall. "Ian was the only soul near enough to help," he continued. "The Great Peace was barely a million years old. Talents were much more limited then. Even the First Chamberlain could do only so much. When he arrived, it was too late to save everyone. He could save the ship, or save himself. But there wasn't any choice. Ian clothed the ship in his own armor and engines, and he accelerated those people out of the gravity well, and the neutron star detonated on schedule, and he was granted a hero's death."

The smile broadened. "You learned that story, did you? As a boy?"

"As a boy, and since," Ord responded.

Then he continued, explaining, "I was promised—in my crib, practically—that if I was very lucky, I'd die like Ian. A perfect, selfless death . . ."

The visitor's response was an apparently humble, much-practiced bow.

"I suppose," Ord continued. "History could be wrong. It often is. Witnesses and sensors could have made the same string of mistakes. It wasn't Ian who saved those people, or maybe he escaped the catastrophe, or he survived it. Somehow. And later, when he learned about his heroic death, he might have decided to let the story stand." Ord set that explanation between them, as if offering a gift. "Being invisible, he gave his children a hero worthy of their love."

The smile broadened, and the blue eyes narrowed. "Perhaps," said the apparition. "Just perhaps, this is what really happened." Then came a big conspiratorial wink. "As you say, this was long ago. Your father had to expend fantastic energies to reach those stranded people. Talents were bulky. Inelegant. Even clumsy. More than today, there were some rather brutal limits to motion and magic." The smile brightened. "What if Ian broke one good law—abandoning functioning pieces of himself—in order to achieve a higher good? What if when he heard about the disaster, he flung aside all the machines and talents that he didn't absolutely need? He sent them racing along one vector, and lighter for his sacrifice, he managed to reach the disabled ship in ample time. Then the star exploded, and yes, he died. What was Ian was definitely killed. But those functioning talents continued following the same course, and after an age, they managed to knit themselves together and build a shared self, an identity and a consciousness. A soul in its own right was born. Then the newborn entity took control of its motions, its actions. And realizing that it was living outside the strictest laws, it decided, quite reasonably, to keep its existence more secret than not."

A pause.

"What do you think of my story, little one?"

Ord shook his head, and a harsh loud laugh bubbled out of him.

The Chamberlain acted offended, but then laughed in exactly the same fashion. "From what I've heard," he warned, "both of us are entitled to our doubts."

"What do you mean?"

For the first time, the man called him Ord.

Then he said, "Your companions, particularly that creepy Nuyen . . . they paint vivid, and frankly, rather incredible portraits of your last few thousand years . . ."

Ord remained silent.

With a snort and a vigorous shake of the head, the Chamberlain exclaimed, "This is all such a peculiar business."

Silence.

"When we envisioned who would emerge from our wormhole . . . well, I'll give you fair warning . . . we didn't anticipate the likes of you . . ."

"You're not imaginative enough," Ord suggested.

Unperturbed, the Chamberlain said, "Obviously. But isn't that the universal failing? The mind's eye is always behind when it comes to seeing."

Ord turned away.

Quietly, fiercely, he asked, "Is this the Core's black hole?"

"Sagittario? Yes, of course." The Chamberlain strolled over to the universal wall, and with a touch of a finger, he enlarged the center of the image. More than a million solar masses created a seamless and elegant mass with no true size, its event horizon embracing a volume twenty million kilometers across. Against that perfect blackness was a speck of matter racing at a healthy fraction of light-speed. It was a pluto-sized chunk of machinery, one of the tools that had once helped make the Core safe for protoplasm. But now the machine was sleeping, tending to its critical parts, probably dreaming of a dangerous future when its powers would be needed again.

Quietly, Ord asked, "Where's Alice?"

"Everywhere," the Chamberlain replied. Then he laughed heartily, shaking his ruddy face, adding with a measured delight, "If I know my daughter, she's everywhere and trying to do everything herself."

She didn't mention you, except once, thought Ord.

The Chamberlain saw his thoughts, or guessed them. And with a sturdy tsk-tsk, he admitted, "That's probably best. Since I don't exist anymore."

Ord watched the machine cross the screen, vanishing for a moment, then appearing on the other side, racing once again across his field of view.

"This is where my talents finally settled," the Chamberlain confessed. "There. On that small, cold body."

Ord touched the rapid speck, and the image changed. Suddenly he was looking up from the platinum-clad surface, staring into the great curtains of stars that moved about Sagittario in longer, slower orbits. With large enough eyes, he could have gazed past the curtains, past the walls of cold dust and hot dust and swirling gases and newborn suns. Thirty thousand light-years away was the sturdy yellow-white light of Sol. In time, Ord might fashion an army of eyes, and if he were patient and precise, he would eventually see the light of his home. Thirty thousand years before his birth, that feeble glow had begun its march. Here, in this place and this time, Ord was nothingness. He was a possibility, unborn and unimaginable. And with that insight, he decided the entity standing nearby could well be Ian Chamberlain. After all, the two of them were much the same: a pair of ghosts trying to climb their way out of oblivion.

He let his father hear those bittersweet thoughts.

And Ian let himself laugh, then patted his son on the small of the back. With a paternal warmth, he told his youngest, "My talents worked alone. For the next few million years, they laid the groundwork for creating a new universe. Here." Again, he gave a soft pat. "Eventually, your sister and the others found me. They're the ones who conjured my old personality and flesh, using shared recollections and my surviving diaries. And when I explained what I was attempting, they decided to help." He shook his head appreciatively. "Honestly, they've done a world of work, compared to my little efforts. But they have better talents, and the raw knowledge. Mostly, I've given nothing but my sturdy, unflagging approval."

"Father," whispered Ord.

He asked, "Are you, or aren't you?"

"This is what I have learned," said the entity beside him. "We are nothing but talents, really. We are genius and power and focus and skills beyond number. These faces we

304 :: ROBERT REED

wear? And these bodies of convenience? In every consequential way, they're nothing . . . nothing but clothes
donned for the narrowest of occasions . . ."

Ord remained silent.

"Nothing about us is human anymore," he heard. "Except
for a thin, perishable skin, that is."

Maybe you are my father, thought Ord, in a secret place.
But I don't much like what you are . . .

Six

*"When Alice arrived home, she mentioned to me that
she liked you, and she respected you and your Family, and she seemed to imply that I should do a better job of appreciating your very difficult legacy,
Ravleen.*

*"Buried in all the other strangeness, I barely no-
ticed those few words.*

*"Yet since then, and now . . . I think about what
she told me. Not about liking you, or respecting you.
I can, and I sometimes I do. And your difficult legacy is obvious and awful. No, what gnaws at me is
this sense . . . this insistent, powerful feeling . . . that
what she really said was, 'I feel sorry for that poor,
pitiful child . . . !'"*

—Ord, in conversation

ONE MOMENT, RAVLEEN was perched on a hard bed, sitting
inside what looked like any apartment lost inside the Sanchex mansion. She was looking in no particular direction,
speaking to Marvel, relating the highlights of the last
thousands of years. Just telling it made her angry. She felt
her heart humming faster, pushing the hot blood around and
around her new body. She felt her voice rise in pitch and
volume, and she heard it rise, and she discovered that her
hands were trembling. Even when she grabbed the muscled

tops of her thighs and held tight, those silly hands trembled.
But she pushed through her rage, ignoring the acidic tears
and the slicing pressure of her clenched fingernails, blood
running now in ten distinct streams, slowly soaking the
bristly wool blanket beneath her.

"Then I went through the wormhole," she reported. "I
caught Ord and tried to kill him. Again. And then you
found me. Whatever you are. Marvel Sanchex, or whatever.
You found us and brought me here." Her heart was screaming, and the pressurized blood began to spout. In a wild,
scorching voice, she said, "The fucking Chamberlains . . .
that bitch Alice . . . leading us into a trap here, in the Core,
with the fucking Nuyens sitting on the side, waiting for the
trap's jaws to drop . . . !"

"Stop," said a voice.

She couldn't see Marvel. Somewhere in the midst of her
telling the story, he had vanished. But his voice returned
now, warning Ravleen, "I don't fall into traps. Not a Chamberlain's. And certainly not one of the Nuyens'."

"Our Family's dead—!" she cried out.

"Am I dead?"

"To me," she answered. "Yes."

"Look at me, Ravleen."

She was staring at her bloodied legs. Against a great,
unexpected weight, she managed to lift her eyes, her face
following slowly after them. The apartment had vanished.
The bed beneath her had turned into a hard stool made of
gray-white bone. She was sitting in one corner of a fighter's
square ring. Marvel, or someone, was sitting in the opposite
corner, wearing a Sanchex body. Besides the ring and themselves, there was nothing to see. A bluish white light came
from everywhere, making her squint. Marvel looked like a
young man. He looked fit and lean, and strong, regarding
her with an inky gaze that made her uneasy, and she returned that look with the hardest stare she could manage.

"Do you know this place?" he asked.

A familiarity teased her. The ring was built from human
shards and scraps. The four posts were bone, each topped

with a fleshless skull. The skulls were bone patched with crude pieces of metal and bone white ceramics, and each skull showed scars partly healed and the wounds that had killed their owners. The ropes strung between the posts were knitted together with human sinews and tendons, and in places, long fingers curled and frozen, then used as simple hooks.

"You don't remember the story," Marvel remarked. "Do you know about our Family, Ravleen?"

She could almost remember, almost, but each time she came close, the truth would skitter out of her view.

"Ravleen?"

Again, she had to force her eyes to lift. She had to work like a demon to keep her massive head level, sitting upright on that hard bone stool.

"This is what I did," said Marvel. "When I was boy, and when I had to make any kind of living—"

"I know," she said. "I remember."

"You don't remember," he cautioned. "I don't think you realize just how mangled you are, daughter."

"That fuck Ord," she began.

"Not all of it is his fault," he countered. "Not in what I see now. And what I don't see." He rose from his own stool. He wore silky trunks and battered shoes, and on each hand was a glove. The right glove was covered with a titanium mesh, while the left glove was smaller, bristling with the canines of hyenas and dogs.

"Are we going to fight?" she asked.

He actually laughed. "Why? Do you want to dance for a round or two?"

But she had no gloves, or shoes. She was suddenly wearing nothing but a woolen dress streaked with her own cooling blood.

"No, I don't want to fight you," said her father.

Then he said, again, "This is where I made my living when I was a boy."

"I remember now," she lied.

He didn't correct her again. Instead, he strolled into the

middle of the ring. The flexing surface beneath him was a durable beige leather made from layers upon layers of human skin. "I was born on Lantana's World. A high-grav colony world—"

"I know that much!" she interrupted.

"Lantana kept bouncing from misery to misery. Wars and several man-made plagues, and there was an ecological collapse, followed by an ugly recovery. Populations expanded again. The economy soared along some very narrow lines. There was a good living to be made for strong young people who would willingly climb into a tiny ring and beat the shit out of strangers."

Ravleen watched him, and listened.

"I was fifteen, and very talented, and exceptionally cruel." He came close to smiling, just for that instant. "That's when the Council came to Lantana. They came and met with our government, explaining that they were searching for a few special people. Only sixty million humans lived there. The chance that one of us would prove worthy . . . well, it was very unlikely. But the government did everything possible to sway the testers. Fifty thousand people, young and with connections, were taken aside and trained while the Council made its preparations. But you couldn't train for those tests, and you certainly couldn't cheat them. That was their beauty. Each person was inflicted with a different set of conditions and questions, and each reaction and answer caused the test to jump into some new, unexpected avenue.

"You don't how beautiful it is. Even now, gazing at the algorithms and protocols, and the bottled genius . . . well, I have to marvel at the elegance and pragmatic beauty of it all . . .

"My given name wasn't Marvel. That was my fighting name. 'Gene' wouldn't put the proper fear into my opponents, you see."

He laughed gently, for a moment.

"Eventually, I was tested. The first questions and a couple AI interviews led to more tests, which was an encouraging sign. About a thousand times, I was asked, 'Do you want to be endowed with godlike powers?' I said, 'Yes.' And sometimes, for whatever reason, I said, 'No, never.' I didn't know it, but I gave the best answer at each turn. That's why they said, 'Okay, Mr. Sanchex. You have one last test. Are you ready?'

"I wasn't, and that wasn't the point. Of course.

"They put me into this ring. They didn't give me instructions, even when I demanded them. Then they threw an opponent in here to fight me.

"It was me. At least in a sense, it was me. An android with my face, my reflexes. My basic strengths. We shared the same nervous system, by the way. The first time I struck him, up here on the arm, I felt the impact. The first time he cracked me in the jaw and got my lip bleeding, he tasted my blood.

"Fight that fight for two little minutes, and believe me, you'll never forget the experience.

"We fought for hours. We hammered and kicked, eroding each other down to pulp and fatigue toxins, then the bell would scream and we'd crawl back to our corners and drink water and broth, scraping together enough energy to crawl back into the middle and batter each other again.

"This is a test, I kept thinking.

"I was in the greatest fight of my life, and I wouldn't quit. I decided that I could outlast anyone, including a machine. Hit the soulless little bastard often enough and hard enough, and I'd come out on the end of this nightmare with the universe at my feet.

"Then I got sloppy, and the machine knocked me down, and it dropped in misery, and watching it writhe on the skin beside me, a different possibility presented itself. What if this wasn't a robot? What if this was a human being? Hell, what if that was me, and I was the robot, and think what that poor son of a bitch was going through?

"That's when I said, 'Enough. I give.'

"My testers came over the ropes and started to patch me up, and they removed the robot's battered head, folding up the arms and legs, making ready to carry the machine to the scrap heap. 'So I'm the real one,' I muttered. They pretended not to understand me. 'How did I do? Did I pass?' I asked. Then this little woman looked hard at me, and without blinking, she said, 'You weren't even fucking close to passing.'

"I was devastated.

"I was relieved.

"Weeks later, healed up and feeling perfect again, I stepped back into the ring. The Council had abandoned Lantana's World. Nobody had been selected, and nobody would be. To help heal that wounded civic pride, a huge prize was offered to whoever beat the reigning champion, and since I was a young stallion, and lucky, I got the first chance.

"He was an asshole, the champ was. A murderer and a monster.

"In a cruel business, he was much too cruel. He had killed half a hundred men in the ring. In fact, he'd murdered two of my best friends. These two skulls here, as it happens." Marvel pointed at two of the battered, infinitely dead shells. "That helped my concentration. The son of a bitch needed to be hurt, or worse. And I came out with every trick ready, getting cheap shots and free shots, pushing the rules until my sworn enemy was starting to get sloppy, and tired, pulling his feet along the skin without lifting them, looking out at me with a sick horror that told me that I'd won. In everything but name, I was the reigning champ now.

"I stopped fighting.

"Really, I couldn't have told you why I stopped. Not then, and maybe not for a couple hundred years. But instead of killing that cocksucker with my hands and feet . . . instead of delivering the vengeance he so richly deserved . . . I let my arms drop, and in a bloody voice, I said, 'Enough.'

"Unfortunately, you couldn't just surrender from this ring.

"I had to let him have his way with my face, my ribs.

My groin. And then because I was obviously giving up, the audience got into it. They felt cheated, and they decided that a payment must have been made for me to throw the fight like that . . . and the riot that followed very nearly killed me. The way I heard it, the Council had to insert soldiers into the mayhem, just to save the father of the Sanchex Family from the clutches of that mob . . . !"

AGAIN, RAVLEEN WAS sitting on a bed, sitting inside a Sanchex apartment.

She was still wearing the wool dress, but her wounds and the blood had vanished. And Marvel was dressed in a dark suit, watching her with a mixture of malice and curiosity. "Tell me your story again," he coaxed. "But slower this time."

He said, "We have plenty of time. Don't worry."

Then when she didn't make any sound, he said, "The Earth. That's the part that really interests me. Describe how you moved a single hand, and tripped an awful trap, and murdered our mother world."

"There's a lot more to the story," she warned. "A lot more than the Earth."

"Really?" Marvel gave her a strange hard smile, adding, "I'm a tough soul. Yes, I am. But, daughter, I think one dead world is just about as much as I can stomach just now . . ."

Seven

"If I'd brought every last one of your talents . . . if circumstances had been that generous . . . we would have been, in effect, two Alices. More than a match for every obstacle stupid enough to stand in our path . . .

"But in the end, what I dragged here is almost nothing.

"Here is what I can offer you . . .

"Although I think there might be some secret intu-
itions . . . notions you hid inside my unconscious self
. . . memes with the mass of a few tamed electrons,
and the irresistible power of a collapsing sun . . ."

                    —Ord, in conversation

IAN SAID, "WITH me. Come."

Ord stepped toward the wall, then the wall was behind
them. Suddenly they were plunging, streaking toward the
platinum-clad machine. It remained tiny and distant, and
swift, but he tasted the first wisps of a deep, deep atmosphere. Unlike any other atmosphere, this was: an invisible
but increasingly dense accumulation of dark-matter talents
and plasmatic talents and baryonic talents made transparent
and permeable, each talent carefully aligned with its neighbors, cooperating with its neighbors, set together like the
elaborate pieces of some grand, secret puzzle.

They were diving into an enormous and perfectly clear
ocean.

Ord was a twist of life swimming inside the enormous
and tireless bodies of the Great Ones.

He could taste and smell several thousand distinct entities, each packed as close to its siblings and peers as possible. Less important talents lay on the surface, while the
essentials of each soul were as close as possible to the
sleeping machine. And still Ord plunged deeper, the ocean
growing dense and fiercely warm, with little pockets of absolute cold slapping against his face.

What looked like a pink mountain was erected on the
machine's northern pole, and straddling the peak was a cylindrical white building of no special size or obvious importance. It was the Chamberlain mansion. Not the fat
modern structure that Ord knew, but the modest five-story
house that the oldest, greatest Chamberlains had known.

Again, Ord asked, "Where is Alice?"

"Close," Ian admitted. "Remarkably close."

Two granite bears flanked the main doorway. One bear

sat, while the other stood on its hind legs, one massive paw raised in what might be taken for a greeting. Passing between the statues, Ord mentioned, "That's wrong."

"What is?"

"Bears don't wave that way."

"But statues do," his father reminded him. Then he touched the boy on the back, urging him forward, and with another step, they had passed through the suddenly open doors.

The cylindrical house looked small from outside, but stepping inside triggered an elaborate set of illusions, cheats, and embedded talents. With his second step, the front room and surrounding hallways exploded outward. Everything except for Ord was enormous. With his third step, it felt as if he were a fleck lost inside some immeasurable vastness. A new set of tricks was stacked upon the last. He allowed his surprise to seep out where it could be admired—earning a knowing nod and wink from the man walking beside him, smiling like his finest friend, a strong warm arm thrown casually around Ord's trembling shoulder.

Softly, the boy asked, "How?"

"Galloping cleverness," Ian replied. "That and catastrophic expense." Another wink. Then he said, "What's a shabby mansion on the outside is a shabby mansion within. But our laboratory hides at the center. Remember, this is fabulously delicate work. For good technical reasons, everything here, including you and me, needs to be even tinier before we can proceed."

Again, tricks were unleashed.

Fifty meters felt like fifty light-years. Together, they soared through the front room and down a hallway that led into the central stairwell. Except the stairs were missing. They passed into a cylindrical chamber that seemed to be kilometers across, and kilometers tall, and lit in the most haphazard fashion by softly glowing orbs that seemed to float where they wanted, in clusters and twos and sometimes alone.

"There's a poetic sensibility in this smallness," Ian assured. "What is the universe if it isn't something born fantastically tiny, yet bursting with infinities . . . ?"

Ian was a glowing sphere, smooth and radiant, and relentlessly ethereal. But not Ord. He still wore a boyish body dressed in decidedly ordinary trousers, even though his body had been compressed into a hyperdense fluid no larger than a fat bacillus. His remaining talents stretched behind him like a great thin tail. Helpless, he was towed to the chamber's center, and on slippered feet, he found himself perched on a platform in front of what looked to be a giant chambered nautilus. The nautilus had a thousand tentacles fashioned from normal sorts of matter, baryonic and dark, while the coiled shell itself was fashioned from strange matter and dark energies—a silvery, impossibly strong shell forged on the lip of the great black hole.

Ord felt the crackle and spark of energies flowing into the shell, spiraling deeper, conspiring with quantum mechanics, hunting the brink of the Planck realm, hoping for a baby universe worth snaring.

He stared at the machinery.

But the strange matter was perfectly opaque, and his best senses had been left at the door. He felt half-blind. He was carefully maimed. And to one degree or another, it was the same for everyone else, too. Smallness was demanded here. Speed was essential. Bulky talents and patient talents couldn't be allowed anywhere near such an elegant, delicate business.

Someone said, "Ord."

A Nuyen was standing near him. Xo was standing there. Like him, Xo wore trousers and slippers and a boy's unfinished body. But what Ord stared at was the smear of light behind his friend. In an instant, the light turned into a Chamberlain. A sister. A sister extruding a confidence and pride that Ord recognized immediately.

"Alice?" he sputtered.

Xo gave him a hard look, shaking his head.

"No," he whispered.

With a tangible despair, he warned, "This one is Adelaide."

Eight

"She's our Two: the first child and favorite daughter of Ian Chamberlain, according to the recollections Alice left for me. Adelaide is exactly the same as Alice, except for the raging differences. Never as powerful, and maybe half as bold. Which makes her more conservative. More perfectly attuned to what is expected and normal. Since Ian's death, she's served as the official leader of our Family—a duty and burden that has shaped every last one of her talents. Nine million years as our matriarch, and until I had Alice's memories to pick through, I'd never heard even a trace of dissent about the great old woman.

"How many of Alice's complaints are real, and how many ride on a younger sister's envy . . . ?

"I can't say, Xo.

"But if you meet my sister, be careful. She's a god drawn with the most ordinary lines . . ."

—Ord, in conversation

"WHY THIS?" Xo had asked. Descending on the moon-sized machine, he had looked at the mansion standing on that granite mountain, and with a faint little laugh, he'd admitted, "This is something of a surprise."

With a sideways grin, Adelaide inquired, "What mansion do you see?"

"The Nuyens'," he answered. Then he clarified, adding, "The original brick building. Fourth Millennia Gothic."

"Maybe you are," she allowed.

"What am I?"

"A genuine Nuyen." The Chamberlain wore an old face, a little fat and very sure of itself. She was touching him by many means, not all of them subtle. The examination had begun long ago, but neither of them had mentioned it. Until this moment, they had said very little, and every word had been polite, and empty, dancing carefully around the important subjects at hand.

"You see the old Chamberlain mansion," Xo guessed.

"Each sees her own, or his own." She led him to the front door and paused, standing on what to Xo looked like a wide brick path covered with a dusting of early-winter snow. "Frankly," she announced, "I didn't think any Nuyen would visit us here. Your Family has a dim view of this work."

"Not dim," he corrected. "They have a very clear and calculated perspective."

"I can agree with that," she said.

They remained in the open, carefully assessing one another.

She told Xo, "There are some peculiar talents still attached to you." Then with a cool smile, she admitted, "I don't recognize most of them."

"These talents haven't been invented yet," he confessed.

"They haven't been needed," she said, correcting him. "I'm sure some soul, in some trivial part of the galaxy, has dreamed them up."

Xo said nothing.

"Maybe I should try to remove them," she remarked. "Before we continue . . . would you like me to do that . . . ?"

He said, "You can try."

"But?"

He shrugged his shoulders. "I'd be interested to see if you could cut me loose from them. Frankly, I wouldn't know how to manage it."

"Exactly. That's what I guessed."

Then they stood motionless for another long moment, ghostly probes trying to decipher Xo's possibilities.

"You hate Nuyens," Xo mentioned.

"That's not true," she countered. "I respect your Family. I understand them. Better than most Chamberlains, I possess a good appreciation of you and your history." Then with a calm laugh, she said, "Hatred is just a small component of my feelings. A spice to the more reasonable emotions."

"But your father despised us."

"Again, that's an inadequate word." She seemed to attempt a smile, then thought better of it. "What he despised were the tricks employed to make you into a Family. To ensure that you would fool the test-givers."

"Nobody was bribed," Xo countered.

"I know that, yes. And all those nagging rumors about blackmail and incompetent AI judges are just rumors. Just noise. The evidence is so paltry, particularly after so many eons and so many opportunities to destroy any graceless evidence—"

"My First didn't cheat," Xo said, using a bristly little voice.

"Again. I agree."

He pretended to care deeply, putting on a tidy rage while telling her, "The test had rules, and the rules were adhered to. Tell me where the testers, or anyone, was fooled by what happened."

"As I said, I agree with you." She began to pull back now, reassured by Xo's responses. "The despot ruling a colony world learns about the coming test. And of course he wants to wear those godly powers. No expense is too much. So he clones himself. He impregnates millions of women with his seed, in most cases against their will. It was a horrible crime, but who was the guilty party? Not his offspring, surely. When the testers from the Council arrived, they decided it was safe to ask the same-faced boys and girls their questions. They believed that none of them would pass, having inherited their father's viciousness and vulgarities . . .

"But one young girl did match every expectation, or exceeded them.

"One girl, different because of mutations and because of her upbringing . . . a poor girl raised by moral, decent colonists . . . she passed every test, and what choice did the Council have? One Nuyen had played the rules to perfection, allowing his clone-daughter to win, and the Council couldn't simply ignore a candidate for that reason. It would have bankrupted the entire process if they had . . ."

"You don't hate me?" Xo asked, his voice soft and sorry.

"I only mistrust you." She smiled with a flickering warmth. "I know your Family and your basic nature, and from this point on, I have to keep a very firm hold on you. Do you understand?" Then she shook her head, adding, "But you came through our wormhole, which means there might actually be a Nuyen who has something important to tell me."

"I do," he told her, using a multitude of coaxing voices.

But Adelaide surrendered to a different logic.

"And who am I to turn you away?" she asked. "Just because you don't have the face that I expected to see?"

Nine

"I understand . . .
"In the end, what happens happens fast . . . !"
     —Ord, in conversation

A SUDDEN PRESENCE emerged to Ord's left, accompanied by a harsh, exhausted gasp.

He glanced sideways. Ravleen was a silhouette, slender when set against a blazing white light. Then the light clotted and collapsed, becoming Marvel. Her father set both hands on Ravleen's shoulders, apparently holding her in place, quietly growling, "Remember now. Behave yourself."

Her face was lean and hard, the body emaciated. Saying

nothing, she gave Ord a wide-eyed stare, trembling as if cold.

The other immortals now dressed themselves in polite bodies and dated clothes. Thousands floated in space, creating a gently bowed wall before the nautilus. Ord searched for the Chamberlain faces. Excluding Ian, there'd be eleven of them. But it took several desperate moments to find the right face. She was high up and near the back—a late arrival yanked away from some critical task. That had to be Alice. He recognized her eyes. Bright and strong and exceptionally smug, those eyes couldn't belong to anyone besides Alice. Yet it was just one face among many, one soul almost invisible, swallowed in that ocean of talent and arrogance, and bounded rationality, and boundless dreams.

Adelaide touched him on the shoulder, lightly. "Tell us," she said. "Every way you wish, tell what you came to tell."

Then she called him Ord.

Suddenly, he wasn't afraid, or sad, or haunted by doubt. This was where he belonged, and he took a bold, micronlong step forward, and with a variety of mouths, he told the Great Ones about the murder of the Core, the ruin of the Peace, the mangling of their lives and good names, and finally, the collapse of their honored Families. If they continued with their perilous work, that was what would happen. He promised them. Then he sighed and shook his head, telling his own story while showing them everything his eyes had seen of death and despair, hatred and revenge. Disaster lay upon disaster, and the miseries still hadn't yet run their course when he abandoned the future, escaping to here. To now.

"You have to end this work," he told them.

Again, and again, in endless new ways, he hammered them with that extraordinarily simple message. He showed casualty figures. He danced with tales of economic collapse and social ruin. He flooded the room with visions of war and wastelands. Then, with a perfect scorn, he looked at each face in turn, promising, "Adelaide will die. Marvel with die. And you will die. And you. And you." Every famous name deserved to be shouted. "Death, death, death!" he promised. "That's what is coming for each of you now."

Carefully, relentlessly, Ord worked his way through the audience, climbing up and around to the face that mattered most.

Finally, with a sudden quietness, he said, "And you."

He said, "Alice."

He told her, "For you, it's everything but death."

She was staring at him—she had never been anything but watchful—her blue eyes bright and unblinking. Was she impressed? But she had to be enthralled. Any sentient mind would have to be impressed, even if it was just a little boy telling the epic.

At least one soul had to believe, What a brave, noble young brother . . .

In a fashion, these dense moments felt easy. Anticlimactic, if anything. Ord reminded himself that he was speaking rationally to reasoning beings, and emotionally to human souls, and how could they resist him? Yet when he paused, there was only a glacial silence punctuated with just enough nodding faces to warm him. He smiled in turn, and because there was nothing else for him to do now, he let himself enjoy the luxury of an unfettered optimism.

Adelaide spoke again.

"You tell it now," she said to another visitor. Her heavy round and excessively calm face said, "Mr. Nuyen."

Xo looked like a youngish man. Like any Nuyen, his face held a simplicity meant to fool observers. But in his voice, there were currents. There were great irresistible pushes of emotion wrapped around armored logic. Xo told the same story, but from his peculiar vantage point. And he admitted what everyone saw for themselves: He had been radically modified, given weapons of mind and spirit in order to subdue the baby Chamberlain.

"But my heart changed," he confessed. "I got sick of the cheating and death, and I joined your camp. Your fold."

"Good," a thousand voices declared.

Then Adelaide waved an arm, saying, "Thank you," to put an end to the speech.

Xo dipped his head, nothing more worth saying.

"And now, you . . . Madam Sanchex?"

Marvel shook his daughter, as if she needed to be awakened. Then with a low thunder, he told her, "Honest, and quick. Spare nothing!"

A withered, devastated Ravleen stared at the Great Ones. For what felt like an age—barely a microsecond, at most— she appeared helplessly lost, nothing left of the great warrior but a terrified splinter, a dried piece of husk. But then a tight little laugh began to slide out of her half-closed mouth. A look of bitterness and cold amusement brightened the face, and the swayed back straightened to where she was nearly as tall as her father. She spread her shoulders while the laugh gained a muscular strength that sounded very much like Ravleen. But it wasn't exactly the same. "You've never seen a worse monster," she promised her audience. "In your tiny lives, you've never dreamed of anything half as awful as me."

It could have been Ravleen's voice. But missing from that simple declaration was the cocky pride, the self-congratulatory joy.

"I murdered the Earth," she confessed. "And I've murdered other worlds and millions of souls. Why, I don't know. I remember hating this Chamberlain boy. Like you've never hated anything, I loathed him. More than you've ever loved, I adored the simple idea of torturing Ord until he was insane." She stared at him, suddenly and defiantly. The black eyes were bottomless, and the face was beautiful again. But the voice was lashed tight to a wild grief, and the eyes were weeping now. She sputtered, "I'm the worst fucking nightmare you can imagine." With her fists, she smacked the flat of her belly. "But I'm nothing compared to you," she cried out, looking at the Great Ones, practically glaring at them. "One wrong move, and you stupid arrogant shits-of-god are going to be worse monsters than anything I ever was . . . !"

Marvel shook his daughter. But he didn't say a public word, and the simple physical punishment was more like a reflex, a mandatory deed.

Again, there was a silence.

Then Ian placed himself in front of Ord, and with an irritated tone, he remarked, "You didn't mention one critical detail, son."

Ord knew what he wanted.

But quietly, affecting confusion, he asked, "What detail?"

"Since you've dropped out of the future," said Ian. Then he added, "Apparently," with a darkness wrapped around the word. And with a weary shake of the head, he said, "You should know the technical particularities. If only to prove that you're genuine, you should have learned them."

Ord looked straight ahead.

"Tell us," Ian told him. Then he put on a smile, asking, "What exactly did we do here, and what went wrong, and to the best of your knowledge, why did it go wrong?"

The great nautilus loomed overhead.

"Or," Ian continued, "would you rather not share those gruesome details with your elders?"

In his most secret mind, Ord thought, *No, don't. Don't do this!*

But there was no choice. In his public mind and with every voice, he described the dense and exceedingly obscure details that Alice had given him. Even now, he barely understood the bones of this science. There were monumental equations, more strange than compelling. Capturing the baby universe was just the smallest part of the magic. Crossing over into the Baby brought the gravest risks. Opening an umbilical wide enough for a soul to pass through, but allowing nothing of the new universe to gush into this realm . . . that's what these entities had attempted, and that's where the calamities lay in wait . . .

Ord recited everything, including data accurate to a fraction of a femtosecond and to the brink of Planck space, and at every critical junction, he gave the names and failings

of those gods most directly in charge. And when he finished, the blame focused and delivered, he again felt a wave
of optimism, confident for every good reason. At long last,
his quest had come to its just and inevitable end.

Hope died a swift death.

The briefest silence ended with a sudden, "Thank you,"
from Ian. From Adelaide. From perhaps another thousand
voices scattered about the great chamber. Then it was Ian
who showed him a wide grin, clapping his hands onto the
boy's shoulders and shaking him with a friendly violence,
telling Ord, "Well, now. Now we know."

To everyone, he exclaimed:

"From this point on, we'll be sure to dance around those
little difficulties!"

Ten

*"When I meet you for the first time, you'll seem so
large and impressive . . . my fantastically powerfully,
unimaginably ancient sister . . .*

*"Yet when I saw you just now . . . when I found
your face, finally . . . you couldn't have looked more
tiny, standing in that crowded place, shoulder to
shoulder with all those elderly gods . . ."*

—Ord, in conversation

XO SPOKE.

With a fierce outrage, he asked, "You still want to finish
it? The Baby? Knowing the whole ugly mess?"

Happily, with a calculated and buoyant indifference,
Adelaide explained, "Not only will we finish our work, but
we will finish it now. Now that we've been shown what
cannot succeed, we'll push past to the logical ends—"

"No!" Ord cried out.

Ian set a hand on his shoulder.

"You can't believe this . . . it's insane to even hope it—!"

"Quiet," Ian cautioned. "Be quiet, son."

With a booming voice, Adelaide asked, "Why did we build the wormhole?" Then she answered her own question. "The wormhole gives us fair warning. It's a portal to the future that allows escape from the inescapable trap. Which in turn lets us do what's best, in the finest way, leaving the galaxy wealthier and happier because of us. Us."

"No," whispered Ravleen.

"Imagine," Adelaide continued. "In another little while, we'll be able to create new universes by the thousands. And eventually, by the billions. Souls born in every portion of the galaxy will live long happy lives, accruing wisdom and maturity and a certain small wealth, and then they'll make pilgrimages to this place." Vivid images accompanied the hopeful words, building a tidy portrait of that very distant future. "Each pilgrim will walk through an umbilical, striding into a universe meant only for him. Each of our children, our neighbors and friends, will inherit their own infinite realm where they rule as they choose, as the forces of Nature, as the irresistible Will of God."

Quietly, angrily, Ravleen sobbed again, and screamed, "No!"

Ord glanced at her. For an instant, he believed that she had managed to retain some hidden weapon. That was her habit, after all. Always hold some little terror in reserve; that was the way of every Sanchex. In a moment or two, Ravleen would shake off her father's grip and, with a thought, or the flick of some secret limb, obliterate the experiment, this laboratory, and every last one of these idiot-souls.

But Ravleen just dropped her head, and shivered.

What others were thinking, Ord couldn't guess. Contrived faces showed precisely what their owners wished to show, and for the moment, they wore a seamless, invulnerable resolve. Even Alice, standing among her peers and superiors, wore an exterior of perfect contentment—immune to any moral judgment delivered by mere children.

"And now," Ian declared, "let's finish our good work."

Hundreds of voices said, "Yes. Finish!"

But what Ord heard best were the little knots and twists of silence. A half-born doubt was simmering, perhaps.

Ian placed both hands on Ord's shoulders. "Would you like to remain with us, son? We'd certainly allow you to watch."

Ord whispered, "Alice."

With a caring, benevolent voice, the ancient man remarked, "We've asked and asked. But it seems your sister wants nothing to do with you."

Louder, Ord called out, "Alice!"

Xo straightened his back, telling Adelaide, "I'll stay here."

"But only here," she warned. "No closer."

"I want to watch," Ravleen remarked. She gave Marvel a blistering stare, adding, "I want a good laugh when you fuck it all up again!"

One last time, Ord shouted, "Alice!"

He was staring up at the nautilus shell—that intricate contrivance of genius and dream. "I have a private, personal message for Alice! From Thomas Chamberlain. From Brother Perfect."

Murmurs passed along a thousand channels. Old gossip was remembered, and enjoyed. Rumors of incest were a pleasant diversion, shattering a tension that Ord had only just begun to feel.

Ian heard the gossipy whispers.

"Enough!" he growled. "She says she doesn't wish—!"

"Wait," said a new voice. Then a third hand dropped on the boy's shoulder. It was smaller than Ian's, and warmer, and even relaxed, the grip was fabulously strong.

Ord closed his eyes.

"What's this message?" Alice inquired, using a private channel.

"Not here," he replied. Using his old-style mouth.

Ian gave a low snort.

But Alice seemed to laugh, savoring that whiff of parental disapproval. "Where would you like to be, little man?"

On a private channel, he suggested a place.

"Why there?" Alice blurted. But then she dragged him across a phenomenal distance, and she made them enormous again, and together, sister and brother stepped inside an obscure storeroom tucked into the basement of the resurrected mansion.

Eleven

"My favorite sister—before I met you, and maybe now, too—was one of the other children living in the mansion. Her name was Maroon. Centuries older than me, she wore a young body and a girlish face. I don't think she wanted to grow up. Like me, she loved the mansion and forests and the churning rivers, and, whenever possible, Maroon avoided the not so gentle tugs of convention and expectation. Really, she loved being a little girl.

"Maroon told me an odd story about our father. A story you know, I'm sure. But then again, maybe you told it differently in your time.

" 'What was our father before he was our father?' she asked me. 'Before the Families, I mean. Before the Council agents tested him and found him to be one of the most qualified souls that they'd ever encountered.'

" 'He was a clerk,' I boasted. Because Ian was our father, and great beyond all measure, I imagined that a clerk had an incredibly difficult and remarkable job. 'He belonged to one of the old governments,' I explained. 'He was very much honored for his long, selfless service.'

" 'Do you know what selfless means?' she asked.

Then she instantly forgot her question, telling me with a secretive little voice, 'That's all true, Ord. But it doesn't tell half the story.'

" 'What story?' I asked.

" 'The Council agents went everywhere to find the Thousand Families. To every colony world and green comet, and even to Minnesota.'

" 'What's Minnesota?' I asked.

" 'That doesn't matter,' Maroon told me. 'What's important was a woman living alone in an isolated district. The wars had scorched the forests and boiled away the lakes, but a few people still lived there. She was the oldest. She was barely two hundred, but in those times, that was practically ancient. The testers did their magic with her, and then one of them spoke when he shouldn't have. He admitted that her scores were very good, if not good enough. She had a decent, caring soul and a natural empathy—'

" 'I know what "empathy" means,' I interrupted.

" 'Which is the easy part of it,' Maroon admitted. Then she went on with her story. The old woman had nodded and grinned. Being a good person, she could accept that she wasn't going to be tested any further. She slowly climbed to her feet, and the testers assumed that she would now show them to the door. But no, she shuffled to a lift that led underground, down into a deep bunker. Bunkers were common during the wars, and in most cases, they were useless. But hers had survived half a hundred bombardments. The testers accompanied her into the crust. She asked if this talent of hers was a little bit genetic, and they admitted that many ethical factors depended on a person's DNA. She said she had a relative. No, she didn't know him personally, but everyone and her parents had said that Ian was always decent and sweet, and smart. He was the sort of man to cry at sunsets, although he could also be very tough-minded when it suited him.

"Of course, the testers referred to the census records, and when they couldn't find any Ian Chamberlains, each decided that the old woman was confused, or worse. But by then, they were inside the bunker and saw the freezer standing in one corner, more ancient than the old woman but still operating in a noisy, durable fashion. She shuffled up to the thick white door, and putting an insulated glove on a withered hand, she asked if they wanted to look at her great-great-great-grandfather.

"Sometimes people from the deep past—those who lived and died before the worst of the wars—did remarkably well with the Council's tests. They weren't hardened by misery and death. They weren't sickened by the idea of machines being grafted into their bodies. Innocent, these occasional dead souls had often fallen just short of being taken as one of the Thousand Families.

" 'Do you want to see Ian?' the old woman inquired.

"Of course they did. 'Please—!'

"She opened the massive door, brittle hinges creaking. The freezer's interior was filled with severed heads, most of which had a passing resemblance to the old woman. With an easy indifference to death, she grabbed one of the frozen heads and, according to what Maroon told me, informed the testers, 'He was a clerk, from what I can remember.'

" 'What kind of clerk?' one fellow inquired.

" 'He sold these little things called stamps,' she offered. 'I don't know why, but they were pretty pieces of paper, and they helped carry all sorts of things into all sorts of places . . .' "

—Ord, *in conversation*

"I USED TO wander into this closet," Alice admitted. "Now and again. When I was a girl, and thought I wasn't supposed to be here."

In a sense, it was just the two of them. But Ord could feel talents pressing down on them, shifting positions like arms hunting for comfort, titanic masses flowing around one another and through the stale, darkened air. A curved plaster wall lay on his left. A tighter curve lay to his right, wrapped around the central staircase. Every wall was obscured behind cabinets and portraits and shelves and the innumerable heirlooms that made the room feel smaller than it was. Everything about the place was exactly as Ord remembered it, except that each item appeared shiny and new, as perfect as the day it was set into this forgotten place.

Ord asked, "Did you rebuild the old mansion?"

"Ian did," Alice mentioned. "With Adelaide's considerable help."

He stepped out of her grip and turned, taking a first close look at his sister. Alice was wearing a youngish face and a stocky body, her red hair shaggy and a little unkempt, her clothes comfortable to the point of being baggy—an ensemble of flesh and fabric that would suit any artist working on her masterpiece.

"More than anyone," he began.

"More than anyone . . . what . . . ?"

"This project is yours," he remarked. "Every success felt your hand, and what follows is yours."

"Good," she replied.

Her face appeared unimpressed, even bored.

"Yet," he added, staring at the bright blue eyes, "you don't have a monopoly on being special. A tweak here, an inspiration there. Somebody else could have accomplished all of this. In another day or another million years. What does it matter?"

"To me, it matters."

Her bored face lifted, staring at a certain portrait. On a sunny day, Ian had posed outside the Chamberlain home, wearing a suit of fine fabrics and what could only be called a forced smile. That long-ago Ian looked weary, and sad, and Ord could almost hear the painter begging him to smile.

"The warm smile of a hero," the painter might have said. "Please, sir. Will you?"

For the world, Ian had tried to look like a man worth trusting. With your life, and your children's lives, and the unborn souls of trillions. And he had been a good, caring person—exactly the kind of soul that should have inherited godly powers. Without question, he helped end the wars that plagued humanity from its inception. He hammered out the Great Peace. And then, on an empty afternoon, the hero had stood in the sunshine, wearing the suit and an honest face, its sad expression centered on a weary, anemic smile.

"Is it our father?" Ord asked.

Alice understood his question, his intent. She shrugged as if the question couldn't be more trivial, observing, "You really insist on being surprised. Why? Didn't I warn you he was here?"

"You might have implied it," he admitted. "But I didn't notice, and I didn't want to believe it."

She acted deaf, and indifferent, and relentlessly bored. With the pale tips of two fingers, she touched their father's portrait. A thick thread of instantly hardened paint emerged from behind Ian's simple gray tie. The old-style optical cable dangled in the sunshine, its roots buried next to his heart, and its sudden appearance, vulgar and honest, served neatly to spoil the illusion of unalloyed humanity.

"That's exactly what you did before," Ord mentioned. "I thought you were being exceptionally rude, vandalizing the memory of our great father."

His comment won a half laugh.

Alice turned to face her brother, admitting, "You're a genuine puzzle. You and your little friends."

"But I know you've worried about some horrible futures," he offered. "The galaxy in ruins, and nobody left to sound the warning but some children."

"I've envisioned every contingency," she purred. "At least once. At least long enough to discount the impossible and put the unlikely in their cages."

Ord was silent.

"And you brought along that Nuyen," she added, her tone disapproving. Disgusted. "For every reason, his Family wants nothing to do with our work. They think it's dangerous. And they hope it is astonishingly successful, since they'll be first in line to inherit their own universes. But if we stumble here . . . well, they'll be ready for that brutal future, too . . ."

"Xo," he said. "His name is—"

"A born liar with some very peculiar talents. I wish I had time. I wish I could autopsy these odd little skills of his."

"Do you think we're lying?" Ord asked.

Then he answered his own question, saying, "No." He stared at her, and said, "You believe. You have no other choice."

"Nothing but success, this time." She said the words by a hundred means, and then with her old-style mouth told him, "Thank you. For your sacrifices, Ord. And your selfless help. Thank you for all of that."

"And if the umbilical fails this time?"

She offered the obvious. Quietly, she said, "The wormhole still exists. Its future end has just roared past Sagittario, accelerated to the brink of light-speed, and if the future is ugly enough, then someone else will return here. Some new incarnation of yourself, perhaps. He'll burst into our time, and we'll make every new correction, all the new refinements, and when they don't work exactly as planned, you'll return again, and again . . ."

"Forever," he muttered.

"Just once," she corrected. "But you'll always return."

Her voice was confident. Defiant, almost. Yet Alice allowed him to glimpse something else . . . a little fear lurking in the blue of her eyes.

"I could have failed," Ord reported.

No reaction.

"Next time, the Nuyens might catch me."

But Alice had already considered every possibility. Even the obscure and unlikely had been recognized, and she would keep playing with those elaborate models until the fun was wrung out of them.

"Maybe you're the last messenger," she offered. "Maybe we've stumbled across the proper way to give birth to a new Creation! The first of millions! Trillions! Until every citizen of the Milky Way can inherit her own infinite realm . . . !"

Ord began to cry.

"You brought me here," Alice reminded him. "Why?"

Shuffling up to one of the tall cabinets, he opened a heavy crystal door and reached past a glittering globe of the old Earth. When his hand emerged, he was clutching a mug carved from pink granite. Quietly, he said, "Thomas gave this to me."

"A talent, is it?"

When he placed the mug in Alice's hands, it turned into a small human head. There was a Chamberlain face and shaggy red hair, and the face laughed until she closed her fingers around it, and suddenly she was laughing in the same boisterous way. Then she fell silent. Looking at Ord with a mixture of disdain and puzzlement, she admitted, "I already have this little talent. It makes you see what's good and funny, even in the middle of a catastrophe."

She asked, "Is this it? Is this Thomas's important, wondrous message?"

Again, the invisible masses slipped around them and passed through them, followed by a fat pulse of energy flowing to where it was needed.

"I know what you're thinking," he assured her.

"You'd like to believe that," said Alice.

Then, after a pause, she prompted him, "So tell me. What runs through my mind now?"

"You're counting the worlds that you've terraformed. The nearest worlds, and others scattered through the Core. You're weighing the colonists living on them. You're playing with the numbers. How many people can die before you grow uneasy? How many worlds vanish before you feel sick? And when does the ruin become so horrible that even someone as strong as you . . . as proud and perfect as you . . . has no choice but to try and stop what's gone wrong . . . ?"

Alice opened her mouth, and closed it.

"You came back to the Earth," he said. "Alone. No other Chamberlain, or Sanchex . . . or anyone else . . . willingly shouldered the blame. Not like you did, Alice. So I have to ask: Why aren't you doing everything to stop this mess—?"

"Maybe I am," she interrupted.

With a baleful look, she said, "During these last moments, I've pleaded with the others. I've admitted that I don't agree with Ian, or Adelaide. The risks are too great. We need to dismantle the Womb now. And afterward, destroy all of the machinery that feeds it." With a grimace, she said, "I've proposed that we finish the work elsewhere. Maybe inside an old globular cluster safely removed from the galactic plane. It would delay our success by a few million years, and the logistics for the pilgrims would always be cumbersome—"

"Or you could stop the work completely," he muttered.

Alice closed her mouth. Then, in a near whisper, she admitted, "I'm not the only doubter."

Another invisible mass drifted around them, then hovered.

"But these are my peers," she warned. "My equals and friends and lovers for the last ten million years. If I can't get enough of them stirred up, then what genuine choice is left me?"

With his most private voice, Ord offered a last detail. "I didn't mention this? And maybe you don't care. But if events play out in the same way . . . if the umbilical turns unstable . . . then one of *them* is still going to slide into the baby universe, abandoning ours when we need him most . . ."

"Who?" asked the blue eyes.

"Ian," he replied.

"You're certain?"

Ord told what he knew and nothing more.

Again, Alice looked up at the portrait. Her face passed through every emotion, her mouth tightening and relaxing again while the bright blue eyes filled with tears, then dried themselves, finding a new resolve. She was in misery. She was perfectly focused. Then she reached past her feelings and found a serene pleasure that won a narrow, wise smile—a smile that could mean anything to anyone who was watching. Then Alice lifted her free hand and, with a touch, wiped away the damage that she had done to their father's portrait.

Ord couldn't stop weeping.

Without looking at his face, she handed back the granite mug. "Here. I don't need this."

A surge of energy, unexpected and scalding, ran up along his arm.

"Do you know me at all?" she muttered, looking everywhere but at Ord's teary face. "Apparently not, little brother!"

Twelve

"I might as well be you . . .

"I'll wear your talents across thousands of light-years, swimming your oceans of memory every moment . . . making myself intimate with your desires and curiosities and very occasional fears, and that boundless fierce hot pride of yours . . .

"Honestly, Alice . . . there will be long reaches of space where my closest, finest companion will be your pride . . . !"

—Ord, in conversation

AGAIN, ORD STOOD before the Womb.

He found himself with Xo, with Ravleen, lost among a legion of entities endlessly jostling—massive and far-flung entities working to place as much of themselves as close to the event as possible. It was exactly like being jammed inside a closet with an army of eager, graceless children. It was claustrophobic and embarrassing, and Ord wanted to be excused from this shameless mayhem. He hungered for solitude, for the chance to watch as much as he could bear from some great distance where he might beg Chance or some far-flung Creator finally to take pity on his siblings.

But when Ord gazed at the nautilus, he discovered new eyes. In this compressed, rapid environment, he saw what the Great Ones could see. The careful, exhaustive preparations had been finished. The coiling shell was nothing now but an inert and convenient vessel helping to protect the delicate business within. And, miraculously, he could see that business. Nestled at the center of the nautilus was a simple, spherical vessel built from some ultimate species of strange matter. There lay a machine forged on the brink of a black hole. Infinitely strong, and nearly infinitely small, but dense, the machine was incapable of leaking light or any other flavor of information. Yet his new eyes peered inside. He gazed at Planck space—that frothy, furious realm where existence and nonexistence shared a perpetual dance. Here was a fantastic wilderness of potential and relentless chaos, and Ord could do nothing but stare, transfixed by the simple, astonishing vision.

At the sphere's center: the Baby.

A single newborn universe lay waiting, indistinguishable from trillions of its siblings and, according to the dreamy geometries, more remote to Ord than the ends of his own universe. Yet he could see it plainly. The Baby was brilliant beyond measure, possessing no recognizable size, or mass, or anything that could be considered an existence. And swirling about its brilliance were fleets of tiny strange-matter machines, each devised and constructed to do some narrow and precise and instantaneous job, laying the careful groundwork for the umbilical.

Someone whispered, "Beautiful."

Xo.

As they watched, spellbound, a thousand baby universes blinked into existence and vanished instantly into the hyperverse. Every universe began with an inflationary burst and ended with an absolute chill or some grand collapse. And between birth and death, what? Not life, Ord knew. In these wild universes, life and sentience and all the blessings and curses that came with them were among the rarest birds. Ord's universe was the grand exception: one creation out of a trillion trillion trillion utter failures. A universe where energy and space were in perfect balance. Where the physical laws not only allowed for life, they demanded it. And where the first slime had time and the means to evolve into other flavors of slime that would eventually accomplish every great thing, and every awful thing, too.

"Closer," someone whispered.

Alice.

Ord obeyed, slipping between half a dozen souls. He was dressed in a boy's body and a boy's simple clothes. He put himself a micron closer, if that, and he realized that he could count the slow, steady passage of the nanoseconds. Here time was an extraordinarily slow business. Whatever was to happen would be history long before the next heartbeat, and the drama would unfold in a space that could hide inside a single proton.

Thinking that, he turned toward Alice, ready with a sly comment . . . some easy noise about how little time it takes to ruin a lot of people's very nice day . . .

But Alice had vanished.

He recognized the only Nuyen face, and he saw the glowering face of Ravleen. But his sister had vanished, or she had never been close. And that's when the obvious struck him, and he realized that the voice urging him to move forward didn't belong to her.

"Closer," he repeated, reaching for the others.

Xo glanced at Ord, then gazed up at the Baby again.

Ravleen was drifting behind an ancient fleck of light. But not a Sanchex. Marvel had vanished, too. And unencumbered by her father's grip, Ravleen slid herself through the body of the near god, leaving it more embarrassed than injured.

"Careful," the entity growled.

Ravleen gave a snorting laugh and took Ord by his offered hand, squeezing until what passed for bone splintered.

Ord winced, and grinned.

Healing the hand before anyone noticed, he looked back into the staring, compressed bodies. He found Ian. He saw Adelaide beside him—the dutiful, relentless daughter. Both were using every eye to stare at the Womb. Three tiny children could not matter less. Keep still, and quiet, and they might be forgotten here.

Here was among the closest of the close, the nautilus hanging over them now—a silvery leviathan larger than some mansions and smaller than an ameba.

"What now?" someone asked.

Xo.

"I don't know," Ord thought. But he felt as if he were lying, so he peered inside himself, every explanation waiting there.

"Something's different," Xo whispered. "About you."

Then, "What did Alice give you?"

Thomas's stone mug. But something else had been tucked inside the mug. He discovered a package of small potent talents, each of them instantly familiar. He had carried them before, but never used them. He was holding the tools necessary to manipulate things too small to be real. Tools perfectly ordinary here. Tools that few would notice, that nobody would question. And with them came the perfect grace necessary to wield them in very novel ways.

Ord started to reply, but Xo was speaking again, almost amused when he said, "Ravleen? You smell different, too."

Ord asked, "What did your father give you—?"

"Everything," Ravleen said, with a smug whisper and a matching grin. Then she opened her hands, staring at them while saying, "Everything," once again. "Plus some very sweet and very potent weapons."

*   *   *

FOR THE NEXT few nanoseconds, they remained unnoticed, and free, and with various secret voices, Ord shared Alice's plan.

But was there time enough?

The Baby was growing, expanding and brightening as vast sums of energy were extracted from the rawest nothing. And the umbilical was growing beside and within it, striving to link the Baby with this frigid, nearly empty universe . . . the machinery as delicate as it was sturdy, and blindly persistent in its duties, every critical event happening too quickly even for the best eyes to follow . . .

"Now," said Ord.

Said Alice.

And like that, a hundred scattered entities were in motion. The children were nearest, and smallest, accelerating to the brink of light-speed and slamming into one of the tentacular conduits, exactly where the nautilus's shell was thinnest. Ord unleashed an elaborate pick that produced a flaw that allowed a quantum fluke to appear. It was a gap that couldn't remain stable for a fraction of a nanosecond. But it was large enough and persistent enough for the others to follow. And as each slipped inside, Ord unleashed another one of Alice's talents, leaving them even more compressed. A hundred white-hot flecks suddenly tiny, almost invisible, were darting around the interior of the shell's outermost chamber, their shared light barely able to fill the suddenly enormous volume.

Ord's pick dissolved, leaving the wall with no memory of a hole.

Marvel shouted, "With me! Sanchexes!"

Ravleen joined her father and siblings, following the coil as it turned and turned, leading toward the center. Toward the Baby.

Alice was beside Ord. There were no other Chamberlains. Just them. She had a few talents, and she dressed herself in a human form, a half smile showing on a thinner, grimmer face. The hair was short and dense. The clothes were simple trousers and a blouse woven from gold-white light. She delivered a serious stare from those infinite eyes. Then with a human voice, she told him, "I'm not going to congratulate you."

She said, "Let's see if we can do any good, first."

For a moment, the nautilus shivered, as if some great hand had carefully taken hold of it.

Then, nothing.

An odd thought occurred to Ord.

"I've been here before," he confided to his sister.

She looked surprised, then intrigued. "What do you mean?"

"When you came home," he said. "When you visited the Earth to find me, and to confess." Why even bother mentioning this? "I was beginning a war game. The Golds were defending a snow fort from the Blues."

"My Golds—?"

"You helped me win that war."

Alice almost laughed.

"Did I?"

What a ridiculous, stupid thing to mention. Ord would have apologized for wasting the time, but an apology would waste even more.

Yet Alice found some reason to say, "Tell me about it."

"About what?"

Her face softened, and her red hair brightened. She touched him. Her flesh was hotter than the interior of a sun, but the hand felt cool, like snow against Ord's forearm, and her strong certain voice forced him to relax.

"Humor me," she told him.

"The history of that little war," she said. "Tell it to me, brother."

Thirteen

"*Maroon told how our father was discovered inside that forgotten freezer, and how the Council's testers had to rebirth him before they could judge his soul's promise. Growing a new body and transferring the surviving mind into that body . . . well, it wasn't routine work in those days, and except for someone like you, it's never been easy. Our sister explained that to me, impressing me with the astonishing luck that carried us from frozen trash to the most powerful Family in the galaxy.*

"*Eons later, the Nuyens told me their version of that noble story.*

"*It seems Ian's mind had degraded over time, an atomic creep distorting the glassy ice of his neocortex. Repairs had to be made. Guesses had to be made. But the testers wanted success, and they knew what they needed . . . and that need almost surely influenced their work . . .*

"*The Chamberlain Family was based on a pernicious cheat, according to the Nuyens . . . a point that they made again and again, trying hard to insult me . . .*"

— Ord, in conversation

THE NAUTILUS SHIVERED again.

Lightly.

Then the Great Ones wrenched open holes in the chamber wall, using the same kind of pick that Ord had wielded. It was a simple and blunt and artless attack. There wasn't time for cleverness, or the need. The besieged rebels were scarce, and without Sanchexes standing on the front lines, they were missing their sharpest and quickest teeth.

Ord raced across his little parcel of wall, patching holes until there were too many to patch. Then he unsheathed a simple device designed to motivate hyperdense twists of

matter. It was a weapon now, blunt and cruel. Effervescent
bodies crawled out of the holes, and he jabbed them, cooking their senses and what passed for flesh. Dozens writhed,
and retreated. For a slender instant, they were soulless monsters deserving every misery. Then one of the invaders
managed to slip past, vast and cloudlike until it compressed
itself into a quark-dense body like his. A face appeared.
She was female, from a minor Family, her features twisted
by a searing pain. An illusion? Or a calculated bid for sym-
pathy?

Reaching for Ord, she begged, "Stop, please! Will
you—?"

He eased his weapon into her exposed belly and flung
her back through the tiny hole.

Twenty more like her emerged instantly, and chasing
them were hundreds more.

From behind, Alice called out, "Retreat!"

Ord grabbed a thread of hypermatter, riding it deeper into
the curling shell. The first chamber ended with a slick
curved wall smaller than the last, and at its precise center,
a doorway had been wrenched open. He dove through, and
all but one or two defenders escaped with him. Then Alice
cut the thread behind them and erased the door, the thread
collapsing upon itself, turning unstable, then dissolving into
hard radiations and a scorching heat.

Like the head of a beaten drum, the wall shook.

Then it grew still again.

The new chamber was smaller, with a smaller outer wall
begging to be defended. The second assault was delayed
while the attackers repaired themselves and made ready to
pry open new holes and charge again. But when they
emerged, it was the Chamberlains who led the way. There
were ten brothers and sisters, plus Ian, shoving their way
through the tiny holes. They wore suffering Chamberlain
faces and angry voices, begging for reason. They demanded
obedience. They promised Alice forgiveness for every
crime. To Ord, they mentioned the pitfalls of youth and
doubt.

"Son," Ian moaned. "My son. Consider these stakes. That's all I want. Stop and consider where you are leading us."

Time was a luxury, and a wasteful temptation.

Ord slashed at them, and mangled them, and inside that next endless femtosecond, he was winning. Then others burst through too many holes, and again, Alice cried out, "Retreat."

They dove into the next chamber, again.

Again, Ord held his post until the fight was lost.

And he retreated with a practiced precision. Most of his talents remained far behind, drifting outside the enormous nautilus. They were alone now. They were lonely. Nobody was trying to steal them away. That chore would have consumed entire seconds, and in this realm, that was the same as centuries. And at these distances, a trusted talent couldn't help him, and he couldn't even pretend to control any of them. They were severed limbs drifting in a faraway solar system, flailing and grasping out of simple habit.

Fight, and retreat.

Rest, and fight, and retreat again.

With grim precision, Ord tallied the lost chambers. They managed thirty retreats, then another twenty. Each attack came faster than the last, but every victory won less space for the time spent. But every retreat meant another ally or two left behind—slow souls too dispirited or exhausted to make the next escape. Every failure meant another partial turn along the shrinking shell. And then at long last: a moment when the attackers seemed to pause, and Ord could count the remaining bodies. Only a dozen of them commanded a chamber no bigger than a ghostly electron, and behind their backs lay very little else.

Xo managed a human face, glancing at Ord with an odd, almost mournful expression before the face collapsed into scorching white fire.

Marvel rejoined them.

With a roar, he announced, "I need help. I need new hands."

Alice wore a colorless face and flat, colorless hair. "I need more fighters," she countered.

"Take this daughter," Marvel offered. "Her temperament's wrong for the work."

Alice regarded Ravleen for a moment.

"Xo," she said. "Help the Sanchexes."

But Xo hesitated. A sorrowful face appeared, and a matching voice said, "I don't think—"

"Yes," Alice cried.

"It would be better, maybe—"

Marvel grabbed him and yanked, dragging the Nuyen down through a fresh hole that vanished in another bite of time.

Ravleen showed the defenders a wide sneer.

"What do you darlings know about fighting?" she asked. Then, with a mixture of rage and serene joy, she reminded them, "I've killed more worlds than you've built, you sorry piss-filled apes!"

THE NEXT ATTACK didn't bother opening holes. This time, the entire wall was demolished, a flash of gamma radiation evaporating every barrier, a chaotic melee erupting and ending almost before any time could be measured.

Ord attempted another retreat.

Ravleen was beside the open doorway, wielding a strange-matter drill. With a clean and happy and much-practiced efficiency, she turned the weapon on anyone foolish enough to come close. For a little instant, it looked as if she might win the war herself. The chamber was suddenly choked with stunned near gods, and wailing voices, and Ord squirmed past them, and paused. He had to pause. Ravleen maimed everything moving, cursing with joy, and at least three blows from elsewhere descended on her together, pushing her into the tiny doorway, leaving it momentarily blocked.

Ord screamed and flung himself forward.

Ravleen gazed out at him with empty black eyes.

Behind her was Alice. She stared at Ord with a longing,

with a massive sense of loss. Then she grabbed the Sanchex and yanked, and the door was no more. The wall had no memory of an opening. A thousand bodies grappled for Ord, and they stunned him, and he wailed, "No," then began to cry again.

He stopped crying when Ian's voice was close, warmly assuring him, "This is for the very best, son."

Then an unwelcome arm was thrown across the gray sketch of a shoulder, and Ian hugged him hard, as if they were the absolute best of friends.

WITH A PRECISE fury, the Great Ones made ready to obliterate the next wall. They were going to press the advantage, bringing this war to its logical, inevitable conclusion.

"The umbilical is nearly finished," Ian reported.

He was speaking to Ord.

"Marvel can't stop it now," he remarked, speaking to everyone stuffed into those cramped surroundings. "The Baby and our connection with the Baby . . . they've reached the point where all of us, working together, would find it impossible to stop their formation . . ."

Ord was silent, glancing at the white-hot faces.

Adelaide was close. She looked like a drab, distracted version of Alice. She looked old, and tired, and in ways that he could just feel, she was sickened by these awful last turns.

"But that's not what Marvel's doing," Ord reported.

His voice was quiet, and respectful.

No one seemed to hear him, or care. But then Adelaide glanced in his direction, as if by chance, and with her own quiet voice, she asked, "What do you mean? What's Marvel attempting to do in there?"

Ord opened his hands and said nothing.

Then he dropped his face, looking perfectly embarrassed.

"Answer me," she pressed. "What's Marvel doing now?"

Ord straightened, and hesitated. "The Sanchexes don't have the proper talents," he confessed. "Not to stop an umbilical, no." Another pause. "But there's someone else who's carrying a considerable talent. A narrowly designed skill that can ruin the umbilical, easily and catastrophically . . ."

A panic began.

It was a deeply buried, extraordinarily private panic. What faces showed gave away nothing of their true emotions. But Ord felt the Great Ones discussing this odd possibility, guessing its source and every possible counter. Given time, they would have seen the obvious. But there was no time. The bulk of their intelligence was light-seconds removed from them, which might as well have been at the far reaches of the universe. What they had brought into this realm were those fragments of their intellect and experience that they could never throw away. They were simple souls, again. They were a little stupid and very scared, and into that extraordinarily human terrain, Ord reached.

With borrowed hands, he grappled with one soul.

"Think," he said aloud, in a thunderous whisper.

"Of the most awful imaginable deceit . . . think . . ."

Fourteen

"Tricks trick because they are beautiful . . . because we love them so much . . ."

—Ord, in conversation

"THERE'S ONLY ONE powerful Family missing here," Ord began.

The Nuyens.

"But they're extremely interested in your work. You know they are. If the Baby slips free—if the Core explodes again—they are willing and ready to ruin you. They'll gut your wealth and eat your good names, and for the foreseeable eons, there won't be a stronger Family. If this explodes in your face, they win. Everything in their grasp is theirs."

Ord paused, a sad and embarrassed look filling the boyish face. "But these are Nuyens. They don't trust easily, and they certainly don't have much faith in your incompetence. So what if they dreamed up a plan to ensure that the umbilical will fail, and fail catastrophically . . . ?"

A perfect silence descended.

"Xo," he whispered. "The Nuyen boy. His siblings enlarged him and twisted him with an assortment of new talents. Then he rebelled against them. Alone, he followed me to the Core, and in countless ways, with every chance, he has helped me. I believe he did everything willingly. No, I won't doubt his sincerity, or his friendship. But what if his brothers and sisters had hidden one more talent inside him? What if they created a single tiny tool that would cripple the umbilical, if it ever found itself close enough—?"

"You know this?" Adelaide inquired, her tone impatient. Skeptical.

"We suspect it," Ord replied. "Xo was injured in the chase to the wormhole, and when he repaired himself, he discovered the talent. By the purest chance. He's studied it ever since, and he's made his guesses, and I don't know how many times he's tried to pry it loose, intending to throw it away. But it's too deeply buried. Whatever this tool is, it's fused to his basic soul. It's with him now. And when Marvel realized that he couldn't stop the umbilical, he had Xo join him. They're huddled around the Baby right now, and if they can't control the talent—if it doesn't neatly cut the umbilical—then it may well wrench it open too far—"

"Ridiculous," Ian snorted. "They wouldn't take that risk!"

But Adelaide saw a possibility. Her Chamberlain face suddenly seemed to be carved from pale white butter, its flesh soft and slick, and tired, and the blue of her eyes had drained away. What should have been bright red hair was now a dull, defeated gray. Adelaide was defeated. She knew it and spent the next little moment accepting her defeat. Then with a public voice, she asked, "What do you want from us?"

"Your surrender," said Ord.

Then he added, "And your help. Now, this instant. Come help try to squeeze off every link with the Baby—"

"No," Ian blurted.

"Maybe we should reconsider," Adelaide conceded. "In light of what we know—"

"Reconsider nothing!" Ian shot over to Adelaide, a booming voice telling everyone, "In a thousand ways, we've nearly reached our goal. We have no right—none— to lose our way now!"

Adelaide stared through him.

Quietly, fighting to sound reasonable, she admitted, "This is nothing but wrong. If it's true, and if Marvel and the boy do this—"

"I know Marvel," Ian blared. "I've known him from the beginning. He's smart and honorable, and he couldn't be that reckless!"

"But this isn't your decision," she interrupted. Then she tried to gain the upper hand, dismissing Ian by saying, "You don't know Marvel. And you're not my father. Strictly speaking, you're a conceit, an embellishment we added to some lost talents . . . because it seemed like an appropriate show of respect . . ."

Ian's face betrayed nothing.

But the eyes brightened, and a sputtering voice emerged from deep inside him. "I am Ian Chamberlain. As much as you're my loyal, loving daughter!"

A silence.

"Although it wasn't real respect," Adelaide muttered. And with a great sadness, she admitted, "Mostly, it was just easy. Making you Ian again."

"I've always been Ian!" he cried out.

She stared at him, her eyes blue again. A cold, cobalt blue.

"You know what's true," he claimed. Then he hesitated, feeling the slightest tug of doubt. But the emotion arose from a place without significance. He dismissed his misgivings with a snort and hard laugh. "When I supposedly died? When I flung myself at those poor colonists? What I gave them was my least consequential part. I was saving what was vital, and rescuing those incompetent children cost me nothing. Nothing but a few scraps of dead skin from the end of my least important finger."

A cold, bottomless silence fell over the scene.

Ian didn't seem to notice. Instead, he cocked his head as if he heard a great crescendo of applause. Briefly, he attempted to smile. Then, with a sturdy and reasoned tone, he said, "We aren't going to fall for your threats, Ord."

To everyone else, he said, "We need to take our positions and make ready—"

A sound intruded. It came from nowhere before finding its source in Adelaide. The ancient and honorable and perfectly devoted daughter was screaming, leaking an incoherent rage, her face twisted in obvious pain . . . a living, fierce redness making the face shine . . . and she placed her hands against Ian's chest, red against the deep gray of his make-believe blouse . . . and with a desperate anger that must have surprised her as much as anyone, she told him, "I won't let you. There's too much at risk—"

Ian made a little gesture.

He had a tool. It was the kind of sharp implement that a man who wants to carve off his humanness would create, and hold close. And for the second time in its existence, he used the tool.

With a calm, surgical skill, Ian sliced away everything that was human from Adelaide. He took away her face, her apparent skin and hair, and the eyes. The human voice vanished, and the ancient protoplasmic memories. Deep-buried instincts, and moralities learned as a girl, and even the name itself. Adelaide. Then he said the name to the incandescent ball that lay before him. "Adelaide," he said, with a measured fondness. "This should teach you." And in the next moment, he used a second tool, and she was no more.

Adelaide was dead.

"But she isn't," Ian remarked, showing a human smile as he stared at the other eyes and the hard-set mouths.

"Dead, I mean. She endures quite well. Her talents stretch out for a billion kilometers. Everything important and useful about my daughter is alive still. Eager still. And she always will be."

The silence was hot. Opinions lay perched on a high, narrow peak, no way to know who would tilt which direction and how many would fall together.

Oblivious to the revulsion, Ian turned to face the chamber wall.

With the strong, certain voice of a onetime general, he announced, "We need to make our next push. Get ready now. This is the perfect moment."

There was no dissent, or even a flicker of genuine anger. But the Great Ones had to stare at the creature that was trying to lead them, their long, glorious lives arriving at this instant and this conundrum . . . and for entities accustomed to an infinite genius, they seemed to be remarkably confused . . .

"Obliterate the wall," Ian called out.

Nothing happened.

"Do I need to do everything?" he asked.

The audience stirred.

Ord tasted shame, and the strangest little beginnings of fear.

Again, Ian said, "We need to make our final push—"

Then the chamber wall evaporated, and for the first moment, it must have seemed to Ian that he had won everything. A consensus had been reached. The attack was under way. But why was that wave of radiation pushing into his face? Had someone done the job badly, the wall imploding by mistake?

Too late, everyone understood.

The chamber wall had been obliterated from within; the defenders were now on the attack. Pouring out of a smaller chamber—from the very edge of the Baby's tiny womb— were Alice and Marvel, and Ravleen, and the other rebels, pressing hard with weapons and relentless, rational voices.

"There's no time!" they called out.

"One choice left!" they promised.

"Help us!"

Then Alice grappled with Ian, shaking him and cursing. Which made him growl back at her, threatening, "I'll do to you what I did to your sister."

"What?" She looked at Ord. "What did he do?"

Ord didn't have to speak.

Alice yanked the tool from among her father's talents, and in a frantic blur, she carved off what was human about him. And to that gray shred, she said, "Stay with me. Watch! I want you to see it. Feel it. Whatever happens, I want you to know . . . you sorry old shit . . . !"

Fifteen

"When I was a boy, and seamlessly predictable, I had a favorite door. Every time I stepped inside the Chamberlain mansion, I'd reach high and gently touch the words carved into a slab of granite.

"PRIDE AND SACRIFICE.

"It was a tradition of mine, and a habit, and usually the gesture was done without any more thought than you'd put into the blink of an eye. But sometimes I'd wonder about my brothers and sisters, about those great souls who'd walked here before me. Perhaps a few of them, like me, had reached up to feel the cool hard stone. I was touching those other hands, in a fashion. There was honor in the gesture. Honor, and a joy. I belonged to a vast and great and enduring thing. That's what I might tell myself, and that's what I would believe.

"It was a silly thought.

"Not because our Family's honor is feeble. And not because our greatness will eventually be gutted and left for dead.

"No, what's silly was the sense of belonging to

*something enduring. Chamberlains have existed for
only a few million years, and that's not a particularly long time. What I belonged to, and what I always will be part of, is far more enduring than any
family name.*

"But you know that, Alice.

"The ancient protoplasm in my hand.

"The eternal genetics buried within.

*"As old as any stone, this life of ours is . . . and a
good deal tougher than most everything else in this
hard cold beautiful universe . . ."*

— *Ord, in conversation*

THE BATTLE REMAINED as vicious and desperate as any
fistfight, but the blows were delivered as salvos of potent
memes and elaborate plans wrapped inside confidence and
bluster and attitudes less pretty. The chamber trembled with
piercing shouts and screamed pleas for cooperation. Everyone spoke about the need to act reasonably and morally.
Yet all combatants, in one fashion or another, seemed to
do their best to ignore everything but their own considerable pain.

Time continued to move in tiny bites, and the Great Ones
were busy bickering among themselves.

Xo fought his way close to Ord.

"Thanks," Ord offered.

Xo had given him a talent and a lie. A potent weapon,
and simple, the talent did nothing but a fill a soul with the
need to be honest, then act on that irresistible honesty. And
the lie had been horrible, and believable. Ord still watched
his friend, wondering if there was a secret saboteur buried
in his nature.

With huge, sorry eyes, Xo regarded the mayhem. And
almost embarrassed, he admitted, "I'm trying. But I can't
make them cooperate . . . can't fool them, or coax them . . .
there are too many minds to play with here . . ."

Ord scanned the fiery minds.

"Too many," his friend repeated.

"Try something small," Ord suggested. His voice was calm and sure, and swift, telling Xo exactly what he wanted.

In that next instant, the same simple question occurred to everyone. Each found it inside him and her, asking, "Whose voice don't I hear?"

Alice's voice.

As a body, they felt her conspicuous absence. Each allocated senses to find the Chamberlain, and all failed in that next fraction of a nanosecond. Then in the wake of their first sickly panic, they realized Marvel was missing, too. Two critical voices, both silent. And together, in a rumbling whisper, everyone asked the obvious question:

"What is Alice doing?"

She wasn't inside the next chamber.

But where the nautilus made another complete turn, wrapping itself inward to the final chamber on the very brink of the Baby, there was someone. Foul souls. Better senses than Ord's spied them. Then it was a sprint across a distance too small to be measured, in the briefest fragment of an instant that wasted even more time. But Ord had already guessed where she was. He moved first, and fastest, plunging into the bizarre, ill-behaved terrain on the frothy edge of Planck space; yet instead of strangeness and serene mathematics, he found himself racing across a familiar if utterly contrived landscape.

He ran beneath a sky of seamless white clouds, running hard across a pasture covered with the most perfect snow. In the middle of the pasture stood a white structure. Not the Chamberlain mansion, no. It was simpler—a cylinder built from tidy, regular blocks of snow. It was like a fort that children would build, then happily fight over.

A tunnel-like gate led into the interior.

To the Baby.

Two figures waited in the open. Each was dressed in white and carved from snow. Like Ord was. He stopped just short and looked at the Sanchex faces, and he glanced at his own cold little hands, and something that could have been Ravleen's voice asked, "Do you know this place?"

She said, "It's my idea. Making it appear this way."

He started to say, "Of course I know it."

Then the Great Ones marched onto the pasture, shoving against each other until no room was left in this pretend world, and nowhere else to move. And in a shared voice, they shouted toward the fort, calling out, "Alice."

Alice crawled from the tunnel.

She emerged from the mostly completed umbilical, and stood up. And of all expressions, she decided on a snowy smile, remarking in a mild, but determined, voice, "There's no more time, and this is what we'll do . . ."

"I'LL TRY TO break the umbilical. Now." Alice said it, then added, "I count three weaknesses. Three opportunities still to come. That's my analysis, and there's no time to debate my math."

Alice was as expert as anyone, or more so.

"And there's no time to calculate odds." She mashed the snow beneath her right foot. "We need to be ready. If it looks as if the Baby's loose, we'll have to absorb the blast for as long as possible." Again, she kicked at the ground. "We need to set up a barricade here. A black hole. If I fail, we can absorb the early leakage. With a black hole serving as our cork—"

"Built how?" a thousand voices asked.

Sagittario was too distant to help.

"We make our own hole!" Marvel roared.

"With what?" the others wondered.

And then they saw what was obvious, and painful. Each winced in some deeply felt, entirely fresh way. And in that next little instant, several hundred of the Great Ones began retrieving those little pieces of themselves, yanking free of the deepest portions of the Womb. They began hauling the pieces out and merging them with the rest of their talents, preparing for that final instant when they would turn around completely, faces pointed at the innocent stars, and with every last wisp of muscle at their disposal, they would run.

They would flee.

Cowards, and criminals. But by all definitions, alive.

The rest of their brothers and sisters continued packing talents into a tighter and tighter and tighter mass, mashing themselves together, all of that genius turned to raw mass, their boundless strength pushing until they were teetering on the brink of collapse—the relentless hand of gravity ready to drive them into an endless, dimensionless hole.

"I'm going back in," Alice announced.

Great masses shifted behind Ord, while other masses carefully held themselves in place.

A new figure appeared beside Marvel. Ian, judging by his appearance, and the disgusted way that the old Sanchex held him tightly around the neck. The ancient, once-dead man sobbed, his human face twisted with misery and remorse. His final mouth was speaking, making no sound. ". . . no no no," he kept saying. ". . . no no no."

"Make your good-byes," Alice said.

Ord thought she wanted everyone's good wishes. But she was looking only at him, speaking only to his face, telling him, "Long ago, I loaned you some odd talents. You've got them here with you, and I don't have time to tease them free."

Alice began to kneel, saying, "I need your hands, Ord. So take this instant, and say your good-byes."

Ord looked abruptly at Xo.

At Ravleen.

They weren't children anymore, and neither was he. But swirling inside their galloping emotions were qualities that neither time nor any grand annihilation could change. Ravleen was still the feral girl, her soul blessed with a rage that couldn't be dismantled or defeated. And Xo was still the boy perfectly able to cheat anyone, on any occasion. Which was why he was here now. Only a Nuyen had enough treachery to turn traitor against his entire Family.

Ord whispered, "Good-bye."

The oddest thought suddenly struck him.

"Be careful," Xo advised.

Then Ravleen said, "Fuck careful. Be brave!"

Alice had already vanished into the umbilical.

Ord knelt and crawled. The snow had no discernible temperature, and he couldn't feel it with any hand. He crawled forward, then hesitated, looking back over his shoulder at the image of a weepy, guilt-ripped Ian. Then to Xo and to Ravleen, he said, "There's this old expression. Have you heard it?"

A strange unease passed through him.

" 'The child is father to the man,' " he offered.

Xo gave a little nod, pretending to understand.

Ravleen just snorted, and with the meat of an illusionary foot, she kicked him in the ass, causing him to plunge toward the fragile, failing umbilical.

Sixteen

"My life . . . my entire existence . . . is built around meeting you, Alice . . .

"Four times in my little life, our paths have crossed, and each time remakes me, changing my nature and all that I believe . . . each brings the same insistent epiphany: I don't know you. I can't know you. And the hand I'm touching is being offered for the first time . . ."

—Ord, in conversation

ORD AND ALICE journeyed to the edge of their universe.

There wasn't room for illusions here. They weren't inside any tunnel, and the whiteness surrounding them didn't resemble snow, and what passed for their own bodies—compressed to the brink of nonexistence—had nothing left that resembled limbs or hearts or any sort of mouth. But Ord could imagine Alice walking beside him, her red hair long and begging to be combed, her clothes disheveled and artistic, and when her words found him, he imagined a solid

and buoyant voice. The fate of worlds was dangling over
the maelstrom, but always some piece of Alice felt nothing
but thrilled: thrilled by what they were seeing, and by
everything they were doing, and how very honored, and
blessed, the two of them were.

Stop, she said.

Ord imagined himself walking, then, standing still.

What is it? he asked.

Here, she told him. Reach here.

What passed for her hand guided what served as his.
Then she explained how to use her little talent, and when.

In a sense, his hand was jabbed deep into the umbilical's
wall.

Waiting.

On schedule, a critical system popped out of nonexistence, suddenly slipping through his fingers, and he closed
his hand and yanked and felt the hand dissolve. Lost now.
Nothing good had been accomplished.

He told Alice, Sorry.

It's all right, she said.

She admitted, Success is a pretty unlikely bird. But I
promise. We'll have a much better chance at our next station.

Ord imagined himself walking again. He had a boy's
body and a boy's simple clothes. In his chest beat an old-
style heart—young muscle driving a cool thick blood down
rubbery arteries, pushing it through pink lungs, then
through the rest of his living body. He was exceptionally
fond of that heart. He felt tiny and sad, and sorry in all the
old ways, and he imagined himself crying as he walked
beside his ancient sister, one of his cool little hands of
blood and bone wiping at the salty tears, trying to push
them back into his eyes.

Perhaps Alice felt him crying.

Everything will work out for the best, she promised. If
not at this next station, then at the third. Or if not today,
then you'll come back through the wormhole again, and
we'll try again.

If it doesn't work today—? he began.

She said, Ord.

She confessed, I've left myself an escape route. Which shouldn't be any surprise, should it? And I promise, I'll hurry back to the Earth and meet you, and we'll put everything back into motion again—

Will it be me? he asked.

The universe was built on innumerable quantum events, each too tiny to be observed completely. Yet their cumulative effects left every detail of the future unknown. Unknowable. Suddenly, asking the question, Ord found himself wielding a talent that explained quantum magic fully and simply. And bringing that abrupt expertise to play, he asked again, Will that Ord be me?

Stop here, said Alice.

He tried to visualize sunshine and green meadow and Alice standing close to him, her nearest arm thrown over his shoulder, lending comfort. But meadows and sunshine were wonders that he couldn't remember anymore. Even the colors of the sky and the sky-fed grass were beyond him now.

Here, she told him.

Ord was standing in the umbilical's path. A trivial, short-distance talent tried to disrupt another key system. And for an instant, the attempt seemed to be working. Success was inevitable. He felt the system pushing against him, then pausing when it met resistance. But his talent had limits, and the umbilical was eager to finish its own construction. The system realigned itself, neatly and swiftly, and Ord was shoved aside. Which was when he discovered another new, unsuspected talent. One of Alice's talents was talking to him, too.

We aren't going to succeed, he said to Alice. Not today.

I know, she replied.

We can walk down this umbilical a trillion times, he explained. And we might stop its formation once. If we are very lucky.

Alice said nothing.

Ord was moving again, dwelling on the enormity of things, and the relentless impossibilities.

Alice caught him again and said, It won't be you. The next time. There have to be little differences in experience, and memories, and in personality, too. But he'll be your age and have your face. And without question, the boy will be a Chamberlain.

At the end of the umbilical lay nothingness.

Ord didn't need to be told what to do. He already knew. But they had arrived before the window opened, and they had no choice but hold their ground, waiting for the narrow opportunity to present itself.

Ord looked for his sadness.

Where was it?

Then Alice was close to him. She was close enough that he couldn't be certain what was him and what was her. And one of their voices was whispering, asking the other voice, Do you know what I thought when I saw you? This time, I mean. After you popped out of the wormhole.

Quietly, Ord admitted, I don't have any idea. What?

That you were a brave, splendid young man, she said.

The words felt warm and slippery and sweet. New talents were being spliced into Ord's nature. They didn't belong to Alice. They were part of the umbilical, knitted into its matrix while it was being created . . . meant to be claimed by whichever entity came through here . . . on his way . . .

On his way.

Where?

Ord looked for his sadness, but instead found an enormous, almost crushing fear.

If I had the honor of building a new universe, said a voice. Said Alice. If I was that lucky person, do you know what I would make sure of?

What?

Very little, said Alice.

And she was laughing. Gently.

But there's one vital thing that I would do, she added. My creation would be enormous and wondrous, full of delicious, unexpected avenues. Of course. But I'd also make certain . . . make it inevitable . . . that its inhabitants could marshal the energies and skills necessary to build more living universes like itself. But that power would come at a cost. An enormous and unavoidable, even damning cost. And do you know why, Ord?

He knew why.

But she was already saying it.

To create a new universe . . . that's an exercise that shouldn't be done without horrific consequences. Otherwise, every half-sentient soul would cobble them together. In their private shops, during their spare evenings, and with as much thought as any hobby deserves. Think of the horrors we've inflicted on our little galaxy, then imagine trillions of universes built by every sort of god . . .

Ord remained silent.

Thinking.

Maybe this is how it works in our universe, she continued. We're destined to build Babies, and the umbilicals always fail us. But each catastrophe still manages to give birth to a new universe, and each universe is inherited by some good soul that desperately wants to fashion a better Creation.

Ord remained silent, waiting for the window.

Maybe that's why you found your way back through time, Alice continued. Despite some very long odds, you reached this place . . . you found me . . . because the soul that invented our universe preordained such perfect things . . .

Unless it's even simpler than that, Ord suggested.

How simple?

You're the only reason, Alice. You built the Baby, and you manipulated the Great Ones, and you always allow the Core to explode . . . and then you run off to the youngest Chamberlain and dress him up in your clothes . . . in your glories . . . and you orchestrate everything to bring him back here again . . . you place him where I am so that you can inject him into the latest in an infinite series of Babies . . .

Alice waited an instant before asking, Why would I do all that?

She was giggling.

Because, Ord said. Inside this loop of time, a trillion of your little brothers are going to inherit a trillion universes, and each of us has no choice but to worship you, Alice ... worship you for all time ...

That would make me extraordinarily cynical, she allowed.

If it were true, she added.

Is it? Ord whispered.

She didn't answer.

Instead she said, Xo. And Ravleen.

What about them?

When I leave—before I race off toward the Earth—I'll carry their souls to Thomas. I'll tell him to set them on a quiet backwater world. He knows backwaters better than anyone. He'll give them good anonymous lives, as rewards for their considerable help.

Thank you, Ord said.

Then he asked again, But am I right? Is all of this your game? Is the Milky Way revolving around nothing but you?

Suddenly he imagined her face—freckles and windblown hair wrapped around an infectious smile—and with a mixture of joy and sadness, she admitted, "I'm just Alice. Just Alice. Whatever that means, that's all I am."

The fear had drained out of Ord, leaving nothing but a strange weepy joy that kept building and twisting inside him.

Maybe he would stop the umbilical, this time.

"Perhaps you will," Alice said agreeably.

They stood together, perched beside the nothingness, feeling the Baby clawing at its cage ... and once again, at the last possible instant, Ord tried to imagine the touch and heat of a hand ... and Alice took hold of him, and squeezed, and then the nothingness began to melt away ...

the last touch of his life
two hands gently holding on to one another
and then
and then
and then, everything.

About the Author

Robert Reed is the critically acclaimed author of ten science fiction novels, including *The Remarkables, Down the Bright Way, Black Milk, The Hormone Jungle, The Leeshore, Beyond the Veil of Stars, An Exaltation of Larks, Beneath the Gated Sky*, and *Marrow*.

Also a prolific writer of short fiction, Reed has been compared to both Ray Bradbury and Philip K. Dick and nominated several times for the Hugo Award. His short stories have appeared in *Asimov's Science Fiction Magazine, The Magazine of Fantasy and Science Fiction, Science Fiction Age*, and many other magazines. A selection of his short work has been collected in *The Dragons of Springplace*.

Reed has gained a reputation for cutting-edge hard science fiction bound together by strong characters and intricate plots. He, his wife, Leslie, and their daughter, Jessie Renee, reside in Lincoln, Nebraska.